D0426193

Virgin and Martyr

Andrew M. Greeley

WARNER BOOKS

A Warner Communications Company

A
BERNARD GEIS ASSOCIATES
BOOK

For the Durkins

Lord God, you gave the law to Moses on Mount Sinai. You also caused the body of blessed Catherine, your virgin and martyr, to be taken mystically to the same place by your holy angels. Grant we pray you that by her merits and prayers, we may be enabled to attain to the mount which is Christ. We ask this in the name of Jesus the Lord.

—Prayer of the Mass for St. Catherine, Virgin and Martyr (whose body, after being broken on a wheel, disappeared and was believed to have been carried by angels to Mount Sinai)

The truth of some images reaches far beyond the truth of most propositions.

—Kurt Riezler

Glory to God in the highest and damnation to all enthusiasts.

—Inscription on a bell, Holy Trinity Church, Cambridge

Grace does not give up easily.

—John Shea

NOTE

The characters in this story are at some pains to assert that their situation is not necessarily typical. Let me reinforce that assertion: None of the persons, institutions, events or organizations is based on a real-life counterpart. All are products of my imagination, save for the imaginary Latin American country of Costaguana, which, as readers of *Nostromo* will recollect, was imagined by Joseph Conrad. Moreover, it is not my intention to imply that the people and events in this story are "typical." I have written a story, not a sociological study of North American Catholicism or a political science study of Latin American Catholicism. Those who attempt to find either in my story do so at their own peril and in the face of the my explicit repudiation of such a purpose.

My tale is rather of a temptation. Paul Tillich called it "idolatry"— the confusion of temporal and contingent political goals, however laudable, with the transcendent and the absolute in religious revelation. G. K. Chesterton called it "heresy"—the confusion of part of revelation, however important, with all of it. Msgr. Ronald Knox called it "enthusiasm"—the confusion of emotional fervor, however necessary, with religious conviction. This temptation is as seductive to the right as it is to the left, to the traditionalist as to the modernist, to the conservative as to the liberal.

Those who deny that their own particular cause, be it "liberation" or "defense of the faith," is immune to the temptation admit by that very denial that they have already succumbed to it.

I intend no judgment as to the extent to which this temptation has not been resisted in North American Catholic involvement in Latin America. Such a judgment is beyond my competence and probably at the present time beyond anyone's competence. To contend, however, that the temptation has not existed or has always and everywhere been surmounted is to have already yielded to it.

AMG
Tucson

PART
ONE

1
BLACKIE

"Look at your hands, Nick. They're dripping with her blood."

Seemingly mesmerized by the fire in Father Edward Carny's eyes, my friend Nick Curran glanced furtively at his hands. They seemed clean enough.

"Her blood was poured out." Father Ed Carny leaned forward eagerly, his big fists knotted like coils. "She died an unspeakable death because of our sins. She's a modern St. Catherine, her body broken on the wheel of American imperialism. We are bound in justice to see that her wishes for the poor and the oppressed are carried out."

Unusual words in a plush LaSalle Street office of Chicago's most prestigious law factory, decorated in bland beiges and browns that would have infuriated old Isaac Minor, the founder of the firm. The language was even more improbable when one considered that Nicholas B. Curran, whose office it was, had been this modern St. Catherine's long-time suitor and short-time lover, and was now, in November 1976, the executor of her estate.

St. Catherine of Chicago, virgin and martyr—my cousin Cathy, who once long ago had wished her name was Kathleen because that was more Irish. A virgin? Well, practically a virgin, a couple of orgasms in this day and age could hardly be held against you. And a martyr? Had not her still living body been torn apart by a chain saw in the courtyard of a South American military barracks?

It was not the time nor the place to note that our presently gloriously reigning supreme pontiff had tossed St. Catherine of Alexandria out of the church calendar on the grounds that, like Patrick and Christopher and Nicholas and Philomena, she was merely a legend.

Nor would I observe to Ed, good dedicated social revolutionary that he was, that psychoanalysts said that of course St. Catherine's wheel represented female sex organs.

"Father Ed," Nick Curran said carefully, pushing his rimless glasses higher on the bridge of his nose, "I admired Catherine too. But I have a legal responsibility, which she entrusted to me before she disappeared.

4 / ANDREW M. GREELEY

If I fail in that responsibility, I will be dishonoring both the law and her memory."

"You're rationalizing, Nick," Father Carny said. "You're hiding behind establishment excuses to frustrate Catherine's wishes for God's poor."

Outside the window of the Minor, Grey and Blatt law factory, high in the Field Building—I rebel at the change of its name to the Lasalle National Bank Building, even if the chevalier was a good Catholic—the sky of Chicago had turned a dirty yellow, like a little girl's spring dress after she has rolled in the mud. Clouds raced over the neat ranks of bungalows and two-flats in the ethnic neighborhoods, swirled by our skyscraper and rushed on toward Lake Michigan, like a galloping troop of cavalry, Chicago's own Black Horse Troop, perhaps.

Before I went to the seminary I thought of such changing skies as Rembrandt weather. My classmates from downstate called it a tornado sky and ruined the artistic image.

At the moment I was hoping for a tornado. My friend Nicholas was in trouble. While Father Ed had gained a martyr, Nick had lost a woman who might have been his wife.

And I'd lost a cousin I'd adored longer than had either of them.

"All I know of Catherine's wishes are stated in her last will and testament," Nick began, his thin face tense. He looked like a quarterback trying to call an audible at the line of scrimmage.

"Which leaves her money to the Movement for a Just World." Ed Carny leaned back and spread his hands expansively, big thick hands with calluses developed building houses for the destitute, who had lived in huts of gasoline cans and tar paper until he had arrived to liberate them from poverty and oppression—whether they wanted to be liberated or not.

"Her last will and testament was drawn up, as I told her, under the laws of the state of Illinois. According to those laws she cannot be presumed dead until seven years after her disappearance."

Carny shook his head, more in pity at Nick's stubbornness than in anger. "Catherine didn't give a hoot about such laws, Nick. You know that." He folded his massive arms across the jacket of his rumpled but carefully fitted black suit, a rock that would not be shaken by the puny blows of Nick's legalisms.

Nick was outclassed in this contest with the big, handsome priest, a welterweight against a heavyweight. Nick would win, of course, but he would appear to be losing. And Joe McNally, the silver-haired, red-faced lawyer who represented the Movement for a Just World, seemed amused to watch one of the best young trial lawyers in Chicago apparently get squashed like a bug.

Nick's high forehead, narrow features and watery blue eyes made him look meek and diffident, a young monk perhaps, one who had not taken final vows and who was nervous about his position in the monastic community. He was the kind of monk, you would guess, who might be deeply interested in art and music and timid on the athletic field, to which the novice master had insisted he make an occasional visit.

You'd be right about the art and music—Orchestra Hall, the Art Institute, the Civic Opera House were among his favorite haunts. You'd be wrong about the athletics, though, perhaps because when he was seated behind his impeccably neat desk, you would hardly notice a solid, disciplined body that served him well at other favorite haunts—the tennis and handball courts at the Chicago Athletic Club and the fairways of Beverly Country Club.

In another and more rational age, I think he would have been a cleric, a studious, responsible scholar of canon law perhaps, with an even-tempered disposition that would fit well into community life. Yet he was the layman and I, a mordant, melancholy, contentious cynic, was the cleric.

A cleric who wore his traditional Roman collar in deliberate contrast to Ed Carny's white turtleneck sweater, a trademark the supply of which would be endlessly and expensively replaced by his admirers among the affluent Irish matrons of Chicago.

Despite his monkish appearance and his mostly monkish life, a streak of romanticism ran through Nicholas Curran, a tragic flaw that drew him to Cathy Collins. Clerics can't afford to be romantics. God knows I'm not one.

And here in his law office, while Joe McNally and I watched, each of us interested for reasons of his own, Nick was matched against perhaps the most charismatic priest in the world. Ed Carny was, they said, a Hans Kung with muscles, an Ed Hesburg who did not change sides after every presidential election. Edward T. Carny of the Franciscan Friars of the Holy Name was tall and massive, with wavy gray hair, commanding blue eyes and a square handsome face, wasted, if you were to believe his admirers, by the suffering he had endured for the poor. He reminded me of a slightly overage colonel in the Bengal Lancers, the sort of leader whose troops would willingly follow him into the mouth of the cannon in the Khyber Pass.

My mother never liked him, a disposition I inherited. When he was ordained, Senator Joseph R. McCarthy was riding high and a dashingly handsome young Ed Carny joined the anti-Communist crusade with lectures on the evils of the International Communist Conspiracy, mostly borrowed from a book by Monsignor Fulton Sheen. My mother, who knew the Party from personal experience, was offended by the young priest's shallow zealotry.

"Clerical discount," she used to whisper unhappily to my father whenever Father Ed emerged from the sacristy of St. Praxides' to say Mass. "Gets away with being a dummy because he wears a Roman collar."

My father's whispered response was a real whisper and not the stage version. "And good looks, Katie. Roman collar and good looks—a potent combination."

When we were in high school, Father Ed would send the outweighed and outcoached teams of St. "Frank's" out to do battle with the semi-professional rivals that played in the Catholic League, often inspiring us to victories to which we had no legitimate claim. More recently, as a missionary in Costaguana, he had galvanized a most unlikely assortment of misfits—priests, nuns and lay people—into dedicated fighters for human liberation.

People like our little quasi-virgin and presumed martyr, St. Cathy of the South Side.

Nick swallowed and tried again. "I'm sorry, Father. My obligation as the executor of her estate is to leave it to a judge to declare whether she's dead or not."

McNally, whose flushed face was partly natural and partly acquired, the result of a surfeit of what my ancestors called the "creature," put in his two cents: "That's true, Nicky, but the court will take its cue from you. If you elect to fight a determination of her death, you can drag it out for most of the remaining five years, regardless."

A massive sheet of rain beat against the windows, rattling them and isolating us temporarily from the rest of the city. Impressive, but not quite the tornado Nicholas needed.

"Her husband will contest the will as soon as it goes into probate." Nick was playing nervously with a Mark Cross pen, one of his rare extravagances.

Nick hated Roy Tuohy, as you may imagine, with an unremitting passion.

And in this matter Ed Carny was in complete agreement. "That traitor." He waved his arms as he had during his spectacular sermons at St. Praxides' in the old days, sermons which were so powerful that hundreds of people would phone the rectory on Saturday to see what mass he was saying the next day. "He's actually writing procapitalist tracts for the American Freedom Institute. He won't get a penny."

"We can arrange a settlement with him," McNally said easily.

"And there's the family...." Nick was not quite ready to say a flat "no" to a priest he had always admired, indeed worshiped.

"What about the family, Father...?" Ed Carny hesitated, after all these years not able to remember my name. But then I am quite insignificant in every imaginable way.

"Can't tell about us Ryans, Ed. We're a crazy bunch."

I might as well have been a statue of St. Christopher, devoid of speech. Ed Carny ignored me and returned to his assault on Nick. "She's dead, Nick; no one regrets it more than I do." His voice broke. "I...we all loved her, but she's dead. We have witnesses now. These two women suffered with her and saw her die."

He reached over to the pile of neatly stacked papers in front of Nick, selected one of them and began to read, with considerable relish and quite oblivious to Nick's distress, the "Acts" as I suppose we must call them in deference to the terms of the Roman martyrology of St. Catherine.

The testimony was quite spectacular: long weeks of humiliation, torture and rape. Although she was beaten, suspended from the ceiling, burned with cigarette butts, violated many times, and tied to a table with electrodes attached to her genitals, Cathy refused to reveal the names of the revolutionaries she had helped. Nor did she once curse her tormentors or cry out for mercy. Her fingers were broken and then her arms and legs. Her face was slashed, nails were pulled from her fingers and toes, but still our brave martyr would not surrender.

The purpose of such torture, Cathy had told me in one of her last letters before she was arrested, was not really to obtain information but to create terror—and of course to amuse the torturers, like Comandante Felipé María Hernández y Gould, the most feared member of the junta that ruled the country.

Finally, on a lovely spring morning in 1975, she was dragged into the courtyard of the Esmeralda Barracks, and while the two witnesses, Paola and Isabella, were forced to watch, she was executed.

" 'They pulled off her clothes and raped her many times,' " Father Ed continued, reading more slowly. " 'Then they shoved their bayonets into her. Then the *comandante* took his chain saw and cut off her breasts and then her arms and her legs, each in two pieces. Then finally her head. She stopped screaming only when he sawed through her neck. The American *señorita* was very brave. Even at the last she did not curse them or plead for mercy....' "

So died my cousin Cathy, who as a girl wanted to be a modern Joan of Arc. Did she welcome martyrdom when it came or, as blood spouted from her severed breasts, did she regret that she had never nursed a child?

Unworthy questions. No one wants to die. Cathy would have died more bravely than most of us, certainly more bravely than I.

"That's what the United States is doing in Costaguana," Ed shouted, slapping the papers on Nick's desk. "Gould was trained in this country. He is a lackey of American imperialism."

Nick looked as if the chain saw had cut through his soul. "The reform government says he's dead," he said slowly.

Don Felipé had indeed put in time at the Command and General Staff School, though he had spent more time chasing the women in the vicinity of Carlisle Barracks than in attending class. Besides, chain saw 101 was not one of the courses.

"Puppets of the military, tools of the United States, employees of the multinationals," Ed raged scornfully, his face purple with fury. "Every citizen of the United States is guilty of her death. Her innocent blood is on our hands. We must expiate by using her money as she wished it to be used—to fight for the liberation of mankind."

"Humankind," I breathed.

Nick was outclassed in the discussion not only because his legal calm was overwhelmed by Ed Carny's flaming zeal. How could you argue with a man who had been a hero to you for twenty years?

When he was dean of students and then principal (that was before Catholic high schools acquired headmasters), he knew almost all the students' first names, the parishes from which they came, their fathers' occupations, the names of their brothers and sisters, even the problems the family might have (widowed mother, alcoholic father). He showed up at wakes and weddings and confirmations, found money for those who needed it, bailed people out of jail, persuaded judges to give them another chance, charmed mothers, placated fathers, reassured pastors. It was universally agreed that he was the best high-school principal in the city.

And certainly the best looking.

And if he spent more time with the parents of the affluent students than with the parents of the poor, no one would find fault. After all, St. Frank's—like every other Catholic high school—needed money. So no one objected to his closeness to the offspring of such affluent families. On the contrary, that too was defended as part of his job.

He missed the Ryans, and that was a mistake—because the Ryans, albeit they were crazy, were also affluent and powerful. But, as I have said, it is very easy to miss me.

The cult of Father Ed on the South Side continued after he left the high school and started a community organization in the black neighborhood. Even the most vicious of racists among the alumni sent him checks. He was a nigger lover, but he was OUR nigger lover. Nor were they put off by his activity in front of the Conrad Hilton during the 1968 convention. Checks pursued him to Costaguana. Even if Ed Carny proclaimed himself a Marxist revolutionary, he was still OUR Marxist revolutionary. And Republicans who thought Nixon was a traitor for dealing with Red China supported Ed's work.

He could do no wrong. When he denounced American war-mongering, imperialism and capitalist racism on Sunday mornings at St. Praxides', the wealthy parishioners smiled and said to one another, "Doesn't he preach a wonderful sermon?" and worried about his health—"Poor man, he needs a vacation."

Nick and Cathy both worshiped the ground he walked on. Of course, Nick's father died when he was a freshman and Cathy's father was a silent piece of furniture in their house.

"I'll do everything I can, Father Ed," Nick replied cautiously. "I certainly want to see Catherine's memory honored as much as you do."

A fair and honorable man, he could accept Cathy as a martyr on Ed's altar rather than a bride on his own bed.

"I know you will, Nick," Ed said in the tone of one who has called an erring basketball captain back to the canons of sportsmanship. "I'm sure it will all work out. You loved her more than almost anyone else."

One of Father Ed's most effective mannerisms was to assume that he had won an argument and then praise the disputant's return to virtue and sanity. In this case he would not budge Nicholas Curran's legal scruples, but in recent years Father Ed had become a little less keen in reading others' reactions.

"What work are you doing now, uh...Father?" he said to me.

The hail shower had swept by and the treacherous sun had returned. Sure enough, the Board of Trade was still at the foot of the LaSalle Street canyon.

"Blackie Ryan," I said, not letting him get away with missing my name. "I teach Greek and philosophy in the seminary."

Which was true, though not perhaps the whole truth.

He shook his head, like a man who can't quite understand. "I know that someone has to do that work, but I don't see how you can stand such irrelevant activity at a time when the forces of liberation and democracy are stirring all over the world."

Another one of Ed's mannerisms was to say something very negative about you and/or your work but with a warm tone, an affectionate grin and a strong pat on the back.

"I guess Greek is irrelevant in an age of democracy," I agreed.

He missed the paradox, lifted right out of G. K. Chesterton, completely.

You will have guessed that I don't like the man. I never did. But I have a father who is very much alive and whose only fault is that he is the white sheep of our crazy family.

So I didn't need a father figure like Ed Carny.

And he had taken away my cousin Cathy. For that I was not about to forgive him.

2
BLACKIE

"She's dead, Nick." I slapped the bare wooden table in the dining room of the Cliff Dwellers to stir him out of his reverie. "We will not see her again in this world."

"I know," he sighed, shaking his head as if to clear away the daydreams. "I know in my gut that she's dead. But my legal head says there is not enough proof to go into probate."

We had walked from LaSalle to Michigan Avenue under the glowering sky, each with his own image of the woman whose limbs Don

Felipé had cut off—doubtless, Nick with memories of his limbs entwined with hers in an act he would have called love.

My memory was of a pretty little seven-year-old who walked down the aisle next to me on first Communion day, giggling beneath her white veil.

And of a brave young woman who could write letters which finally were uncompromisingly honest about her own self-deceptions.

Clergyman or not, Christian or not, I would have strangled Don Felipé if he'd been available for such an exercise. In his absence Ed Carny would do.

Nick would have wanted to put the *comandante* on trial—and call Ed as a witness, and probably settle for a life-in-prison plea bargain.

If you had watched him stride across the Loop with me, broad-shouldered, confident and strong, you would have revised your image of him as a pleasant, studious young monk. At noon the Loop becomes a network of Indian paths with lawyers doggedly pursuing their prey, swarming like Indian braves hunting in the forest, simultaneously hostile and friendly, ready for combat, but also ready to strike a deal. In this forest Nick was one of the most powerful of the young chiefs, energetic yet deliberate, vigorous but gracious, a man who could smile quickly and crack a joke as he moved through the forest and still be absolutely sound in a crisis. Perhaps he was more cautious than some of the reckless young braves, but only because he reserved his flair for the times when flair was essential. You knew when you saw him move briskly along the forest trail that in the moment of truth, his insights would be deadly accurate and his instincts totally reliable.

And your analysis of Nicholas Broderick Curran would have been absolutely right, unless the prey being pursued in the forest was a woman. Raised by a land-grubbing, penny-pinching, perpetually whining mother and surrounded by three bitchy sisters, Nick was defenseless when the subject was women.

"There are witnesses," I said tentatively.

It was characteristic of Nick that he would take me to lunch in the spare, turn-of-the-century dining room (no air conditioner in summer) on the top of Orchestra Hall. Not for him the plush, important eating clubs of which his firm had undoubtedly made him a member. None of those clubs, you see, had been founded by the great architect Louis Sullivan.

"You know how naive Father Ed is," he poked unenthusiastically at his mushroom omelet. "He thinks everyone is as sincere as he is. I'm not convinced by their affidavits. It could have been anyone who was executed that morning. At the least, I want them on the witness stand."

"Ed stands to profit if they're telling the truth."

He seemed surprised. "Oh, sure, but Ed doesn't pay much attention to money. He was in no hurry for the will to be probated until the witnesses appeared."

I broke a piece of Ry-Krisp, my one concession to the fitness craze. "The American ambassador says there is no reason to doubt that they were in Esmeralda."

Nick dismissed the ambassador's assurance as irrelevant. "Six months after the reform government takes over and they are freed, almost two years after the event, they come forward with testimony. I suppose that they are telling the truth, but as a lawyer who is responsible for Catherine's estate, I can't take that for granted."

He pushed the half-eaten omelet away. No appetite at all after Ed's recitation of the Acts of St. Catherine.

"And as much as you like Ed Carny, you are not eager to see Cath's money go to his crackpot organization."

Nick glared at me. "You know too goddamn much, Blackie."

I considered not buttering the Ry-Krisp, but decided against such austerity. "And you wonder why an Outfit lawyer like McNally is representing the Movement?"

I quickly examined my refusal to share her letters with Nick. Was I jealous of him because for one hate- and passion-filled weekend he was her lover and I merely loved her? My usually cooperative conscience assured me I was clean. But I didn't trust it.

"Ed is so..." He gestured like a man apologizing for a lovable but incorrigible child.

"So naive. He doesn't know that you might think the Mob is after Cathy's money."

"I didn't say that," he responded hotly.

I refused to rise to the bait. We looked out the high windows of the Cliff Dwellers at the gray lake, churning and foaming beyond the tracks and the park.

"She was born in the wrong time," Nick continued, speaking very softly. "Ten years earlier or ten years later and none of this would have happened."

"Hmmn," I said, taking another Ry-Krisp. Yes, of course, Cathy was a product of the sixties, one of the few would-be martyrs of the decade whose offer was taken seriously by those who are in the business of carving up young women's bodies.

"I often think I might have been able to stop it," he continued. "Maybe I didn't insist strongly enough. Particularly when I saw her the last time in Río."

"No one resists grace, Nick. It's a combination of mist and quick-silver. It sneaks in through the cracks and the crannies, fills up the interstices that our plans and programs and personalities leave empty, takes possession of the random openings we give it and then, when we least expect it, when we've done everything in our power to stop it, BANG! there's the big surprise."

He had not the faintest notion what I was talking about.

"Catherine as a saint is certainly a surprise.... By the way, Blackie, will you ride up to the Hill with me for the dedication of the statue? I promised Rosie O'Gorman that I'd be there."

An invitation to dedicate Rosie's statue to her martyred friend was about as appealing as an invitation to a ball in Seville while the black death was raging in the city.

"Why did you agree to go?" I demanded impatiently.

"You know Rosie." He shrugged. "She wouldn't accept a refusal. The bishop will be there...." His voice trailed off apologetically.

Nick Curran is a lawyer of enormous integrity, strength of character, skill and wisdom. He will probably end up in the United States Senate before he is forty-five. Alas, he was the youngest of four children, and the only boy. So Nick is utterly powerless to resist the whims and wishes of women.

Which is one of the reasons Cathy's dismembered body lies under the ground somewhere in Costaguana.

"All right," I said. "I'll come along and try to protect you from Rosie's charismatics, but I warn you it will be a freak show."

"I don't think it will be that bad," he said lamely. "Anyway, I guess I owe her something."

"Let the dead bury their dead, Nick," I snapped. "Cathy would want you to go on with your life."

Nick was thirty-four. He should have been married long since. He loved children and should have had kids of his own in grammar school by now. He had carried the torch for Cathy for twelve years. It was time to put it down.

"I know," he said sadly. "But this estate keeps her on my mind. I don't like..." He hesitated, then reached into his jacket pocket, pulled out a battered airmail envelope and passed it across the table.

I recognized the small, neat handwriting—long antedating her convent years—instantly. My fingers trembled slightly as I took the letter, not enough, however, for Nick to notice.

Dear Nick,

I'm sorry I was so stupid about the will. You were right as you always are. You should have been tougher with me. I've had some second thoughts since then. I'll be back in the States shortly to change the will. See you soon.

Fondly,
Cath

Typically direct and to the point. Cathy was as flaky as a bowl of breakfast food, kinky as a telephone cord, and indecisive as an archbishop. But once she had made up her mind to do something, she acted with the brisk vigor of a 747 touching down.

There had probably been only one earlier version of the letter, which closed with "love" instead of "fondly."

I felt like someone had turned on the nonexistent air-conditioning of the Cliff Dwellers.

"This puts things in a different light," I said, though I was not as surprised as Nick must have been when he opened the letter.

"You'll note that it's dated October 14, 1974—a few days before she was arrested."

"I noticed that. What are the implications; legally, I mean?"

"If anyone else has any indication of how she was going to change the will, this letter would be powerful evidence in probate. Under ordinary circumstances, it would have no impact on Ed's motion to have her declared dead."

"To be heard, appropriately enough, just before your namesake comes down the chimney with his bags of goodies."

"I think the letter would upset Ed."

"It might at that."

"It could be interpreted as a sign that her dedication to the Movement was weakening."

How Nick's hopes must have soared between the time he read the letter and the news of her arrest. And then what hell afterward. Poor bastard.

"And Rosie and her crowd of charismatics and all the other cultists of our St. Cathy would be terribly upset at that notion."

"I don't want to tarnish her memory." Nick's chin sank in his hands. "Yet..."

"Yet, someone may have found out that she was changing the will and called in Don Felipé? And if that's the case, the motion Judge Fielding will hear next month might give a clue to who that someone was."

Nick looked up at me, his handsome face reminding me of a painting of Jesus with a crown of thorns. "Ed has some strange people in that movement."

"He has indeed." There would be no peace for Nick until Cathy's ghost was put to rest. And that might take a long time. "When's the dedication at the Hill?"

"Next Monday." He shook his head as if to clear the demons out of his brain. "Feast of St. Catherine of Alexandria."

"There is no more feast. The scholars claim that she is merely a legend, wheel and all. So she has been ejected from the Calendar of the Universal Church. And, anyway, next Monday is not the twenty-fifth of November. It's a week early."

"I think Rosie said something about changing the feast because of the Thanksgiving vacation."

If you were a Charismatic matron, married to a fabulously wealthy Silicon Valley president, you could, I suppose, do anything you want with the feast of an excommunicated saint.

"Okay." I marked it in my calendar and finished my tea. Bring this bicentennial year of our republic to an end by praying at the foot of my cousin's statue. I hoped that Rosie restrained the lunatics at the Hill from an abstract representation of Cathy's martyrdom.

"You'll help me?" he pleaded, his eyes so sad that if I had a heart it might have felt like breaking.

"Put the ghosts to rest? You bet." Goddamn right. And then in an ineffectual effort to get his mind off Cathy I asked, "Going to the concert tonight?"

"No. Mom is having the family for dinner."

And of course you must be there. Mom has never forgiven you for the disgrace that she thinks you caused when you moved out to your own condominium. Imagine a boy of twenty-six who doesn't want to live at home with his mother and unmarried sister! What will people say!

Bitches. If their necks were available I would add them to the list of appropriate strangulation victims.

Oh, yes, Cathy, I won't spoil the legend. But I'll be damned if those crackpots are going to get money you didn't want them to have. And I'd show Nick your damn letters if I was not afraid they'd make him love you even more than he does and prolong his agony of loss.

3
NICHOLAS

I met Joe McNally in the steam room at the Illinois Athletic Club. His eyes were bloodshot and his flesh flabby and inflamed.

I was feeling good. Coming out of the pool, I had encountered counsel for the defendant in a big breach-of-contract construction suit.

"Two-five," he'd said, meaning million, and offering a settlement.

"Two-seven," I'd replied, having been willing to settle for two-three.

"A deal," he said, diving into the pool. "Lunch Friday," he added, coming up for water.

"The Attic," I'd said, walking toward the steam room. I probably could have got two-eight for our client. But you have to leave everyone some room.

Such exchanges run on pure instinct and I love them. I might not be good in the pits at the Board of Trade—I think a little bit too much for that sort of work—but I like my quick, sharp combats occasionally.

The first couple of cases for the government back in the sixties, I didn't trust my instincts and lost. Then came the day when on pure gut I offered a petty hood immunity and blew a cozy little extortion racket wide open.

Since then, my instincts have been wrong sometimes, but not as often as when I trust my brains. Mind you, instincts are no substitute for hard work, careful research, smart colleagues and intense preparation. However, you can't win without them.

Except with women. And Monica says that my woman instincts are not bad instincts, only undeveloped.

I told myself it wouldn't do to think about her while I was walking around naked at the IAC (Illinois Athletic Club). So I wasn't quite ready for McNally's opening ploy.

"Probate work is a little unusual for you, isn't it?" he said, with the Irish lawyer's typical indirect opening.

"I've been close to the family for years. Ed Ryan got me my first job."

"Yeah.... Have you decided what to do about my client's petition?"

"Not really. I'll have to see what the witnesses say under oath."

His eyes flashed. "You're going to put them on the stand, huh?" He wiped the sweat off his torso with a soggy towel.

"I don't see how that can be avoided," I replied, feigning surprise. "Do you?"

A hell of a lot of good my precious instincts did that Monday morning in Río when I might have saved her life.

"I suppose not," he sighed.

"Why are your friends so interested in the case?" I asked bluntly.

He laughed as Outfit lawyers always do when their "friends" are mentioned, conveying the impression that they think of their employers as charming and delightful peasants.

"My friends are good Catholics, you know that. They send their kids to Catholic schools. Fine family people. They merely want to help out the missionary work of the church."

"A Marxist Catholic 'liberation' group?" I said skeptically.

"Well, you know how persuasive Father Carny is. Maybe my friends like him."

"Maybe."

"I don't suppose they'd mind my telling you a little more," he added. "Sort of off the record."

What he meant was that his friends had given him a message for me.

"I won't be on the stand."

"Let's suppose, just hypothetically, mind you, that some good Catholic people in those spic countries have a lot of money that their families have saved by years and years of hard work. And let's suppose that they are afraid that the government—it doesn't matter what political hue, governments are governments are governments—might take this money away from them. And they know my friends have friends elsewhere who might help them by seeing that the money flows smoothly, if you know what I mean."

"An interesting set of suppositions."

"Yeah, now what if someone with a chain of mission stations in a number of these countries sets up a little messenger service, a kind of small United Parcel, let's say, to bring my friends and these people in contact with each other and what if this someone gets a small commission for his work?"

Was Ed Carny involved in smuggling currency?

"That would be pretty risky for him, wouldn't it?"

"Naw, my friends might welcome the help of such a messenger service, as long as everyone was honest. You know what I mean— couriers who could carry a neat little attaché case with large denomination bills, maybe switch the case somewhere for one that looked just like it, only with dollars in it. That kind of thing, you understand?"

"But if someone has begun to dip into the funds, your friends would be very upset and might want repayment real quick."

"They become very impatient when they think someone is trying to rip them off. They feel it shows a serious lack of respect."

"How much?"

"Nowhere near all of it, but it's the only reserves he has left. Mind you, he didn't act disrespectfully himself. The man is incredibly naive, sincere but naive. I don't think he knew who he was dealing with at either end. He merely wanted the money for his mission work, if you know what I mean."

"Will they put him down?"

"Come on, Nick, they're good Catholics."

I rose from the bench, tying a towel around my waist. "That didn't protect the provincial of a certain community who woke up strangled a few years ago."

"That's an entirely different case."

How did a guy like McNally sleep at night?

I waited for more. I'm following a gut feel for you now, Catherine. Too late, I know.

"I don't think they'll put him down. He's too popular. They might close down all his missions, though. That's why he's in such a hurry to get the money."

"They could close down the Centers?"

He seemed surprised. "Why not? Think about it, anyway. That's all my friends ask."

"I will," I promised him. "I certainly will."

His friends were everywhere and could do almost anything they wanted, including murder a woman courier.

4
NICHOLAS

I suppose that the appropriate adjectives for my affair with Monica are "torrid" and "tender." It started out as torrid sex and had somehow, without either of us quite intending it, become tender love, a love so sweet that it frightened both of us.

As I drove from my mother's house in Oak Lawn to Monica's apartment near Lincoln Park, I wondered not what my mother would think of the exercises which awaited me—Mom would assume that since I was unmarried I was still a virgin—but what John Blackwood Ryan would think.

There are a number of theories as to why Katie Ryan—God rest her wonderful soul—gave him that middle name. One is that she had made a Blackwood convention at bridge the night she conceived him. Another is that one of the ancestral Collinses was actually called "Black Blackwood" when he led an eighteenth-century group of Irish revolutionary Whiteboys. You can never be sure with the Ryans, but Blackie seemed to want to be called nothing else.

I'd met Monica at a trial in which her market research skills made her an expert witness for the other side. I'm afraid I tore apart survey-taking during my cross-examination and made her a little angry.

We met in the elevator at the end of the day, just the two of us, and I offered my halfhearted apology. Her gray eyes flashed merrily and she said I would be forgiven if I took her to supper.

She was a tall woman, at least five-ten, with long blond hair, a round gentle face and a voluptuous body. She was Polish, from the Northwest Side; her husband, Tim O'Connor, had been a marine captain till a scrap of a Russian mortar shell tore through his skull at Khe Sanh. Monica was the vice-president of her company, well paid, well challenged and well adjusted to widowhood and to single-parenting her two teenage children, who were away at school, if one was to believe her.

She was also smart, and fun and funny. I asked her to hear Solti do Bach and Mozart the following week. When the concert was over, she invited me to come home with her.

"Why?" I asked, confused and uncertain.

"Because I want to go to bed with you."

I was shocked and astonished. In my milieu women don't talk that way—though Catherine had on occasion. Still, I was secretly pleased and not a little surprised that a woman would find me attractive.

"I'm afraid I'm not a spectacular lover," I responded, feeling my face grow warm.

"I bet you are too."

Sex, she insisted, was recreation, exercise, natural activity. It would be unnatural for two people our age who were becoming friends not to explore each other's body.

I wasn't so sure about that. But there had not been much sex in my life and I was hardly able to resist such an attractive temptation.

Sex with Monica was delightful. She was spectacularly skillful at giving pleasure and at teaching me to give pleasure in return. She completely ignored my inexperience and naiveté until I was neither inexperienced nor naive anymore.

Moreover we liked each other. We were not only lovers, but confidants and friends. The conversations before and after lovemaking were as rewarding as the sex itself.

Then suddenly there was respect, affection, concern—and an emotion for which there was no other name but love. It would have seemed almost inevitable that we would begin to talk about marriage. Blackie would have said that there is a propensity toward permanence in every sexual act. Surely there was a tendency in that direction for Monica O'Connor and me. We both tried to duck the issue, because we both were still grieving for the loves we had lost. And we knew, without exactly saying it to each other, that our love would soon demand that we abandon our grief and face the challenge of a new life.

She was waiting for me in film and lace when I got off the elevator on her floor, despite my warning that such appearances might pique the interest of the neighbors. As was always the case when she knew I had been at my mother's, her antics as soon as we were inside the door were especially mind bending—"so that you'll know that all women are not like your family."

After our first round we drank cognac, a ritual on which she insisted. Monica was curled up on the couch, frankly admiring me in a way which was both flattering and embarrassing.

"A lot about Catherine today?" she said, rearranging her lovely legs.

"Can you tell? I'm sorry. I didn't mean..."

"I'm insanely jealous of any other woman." She laughed. "But, no,

I don't mind." She put her glass on a coaster on an antique end table. "Only I can't get a picture of what she was like. As you know, I'm an old-fashioned Catholic who can't stand these radical nuns who sound like nothing had happened for a thousand years until they came along."

She was indeed an old-fashioned Catholic who went to Communion dutifully every Sunday, quite convinced that our romps were "at the most, venial sins."

"She was something like that some of the time, but there was more.... I don't want to bore you...."

"I won't be bored. You should talk about her tonight, I think. Come here. Sit beside me."

"My mother told me never to sit next to naked women."

"And my mother told me never to take the slip covers off the couch, especially when naked men might sit on it."

Her comfortable, Scandinavian Modern apartment was incredibly clean—a Polish trait, she insisted. And I wasn't sure that the slip covers were not stored away to be returned as soon as I left.

I huddled in her arms and she drew a blanket around us to keep us cozy for the hour or so we had before we would go to her bedroom again, experiment with some new sexual gymnastics and then, at her stern instruction, get the sleep we needed if we were to work efficiently the next day.

She stroked my forehead and face with sensitive fingertips. "I love you, Nick," she whispered. "I didn't mean to fall in love with you, but I have. Trust me with your pain. Maybe I can help make it go away."

I was caught between a dead love and a living love. I couldn't keep them both.

"A lot of the radical nuns you don't like have merely substituted one kind of piety for another," I began hesitantly.

"Feminism for the sorrowful mother novena," she observed.

"Right. And Catherine certainly did some of that. But I don't think there's much sensuality in such people. Catherine was the most sensuous woman I knew until I met you."

"Really!" She laughed and drew me closer.

"Not the same way. She never had a chance. But that's not the point. If she had only been pious or only been sexy, I probably wouldn't have been attracted. It was the combination, I guess."

"Poor kid. And I suppose the combination is what killed her too."

Without any warning, which would have enabled me to control myself, I started to cry. I may have wept as a child, but I have no recollection of it. These tears for Catherine were the first I had shed in my conscious life.

I wept and I wept and I wept. Monica hugged my face against her splendid breasts and hummed softly as though I were a little boy being consoled by his mother.

Which I guess, in a way, I was.

Over and over and over I repeated my cry of protest, "Why did she have to die, Monica? Why did she have to die?"

5
NICHOLAS

"You understand that officially this conversation is not taking place?" the thin and nervous assistant to the assistant director of the Federal Bureau of Investigation said, drawing tight little circles on his desk pad.

"I'm not here at all," I said wearily.

For all I had learned during my day-long visit to the J. Edgar Hoover rabbit warren, I might just as well not have been there. The Bureau owes me a lifetime of favors, but unlike local police forces, the Feds have a poor collective memory for favors owed. Officially they knew nothing about Father Ed Carny. Officially they knew nothing about any connection between him and the Outfit. Officially they were unaware of any international ring of currency smugglers.

But the official line was always uttered in a tone of voice which promised that if I had enough clout they could tell me stories which would curl my hair.

The Bureau also routinely exaggerates how much it knows and how secret its secrets need to be. So I called a friend in a very high place beyond the boundaries of the Department of Justice and leaned on him. He was in a business in which one never forgets favors.

Therefore my assistant to the assistant was anxiously warning me that our conversation did not exist before he told me what he had been warned he had to tell me.

"There is no violation of American law in removing currency from a Latin American country and transferring it to banks in a third country," he began cautiously.

"I understand," I agreed.

"Nevertheless, when we learn that certain American cities are being used as exchange points in this process, we feel obliged to maintain a certain interest."

"Sure." I nodded. "International currency and international drugs are often connected—and international guns too."

I didn't add that the Bureau often collected information for the same reason the man said that he climbed Mount Everest—it was there. And someday it might be useful.

"There is hardly a Latin American country," he went on, "in which a considerable number of individuals—on the right or the left, as the case may be—do not have a substantial interest in transporting money, often U.S. dollars bought on the black market, to other countries, most notably Switzerland."

"Against the proverbial rainy day."

"Precisely," he said, as if I were a student with a quick and accurate insight. "Nor is it unusual for the representatives of organized crime to become involved in such traffic."

Either because they were asked or, more likely, because they had muscled their way in.

"American missionaries theoretically would be extremely useful couriers. A host country would not be likely to search them too carefully before they left. Moreover, at the present time missionaries move about Latin America and indeed the world with a good deal of freedom."

"So I understand." Would he ever get to the point?

"Mind you, we are not questioning their consciences in these matters. For example, they might be smuggling church investments to the Vatican."

"And in such cases the Outfit would give them a twenty percent clerical discount."

"Hardly." He made a face to indicate that he did not appreciate my sense of humor.

"So Ed Carny has been smuggling currency from Latin America to Switzerland?" I said, forcing him to the point.

"Not at present, of that we are certain," he said, playing nervously with an eight-by-ten manila folder.

"And before he was thrown out of Costaguana?"

He passed me the folder, permitting me to make my own judgment.

There were eight pictures, all of them in airports. I guessed that there were three different backgrounds, San Juan, Miami and JFK in

New York. In each of the pictures briefcases were being exchanged. In five of them the broad shoulders of Father Ed were unmistakable.

I experienced an instant of revulsion. Father Ed was a hero with feet of clay, doing dirty work for the Mob.

"And who are the couriers in these three shots?" I asked, showing him those in which Ed did not appear.

He shrugged. "There were a number of different people."

"Catherine Collins?" I asked, examining the photos carefully. They were sufficiently blurred so that I could not tell the sex much less the identity of either partner in the exchange.

"Not to our knowledge," he said cautiously.

"Would you tell me if you did know?"

"I cannot answer that question," he replied smugly.

I gave up and decided to try for the six o'clock flight to O'Hare.

Nine chances out of ten she was one of Father Ed's runners and the Bureau knew it. Why hide the truth from me?

Why not? What good is there in knowing a secret unless you can hide it from someone else?

Anyway, it didn't make much difference to the only question in which I was fundamentally interested: Was Catherine Collins really dead? Whether she was a courier in illegal currency movements before she disappeared into the prison camp at Esmeralda was, presumably, irrelevant to what happened to her in the camp.

It might not, however, be irrelevant to a hasty legal decision that she was dead.

And who was Catherine Collins, who might have been one of the couriers in the three blurred photos? Blurred, perhaps to confuse me.

A thrill hunter who loved the mystery and the excitement of dealing with the Outfit? A radical Marxist unshakably committed to the cause of world revolution? A pious nun dedicated to healing pain and misery? A lonely and frightened woman trying desperately to repudiate past mistakes?

Or an appealing woman whom I had always loved?

It had been so long that I could not even remember what she looked like.

The last time together in Río, when we had made angry, hurtful love, she was surely not a pious nun.

I phoned Monica from National Airport and proposed a late supper.

"Sure," she said. "Call me from O'Hare. Love you."

We were saying that to each other, however casually, more and more often. Monica was willing to give up her grief.

Was I?

If my wild-goose chase to Washington was any indication, I was not.

6
NICHOLAS

I had had no intention of attending Catherine's New Year's Eve Party in 1960. At the time, I was a freshman in college and she was only a sophomore in high school, hardly worth my notice even if she was the prettiest girl around. However, Pat Ryan, her cousin and a classmate of mine at St. Anthony College, was going to the party and he urged me to come along. "Free booze and free girls," Pat argued.

In those days in the Neighborhood there was rarely booze and the girls were certainly not free. Neither Pat nor I would have known what to do with free girls anyway. But Pat's presence at the party made it more acceptable for me. It was not merely a gathering of silly sophomore girls.

Pat's younger brother, Blackie, would tag along as he did when Pat and I were together during summer vacations. We didn't mind Blackie, who even then was a strange little kid, because after a few minutes he seemed to become quite invisible.

Nevertheless, I felt awkward when we drifted into the big old Collins house at the top of the ridge on Glenwood Drive about eleven-thirty on New Year's Eve. My mother insisted that Erin Collins spent more money on antique furniture for one room than most people spent on their whole house. Surely the recreation room, where "The Sound of Music" was playing on a monumental stereo and some couples were already dancing, had the look of an uncomfortable and oddly assorted museum exhibit.

One quick scan of the room reassured me that I would escape the horrible fate of losing caste by associating with "kids." A law school student was dancing with a well-developed sophomore. The youngest boy in the room was a high-school senior, save for Blackie, who disappeared into the library and was not seen again till midnight. Catherine's bevy of sophomore girls were dressed up and made up to appear seven or eight years older than they were and, except for the vagrant adolescent giggle, were able to maintain their pose of sophisticated women of the world—

what we and they thought were sophisticated women of the world—with cigarettes, hard liquor, an occasional "shit" and cheek-to-cheek dancing.

And Catherine's court of young women was uniformly attractive. She was not one of those pretty women who are threatened by other pretty women.

"See," said Pat Ryan, reading my thoughts. "You don't have to feel you're spending New Year's Eve with children."

That concern was only half my problem. The other half was Catherine, lustful thoughts about whom invaded my mind when I least expected them.

She pecked Pat on the cheek, hugged Blackie affectionately and shook hands with me.

"Hi, stranger. Getting straight As in college too?"

"We don't have finals till next week." I stumbled over the words, disconcerted that weird little Blackie seemed so at ease in her warm embrace.

She often appears in my memory the way she was that night, in the first flush of her womanly beauty, dressed in a white bubble dress with red polka dots and a matching stole to cover her bare shoulders. She was too young to dress that way, my mother would have said, and perhaps rightly. Erin Collins pushed her daughter too fast toward physical and social maturity.

Just the same, Catherine filled the dress perfectly, a slim, perfectly proportioned young body that you wanted to touch as much in admiration as in desire. With her high cheekbones, pert, upturned nose, sharply sculpted face, dark skin, short curly hair and vast brown eyes she looked more gypsy than Irish, a young woman who perhaps ought to be dancing the flamenco in a café in Barcelona or playing a violin in a student beer hall in Vienna.

I was a romantic in those days. Blackie wasn't, however.

"You'll catch cold if you go out in that dress."

Catherine blushed. "You're not supposed to go out in them, dear Cousin." Despite her momentary embarrassment, her eyes were dancing with mischief—as they usually were. "Anyway, don't you like my dress?"

"I like the stole especially," said her cousin. "I'm delighted to see that our passions will not be aroused by dresses that are not Mary-like."

"You clown." She hugged him again and grabbed my hand. "Let's see if college has improved your dancing, Nicholas."

In those days there was a decent-dress crusade in Catholic high schools that advocated "Mary-like" women's apparel, which was defined by an intricate system of measurements of various parts of a woman's anatomy. Father Ed Carny joked that reading the measurement norms was more likely to lead to sin than looking at a girl who didn't follow them. As prefect of the Sodality of Our Lady in the sophomore class at Bethlehem High School for Young Ladies, Catherine vigorously advocated chaste and Mary-like dresses. But she did not always practice what she preached. The stole was a mere token concession, which I devoutly hoped—or perhaps not so devoutly—would be discarded before the evening was over.

The Ryans' little girl cousin, as they invariably called her, was hard to miss during the summers at Grand Beach when I was in high school and spent much of my weekend time and the whole of the last two weeks in August at the rambling wooden house where the Ryan clan came and went from Memorial Day to Labor Day. Mrs. Ryan, Katie, the one who had been a Communist as a girl, was still alive then and presided over the summertime festivities with charm and energy and extraordinary tolerance. Every guest became a member of the family to be praised, reprimanded, ordered, encouraged and consoled, as though the guest was one of her own.

I felt more at home with the Ryans than I did in my own home in Chicago. Even though my mother objected to my associating with the "wealthy" (despite the fact that she had amassed a considerable amount of money buying and selling real estate—the classic Irish "woman of property"), my police lieutenant father, before he died of the incurable disease of stopping an armed heroin addict for a traffic violation, insisted that the Ryans were "decent" people. He dissented rarely in family matters, but when he did, the issue was settled. So I could go to the Ryans whenever I wished, despite my mother's sighs and my sisters' sniffs.

And, although the Collinses had their own smaller and newer home farther down the beach, Catherine spent most of her time at "our" house. She was an only child; her father rarely came to the lake, and her mother's principal activity was arranging tea parties for those who shared her religious enthusiasms. In her own home Catherine was a hothouse plant, a doll dressed up to take bows for her mother's guests. At "our" place, she was an imp, a tomboy, a troublemaker, a trial, and a beloved blessing.

Katie Ryan insisted that Catherine was her namesake even though Katie stood for Kathleen and everyone knew Erin Collins was not close to her brother's wife, never quite able to forgive her for her Communist past. So, in a family where everyone was a favorite, Catherine was a special favorite, treasured by both Katie and by her eldest daughter and assistant matriarch, Mary Kate.

In such an environment Catherine turned into a hellion. And I was a special target for her tricks, never sure when my sheets would be frenched, my lemonade salted, my Coke laced with vinegar, my hair doused with sand.

None of the older boys found her antics amusing, especially Pat and me, though she and Blackie were usually in cahoots. She later denied that it ever happened, but I lost my temper and gave her a sound spanking one of those summers in the middle fifties, when she put not salt, but sand, in my lemonade. She wailed like a wounded banshee. When I calmed down, I feared I would be banished from the Ryan house forever. No one dared raise a hand to Katie's favorite niece.

But Catherine didn't squeal.

"No more sand," she giggled, bringing me and Pat a large ration of lemonade—the Ryans consumed it by the gallon—on the beach the next afternoon.

That was another part of the Catherine mystery. An only child who had most of her whims gratified even before she knew what they were, she was amazingly generous with her time and energy—the first one to clean up the table after dinner, an unasked bearer of cool drinks to all of us, a solo pilot with apparent monopoly on the Ryans' recalcitrant vacuum cleaner and the infallible window closer when the rain clouds gathered.

"You'd think she was the maid or something," said the golden-haired Mary Kate.

"She likes to help," her mother responded. "Nothing wrong with that. I wish some of it would rub off on my children."

Even to the inexperienced eyes of a fourteen-year-old boy, it was obvious that Catherine would mature into a lovely woman. When she ran down the beach, screaming at the top of her voice, the tomboy style could not altogether efface the trim little body or the carefully molded angles of her triangular heart face. You had to pretend that she was a nuisance, however, because, after all, she was still in fifth grade.

And heaven knows she was a nuisance—until you wanted someone to bring you lemonade.

Catherine never walked on the beach. Wherever she was going in those years it was at top speed, save when she donned her little doll dresses and went to church with her mother every morning, the only part of the day when she was not with her cousins. Her piety wasn't feigned, not even then. Later on, when her mother became so taken up with her "little group" in Chicago that Catherine spent the summers in the care of a housekeeper at Grand Beach, she still went to church every morning, even if it meant dragging a reluctant Ryan—or an even more reluctant Ryan guest, like me—out of bed to drive her to New Buffalo.

The doll clothes worn previously had been replaced by Bermuda shorts and a T-shirt, but the intense seriousness of her religious devotion was unchanged. I wondered often what she was saying to God and what she was hearing in return.

By then she was much too pretty to be written off as a tomboy nuisance.

By the summer of 1959 she had become a regular feature of the Friday night and Saturday night beach parties, obtaining entry by means of her portable stereo and her limitless collection of such staples as Elvis, Chubby Checker and the Beach Boys. The older girls were not pleased at first, but Catherine's energy and willingness to do all the work overcame their resistance.

And the sound of her musical-comedy voice, light and clear in the babble of teenage female sounds, was enough to fill my mind—and I suspect the minds of every male my age on the beach—with anguishing thoughts. The adolescent male imagination makes *Playboy* seem mature and sophisticated in comparison. Such imagination is essential, Blackie would later lecture me, for the continuation of the human race. Fortunately, in that era, while most of us thought and talked about nothing but girls, we did very little with them or to them. And when we became involved with a girl, usually she became a person quickly and we turned fiercely protective of her.

Others did, that is. My romantic attachments were limited, not so much for lack of opportunities—girls always needed prom dates—as for the lack of confidence. My mother and my sisters ridiculed me whenever there was a rumor that I was "falling for" a girl, and I discreetly avoided young women.

But Catherine, that summer of "Personality" and "Mack the Knife" and "Tom Dooley," was not to be avoided.

It happened in mid-July when the party was breaking up lest the Grand Beach police force find fault seeing us all in one place. Pat had gone off with his girl of the moment. Blackie was somewhere reading either *Goldfinger* by Ian Fleming or *The Phenomenon of Man* by Teilhard de Chardin. And I found myself and Catherine alone on the dark beach as if we were the only two persons left in the world.

The summer air was heavy with the threat of a coming rainstorm.

The night clouds obscured both moon and stars. You felt you had to push your way through heavy drapes of humidity.

A boy and a girl alone and invisible on the beach on a steamy summer evening—made to order in those days, and maybe in any days, for necking and petting. Especially as my mother and sisters would never find out. And I felt that it was time I overcame my inexperience.

I wasn't given much choice about it. Catherine said, "Hey, Nick, don't walk so fast, wait a minute." And stood on her tiptoes to kiss me, a wet, inexperienced and very intense kiss.

And so it started. In retrospect our games that night were harmless enough. The chances of our straying over the line into intercourse were almost nonexistent—neither of us knew how and I would have been terrified of hurting her. But, unlike other girls, Catherine drew no lines. And I had never felt, much less kissed, a girl's breasts before. By the standards of our group and that time, we went pretty far.

And, of course, Catherine continued to receive Holy Communion every morning.

As summer came to an end, so did my increasingly pleasant amusements with her willing young body. During the first week at college, we endured grim retreat, preached by a terrifying former military chaplain, a retreat in which we were bombarded with images of young men and young women horribly killed after they had committed "sins of the flesh" and thus were doomed to hell for all eternity. World War II, it seemed, was little more than the occasion of the damnation of millions.

I suffered acute guilt feelings about what I had done to Catherine, tried to count the number of times we had sinned—it seemed that there must have been hundreds—and spent a half hour in the confessional being shriven of my evil deeds.

I wondered whether Catherine had confessed them. I never did ask her.

Part of my "firm purpose of amendment" was a promise to avoid her for the rest of my life. Indeed, the chaplain, a bald, fat little man who reminded me of an unhappy and unhumorous Friar Tuck, made me swear never to see her again, before he gave me absolution. And, not wanting to be tormented in hell, I so swore.

But the flesh is weak. I told myself that I would be safe in the protection of Pat and Blackie, ignored my sisters' ridicule and went off to the celebration of the coming of the year 1960.

I think the music playing while we danced was something from Ray Charles, but the softness of Catherine's cheek against mine made the music seem unimportant. All my sinful feelings returned and didn't seem sinful as I held her in my arms, hardly conscious of anything but Catherine, not even the elaborate infrastructure which was deemed necessary in those days to maintain a strapless dress in place.

"Hmmn..." she cooed. "As cute as ever, but you still can't dance. Why do boys who are so graceful at shortstop and other silly places turn awkward on the dance floor?"

"Girls in our arms," I mumbled.

That sent her into spasms of laughter. Despite my inexperience, she seemed all wound up. Looking back, I see that the demons were already after her. Maybe they had plagued her all her life.

At 11:50, Mrs. Collins came into the room and turned off the stereo. "Sit down, boys and girls," she said. "I want to talk to you for a few minutes."

We were surprised. Parents were usually in evidence at the beginning of a party, but then they were supposed to quietly drift away, like the practically invisible Mr. Collins had already done, to some appropriate parental place.

Mrs. Collins was in her early fifties then, a slender woman with pale skin, a thin face and long white hair, clad always in black and looking like a poster for Lady Macbeth—or maybe one of the witches. Her eyes were permanently wide in the kind of expression of awe you would expect from someone who had just seen a vision of the Sacred Heart, and her voice was soft and breathless, as though she expected the cardinal to walk in any minute.

It was Someone more than the cardinal that she expected.

"I want you boys and girls to have a wonderful time tonight," she said rapturously, "because this is the last New Year's Eve party that will ever be."

Catherine's face was expressionless, neither angry nor embarrassed, nor surprised. Blackie had drifted back into the living room, with his finger in a copy of *Goodbye Columbus.*

"You know that when poor Pope Pius opened the Fatima letter two years ago, he broke down and wept for three days and then died a few weeks later. You know that Padre Pio has told some holy nuns the secret in the Fatima letter: we have not prayed enough and Russia will not be converted in time. The world will come to an end this year because of our failure to pray. It is too late now. All we can do is prepare for the end. There will never be a New Year's Day 1961. The earth will be a burned-out cinder before Labor Day. I want you to enjoy yourselves tonight and then begin tomorrow to pray and ready yourselves for the end."

"My mother says the letter from Lucy isn't about the end of the world," protested Rosie O'Gorman, a plump and lively little classmate of Catherine's. "She says it's about the obscene clothes women wear on beaches these days."

"Bikinis," said a whisper that I knew was from John Blackwood Ryan.

Not having heard her nephew's comment, Erin Collins smiled sweetly at Rosie. "Of course, darling, but dear Sister Lucy of the Sorrows has already told us that the Lady who appeared to them is upset about indecent dress. The secret letter is about the end of the world."

The Fatima secret, allegedly in a letter written by one of the three children who claimed to have seen the Virgin at that Portuguese town in 1916, had been the subject of much speculation not only in the "private revelation" circles in which Erin Collins moved but even among many Catholics not normally concerned about such things. Some of the nuns in the parochial schools used the "secret" as a bogeyman to frighten into line rambunctious boys who did not respond to other disciplinary sanctions.

"There is so little time left," Mrs. Collins went on serenely. "I know that you are all very good boys and girls and that when the end comes, the Blessed Mother will wrap you in her blue mantle and bring you home to Jesus. So that's why I want you to have a good time tonight. Those whom God loves have nothing to fear. But promise me that tomorrow you will begin to prepare."

She looked from face to face, sweet love mixed with a gentle demand for a response.

The grandfather clock in the foyer of the Collins house began to toll twelve. Outside one could hear the rattle of small arms fire, a Negro (as we would have said then) New Year's custom which had spread to white neighborhoods the last couple of years.

"Yes, Aunt Erin, we sure will," said Pat Ryan, who was impressionable enough to be frightened and to mean his pledge, although he and everyone else knew that by the next morning it would be forgotten.

"Yes, we sure will," agreed Rosie O'Gorman.

There was a chorus of agreement from the rest of us, including a movement of lips from the still impassive Catherine. Only Blackie's cherubic little face expressed dissent.

"God bless you and keep you all and have a wonderful new year," Mrs. Collins blessed us like a mother abbess and glided out of the room.

It could not have been more quiet before the closing of a casket at a wake.

"Pope John lost the letter," said Blackie. Then assuming an Italian accent, he imitated the wonderful fat Pope, whom we all worshiped. "I donno what I dida with it…it wasa here somawhere…donna worry about him…I finda pretty soon…issa verra important letter…what was thata name again? Fatima? Lika the cigaretta, ya mean? Hey, thata reminds me of a story…"

We laughed nervously. Blackie was going to be a priest, so we supposed that it was all right for him to make fun of "the Secret." Still…

"Actually, when he opened it," Blackie continued, "he found it was a bill for the Last Supper and he said he wouldn't pay because Jewish catering services always charged too much."

More laughter, now with less nervousness. Even Catherine was grinning.

"No, what it really said was 'Vote for John F. Kennedy.' "

Now loud cheers.

Blackie grabbed a beer can. "To the next president of the United States, John Fitzgerald Kennedy!"

"And a happy new year!" Pat joined in.

The spell was broken. We all drank to Kennedy and 1960. Catherine hugged Blackie enthusiastically again and pecked quickly at my lips.

I wasn't a very sensitive eighteen-year-old, but I saw the darkness lurking in the depths of her wonderful brown eyes. For the first time I worried about Catherine.

She willed that the rest of the party be a success and threw herself into the singing and dancing and drinking with madcap energy, the mistress of the revels while the Plague lurked outside the town walls.

And the polka-dot stole was quickly discarded. Which made it easier for me to kiss her throat and shoulders after everyone else left at four o'clock in the morning.

It was a more frantic and passionate session than those of the previous summer. I had more accurate information about intercourse now, as a result of freshman biology, and was dimly aware that we were headed in that direction.

I stopped of course. I was a good Catholic boy, even though the lack of answers to my questions in the theology classes at St. Anthony was even then shaking my faith. I realized vaguely that there was a connection between fear of the world's end and the passion of Catherine's willingness to surrender. I did not want to take advantage of her.

The 1961 party was at the Ryans. As their clock began to toll the magic hour, Blackie glanced at his watch and sighed, "Aunt Erin loses another."

A year-old picture of Catherine's swelling young breasts flashed in my mind. They were so wonderfully, delicately beautiful. Nothing will ever erase that image. But on January 1, 1961, I piously thanked a God in whom I was not sure I believed anymore for having prevented me from impregnating Catherine the year before.

Now I wish I had.

7
NICHOLAS

I woke up screaming twice that night, with shatteringly realistic images of Catherine being torn apart following me from nightmare to wakefulness. Both times Monica nursed me back to sleep.

She let me sleep the next morning till just before she put on her dress—the decisive sign that she was leaving for work. She put a tray of orange juice, toast, bacon and coffee on the bed next to me.

"You didn't have much sleep last night. Don't assume that this is an automatic service at this hotel."

"Thanks," I mumbled, still not sure that I was awake.

She considered me carefully, her gray eyes troubled. "Call them and tell them you won't be in till noon. You're important enough."

"I can't do that."

"She should never have gone into the convent," Monica said firmly. "You shouldn't have let her."

"How could I have stopped her?" I said.

"You don't know much about telling women what you want, do you?"

I tasted the coffee. Excellent, as always. "I don't know what you mean."

"You don't know how to lay down the law." She glanced at her watch. "I have to run. We'll talk about it later."

I kissed her bare shoulder and watched admiringly as she slipped her jersey dress over her head and gracefully dropped it into place on her luscious body.

Then she left and I was alone with my breakfast and my memories.

And the certainty that Monica was right. But how could I have stopped Catherine, then or anytime afterward?

8
BLACKIE

"The child is a changeling," my mother insisted. "Have you ever known anyone Irish who does not sunburn? She turns tan. Erin and Larry have themselves a little Pict on their hands. At least."

I felt a troublesome stirring in the back of my head. A slight twinge, like the first hint of a toothache you think you might have in six months. I was not yet old enough to worry about Cathy, but I was old enough to sense that sometime I might have to worry about her.

My mother's ordinary conversational style was what my father called adversarial. She would take a position, certainly exaggerated and often totally absurd, and argue it with conviction and passion so as to challenge others to respond. She would, Dad said, have made a wonderful lawyer. As it was, he said with his shy, sly grin, not bad as a politician.

And Mary Kate was cut from the same cloth, naturally enough. Another great lawyer was lost when she turned to psychiatry. She loved to play my mother's game, as often baiting her as arguing back.

"Probably some Spanish genes from the wreck of the armada. Or maybe some black slave...."

"Hush your mouth, child." My mother laughed. "If the South Side Irish think that, they won't let us come to Mass at their church."

Even though the family had migrated to the South Side when my father came home from Iwo Jima after the war, my mother still thought of herself as living in exile among a culturally deprived people.

Mary Kate was either a junior or senior in college, so I was either ten or eleven years old. It was probably 1957, because if it had been the year before, Mom would already have been working in the second Stevenson campaign. So it was the year that Cathy put the sand in Nick's lemonade and finally managed to get herself spanked, a feat of which she was enormously proud. I remember distinctly the music from *The Bridge on the River Kwai* as they talked. They were setting the table for some family celebration at Grand Beach—we had, my mother said, 2.7 celebrations a month.

They knew that "Little Mr. Big Ears" was listening, but as my mother had said many years before, "He's going to know all the family secrets anyway, so why not just pretend he's part of the furniture."

I can also remember thinking how pretty both my black-haired mother and my blond big sister looked in swimming suits—the only approved form of dress for Ryan women in the summer.

"She has to be a Pict," my mother continued, arguing her case. "They were the small dark people, aborigines who were there before the Celts came. Quite uncivilized and mostly faerie. I think she's fey. It must come from the Murtaugh side of the family because there's not a trace of leprechaun blood in the Collins side."

"I disagree," said Mary Kate, "it must be from the Collins side. Otherwise why would she and the Punk be such close friends? He's fey too if you ask me. Aren't you, crazy little leprechaun Punk?" Mary Kate embraced me and messed my hair with no regard for my dignity as an eleven-year-old.

Most eleven-year-olds, I have since learned, do not like to be embraced by women of any age. Alas, I was a deviant even then.

"It's simply impossible that my dull brother and his pious wife could have produced a child with such energy and good looks," my mother continued. "Oh, she's a changeling all right. Your psychology can't explain it. Why, my brother Herbert was never happier than when he was a hobo during the Great Depression. He made all that money building radar sets or somesuch during the war, and I'm sure if Erin hadn't nailed him, he would have gone right back on the road, except hobohemia was a casualty of prosperity. Give old General Ike a chance, though, and he'll bring it back."

Politics was never far from my mother's mind.

"They did marry late, didn't they?" Mary Kate mused as she distributed the salad bowls. "Uncle Herbert was quite old, wasn't he?"

"No older than I am now," my mother protested with undisguised merriment, "though poor Herb was born old. And born a bachelor too. He has his money and he has his commodity market to play with, and he doesn't need a wife and child."

"She was forty, wasn't she?" Mary Kate continued. "And Cathy was a month or two premature?"

"At a healthy seven pounds," my mother replied, "and himself there at full term plus, only five and a half."

"Small Punk," I said and waited for them both to look at me in astonishment.

When that ritual was finished, they went on in their discussion of Cathy. I was precisely at the age when I no longer took my cousin for granted. She wasn't a person in her own right quite yet, but neither was she a given in the environment. Listening to Mom and Mary Kate talk about her was like fitting together the pieces of a jigsaw puzzle.

"Changeling or not," said Mary Kate, "it is astonishing that with a background like that, she has so much energy and enthusiasm. And that she'd be mad about Nick Curran, even if he is cute. Maybe she's looking for a father."

"Poor little tyke." My mother was not about to retreat from her original stand, she never did. "It's not easy for a changeling. She's so pretty and so lively. I don't know what's going to become of her."

Mom would never have guessed that she would end up a virgin and martyr.

Nick said to me much later that while I doubtless loved her too, my feelings for Cathy were not sexual. I let him think that. But, of course, they were sexual. If I had not been destined to be a priest, I would have taken her away from him and there would have been none of the subsequent nonsense.

For many years I was able to tell her to stop her foolishness when it appeared and she obeyed. Such a relationship either ends up in marriage or it merely ends. By the time we were teenagers, my ability to slow her down was already waning. I could stop her from climbing fences with barbed wire on top. I couldn't stop her from dating some of the creeps she went around with when Nick wasn't available. And I could not prevent any of the subsequent lunacy.

But I remember clearly the day when I finally experienced Cathy as a distinct person—and began to actually worry about her. I ended that particular bit of folly, but sensed that this budding young woman was in for trouble from which I could not protect her.

We were in seventh grade at St. Praxides' grammar school. It was a soft golden Indian summer day and I was walking down Coyne Avenue wondering how long I could keep my mouth shut in Sister Mathilde's class. That worthy nun insisted day in and day out that we were spoiled rich children and that we all were going to ruin our lives because we had no self-restraint.

Moreover, Sister Mathilde, a tiny, crotchety nun with a little bell that she rang compulsively, did not like Cathy. So great was the unspoken identification between us inseparable cousins that not to like Cathy was not to like me.

Nuns mostly did not like Cathy, though her grades were high and she worked hard in school. Perhaps her enthusiasm and generosity made her too popular with the other girls, who by rights ought to have envied her attractiveness. Perhaps Cathy, for whose animal energies the class-room was unbearably restraining, squirmed and twisted too much. Maybe she was too interested in boys, and the charge of being "boy crazy" was, God knows, certainly not false. Or maybe she was caught too often with her drawings. Cathy drew airplanes, mountains, rivers, lakes, nuns, priests, and boys, boys, boys. As soon as a dull interlude threatened in the classroom—and there were many such—Cathy would reach for a sheet of scrap paper and begin to sketch.

And that infuriated the nuns. One year she had been elected by the other girls to crown the Blessed Mother at the end of May and was banned the day before the sacred event because our teacher found her drawing boys' faces.

It was patently unjust and I began to organize the troops for revolt until Cathy said simply, "Drop it, Coz."

I dropped it, of course.

So when I saw Cathy on the school steps that glorious autumn afternoon, I assumed that Matty the Mad, as we called our teacher, was persecuting her again.

Cathy was sitting on the steps, in school uniform of blue blazer and plaid skirt, head buried in her hands.

"See Nick with another girl?" I said, sure that it would get a rise out of her.

She didn't even look up. So I walked up the stairs and sat next to her. "What cooks, Coz?"

An immemorial greeting between us.

"I wish God would take me and let the others live," she sighed.

"What others?" I asked. "Are you Joan of Arc again?"

"Some of the kids from high school were telling me about it. Padre Pio has predicted that on the coldest day of the year, the Bear will fight the Eagle and that the Eagle will win but will lose one-third of his children."

"There'll be a war this winter between us and Russia and we're going to win but a third of us will be killed and you want God to take you now and spare the rest of us?"

She looked up, her vast eyes heavy and sad, and nodded solemnly, "I'll never amount to anything anyway, so why not let all the others live?"

"Including the children of the Bear?"

"Why not?" She shrugged. "If you're going to die for one people, why not die for two?"

There were new Padre Pio predictions every year. I don't doubt that the Italian stigmatic was a good and holy man. I only hope he was not responsible for the predictions that swept the Catholic superstition grapevine every year. They were invariably wrong.

Which didn't stop folks like Erin Collins from believing the next prairie fire rumor.

"Does your mother know?"

"Not yet; I'm afraid to tell her."

That was all. We never talked about her mother. Cathy was obedient to her mother and never argued, behavior which was neither required nor tolerated at the Ryan house. I don't think the question of love arose between her and Erin.

"You might jump off the Board of Trade," I began, "or slash your wrists or burn yourself at a stake, if you can find a stake. Or lie down and let the Rock Island run over you?"

"What?" she demanded.

"Well, since God obviously isn't willing to take you up on your offer, maybe you should make him. End it all yourself and save the world."

She began to giggle. Then the giggle turned into a laugh. Then tears.

"You're so wonderful, Blackie. I don't know what I'd do without you." Then momentarily serious again, "You don't think there's going to be a war?"

"I'll bet my portable radio against your stereo that there won't be."

"No bet." She punched my shoulder and laughed again. "You always win. Come on. I'll race you to Eighty-ninth Street."

Honesty compels me to say she won.

And that night I worried about her. It was, I think, the first time I consciously worried about anyone. Why should Cathy think she wasn't worth anything? Why should she be afraid of her mother? And why should she believe such stupid things about the Bear and the Eagle? And how was all that connected with my mother's worrying about her that day in Grand Beach?

The Bear and the Eagle rumor swept the city until finally the Chicago chancery office issued an "unofficial" denial—whatever that might have been. As you may have noticed, the prediction was wrong—that year, anyway.

I've worried about Cathy ever since. And I am furious at her death. It is strange, when I think about it. I mourned my mother deeply, but even though she died at the age of forty-seven, long before her time, I was never angry about her death. It's easy to be angry when someone you love dies, even if it is with a joke on her lips and a laugh, but anger didn't seem appropriate. I certainly was not enthusiastic about Dad's remarriage, even though I knew his second wife had been selected by Mom before she died. (You do not leave the care and love of an adored husband to chance, not if you're Katie Collins Ryan, you don't.) There was an incident in which Mary Kate and I were involved that swept that objection away rather definitively, an experience which still makes me shiver.

But even at my worst during those troubled times I was never really angry. As I said, it didn't seem appropriate.

But I'm madder than hell about Cathy.

And I propose to get even.

9
BLACKIE

The Sunday evening before our pilgrimage to Our Lady of the Hill and the shrine of St. Catherine, virgin and martyr, I phoned my sister Mary Kate.

"Doctor Murphy is at home," said Caitlin, one of her teenage daughters, trying to sound like the receptionist at either an expensive medical building or an even more expensive bordello, "and will be happy to converse with her clerical brother."

"Nerd," I responded.

"Geek," she observed.

I presented to my sibling the psychiatrist my problem of whether to give Nick my correspondence with Catherine. I would be violating a trust. On the other hand, when Cathy and I would meet in the Many-Splendored Lands, she'd probably bawl me out for not sharing the letters with Nick long ago.

That was Catherine, blunt and direct.

True to type of all the Ryan women, Mary Kate ignored my question. "You're not going to Rosie O'Gorman's gross-out at the Hill tomorrow, are you?" she demanded, long since a victim to the teenage language with which she was surrounded both at home and in her clientele. "Janet Cline tells me the place has turned into a zoo, pentecostals and radicals and now miracles."

Janet Cline was a classmate of Mary Kate who had survived the late sixties and with considerable vigor taught English literature to a new generation of late adolescent women at Our Lady of the Hill, a generation which reportedly no longer asked whether D. H. Lawrence or James Joyce (God be good to him!) was "relevant."

"Miracles...?"

"Mr. Benetta, the president of the college, is into the charismatic renewal in a big way—tongues, baptism of the Spirit, healing, the whole bit. So is the young idiot who's the new bishop up there. They've turned an exhibit of Cath's paintings into a chapel to which hysterics come to be cured from their illnesses. And Cathy's paintings up there are so unspeakably bad."

So Nick had assured me.

"Is there not a value judgment in the word 'hysterics,' perhaps a chauvinist one at that?"

"If you can't find a martyr's body"—Mary Kate ignored my observation about the Greek roots of 'hysteria,' as she ignored almost everything I said—"you collect some of the execrable art she did there because you were too busy recruiting her to the convent to teach her how to paint, and you turn them into second-class relics."

I was impressed that she knew what a second-class relic was. "You're saying our saint's college-age paintings are shitty?"

Occasionally I would rate a response to my wordplay on the order of "Punk, this is too important a matter for your pedantry."

Today, however, was not one of my lucky days.

"Poor Erin. She should have lived long enough to see her daughter become one of those creepy saints to whom she prayed. What does Cronin think of Bishop...Bishop Whatever-his-name-is?"

Sean Cronin is our auxiliary bishop and the man for whom I am alleged, not without some justification, to play the role of an eminence grise.

"Cafferty. My Lord Cronin says that he is so dumb that even the other bishops notice it."

"So why the hell do you want to give Curran those letters from Cathy? Isn't he enough of a necrophile as it is?"

I explained that they might reveal to him more of how Cathy lived and why she died and that Nick would not have peace until her ghost was laid to rest.

"There may be a lot of worms under that rock, Punk."

"Yet Nick must turn it over."

"I suppose...Why don't you see what happens at the Hill tomorrow?"

Then Caitlin was on the phone warning me that I would be a true gelhead if I did not show up later in the week to hear her sing Ado Annie in *Oklahoma!* I resisted telling her that not so long ago seminarians had been forbidden to attend that play because it was "dirty."

Caitlin was now as old as Cathy was the summer after my mother died, and terrifyingly like her in temperament, though far more mature.

After I hung up, having made my solemn promise, I thought about a conversation I had had with Cath that summer, one that deepened my worry and made me feel more helpless.

We were sitting on the porch overlooking the lake after several hours of water-skiing. Cathy, in her standard garb of bikini and shirt, was silently nursing a Coke. Nick was in Chicago, of course, working on his beer truck.

"What cooks, Coz?" I asked, knowing now the mood of self-rejection and wondering whether she would talk about it.

"Last night's date with Ernie Crawford."

"Bad?"

She shivered. "He really is an ape-man. He stopped short of rape, I guess, but he plays for keeps."

"Not nice like Nick?"

"I didn't know boys were that passionate. Father Ed kept warning me, but Nick...well, Coz, he's different."

"No, he's not," I said. "He gets turned on just as much as any one of the rest of us. But he controls himself better."

"Hmmn...." she mumbled, contriving to look both enlightened and confused. And my mother was no longer around to provide answers.

"So take it easy," I said inanely. "You don't want to find yourself pregnant."

"Oh, that." She dismissed it with a quick wave of her hand. "That wouldn't necessarily be bad. And least a baby is something worthwhile. I'm probably not good enough to do anything but bring babies into the world."

"That's crazy, Coz," I protested.

"No, it's not," she responded listlessly, pounding her little bare feet on the wood of the porch. "Name me one good thing I've ever done."

"Those cartoons of Monsignor, for starters."

She gathered my two empty Coke bottles and her own with a sigh and walked toward the screen door. "I don't want to talk about it anymore, Coz. Sorry."

Not nearly as sorry as I was. And am.

The phone call to Mary Kate confirmed my instincts: If Nick was still interested in turning over the rock after our ordeal at the shrine, then turned over it must be.

No matter what we might find.

10
MARY KATE

Caitlin was practicing "I Cain't Say No" on the piano, while I was considering my sibling's phone call. I made a mental note that the piano needed tuning, as it had for nine years.

I saw no problem in Nick's reading Cathy's letters. Nor would Cathy herself object, God be good to her, in whatever part of the hereafter she was currently resident—my own guess was that despite the charismatic canonization at the Hill, she was located in a comfy part of purgatory, getting her act together before the big party began.

Like the rest of the women in our family, Cathy had a strong streak of the exhibitionist in her. Before she died she reveled in strolling down a beach in Brazil dressed in a swimsuit that would have led to her arrest in the great state of Michigan. She competed with those luscious Latin adolescents purely for the hell of it. No, she wouldn't mind Nick learning more about her. That's not the problem.

The Punk is my favorite sibling (and all our other siblings' favorite sibling) and knows more about women than most men, but he can't cope with the sexuality that pervades her letters. Doesn't even see it. He perceives that her life was a half-intoxicated drive down a mountain road, on one side of which was comedy and the other side commitment. He understands that at one edge of the road there was superficiality and at the other zealotry, and that Cousin Catherine spent a hell of a lot of time on the edges.

But he can't see—or can't permit himself to see—that the engine which drove the car at such high speed and the intoxicant which made her swerve from one side to the other was sex. Or to be more candid about it, SEX.

Where does he think the vitality and the enthusiasm and the manic humor and crazy generosity and the giddy flakiness and the burning affection came from? I guess he finds it hard to cope with how much sexual feeling there was in his relationship with her.

If it's too much for the practically perfect Punk, what about poor Nick? And damn it, I must stop using that adjective every time I think of him.

Sure, I'm a Freudian. But SEX was more important in her life than in the life of most women. And it's more important in the lives of most women than most men (and most women too, for that matter) are prepared to face. Cathy could have kept comedy and commitment in balance if her sexual energies had not been so abundant. And if she'd had any role model in her family to show her how to avoid superficiality and zealotry, she would not have had so great a problem integrating her sensuality.

As it was, the raw power of her lusts, hungers, needs, desires—call them what you want—drove her at high speed. Toward the end she realized that and tried to solve it all by grasping for the quick solution of good fucking.

And that didn't work either.

On the Christmas vacation of her first year in college—the year before she joined that damned nunnery—she and I were alone in our house in the Neighborhood and I was nursing, let me see, it must have been Petey. Naturally enough we talked about sex. It was a conversation that as big sister and surrogate mother, I should have had with her before but, Freudian or not, I am still sufficiently Irish to dodge such conversations with kids or surrogate kids if I can.

At first, Cathy pretended to be uninterested in clinical details. She wanted to know about saying "no" and "yes"—how to say those key words, and when to say them, and the most effective ways of switching from one to another. And she was also concerned about how you could avoid hurting with sex and how you could better help.

Why don't men realize that we are such lustful creatures? Generally speaking, our hungers are more diffuse, slower, more unpredictable, more varied and, once stirred up, often more voracious.

As I tell my Pirate, Joe, we don't always need an orgasm. Sometimes it is enough for us to cuddle. On the other hand, if we are capable of a lot more skyrockets in one session than they are, it's because we often need more pleasure.

And damn it to hell, we're entitled to more too!

We are also a kinky stew of blatant exhibitionism and fragile modesty, not always predictable even to ourselves, and utterly baffling to all but the most self-possessed men. Not comprehending that we identify much more with our bodies than they do and hence are caught in a deep and powerful rhythm of mystery and disclosure, your typical male is terrified by our quick shifts from wanton to prude and is quite unable to enjoy those shifts, which in part, after all, are designed to amuse, entertain, delight and intrigue him.

Now I ask you, are not the persons I've described in the last couple of paragraphs more attractive bed (couch, desktop, carpet, bathtub, shower, front seat of the car, beach, lawn—you name it) partners than your *Playboy* Playmates?

The Pirate, by the way, is my husband, Joe. He is called the Pirate because he looks like a fierce west-of-Ireland pirate, especially when he is wearing his sexy black and silver beard. You can easily imagine him sacking monasteries and carrying off the sacred plates and ravishing all the women in the countryside. (Images which are to be attributed totally to my kinky sexual fantasies. Joe is the most peaceful and gentle of men and deserves a much better wife than the one he has.)

I can't figure out why men don't think that way. Maybe because we are more mysterious and hence more interesting and hence more frightening than the Playmate. And why can't even as clever a man as the Punk see SEX as something more than merely episodic in Cath's crazy spin down the short highway of her life?

Anyway, when Cathy and I were having our heart-to-heart, and me trying to satisfy another future male chauvinist with a breast fixation, I felt that perhaps we were being too ethereal. So I told her about oral sex. Can't hardly survive these days without knowing about it. Sure enough,

Cathy was barely aware of its existence (it was 1962, remember) and knew none of the details. She was fascinated. "Is it fun?" she asked, her brown eyes as wide as our stereo speakers.

"For some people sometimes," I said, drawing a deep breath.

From that we went on to one thing and another. Like most young Irish Catholic women at that time, her sexual knowledge was a mixture of ignorance, misinformation, modesty and insatiable curiosity.

Not as much ignorance, mind you, as in my age peers.

"Have you ever had sex with a man you didn't love?" she asked finally. "What's that like?"

"I've had sex with a husband at times when I've hated his Boston shanty Irish guts."

"Why have it, then?"

"Horny."

"You or Joe?"

"Regardless."

"And what is it like?"

"Strictly personal reaction, hon. No obligation. I tell myself I'm doing it because I'm afraid my damn Pirate will find someone else or because I'm afraid I'll try to find someone else and fail. I insist that I'll still hate his guts afterward."

"Do you?"

" 'Course not. Mostly I fall in love all over again. We race each other to see who apologizes first."

Cathy blushed with delight, not shame. "Oh, M.K., how wonderful!"

"I guess," I said, shifting Petey, the product of one such night, to the other faucet.

She then established that it was not abnormal for a woman to enjoy the bodies of other women, "so long as she likes men more." And told me in considerable detail what appealed to her about the bodies of both sexes. "Tight buns," as I remember, among other things.

My cousin/sister was not the kind of woman who would strike many men as sexy. A woman who was sensitive to the nuances of her own and other people's hunger would have known instantly that the seemingly prim girl talking to me that day—brown skirt pulled discreetly over her knees, beige sweater not too tight (but tight enough), no makeup, hands folded in her lap as if she was a novice already, soft voice, soulful brown eyes—was a ticking sexual bomb.

How would you know? White knuckles, vulnerable throat, eager shoulders, shy invitation lurking in those soulful eyes, gracefully twisting torso, the lazy opening of her lips when she smiled, one ankle appealingly over the other. You need not be polymorphously perverse—and I'm not, well, only a little—to find her intensely appealing. A demure Irish Catholic Venus whose clothes might fall away with the smallest movement and whose arms would then extend in a fragile offer that was both conquest and surrender. If you accepted the offer, you'd find yourself riding a sweet-tasting ballistic missile.

Did Cathy see herself that way? My God, it was 1962. How could she?

When the tension of the conversation increased, she reached into her purse—neat, quiet movements, almost nunlike—and pulled out a pad to sketch me and Petey. A bare-shouldered, somewhat overweight Viking madonna with a breast-fixated boy child. Sexual bonding between mother and son. I still have the sketch. I cry whenever I look at it.

Artistic vision and sensuality correlate highly. Which comes first is a chicken-and-egg question. Regardless, Cathy was at the upper end of the sensuality scale. Can someone that preoccupied with the flesh be a good nun or priest? Sure. The Punk has probably never let a nice ass or a cute boob go unnoticed since he was five. But he has his act together. He was born, I think, with the act together. At no time did Catherine have a chance to drive down the road at a slow enough speed to figure out where she was going.

"How long did it take you to be good in bed?" she asked thoughtfully.

"Depends on your source of information." I burped Petey, a process he loved more than any of the other Brats. "Joe will tell you 'right away.' I think I'm still learning."

She grinned at that. "Do you think I will ever learn?"

"A lot quicker than I have," I replied fervently.

There was a faraway look in those soulful brown oceans. She kind of thought, I'm sure, that she'd be a pretty good lay too.

"Do you want Joe a lot?"

"Some days I hate to come home from the office because I know he'll be there, lean and handsome black Irish pirate with cute dimples and curly hair, wanting to screw the first moment he sees me. Other days I can think of nothing else. We're a lot more variable than they are. They'd say we're more erratic; but, poor single-minded dears, they have no feel for the rhythms of life, like we do. Joe knows how to read the signs pretty well and how to break through the barriers when he has to or when he should."

Fed and burped, Petey wanted to play. Mama wanted to reassemble herself, so Petey, who was polymorphously perverse, ended up in Aunt Cathy's arms.

"Will Nick ever figure that out?"

First mention of Nick all day. I take a very deep breath this time, searching for truth.

"All men need help, Cath. So do all women. But men need it more; that's okay because we're better at giving it. Nick'll be all right if he receives a lot of help."

At this juncture your average nubile miss will want to argue that it's not fair that men are entitled to more help, and I will go into a long discussion about external versus internal organs, etc., etc. Catherine doesn't do that at all.

"I think he'll be all right too," she says simply.

And I say to myself that this Nick is a lucky bastard. Given half a chance, he would have been all right too. Only he got much less than half a chance. Meanwhile traitorous Petey has fallen sound asleep in Aunt Cathy's care. Little bastard.

"I want one of these," she said, fiercely nestling perverse Petey against her breasts, as if she wished she could nurse him too.

"Sell this one to you cheap," I said, recapturing Petey with some difficulty. Who says I'm not bonded to my Brats?

"I want a man too, M.K.," she said, bowing her head in proper modesty. "All the time. One to hold in my arms. And to hold me. Nick especially but almost anyone will do. Even more than chocolate ice cream. Is that abnormal?"

"Couldn't be more healthy." Petey took his own sweet time about settling down. Like Aunt Cathy more than Mommy, will you, you little fraud?

She looked up at me, still acutely embarrassed. "I mean, I REALLY want one."

"Great. They have what we need and vice versa. You're not an archangel, hon."

She nodded as if she understood. But she didn't. How could she, growing up in the house she did?

Let me tell you, students, when a woman imagines men and chocolate ice cream in the same picture, you have one highly charged libido on your hands. I was too young then for a daughter that old. I had an opportunity much later to pursue the subject again with her, but I thought I had plenty of time. It turned out that time ran out more quickly than I thought it would.

Where were all that energy and comedy and commitment going? In the direction of what my Boston Irish pirate calls the "Absolute Ultimate." She looked in the wrong places, I guess. The Punk says that our sister/cousin had the raw materials of greatness. Lots of people do. She didn't have a quarter of a chance. Maybe in those last few minutes when they were chopping up her lovely body, she found greatness and the "Absolute Ultimate" too. I don't like the way God worked that one out, but as my mother taught me in her dying weeks, you do it God's way.

STILL, I suspect that God only put up with Cath's end. He didn't like it any more than I do. And if He REALLY had His Ultimate Absolute way, she'd still be with us, stirring up a storm.

The night of our heart-to-heart, Cathy stayed for supper. Reassured of her normality and her prospects, she flirted outrageously with my black Irish pirate, harmless, comic flirting, which the pig loved. I warned her as she left that she could be in deep trouble if she kept it up.

We both laughed, confident of the power of the secrets we shared. The power wasn't strong enough.

Caitlin was standing at the door, Ado Annie replaced by the daughter on whose shoulder her mother cried, the shrink's confidant, poor kid.

"Aunt Cathy?" she said gently. "Were you and Uncle Punk talking about her again?"

I nodded my head, wiping away the traces of my sniffles with a crumpled piece of tissue.

"Did she have to die, Mom?" Caitlin put her arm around me.

"Maybe, kid," I said, praying that I could protect her as I had not protected Cath. "But, damnit, I don't think so."

11
NICHOLAS

I fortified myself for the trip to the Hill by spending the weekend with Monica. Our pleasures, our affection and our conversation were more leisurely than they were in our hasty evening sessions. I enjoyed Monica in every way, physical and spiritual, that a man can enjoy a woman. I was close to love's tender net and not sure that I wanted to escape it.

We were curled up on her vast couch, drinking white wine and watching the Minneapolis Vikings tear to shreds the hapless Chicago Bears, warm and comfortable while the autumn rain beat against the windows of her apartment. The sound was turned off so we could see the Bears go under and be spared the pain of hearing it too. Monica was wearing a thick gray robe, under which my hand rested peacefully.

"You shouldn't go there, you know," she said.

I had said nothing during the last two days about the dedication of the statue. "I suppose you're right. I couldn't turn down Rosie's invitation. She was Catherine's closest friend in college."

"You never do turn down women, do you?" she said, returning to her favorite theme.

"I'm glad I didn't turn you down," I said, moving my hand across her pliant body.

"That's different," she laughed.

It was, I suppose.

I remembered the time I agreed, against my better judgment, to accompany Catherine to Little Angelica's house and told Monica the story.

It was the summer of 1962, after the missile crisis. Katie Ryan had been dead for more than a year and a half, having breathed her last at Grand Beach in the Easter Week of 1961. Edward Ryan had remarried, and Helen, his new wife, brought joy back to the old house, a somewhat more orderly joy, perhaps, but one in which the Ryan family seemed to prosper. She was already pregnant with her first child.

I suppose I was more uneasy in the new regime than her stepchildren were, especially since Helen deferred to Mary Kate (now Dr. Murphy), who was only two years younger, as the new matriarch of the clan. Yet I was not quite certain that I was as welcome as I used to be.

By that summer of "Days of Wine and Roses" and "Blowing in the Wind," of Sonny Liston and Rod Laver, of *Lawrence of Arabia* and *The Manchurian Candidate*, I thought I was in love with Catherine, though I did not know what love was or who Catherine was—not that I have learned to understand either subject in the years since. She had graduated from high school (and spent June in Europe) and would be at the Hill in the autumn, across the river from St. Anthony's. I would go to law school the following year and finish the year she graduated from college. And then we would be married. I took it for granted and Catherine did not seem to disagree, though we did not discuss it much.

The Second Vatican Council was about to convene in Rome, but I was barely aware of that fact and certainly could not have imagined that because of it I would be worrying about the probate of Catherine's will fourteen years later.

I was fascinated by her—no, better to say obsessed with her—in a heavy-handed, unperceptive male adolescent way. Catherine dazzled me, and stupidly I did not seek to find who the person was behind the dazzle. So much beauty, so much vitality, so much mystery. Was that not enough?

She was moonbeams dancing on the water, a spring breeze sweeping down the beach, a brief snow flurry on a sunny day—light, airy, mystifying, delightful.

She would plan a birthday present to a friend for weeks, travel across town to just the right store to buy it, phone me at school for last-minute advice about the present, wrap it herself—often with my supervision— and then take it to the recipient in a solemn high procession, in which I was, of course, her acolyte. And it was all fun to her, not a responsibility, not a burden but a wonderful adventure, like exploring the Gobi Desert.

She dragged me off to Orchestra Hall and the Art Institute, buildings of whose existence I was barely aware, and watched with anxious eyes for my reaction. Solti was conducting his Mahler's Sixth the first night at Orchestra Hall and I felt stiff and awkward, a longshoreman at a society party, among all the nose-in-the-air music lovers.

Then I heard the first bars and was hooked. She sighed with relief and held my hand through the rest of the concert, gripping it very tightly at the posthorn passage.

And then I was conveyed to the impressionists across the street and similarly hooked. She bought me books and records and soon I knew more about music and art than she did. Only then did I begin to realize that her "drawings" displayed considerable raw talent. One of her high-school nuns had spotted the talent and was giving her special lessons because her mother absolutely forbade her attendance at the immoral Art Institute classes.

Never once did it occur to me to wonder how the only child of a miracle-obsessed mother and a man whose life was hidden behind the pages of the *Wall Street Journal* could have found out about Orchestra Hall or the Art Institute. I still don't know.

Nor did I ask myself why a girl from such a morbid background would be so vivacious and charming. It did not occur to me that there might be another Catherine behind the young woman for whom every movie, every visit to a hamburger stand, every night watching basketball on TV was high adventure.

When we walked down the beach together, Catherine would literally bounce around me, like a child following a clown in a circus parade, so great was her enthusiasm about what had happened yesterday or what would happen tomorrow.

She visited the old people's home at Oak Forest (the County Infirmary, to give it the proper name in those days) and the Marillac settlement house every other Saturday, and she wrote large checks for every good work recommended by the nuns at Marillac.

She loved running gags—I was "Ape-Man" and she was being "dragged back to the jungle by the hair of her head"—and practical jokes. But the jokes were always benign. One night during Christmas week she had a "Blackie party" in which everyone was to dress in black and bring presents made out of black wood. It wasn't his birthday. She just wanted to have a party for her beloved cousin.

And on the day after my twenty-first birthday—I could not abandon my mother and sisters on the day itself—she insisted that I leave my beer truck and come to Grand Beach for a special supper. We had a hamburger at Roxanne's and she gave me a paperback book of the stained glass of George Roualt. I felt let-down and mourned the money I might have made on the beer truck that day. But she was bouncy and sprightly as though it were all very special. So I tried to pretend I was delighted.

Normally Catherine was very sensitive to my imagined poverty, so we ate cheaply on dates save on those rare occasions when I permitted her to treat. I wondered, as we entered the Ryan House at the beach, whether I was being needled on my twenty-first.

And there were a hundred and fifty people and a stack of art books two feet high waiting for me when the lights went on.

My mother and sister had been invited, of course, but could not come.

When Katie Ryan died in her room at Grand Beach watching the sun rise over the lake, the Ryans fell apart, even though they'd known for months what was coming. Catherine took charge for a couple of hours, cooking meals, making phone calls, holding hands, hugging visitors. And at the wake she was in the thick of the mourners—reassuring, consoling, loving.

God, how I loved her those nights.

And her mother sat in an oversized chair at the back of Kearney's funeral home, beaming happily, not at her daughter but at the "beatific vision" which had been awarded to Katie. "There's nothing to be sorry about," she said, as though she were doing a commercial for God. "She lives!"

Father Ed Carny, who was Catherine's spiritual director then, even though the nuns at Bethlehem High didn't like him much, finally said, "Sure she lives, Erin, but so do they and they miss her."

His words had no effect on either the smile or the slogan.

Herbert Collins discussed the latest permutations of the soybean market in the lobby of the funeral home, showing no sign that he knew that the sister who had brought him out of hobohemia was dead.

And after it was all over, Katie in the ground, the Ryans back in their empty home on Glenwood Drive, Herbert behind his *Wall Street Journal*, Erin at a tea party with her mystics (which prevented her from being present at Katie's grave for the final blessing) and Catherine and I driving to the bus depot for my return to St. Anthony's, she broke down and sobbed for a half hour in my arms.

Still, I never thought that there were contradictions in my future wife's personality, that there might be pain behind the dazzle.

She wasn't without faults. Her black moods were unpredictable and deep and she would let no one help her. And her effervescence frequently went over the line and she became flibbertigibbety, not only dazzling but dizzy. She was a fine swimmer and a superb water-skier. In fact, Catherine in a bikini on a single ski was hard to beat for outdoor entertainment. Whenever she wiped out—which was every time she skied—she dove underwater quickly to make sure everything was in place before she climbed into the boat.

She was, however, useless in sports that required time or concentration. She had some natural talent at tennis but refused to concentrate, and argued that the only reason I took her on the golf course was so I could put my arms around her to teach her how to swing. Save in her black moods, a couple or three times a year, she was never serious and refused to concentrate on anything serious. In the black moods she was very serious indeed but wouldn't talk to me. I think now that such traits would have made us a poor match in marriage—Catherine was not serious enough at ordinary times and too serious in serious times, while I was too serious at ordinary times and flippant in times of deep trouble. I thought a golf game was deeply important and she thought it was absurd.

I refused to worry about my own death. She worried terribly about her death.

I remember as though it were yesterday the night of her junior prom in May of 1961. It was before proms became unfashionable in the "relevant" later sixties.

Junior proms are bizarre events, tribal rituals for young maidens in which the maidens are more aware of the role they are playing than they are of their partners in the rites, who are present mostly for reasons of social necessity.

The girls are sixteen or just turned seventeen, still prone to giggle and swarm with one another as if they were at a parish teen-club dance. Their dates may be as young as sixteen and as old as twenty-two and awkward with the suddenly radiant young women, self-conscious as they are in their beauty and their obligation to enjoy this magic night in their lives. The young dates want to swarm with their own kind and drink beer to overcome their embarrassment. And the older dates feel ridiculous because they are associating with children.

Catherine and I were immune to the rituals and indeed to everyone else, even to Blackie and his date, with whom we were doubling. We danced together as though we were floating on the top of cumulus clouds, basking in the sunlight of each other's happiness. Catherine was reveling in her magic night and I was reveling in Catherine.

The songs the orchestra played at the Drake Hotel that night were "Love Makes the World Go 'Round," "Moon River" and "Let's Do the Twist." I had learned how to behave passably on the dance floor and had matured sufficiently to be protective of her. And she wore a pink Roman-tunic off-the-shoulder gown in the fashion the president's wife had made popular, the kind of dress that required no elaborately engineered support mechanisms, but only Catherine to keep it in place.

"You look great in a summer formal jacket," she murmured, looking up at me, her eyes a mixture of amusement and adoration. "Did your family approve?"

The adoration deprived me of my breath and my speech.

"Sorry." She buried her head in my chest. "Shouldn't have asked. Thought they couldn't help admire you."

For all we talked about each other's families, the two of us might have done a Venus from the waters of Lake Michigan.

"I dressed at the Ryans'," I replied sheepishly. I knew what my family would say about a jacket that matched the color of her dress. "And I was speechless because of a certain pair of brown eyes."

Her shoulder blades convulsed in a giggle. "Nick, you're too much."

My face, already quite warm, became as hot as it would have been if I'd been walking under the desert sun.

Catherine, Catherine, Catherine. How did I lose you?

After the prom we went to the Cellar, a bar in the Wacker Drive underground which had been taken over by a group of parents who argued that it was better that the promsters drink themselves sick under parental supervision than without parental supervision. We caught each other's eye after the first, drunken half hour and slipped out. Blackie led us to an old-town French bistro where we sipped white wine, nibbled strange sausages and discussed foreign films—*Jules and Jim, Boccaccio 70* and *Viridiana*.

Despite his posture as the man whom no one noticed, Blackie never lacked for dates with gorgeous and intelligent young women in high school. His date that night was a lovely redhead who is now a famous movie actress.

My Catherine was able to hold her own in the serious conversation. She expressed ideas and opinions that I would not have dreamed she had. Moreover, her wit kept the discussion fun. Not a typical prom evening, I told myself, but then I don't have a typical prom date.

We drove to North Avenue Beach to watch the sun come up over the lake. Blackie and Lisa walked down the beach hand in hand and Catherine and I sat on a park bench as the sun peeked over the rim of the lake and bathed first the smooth water of the lake and then our faces and arms in a glow of golden promise. We were both tired and knew we should go home for a few hours' sleep before driving to Grand Beach for the "day after" beach party. I put my arm around her and she rested her head against my shoulder. I tightened my grip on her bare shoulder. I felt very proud of myself. I was doing what men do—loving and taking care of their women. For a few moments we were enveloped in the gentle protection of the rising sun.

Then I noticed that she was silently crying.

"What's wrong?" I asked, assuming that I must quickly set the whole world right for her.

"It's so empty and foolish—the money wasted on dresses and rented suits and flowers and music and beer. What must God think of us? And what good does it all do anyway?"

"You seemed to have a good time," I said dubiously.

"A wonderful time." She hugged me. "A night I'll always remember. That's why I feel sad. Even the nights to remember are empty."

Soon she stopped her tears, Blackie and Lisa reappeared, and off we went for breakfast at yet another French restaurant that Blackie had discovered and which made, he insisted, "perfect croissants." No sleep on a double date with Blackwood. Catherine was the life of the party, the leader of the revels for the rest of the day. I dismissed her tears as the same sort of nervous release which led eighth-grade girls to sob their hearts out on graduation day.

I had no idea who she was. Hints like the tears after the prom escaped me completely. Even now I don't know who she was. I was in love with a creature of my imagination, an image I had created and projected on her.

Yet we might have worked it out. And I would not have sulked on my beer truck after a wasted golf match if I had realized that I had only one more summer with her, instead of the lifetime of summers that I had expected.

I don't wish to be harsh on myself. I was twenty. At that age young men are dullards, more ape-men than Catherine realized, when the subject is women. But I was duller than most.

Although I was immune by then to their ridicule when the subject was Catherine, my mother and sisters continued to snipe at her, insisting that she was "free with her favors" and that everyone in the Neighborhood was talking about her "promiscuity." Actually they were wrong on both counts. Catherine's reputation was unblemished and she was not free with her favors, save with me. And between the two of us there had been ratified an implicit treaty about sex. We were cautious and restrained— I because I did not want to hurt this Ariel who had spun into my life and she because...

I don't know why. It simply came about that she was deft and brief in our embraces. I hardly noticed the change, did not talk about it and did not wonder why it had happened.

Yet when we were in each other's arms, it was like a few minutes in heaven, even if I didn't believe in heaven anymore. The subject of sex was never explicitly mentioned between us, even if the remote promise of sex with her was enough to bring me mind-breaking happiness.

If Catherine and I had married, as I was sure we would, I suppose we would have lived together in amity for fifty years and not talked about ninety-eight percent of the things that were important to us. Certainly not about our sexual relationship.

I did not have then and I don't have now the slightest notion of what she thought about her mother's cult of private revelations and miracles. It was something that some of the people in the parish did and that was all.

Now, of course, I wish I knew what she'd thought about them.

But the day she phoned me at the Ryans' Grand Beach house in the summer of 1963 to ask me if I would drive her to Chicago to meet her mother at "Little Angelica's" house, I simply said yes. I knew that Catherine accompanied her mother on some of her mystical excursions, and if Catherine's own car was being serviced in Michigan City, I would borrow a Ryan car and drive her to Chicago.

Her parents now came to the summer resort only on weekends and Catherine was alone in the Collins place with a housekeeper and two rooms filled with paintings of the lake in its many moods.

I had requisitioned from Mary Kate the old orange VW, about whose cuteness Catherine had been ecstatic, and picked her up.

A very different Catherine was waiting for me when I turned into their driveway. Her summer costume was invariably a bikini and a T-shirt, but today she wore a modest, long-sleeve navy blue dress, nylons and high heels. And she did not notice the beloved orange bug.

"Little Angelica," she explained to me as we drove in on the Indiana toll road, "died of tuberculosis of the bone when she was seven years old. She suffered terribly but never cried. When she died, the room was filled with the odor of roses. Her body never became stiff or hard. Miracles happen in her house and at her graveside. Isn't that wonderful? Monsignor McDonagh will lead the rosary today and her family and her friends will pray for her canonization. Wouldn't that be super? A saint from Chicago? Wouldn't that be something to make us all terribly proud?"

I agreed that it would. You agreed with your steady even if she wasn't quite so steady as to accept your class ring. (Father Ed warned all his advisees against going steady. Good advice, I guess.)

The Maguire home was a frame two-story on the "East Side," which for us meant anything east of State Street. I think it was off South Chicago Avenue but I can't be sure. Even then, it was a racially changing neighborhood.

There were no blacks inside the house, although I suspect that if they had come to pray for Little Angelica's canonization they would have been welcome—more welcome, to give those people credit, than they would have been at the local parish church.

At first I felt sad for the Maguires, simple, uneducated people caught up in a mania. The father was a retired transit employee, the mother still taught school. The two boys worked at "South," which meant the steel mills. Honest, hardworking folks whose only goal now was to live up to the canonization.

And their home invaded by an odd collection of creeps. There were three or four young women about my age—none of whom would have occasioned the slightest immoral thought—and the rest of the group must have averaged well over sixty. Mrs. Collins was relatively young compared to the others. There were some ancient nuns and some doddering priests and some vastly overweight lay women and some vastly underweight old men whose red-veined noses suggested a life of struggle with the "creature."

They all greeted Catherine, whom they apparently knew well, and she responded with the same cheerfulness with which she talked to her friends on the Beach. The group chattered in low voices, like Erin's on New Year's, about apparitions of the Virgin in the Philippines and in Wisconsin and about marvelous cures at the grave of "Little Jane." There seemed to be some rivalry between the supporters of "Little Jane" and the supporters of "Little Angelica" as to which of these suffering children would be canonized first.

When Monsignor McDonagh, a fat, bald little man with a cane and a wheeze, arrived, the atmosphere changed. He began the rosary as soon as he entered the room, kneeling in front of a little shrine with a picture of Angelica, a candle and some weary roses. The Apostles' Creed generated an almost palpable electric current as though someone had thrown a switch, or the house had been hit by lightning.

I was scared. I didn't know why—and still don't—but the uncanny was present in that room as we prayed. I wanted to run as fast as I could, but I couldn't desert my Catherine, whose wonderful face was bathed in a beatific smile.

She buys it all, I thought, my head ringing with confusion. But maybe, after all, there was something there to buy.

It was hot and uncomfortable in the tiny parlor with its old-fashioned, mail-order-house furnishings—the Maguires apparently had put all their money into the "cause" and hence could not afford air-conditioning. Most of the cultists clearly did not believe in deodorants. The heat and the smell and my rising sense of the uncanny made me dizzy.

I fidgeted through three decades of the rosary and then my eyes began to wander. There was a mirror on the wall just above the monsignor's bald spot. I focused on three sweat-soaked strands of hair to distract myself from the discomfort.

The mirror filled with smoke. There was someone in the mirror looking out at us, someone evil and hideous. The smoke cleared momentarily and the face was revealed. It was a visage of pure horror, maniacal, evil; ugly, distorted hatred; a medieval gargoyle come alive among us.

I heard my own voice screaming, but it was drowned out by other screams. "She's back! She's come again! Blessed Angelica protect us!"

Then it was over. The smoke vanished, the face disappeared, the electricity in the room turned off.

To be replaced by bubbling joy over what had happened. Some of the assembly admitted that they had not seen "her" and others claimed that it was "him" this time. But whether it was a "her" or a "him" or maybe nothing at all, there was still agreement that we had been present at a great event and that the "cause" must be advancing for the powers of darkness to attempt such a dramatic attack on the supporters of Little Angelica.

And there were three thin black lines on the child's face in the picture that had not been there before.

I realized that my sport shirt was soaking wet and that I was shivering. I wanted out in the worst way. Dear God, Catherine, let me take you home.

"Wasn't it wonderful?" Erin Collins exulted.

"Did you see anything?" Catherine seemed more curious than moved by the "event," as we were calling it. Crisp and cool, though usually, much to her embarrassment, she perspired when walking up a flight of steps, she was calm and her brown eyes peaceful.

"I screamed, didn't I?"

"First one," she agreed. "I didn't see a thing. I never do. Probably not holy enough."

I started to laugh and then realized that she wasn't joking.

I was in the early part of my agnostic period, brought on by Katie's death, I'm sure. I believed in very little. Yet I saw the face and Catherine didn't.

I may believe in even less now, but Blackie says that the good Christian believes only a few things, but those very strongly.

Many years later I told him and the Murphys one night at supper about the incident.

"Collective psychotic interlude," said Mary Kate.

"With overtones of paranoiac delusion," agreed Joe Murphy, who is also a psychiatrist.

"But I saw it and Catherine didn't," I insisted.

"Cathy's grip on reality has always been stronger than yours," said Blackie calmly.

On the way back to Grand Beach I was already trying to persuade myself that it hadn't happened.

And Catherine exclaimed about how wonderful it must be to know that you are a saint. She even quoted the writer—Leon Bloy I guess, he was popular in those days—who said that there was but one tragedy and that was not to be a saint.

And I resolved that once we were married, Catherine would not attend such crazy gatherings.

"You wouldn't have stopped her, though, would you?" Monica demanded.

"I don't suppose so," I admitted.

We were eating Polish sausage and drinking yet more white wine in her kitchen when I finished my story.

"You only come here when I invite you," she continued. "You never invite yourself."

"I don't want to intrude."

"And you don't make love to me in the morning, even though I can see the hunger in your eyes."

"You think morning is for going to work. I don't want to push."

"I look good when I'm half-dressed in my work clothes?" She filled my wineglass again.

"Fabulous, even better than the night before."

"And maybe I'd want you to push a little?"

"You'd let me know." I was feeling exasperated by her catechism. "What's the point of all this, Monica?"

"And maybe I'd love you just because you wanted me to?"

"I won't be selfish with you."

"You should have been more selfish with Catherine," she said.

I knew what she meant, of course. There was no way to explain how and why I could not have been.

"Do you think you have the picture on her now?" I asked, trying to duck a response.

"I'm not sure. Why would someone with that energy give up her painting? Didn't anyone try to protect it?"

"I don't know that anyone thought it was important. How do you save the world with painting?"

12
NICHOLAS

It was the same summer, the year that she went to Rome and flirted with the pope, that I found her with the copy of *Playboy*.

It was a Friday afternoon in mid-August. I had left the beer truck early and driven up to Grand Beach in my jalopy. Her parents' car was not behind the house, so I rang the bell.

"Come in, Ape-Man."

"Where are you?"

"In my studio. Come on up."

"To see your etchings?"

"Don't be fresh."

She was in T-shirt and swimming suit at her drawing easel, working away. Elvis was singing in the background, as he always did that summer.

"I found this wonderful way to draw nudes without going to the Art Institute," she said enthusiastically. "I'll have to hide it before my mother comes. But I've always wanted to do it."

I walked around the easel and saw a *Playboy* centerfold on the edge of the easel. A reproduction of the big-busted young woman was emerging on her canvas.

"That's a *Playboy* centerfold," I said, not very intelligently.

"Yeah, isn't she gorgeous, if you go for that type. But, hey, you shouldn't look at that." She snatched the centerfold away and stuck it behind a book of the work of Claude Monet. "It's an occasion of sin for you."

"Not really." I tried to laugh. "Can I look at the painting?"

"Oh, sure," she said, dabbing vigorously with her brush. "It's art."

Oddly enough it was. It was the same full-bodied young woman in the same languorous pose, but Catherine had transformed her. The Playmate had become a revelation of bodily beauty, with the soft-core porn, as we would call it now, filtered out.

"That's remarkable, Catherine. You've transformed the picture, made it lovely instead of salacious."

"That's what art is supposed to do, silly." She jabbed the handle of her brush playfully at my stomach. "I've always wanted to paint bodies. I think they are sooo beautiful. I'd like to paint you someday."

I felt my face burning. "Really?"

"Sure, girls' bodies are nice"—she laughed—"but boys' bodies are nicer. Oh, oh, I hear the family Caddy. Let's hide this."

"Did you just walk up to the stand and buy *Playboy*?"

"No, silly. I asked some of the freshmen boys to lend me theirs. That way I didn't have to pay. I suppose at the Hill I'll have to buy my own."

The thought didn't seem to phase her in the slightest.

I've never forgotten what she did with that picture. It was sheer raw talent. She saw something in the centerfold that no one else had seen, probably not even the model herself.

But in those days, a girl's talent was not all that important. Catherine "took" drama and singing as well as art in high school. She had leads in both *Oklahoma!* and *West Side Story*. The last time Katie Ryan went out of her house before she died was to see Catherine play Ado Annie. Katie was gaunt and pale and frighteningly beautiful. And she called me and warned me that I would be expelled from the family if I didn't have roses for Catherine.

I would surely have forgotten. As it was, when my mother found out—someone ran to the phone and called her right after the curtain bow—she wouldn't speak to me for a week. "A sinful waste of money," she said.

And Catherine's mother didn't have time to come to the play.

There was one marvelous interlude that night. The girl who was playing Laurie had some kind of stomach attack, virus or nerves or maybe a combination. So Catherine improvised for five minutes, sang a couple of songs a second time and made up a monologue on the spot, improving on Oscar Hammerstein, if you ask me. It was so well done that only a few people even noticed.

When she didn't want to be a female Michelangelo, she wanted to be a female Laurence Olivier. She was good at it too, especially at mimicry, which is why she picked up Spanish so quickly, even in high school. She found a couple of Mexican-American kids and practiced with them every day.

Looking back on those years, I don't think we realized that we had a magic young woman on our hands. I adored her, but it would never have occurred to me to tell her that she ought to do more than merely fantasize about art or acting.

The most amazing thing was her way with kids—more than magical, it was almost scary. She was an only child and even the youngest Ryan kids, before Helen, were not much younger than she. Yet she was the best baby-sitter in Grand Beach. She didn't need the money, of course, but she loved the work. Even the most obnoxious brats—and there were more than a few of those among the South Side Irish—settled down when Catherine came into the house.

And on the beach little kids swarmed around her whenever she appeared, to ask her to fix the straps on their swimsuits, wipe their noses, dry their tears, heal their hurt feelings, put a Band-Aid on their "owies" or even just come play with them.

She always had a box of Band-Aids in her beach bag.

"Why do they always flock to you?" I asked one day when most of our sun time was disrupted by adoring little ones.

"They see another obnoxious little brat, just like themselves," she said flippantly.

"Or maybe someone with childlike goodness."

"Nick, you're wonderful." She kissed me enthusiastically, her eyes misting with her usual quick tears.

I was sure someone would call my mother within the hour and report that too.

<u>13</u>
NICHOLAS

"The poor kid needed someone to protect her," said Monica thoughtfully.

We were lying in bed, enjoying the leisure of conversation before love.

"I know that now. Hell, I knew it then too. But I couldn't figure out—"

"Don't be too harsh on yourself," she said, patting my arm reassuringly. "Maybe you needed some protection too."

We did not, however, make love the next morning. I had to leave to pick up Blackie for our pilgrimage to Catherine's shrine.

14
NICHOLAS

"She was basically a Crusader saint," Blackie said, his nearsighted eyes blinking as he drove northwest on the interstate under a threatening gray sky. "There was a lot of traffic between East and West, sort of on the fringes of the Crusades. Sometime after the Third Crusade, a monk on the run from the East showed up in Rouen with a couple of vials of oil and a few tiny bits of bone. He tells the local duke, a well-meaning rummy named Richard, that he's from the monastery on the top of the holy Mount Sinai and that he was responsible for collecting the oil that oozes from the tomb of St. Catherine near the monastery. The bits of bone came out with the oil, which has marvelous curative powers."

Blackie looks like a modern Father Brown, short, pudgy, cherubic, with curly brown hair, apple cheeks and an expression of impenetrable composure. He is the kind of utterly unimportant-appearing person that you wouldn't even notice if he was on an elevator when the door opened and you walked in. He is also the brightest man I know, ruthlessly loyal, and as much a pixie as his cousin, though he hides that last attribute behind his guise of mordant cynicism.

"And Duke Richard says?" I asked, knowing my lines in the dialogue.

"He wants to know more about St. Catherine, since he's never heard of her. The monk, a certain Simeon, was a wonderful con man. He spins a yarn about a young woman of a noble family, vowed to chastity and brilliant in philosophy, who refutes all the pagan philosophers, is tortured to death by being strapped to a wheel of an ox cart at the order of the cruel Emperor Maxentius—who had propositioned her, by the way—and then beheaded. Her body disappears because some passing angels steal it away from the wretched pagans and carry it off to Sinai where the monks discover it later and build a shrine, which also produces this wonderful oil they market."

"And?"

"And Catherine is an overnight sensation in medieval France. She joins the ranks of the great wonder-workers, along with your man Nicholas, who also probably never existed, and her oil turns up all over France healing the sick and restoring sexual potency to both men and women."

"What!"

"Precisely. The Freudians who specialize in saints say the reason is that the wheel represents the female sex organs—"

"Oh, my God!"

"And Catherine becomes the most popular nonbiblical saint of the Middle Ages. Joan of Arc hears her. More hymns and poems are written about her than about any other saint. She becomes one of the three great winter saints who prepare us for Christmas and promise us spring—Andrew and your man being the others. And after six hundred years of stirring up devotion and good works, she is stricken from the lists by scholars and our presently gloriously reigning pope on the grounds that she never existed."

We had left the interstate and were riding through the rolling countryside toward the river and St. Anthony's and Our Lady of the Hill.

"How come?"

"There's no record of any such saint in the Eastern church and no record of a devotion on Sinai either. Catherine was a fake, or rather Simeon was a fake—kind of hard on all those poor people whose potency was restored."

"And who spoke to St. Joan?"

"Ah, that's a good question, isn't it?"

"It's a shame to lose her," I said, as the steeple of the nineteenth-century chapel on the Hill appeared.

Blackie sighed. "It's what happens when you let scholars take over from the storytellers. In any event, the similarities will not escape you—talent, noble family, torture, death, disappearing body, miracles."

"Except our Catherine really existed," I said sadly. "She really went to school here."

"At least you don't question the nobility of the Ryans," he said, with the tiny smile that was the most Blackie would permit himself when he was playing his pedant role. "The point is that if one gives Ed Carny and Rosie O'Gorman time, our saint may have as little connection with reality as her namesake."

"That's too harsh," I said.

There are four components to Our Lady of the Hill: a rural estate a beer baron willed to the sisters—a crazy, sprawling nineteenth-century Gothic castle, which is the heart of the college and now the administration building and student activities center, to which is attached a chapel that Blackie once described as "hemorrhoidal Gothic"—a group of early twentieth-century Jesuit Ugly academic buildings added to the "castle" (which is what everyone calls it) in haphazard fashion before 1940; some cement-block dorms and labs built behind the castle during the post-World War II heyday of college expansion—which are now coming apart at the seams—and the new glass and steel Rosemary O'Gorman O'Malley Athletic Center and Library, which reminds me of the wild-animal building in an Austrian zoo.

The whole complex is outstandingly unattractive, a successful effort to deface a lovely Midwestern vista of hills and fields and river.

And if one looks down from the "Hill" to the "Valley" across the river where St. Anthony's stands, one can see that this is not that rare event in American Catholicism, a place where the men had better taste than the women. We don't have an athletic center the likes of that at "Rosiville"—as the new generation irreverently and ungratefully calls the O'Malley Center—because none of our alumni married a Silicon Valley wunderkind.

"This whole scene must be preserved in some Disneyworld of the twenty-first century," Blackie murmured as we drove around Circle Drive in front of the castle, "as evidence of just how far we've sunk from Chartres."

"Oh, my God," I exploded. "Right in the center of Circle Drive."

A small crowd of people had gathered around a low platform and a cloth-covered object, including a couple of young women in wheelchairs. One of the men was donning, with the help of a priest, episcopal vestments. We were just in time for the ceremony.

"We must inquire whether the statue secretes oil," Blackie said grimly.

Rosie O'Gorman O'Malley had been cute and plump in her nubile days. Now she was plumper, but still not unattractive. The beauty spas she could afford a couple of times a year helped. And her spacey-eyed husband in crew cut and horn-rimmed glasses—who Blackie claimed thought in Fortran—was obviously still in love with her.

Blackie and I were hugged, and introduced to the dignitaries. Doctor Benetta, the lean, dark, deep-eyed college president, looked like an up-and-coming Mafia hit man. He was a civil engineer who had not quite made it to tenure at State but who replaced a nun with excellent credentials in medieval English when the order decided that it needed a lay president. Bishop Cafferty, a thin, short Telly Savalas, whose wild eyes suggested an escapee from a halfway house for the harmlessly insane. And Friar Mark Goodwin, a tow-haired classmate of mine at St. Anthony's, who had been center on our basketball team and had a doctorate in Ugaritic.

"The only reason I'm here is that I knew how hard this would be on you," he whispered as we shook hands. "The respectable marrieds in the crowd are the charismatics. The bearded, beaded jeans types are from the Emmaus Commune down the river—priests, nuns, ex-priests, ex-nuns, you name it."

"Ed's crowd," Blackie said.

"You better believe it."

"No students?" I asked with some surprise.

"Quarter exams and too cold," Mark said.

Despite the cold November wind and the glowering gray sky, Ed was not wearing a topcoat. His face was pinched and red, from the wind and from the pain of the event.

"It's not easy, is it, Nick?" he said, gripping my arm. "Even though you know she's in heaven and is as much a saint as any of us will ever know, it's still not easy."

"I hope you like the statue," Rosie said, huddling in her mink coat for protection from the wind. "The art department wanted something abstract, but I wanted it to be Cath, just the way she was the last time I saw her in the Miami airport."

"Miami airport?" Blackie cocked an inquisitive eye.

"Just before she died," Rosie bubbled enthusiastically. "You know we have a condo at Biscayne. I saw her there twice, dressed in expensive clothes and wearing dark glasses. The first time she recognized me and ducked away. The second time I kind of hid and watched her climb into a big Mercedes. She must have been doing something important for you, Father Ed."

Father Ed looked mystified. "She never left San Ysidoro, except for that time she met you about the will, Nick."

"I'm sure it was her," Rosie insisted. "Well, it doesn't matter. The bishop is ready. Do I go first, Doctor Benetta?"

No, she did not. Dr. Benetta went first and delivered himself of ten minutes of unmemorable remarks about sanctity from an engineer's point of view.

Rosie had the sense to be brief. "Catherine Collins was my closest friend in high school. We were roommates here for a year. We went into the novitiate together, though I only lasted two weeks." Reasonably dignified giggle. "I loved her. I miss her. I always knew she was special. I hope she'll stand as a symbol of goodness and excellence for future generations of Hilltoppers."

Bishop Cafferty gave a rambling talk about the last three popes, Pius

XII, John XXIII and Paul VI, and how they were involved in our celebration.

Then Rosie pulled the cord and the covers fell away.

It was Catherine as we had known her, small jaw tilted defiantly upward as though she were planning a special party, hands jammed into her blazer pockets, lips about to explode into a smile, jaunty shoulders prepared to swing, trim legs under a short skirt (though not as short as the miniskirts she wore when she was a freshman), ready to bounce around you in Ariel merriment.

"My God," said Blackie. I saw a quick spasm of agony race across Blackie's face.

And on the bronze pedestal was the prayer for the Feast of St. Catherine, virgin and martyr.

Lord God, you gave the law to Moses on Mount Sinai. You also caused the body of blessed Catherine, your virgin and martyr, to be taken mystically to the same place by your holy angels. Grant we pray you that by her merits and prayers, we may be enabled to attain to the mount which is Christ. We ask this in the name of Jesus the Lord.

The crowd applauded enthusiastically. I wanted to weep as I'd done in Monica's arms. But I had done my weeping for the half-century.

Then the bishop said a short prayer blessing the statue and sprinkled it with holy water. I wished it would end quickly, that we could eat our lunch at two-thirty in the afternoon and get the hell out of there, never to return.

As he ended the prayer, Bishop Cafferty's voice quivered and then he began—I can think of no other word for it—to warble. His voice sailed up the scale like a kite in a high wind, wavered and then plunged back to earth, only to soar off again, like a drunken canary.

The bishop's body jerked rigidly upright and then began to sway, not in tune with his warbling, but slightly behind it. President Benetta joined in almost at once and in a few moments half the little group was singing with them.

"Oh, Catherine, Catherine, save us," shouted the bishop.

"Catherine, Catherine, save us," the chorus intoned.

"Charismatics," muttered Mark Goodwin unnecessarily.

And, despite myself, I wanted to speak in tongues with them, to celebrate my Catherine's immortality. Only the memory of the day at Little Angelica's and the Ryan family's dismissal of that as collective neurosis stilled my tongue.

Finally it was over. And, soaking wet again under my coat, I walked with Blackie to the castle for our late lunch.

"Catherine would have been pleased," I said inanely.

"She would have done what no one else had the courage to do," he replied. "Cathy would have laughed. She'd still be laughing."

15
BLACKIE

I'm always amazed at the ease with which charismatics recover equilibrium after one of their wild excursions in nonverbal celebration. We walked into the refectory in the bowels of the Castle as though nothing extraordinary had happened. And, by their standards, perhaps nothing had.

Margaret Aimes, who had been Cathy's assistant novice mistress and had worked with her in Costaguana, stopped me as we were walking down the stairs to the refectory. She was a solid woman with a "German mother's" face, blond hair turning gray, kind blue eyes and the gentle manner of a professional nurse. "Father John, can I talk to you and Nicholas over at the House of Hope after lunch? Please don't tell anyone. I'd be in terrible trouble if they knew."

I wasn't sure who "they" might be, but I agreed. The House of Hope, incidentally, was the former novitiate converted into a rest home for aging nuns. Many of them would die in the same building in which fifty or sixty years earlier they had first become part of the community—and with the melancholy thought that they were spending their last days in the novitiate because there were no more novices.

Many things have changed in the church and the academy since the sixties, but not the quality of institutional food. I had a cup of tea and waited hopefully for the ice cream.

In the meantime there were entertainments.

Midway through the meal, a little character in a poncho, with hair and beard modeled to make him look like Jesus, rose from his table and demanded our attention. "Catherine died for our sins." He began his reprise on a familiar theme. "She is every black, every Hispanic, every gay, every lesbian, every native American, every woman that Amerika has ever killed..."

"Priest?" I asked Mark Goodwin.

"What else? His father is a bank president. Wearing designer jeans, I bet. Notice he left out certain ethnic groups?"

The burden of the young cleric's harangue was that we ought to vote a motion of censure against those legal lackeys who were responsible for keeping Cathy's money out of the hands of the poor to whom it belonged "as a matter of justice."

Enthusiastic cheers from the great unwashed of the Emmaus Commune.

Vigorous and dashing, Ed Carny took the floor and in a good imitation of Ed Hesburg preaching social justice said that it was not proper to say those things about Mr. Curran without giving him a chance to reply. Note well, he didn't tell the damn fool to shut his diarrhea mouth, he'd rather put Nick on the spot.

The reaction to Nick's reply must have wiped out whatever residual claim purgatory has on Nick. He tried to talk about the laws of the state of Illinois and was silenced by the hissing of the communards.

Ed intervened even more sternly, demanding a fair chance. The charismatics and the speakers' table—Benetta, Cafferty, the O'Malleys—writhed silently.

"No point to it, Father Ed, but thanks for the support. I have nothing to say."

I shuffled to my feet, ready to destroy the bearded punk. Before I told him what an idiot he was, I felt Mark Goodwin's firm pressure on my arm. "Leave it, Blackie. It doesn't make any difference."

It made a hell of a lot of difference, but I left it.

The motion to censure passed with only my voice dissenting. There were a lot of folks who didn't exercise the franchise. The meal went on.

"No one pays any attention," Mark argued. "They'll go away eventually."

"Doubtless," I said, "but in a perhaps better age we would have disposed of them more summarily."

The charismatics did eventually leave, and then we were taken on Nick's final ordeal—a tour of the permanent exhibition of Cathy's paintings, an indoor shrine to match Rosie's outdoor shrine.

I imagined pictures of both in the college's catalogue and fundraising literature.

Nick was convinced that Cathy had had extraordinary artistic talent—a notion I had confirmed for myself in second grade when she did devastating cartoons of our pastor at St. Prax's in those days. Nick also felt that in high school, under the direction of Sister Fionna (who oddly enough was still a nun and still teaching art), Cathy's abilities were rapidly developing. Then as a freshman at the Hill she had been directed toward religious magazine-cover piety and, in the one course she took after the novitiate, toward unintelligible abstraction.

The paintings stopped when she went to Latin America, never to begin again.

So it was another violation of Catherine to be dragged through an exhibition of sweet, feminine Jesuses and twisted abstractions that for all the world reminded me of instruments of torture. Doctor Benetta conducted the tour with two women whose pantsuits and low-heeled shoes revealed them to be nuns, the bishop, his officious young secretary, the O'Malleys, Mark Goodwin and the two young women in the wheelchairs.

The "Catherine Collins Exhibition" was simply one of the castle's many useless corridors, brightly lighted so as to expose every failure of technique and every inappropriate mix of colors in works of art which were so bad as to deserve to be buried in the ground and indeed without any of the rites of Christian burial. Drooping flowers and wavering vigil lights added to the charm.

Everyone agreed that the talent displayed was incredible, lamented that it was no longer with us and celebrated the fact that the art of Cathy's life had been more important than the art of her paintings.

I knew what Nick thought of the latter. If he did not use scatological language, neither will I.

Then we had our cure. Of course, we had a cure. The kind of cure which would have brought joy to the late and not greatly lamented Erin Collins.

One of the scrawny adolescents in the wheelchairs began to cry as though she were having a charismatic seizure. The bishop and his officious young secretary and then Doctor Benetta joined in the rising hysteria. I grabbed Nick's arm as hard as I could and dug my fingers into it, hoping that the shock of pain would keep him from crying.

The young woman threw her crutches away with open contempt and, tears streaming down her unappealing face, walked the full length of the room to embrace the screeching bishop.

"Catherine, save us. Catherine, save us," chanted everyone but Nick, Mark and myself.

"Augustine, Albert, Aquinas, Bonaventure, Newman, Teilhard and Karl Rahner preserve us," I said, I hope audibly, to Mark.

"Psychosomatic paralysis for the last two years," he replied, much more quietly. "Hell, Blackie, she can walk now."

"For how long?" I countered.

"Anything is better than nothing," he said; not unreasonably, I suppose.

I then conveyed a frayed and nearly exhausted Nick to Hope House.

Before that repository had become a novitiate, it had been the caretaker's lodge on the beer baron's estate, down in the thick grove of cottonwoods near the river. It had the usual early-fifties concrete block additions.

Margaret Aimes, lean, weary and, I thought, hopeless, waited for us in the parlor of Hope House, a parlor that somehow had escaped aggiornamento and still had not only lace doilies on the worn blue serge chairs but also the novitiate's portraits of Pius IX and Leo XIII on the walls.

"So many things have changed," she mused when we were seated. "Sister Amabilis, Catherine, of course, was in the largest class of postulants we ever had—sixty-five. We haven't had a postulant in the last three years. And it was only thirteen years ago."

"How many of them are still in the community?" Nick asked, out of politeness rather than interest.

"Ten," she said sadly. "No, nine now. We have become a community of old women. Soon there won't be any of us left."

I felt sorry for her. She had labored in the heat of the day and deserved better. Remembering Eloise Fenwick in Wilder's *Theolophilus North*, I said, "The religious life has served human needs for fifteen hundred years, Marge; it will survive."

"I hope you're right, Father John." She sighed. "I don't see any signs yet."

"Maybe Catherine will inspire other young women," Nick said with commendable gallantry.

"I want to talk about her." She hesitated. "You must promise you will quote me to no one. I would be in terrible, terrible trouble. But I have to tell you. I'm so confused...."

We assured the poor woman that her secret was safe with us.

"I think Catherine was about to quit the Movement before she died."

Outside, the November wind was blowing with increasing anger. We would have snow flurries at least on the way home. Inside, the clock in our room was ticking loudly.

"Quit?" Nick broke the anxious silence.

"The killings, the killings," Sister Margaret said, beginning to weep softly. "Neither of us could stand them. I wanted to leave too and had worked up my courage when the reactionary government took over."

She meant the group of young officers who eventually overthrew the not-so-young officers of the junta. They made way for the election which put in power the reform government which was now ruling the country, a coalition of Social Democrats and Christian Democrats— lackeys of the multinationals, according to Ed Carny.

"Killings?" Nick asked in dismay.

"One night the revolutionaries Father Ed was supporting came to San Ysidoro and killed the mayor and his family. Lined them up and shot them with automatic weapons. They were not bad people. He was a little corrupt but not terribly bad by the standards of Costaguana. Most of the townsfolk liked him. And of course his wife and three sons had done nothing. Lorna, a Sacred Heart nun from New York who was part of our team, said it was an essential action of revolutionary justice. I should have had better sense, but I said it was murder."

She tried to explain her agonies to me. "The evangelicals are making thousands of converts in our area because the peons are afraid of violence and they think the *padres* encourage the violence. Anyway, when Father Ed came back from the hills we had a sensitivity session, and Lorna and the others tore me apart for bourgeois sentimentalism. A revolution, they said, had to have its own ethics. Father Ed said that only by disorganizing the society could the revolutionaries reorganize it. I didn't have the courage to disagree and confessed my capitalist and imperialist sins. It was worse than any of the Chapters of Faults when I was a novice mistress."

If the poor woman had not been so close to tears, I would have rejoiced at a novice mistress's getting some of her own.

"And Catherine?" Nick asked.

"She never said a word at the sensitivity session. She was white-faced and grim, eyes rock hard. But no one challenged her. Later she took me aside and hugged me and said I was right and she was sorry she hadn't had the courage to support me."

Ah, my wonderful Cathy.

"Then?" Nick leaned forward, his fists clenched like a prizefighter's.

"The next week the revolutionaries ambushed a government patrol only two hundred meters from our compound. Five of the soldiers were killed and one badly wounded. He was only about fifteen. On both sides, Father, they're only kids who are fighting because someone has a gun at their back. Lorna, who is a nurse, refused to treat the boy. He was going to die anyway, I suppose, but she said he was a capitalist tool and didn't deserve our help. And Father Luís would not give him the sacraments..."

"Ed wouldn't, either?" I shouted.

"Father Ed was back up in the hills," she rushed on, like all the others so eager to protect Father Ed. "Cathy held the boy's head in her arms and prayed with him—you know how good she is, I mean was, in Spanish, Nicholas. She even sang a lullaby to him as he died. Lorna was furious. So was Father Luís. As soon as Father Ed came back, they demanded another sensitivity session. Poor Catherine! They called her everything—a capitalist dupe, a chauvinist lackey, a bourgeois sex object. They said she was a rich, middle-class whore and that her consciousness had never been raised."

"She agreed? Did she confess her faults?"

"No more than she did when she was a novice." Margaret smiled wanly. "She just listened, tight-lipped and somber. And then Father Ed asked her if she didn't want to reply to her friends' criticisms and she said no she didn't. And she walked out of the session and back to the room she shared with Lorna and me."

"Was that the end of it?" I asked.

"It was late at night and the next day things at the settlement went on as usual. I think she surprised them by refusing to give in. Then a week later she was arrested by another government patrol and we never saw her again."

16
NICHOLAS

"What went wrong with them?" I asked Blackie as we entered the car to drive back to Chicago.

We had agreed to divide the driving. He would pilot my Fairlane to the Hill and I would bring it back. But I yielded quickly to his insistence that he drive it on the return trip too. I wanted to arrive home alive and I was in no shape emotionally to wrestle with the falling snow and the toll road.

The last act came as we were turning down Circle Drive after returning from Hope House. A young couple, coat collars turned up, shoulders hunched against the wind, walked across the drive to Cathy's statue. Blackie stopped the car and we watched. They knelt down in front of her and made the sign of the cross. Then, after a few moments of prayer, they repeated the sign of the cross and rose. The girl bent down and placed a bouquet of flowers, wrapped in plastic, at the foot of the statue.

"What's that about?" I asked.

"Weeknight date before Thanksgiving, probably one lives in Minneapolis and the other in Cincinnati. The students don't speak in tongues or vote resolutions. They just pray to her."

"The way she and I used to pray to the Our Lady of Perpetual Help in the chapel before dates when she was a freshman and I a senior..."

"Right. In its own way worse than the warbling and the protests?"

"You were right. She would have laughed at the tongues-speaking. She wouldn't laugh at those two."

"No, indeed."

So I wanted to talk about the fall of the religious orders, anything to drive away the image of Catherine and myself praying together in front of that statue. Blackie obliged me.

"The religious orders? They had a wonderful ideal, which, toward the end, they imposed mostly through power and envy. Then when the big changes came in the church and power and envy were turned into different forms, they found they no longer understood what the ideal was."

"Oh."

"You can't expect to maintain order among a group of seventy novices, young women filled with bodily energies, unless you claim a monopoly on knowing God's will and unless you use group control to keep the aberrant and the gifted in line. That's how it was done. You went through the motions teaching them what the religious life was and helping them to freely assimilate its principles. You talked about the spirit of the Holy Founder, whoever he or she was. But in practice you governed through fear and thought-control and group pressures. You wanted internal conviction and commitment, but you settled for external conformity because you had so many classrooms to fill with teachers, so many hospitals to staff, so many Latin American missions to maintain. Cathy's talent with a brush was a luxury you couldn't afford. You didn't need art teachers, and special training for her would have created unrest among those who were less talented. Even if you didn't have an excuse like sending her to South America, you had to repress her special gift. It all

76 / ANDREW M. GREELEY

worked fine until someone said there were changes going on and you began to examine what you were doing. Then you destroyed the old power structure, denied that the superior was the voice of God, wiped out the old tools of social control and discovered that there was nothing left to love and hate, to lean on and rebel against. The very people who destroyed the old mother in the name of the new mother found that with the old mother gone there was nothing left, and departed in droves. And those who remained shaped the new mother in the image and likeness of fashionable liberalism—social advocacy or the peace movement or feminism. And you don't have to be a religious sister to support any of those things."

"The baby went out with the bathwater?" I said.

"Worse than that. There was so much bathwater that they forgot who the baby was or what it looked like. Take Marge. In a habit, she looked mysterious and intriguing. Now she merely looks dowdy. Remember those St. Joseph nuns at Selma with Martin Luther King, God be good to him, on the front page of every newspaper in the country? If that happened today, we wouldn't know that they were nuns. They don't have to look weird, but unless they look like nuns, no one is going to give a damn about what they do."

"Catherine?" I sighed, still not resigned to her being a saint, a martyr.

"I don't think she belonged in the order. Any human organization that considered her abilities with a paintbrush irrelevant deserves to disappear from the face of the earth. But maybe I'm wrong. If we hadn't had the big change, she would be teaching trig, not art, in a high school in Nebraska and probably be not more unhappy than Rosie O'Malley—which is not necessarily bad. Instead she's St. Catherine, virgin and martyr, wonder worker and patron of revolutions."

"You told Meg Aimes that the religious life would continue."

"Oh, sure. In new forms. In communities that support instead of control, that fight envy instead of institutionalizing it, communities in which power is in the service of love. Isn't that nice rhetoric?" he added bitterly.

"And how long will it take to develop such new forms?"

"A hundred years, at least," Blackie said nonchalantly. "Not nearly soon enough for Cathy."

"She may be the patron of such communities."

"Hooray!" Blackie shouted angrily as we turned onto the toll road.

Yes, I would appear at Monica's apartment tonight. Let the church worry about the long run. This night I would only worry about the short run.

17
BLACKIE

He didn't want to come into the rectory with me when we finally limped off Eden's Expressway through the worsening blizzard. I insisted. I did not look forward to what was to be done. No way. But it still had to be done.

We went to my room, which I admit is more confused and disordered than it might be. I mixed him a strong J&B and soda, assuming that the alcohol would not take full effect until he arrived at his mistress's and then it was her problem.

I was sure that Mary Kate would approve the next day. Still I hesitated.

Cathy was dead. She would not mind now if I permitted her lover to know who she really was. I was betraying a confidence, violating privacy, exposing my cousin to the man she loved the most and feared the most. And giving up all that was left of her that I still possessed.

I told myself that, even if she were alive, she would approve. Yet, I was not certain.

"I will tick off the matters which trouble you, Nicholas," I began, trying to sound like an objective Aristotelian philosopher of the sort that I am ten minutes every day. "They are, unless I am mistaken, five in number. First of all, you are uneasy about the presence of the Outfit in the litigation on Cathy's estate. Secondly, you do not fully believe Doña Paola and Doña Isabella, if my memory serves me correctly about the names of the witnesses. Thirdly, you have a letter from Cath suggesting that she was about to change her will. Fourthly, you discover that she made secret trips to Miami, at least twice the year before she died. And fifthly, whatever her ideological orientations and whatever her attitudes toward Ed Carny—a subject on which you and I have historically differed—there is the strong possibility that she had had it with the Centro San Ysidoro. Is my catalogue comprehensive enough?"

"That covers it," he said, carefully nursing his drink.

I paused, knowing what I had to say and yet still uneasy.

"Cathy kept a diary from the time she went to college until a few weeks before she died. Being who and what she was, she was quite incapable of keeping it only for herself." I unlocked my file cabinet and took out the thick folder of letters. "So she wrote her diary in the form of letters to me. They are remarkably candid. Probably they could be written only to a cousin who was going to be a priest and a lifelong friend."

I handed the letters to him with the ceremony of King David bearing the Ark of the Covenant, except that I did not dance. Nick hesitated, no more eager to accept the remains of Cathy than I was eager to relinquish the relics to his possession.

His expression was a mixture of curiosity and pain. "I don't think…"

"I hesitate too, Nick, but my instincts tell me the answer to what happened may be in these letters. I can't find it. But two heads…"

"Something that fits in with what Sister Margaret told us?" He touched the folder as if it were white-hot metal. "Would she want me to read these letters?"

"Under the circumstances"—I crawled out on the shakiest limb of my life—"I'm sure she would."

Forgive me, dearest cousin, if I am wrong.

He took the folder from me, firmly and decisively. "All right. We've got to find out why Catherine died."

"And," I added, "who killed her."

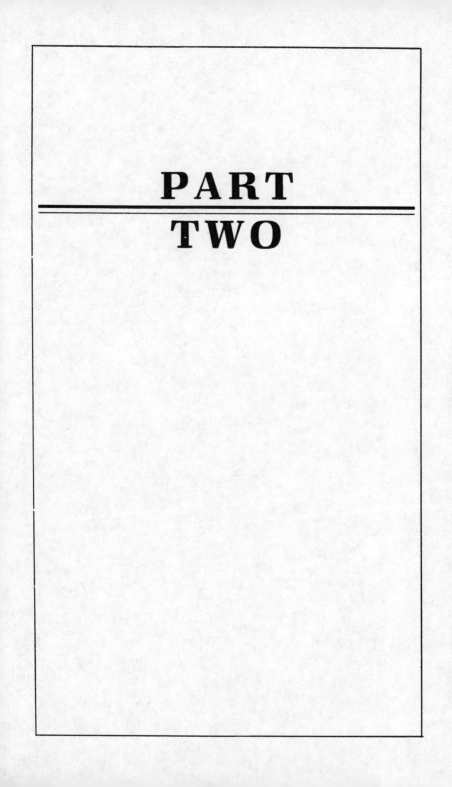

PART
TWO

18
CATHERINE

June 14, 1962
Rome

Dear Cousin,

Well, I may be the youngest of the four pilgrims, but I am
still the undisputed winner in the ass-pinching contest, much
as it offends your sister Nancy to admit that Italian men like
dark-skinned types better than they like blonds.

My score after two weeks in this wonderful city is twenty-
nine, actual and attempted. Nancy wants only to count
successful attempts but that is not fair. It rewards vice, I tell
her.

Nancy and her two friends don't think Italian men mean
anything evil when they pinch pretty young girls. I argue that
they mean less than an American would who tried the same
thing, but that they still mean plenty.

Can you imagine Nick trying something like that? The last
time he approached that part of me was when he spanked me
for putting the sand in his lemonade.

Wasn't that a wonderful summer, Blackie? There hasn't been
one like it since. What a shame we have to grow up.

I miss the Beach, even if we'll be back by July 4. Summers
there are the happiest times. And I miss the Big Lug too, even
if he will spend most of the summer on his damn beer truck. I
keep wishing he was here with me. He knows so much more
about art and takes it so seriously, while I am a superficial
flake like I am about everything else. He would enjoy the trip
more than I do.

Which doesn't mean I don't enjoy it, Cool Coz. It was a
consolation prize, I know, and it didn't seem right for me to
come. But now I'm glad I did. The weather is mild, the sky is
clear and light, like a summer sheet, and Rome is the greatest
museum in the world.

We're going to see the pope the day after tomorrow. Father

Sean Cronin, from down the street back home, is studying
here, and he arranged for some kind of private audience.
Chicago clout. Helps to have a brother who works for President
Kennedy, I suppose. I can hardly wait. I'm sure he'll be the only
saint I ever meet.

And why is my zany, babbling cousin writing me such a long
letter, distracting me from my study of Greek and other
IMPORTANT things, you ask?

WELL, all the others are keeping diaries and I don't think
that makes much sense. Why write things only for yourself?
SO, I decided I'd write to someone else. Nick is the first choice,
but as we both know, there are things on my mind that I can't
tell Nick yet. And I'm scared silly of the day when I try to
explain. SO, who else to write to but Cousin Blackie?

I do so envy you, but not in any bad way, I hope. You're able
to pursue your vocation right away. And I have to wait for
another year and pretend that I don't have any special goal in
life. As Father Ed told me for the last three years, once you
have made up your mind you belong to God, nothing else will
satisfy you.

And he also says that if you turn your back on God and
permit yourself to be tangled up in worldly things, you may
lose Him.

I don't want to lose God, Blackie. I'm a shallow and
immature person and worldliness is my most serious
temptation. I only hope I can keep my vocation despite all the
worldly distractions that will tempt me for the next fifteen
months.

Fifteen months. It seems like fifteen years.

Later

We had lunch with Father Cronin and an absolutely gorgeous
priest from New York, Father Roy Tuohy. He's studying
theology here and is terribly bright. He looks just like
Mastroianni—thin, sallow, soulful brown eyes, worn-out face.
Makes poor Father Sean seem like just a dull restless South
Side Irishman, of which I already know too many.

Anyway, we have to wear black dresses with long sleeves
when we meet the pope. Nancy thought this was pretty funny.

Did they really think we'd give that wonderful old man bad thoughts with our bare arms?

Father Tuohy, who is studying something about the early Middle Ages, was very serious. He said that girls should realize that modern fashions cause many terrible sins and that we will have to answer to God for the way we lead boys on. Because he is so cute and so sincere we didn't say anything. Father Cronin told him that he thought women's bare arms were not what really kept the human race going, but that they helped.

Father Tuohy didn't smile. He said the church needed a lot of reform, a return to the old-fashioned moral values. He also said that the present pope had that in mind when he summoned the council.

Sean just laughed, that reckless Irish laugh of his. He kind of scares me.

I wanted to see the Church of St. Andrew of the Valley, where part of *Tosca* is set, so I walked back in that direction with Father Tuohy while the other girls went to the hotel for their siesta. He was very grim and somber, kind of like Nick when his mother has been chewing at him, and I felt like the dumb bunny I am. He talked about his studies and about how the church had to resist the temptations of modern fake sciences like psychology.

I was sure glad Mary Kate wasn't around.

And then he said that frivolous young women like us were part of the problem. We didn't have any values and we would raise children who would be no better than Communists.

Honestly, he is really cute.

I didn't tell him that I was going to be a nun, and that the only reason I am not entering this fall is that my father surprised me by insisting that I attend college for a year first.

I was kind of ashamed of my lack of willingness to sacrifice for my vocation.

Father Ed says that I'm doing the right thing and that God will protect me through the temptations of the year. I hope He does, because I think it would be terrible to lose a vocation.

And I feel so sorry for Father Ed. You can see the heartbreak in his eyes. I can't understand why, because there was a dumb provincial election and they took his high school away from him. I guess that even Jesus was a victim of envy.

Why would anyone envy Father Ed? He is the best high-school principal in Chicago. Shouldn't the order be proud of him? I don't understand that at all.

I'm sure he'll be a wonderful parish priest, even though there aren't any white people left in the neighborhood.

But it's still not fair.

WELL, Cousin, this is the end of my first day's diary. I don't know whether there will ever be a second day. We're going to some *trattoria* for supper to meet some boys that Nancy says are cute. She certainly knows how to find cute ones. She has been very sweet to me, part big sister and part little mother. And it was nice of her to let me tag along on their trip, even though I'm four years younger.

Give my love to Nick, if you see the Ape-Man. I send him a card every day of course. And then I can hardly wait till the next day when I can sit down and write him again.

Love,
Cath

<u>19</u>
CATHERINE

June 16, 1962
Rome

Blackie Darling,

I am riding the clouds. I am so pleased with myself that I'm unbearable. I don't think I'll even talk to the Ape-Man and you when I come home. I am too important to talk to anyone.

I had a personal conversation with the POPE! That's right: The successor to St. Peter, the Vicar of Christ, stopped to chat with dumb old Catherine the Flake!

Would you believe it?

We all dressed up in our funeral clothes and went over to the Vatican. Father Cronin, looking like some kind of wild Irish monk, met us and took us up the stairs and through the most gorgeous rooms in the world and I was too nervous to look at the frescoes. (Please don't tell Nick that!) I wasn't too nervous to notice the Swiss guards, who are terribly cute and have to pretend they don't see any difference between you and the elderly ladies from a Catholic women's organization that were walking in ahead of you.

Anyway, we get to this big room with a throne in the center of it and a lot of very important priests in purple standing around. There's about twenty of us, which is very small for papal audiences, and Sean Cronin is kind of in charge. They're mostly old people who have good friends in the archdiocese and will go home and talk for the rest of their life about the day they met the pope.

Which I'll NEVER do.

So the door opens and this little old man in white comes in with a fat belly and a funny face and the most beautiful smile in the world. I want to laugh because he is so much like Santa Claus.

He moves very quickly for an old man and bounces up to his throne like a kid. And he talks for a few minutes, waving his hands, like he's selling fruit. His voice is strong and vigorous and some of the important priests grin and even laugh.

Then a very pompous priest in purple translates into English and doesn't say anything funny at all. So I don't think we're getting the full translation.

I don't really remember what the pope said, except that he's glad to see us and he'll bless our rosaries. So I hold up about twenty rosaries and he blesses them all.

Then he begins to walk along the line of visitors, and Father Cronin introduces each of us to him. Your sister and your cousin and their two friends are at the end of the line because we're just silly kids. And since I'm the youngest and the silliest, I'm at the end of the line.

Everyone genuflects and kisses his ring. Even Nancy remembers to do it right, though I know she's thinking about this boy from Stanford we met night before last.

Then they come to me and Father Cronin says, "Caterina Collins."

Caterina is Italian for Catherine.

Now isn't that a dumb thing to tell you?

Anyway, I forget everything and stand there like an all-time dumb bunny holding the pope's hand and grinning.

And he grins back at me, like we both have some secret joke, and we both laugh.

"Sienese?" says the pope.

"Is St. Catherine of Sienna your patron?" Sean translates.

"No," I say and giggle.

The pope shakes his head and raises his eyebrows as though I have refused to buy his fruit because I think it's too ripe.

"Genovese?" he says, like he can't really believe that. I mean, does this dumb kid look "Genovese"?

"St. Catherine of Genoa?" Sean is breaking up now.

"No way," I say, still giggling and wishing I knew who St. Catherine of Genoa was.

The pope shrugs and waves his hands like, "Who is this kid anyway?"

"*Quale Caterina*?" he says.

This is too much for Sean. He's laughing now. So is everyone else in the room. And I'm feeling very warm.

"What kind of Catherine?"

"St. Catherine of Alexandria, virgin and martyr," I say promptly, like I'm a second-grader.

The pope rolls his eyes like he is completely impressed with me. "Verra brava woman," he says, just like he's imitating you imitating him. "Verra brava woman."

"Maybe I'll be a martyr like her," I say, and wish I could cut off my stupid tongue.

The pope kind of frowns and shakes his head. "St. Caterina was a verra wisa woman, philosopher, teacher. You be a wisa woman, Caterina. Teacha others. Is harda to die, but isa much harda to be a wisa teacher. You be a wisa teacher, eh?"

And then he lets go of my hand and walks briskly toward the door. But he turns and comes back.

"Is verra harda to teach, Caterina. I ama the pope, teacher for all the world. Isa *terrabile*. Ima not a gooda teacher. But, Caterina"—and he smiles and winks at me. Honest, Blackie, Pope John XXIII winked at me—"You'ra smarta girl. You be a good a teacher. Teacha lota people about God. Hokay?"

"Hokay, pope," I says and we both giggle and the whole room breaks up.

Your sister and everyone else pretends to be insanely jealous. They say it's only because I have dark skin and the pope thinks I'm Italian.

I don't care. I'm as high as the Alps.

I've already written to Nick. And you have to tell him it's all true. I must write to my parents, but I'm kind of afraid to. I don't think they'll approve.

Isn't it wonderful, Blackie? I can see now that it was God's will that I come to Rome instead of entering the order this year. Because now I know from the pope himself that I'm supposed to be a nun.

Well, I have to run. I met the cutest boy from Santa Clara the other night. You know how I am. I kind of took over the singing at the *trattoria*, even hammed up some opera stuff. And he thinks I'm wonderful. So he is taking me to hear *Aïda* at the Baths of Caracalla tonight. Do not, I repeat, do not tell NICHOLAS about him.

> Love,
> Your Cousin
> And
> The Pope's friend
> Caterina

P.S. Father Cronin just left the pictures and I am so embarrassed. There's dumb Catherine holding the pope's hand and grinning at him like an absolute nitwit.

But the pope is grinning back.

20
CATHERINE

September 9, 1962
Our Lady of the Hill

Dear Blackie,

First night of college. Lights out. And I'm scared.

I've spent exactly one day in college and I'm so homesick that I want to leave tomorrow. The rooms are small and crowded, the beds are like rock, the food is miserable, the sisters are creeps, the chairs are hard, the air is hot and the whole place smells!

Goddamn penal institution.

St. Catherine, virgin and martyr, big brave heroine, already missing the comforts of home. Spoiled only-child brat, like everyone says. What would have happened to me if I'd been over in the postulancy tonight?

I wish it were next weekend, so I could come home. Only I can't come home any weekend till Thanksgiving because NICHOLAS has me lined up for something every weekend. Show off the little prize to all the big guys at St. Tony's.

I hate it all.

And I know you won't be able to read this letter till you come home in January because you can't receive any mail. It's not fair, Blackwood, dear. I want someone to feel sorry for the little spoiled brat.

I know that Rosie is here in the same room with me—she snores. Can you believe that? Rosie snores. And poor dumb wonderful Nick the Ape-Man is right across the river. I can talk to him every day. That was the big reason for coming here. I would see Nick and talk to him every day.

Now I never want to see him again!

Oh, Blackie, I'm such a dumb twit. If you were here, you'd be saying that I'll be all right in the morning.

If I live till the morning.

And half the time I'm afraid I will live to the morning and the other half of the time I'm afraid I won't.

I'm going to stop now and pray on the rosary the pope blessed for me. I'll ask God to make me a "verra wisa woman." And get me through this night.

I love you, Coz. Pray for me, even if you don't read this letter till January. God doesn't care about time.

Scared,
Cath

P.S. Two weeks later. What a dope. I love it here now. I love the autumn colors. I love football games. I love the school. I love the nuns. I love my art classes. I love the part I have in the play. I love Rosie. I love everyone. And, oh, yes—though I didn't have to tell you this—I especially love Nick.

_21_
CATHERINE

December 8, 1962
OLH

Dear Blackie,

I am confused again.

I think I have been trying to forget about God. That's what Sister Intemerata, my art teacher, says. I haven't been paying much attention to her because I have been having so much fun, fun, fun here.

Nick is an incredible young man. I can't believe some of the things the other kids have to put up with. Their dates are savages, beasts. My God, you would need to dress like a football player or a knight in armor to be safe with them.

And Nick is so gentle and kind and sweet.

And popular with everyone. Did you know he is senior class president? I mean, he seems so quiet, you wouldn't think he'd have that kind of influence. I guess he has to get away from that TERRIBLE family to blossom.

Of course, I never tell him that they're terrible.

He wants to marry me, Blackie. Can you imagine that? He wants to marry me. Oh, he hasn't popped the question or anything like that. Our Nick the Ape-Man doesn't rush into anything.

But I can tell. And he wants me to tell. There are little hints here and there about our traveling to Europe together or coming back for reunions—when you're a senior I guess you think a lot about coming back. I don't know how I'll survive next year when he isn't here.

Anyway.

Anyway, what?

Oh, yes. I love him, Blackie. I have no trouble imagining the rest of my life with him. He'd have to be tough with me when I turn flaky, and he isn't able to do that yet. But he'd learn. And we'd probably fight and I'd win most of the fights, because he's a gentleman and I'm not much of a lady. But we would be happy, I think.

No, I know we'd be happy. I'm so happy when I'm with him, I don't notice the time pass. He loves me and I love him. And we'd be happy together for all our lives. And have wonderful children who would be like the Ryan kids.

And if I give him the slightest signal, Blackie, I swear, I'll have a diamond by the end of the summer. Only eighteen, going on nineteen, and I'll be ENGAGED!

And to a boy I have always loved. I mean, I never really thought I had a chance with Nick. Why would he waste his life with a flake when there are so many more gorgeous and more sensible girls?

That makes me think about it. He deserves better than me.

Still he wants me. And I want him.

Of course, I don't tell him that. When he makes his shy, embarrassed hints, I just laugh gaily and away we go.

I am really getting good at the merry laughter act.

And I come back to my room and cry my eyes out, though quietly so I won't wake anyone up, because I know it's all wrong. I have a vocation. I'm going to enter the order in the fall. I will not marry Nick or anyone else. I am reserved for God. I must be a bride of Christ. To tell you the truth, I'd much rather be a bride of Nick right now, even though that's a terrible thing to say.

What I want doesn't matter. It's what God wants. And I have this strong inner feeling that God wants me. So I will have to give Nick up. I haven't told him that yet. At the beginning of every day I say to myself, Cathy, you are going to tell him tonight. You must tell him tonight. You are a dishonest faker if you don't tell him tonight.

And then I lose my nerve as soon as I see that strong, smiling face.

Oh, damn!

Sister Intemerata is very gentle with me. She talks quietly and softly while I'm drawing sketches—about how much God loves us and about how special we are who are called to be brides of Christ. She's in her middle forties and was prom queen here the year before she entered. Her date that night is the governor of the state. She is a beautiful woman who has given up everything for Christ. Why can't I do the same thing?

I will do the same thing. I will enter in the fall.

I'm not living the kind of life of someone who is committed to Christ. I'm a silly worldling, flitting around on the surfaces of everything, afraid of the depths.

Father Lyons, who teaches our social ethics course, tells us that the way we Catholics witness Christ in the world is by being good at what we do. If we're bakers, he says, we win people to Jesus not by using our bakery shop as a convert center but by making good bread. Jesus deserves the best and we win people to Him only when we're the best.

I want to be the best, Blackie—oh, how I want to be the best. I've always wanted to be the best, even though usually I end up being the worst. I want to be a great painter so that when people see my great paintings they'll see Jesus, even if I'm not painting pictures of Him, as is true now in art class.

But my paintings are sloppy because I'm distracted and

because I'm living such a dishonest and sloppy life. Sister doesn't say that, but she does say you can't separate life from art. Dishonest life produces dishonest art.

I'm in Father Lyons's YCS group and am getting a lot out of it. We first OBSERVE. We study some problem like lack of respect for ideas in the school. Then we JUDGE. We ask whether in the light of the gospels this is the right way for Catholic students to be. Then we ACT. We resolve to do something that will promote a climate of greater respect for learning here at the Hill. It's not enough to study more ourselves. We have to change the environment, like by having serious discussions about good books with our friends. It is all very exciting and I really believe we can change the environment here. There's so much giddy superficiality.

Then I think of what a hypocrite I am. There is no one in all the world more giddy and no one more superficial than I am. I'm trying to renege on my promise to Christ and I'm deceiving a wonderful boy.

But I can't stop.

Father Ed came up to see me last week. Right after the Thanksgiving break. He's happy now in his new work and bubbling with enthusiasm about the community organization in his parish. He and Father Lyons are friends, and they had a wonderful argument about whether the priest ought to be the president of such organizations. Father Lyons said it was the layman's proper role. And Father Ed said the laity would only do it when we showed them how.

Anyway, Father Ed had a long talk with me. He was very gentle and very nice, but also blunt: I'm being unfaithful to my vocation. Christ will be disappointed that one of his intended brides is trying to run away. I have to settle down and make the most of this year of preparation instead of living like a little nitwit.

And I must tell Nick the truth or he will never forgive me when I do.

Those are about the same things that Sister I. tells me. I know they're both right and I'm wrong.

But I'm so weak.

In another month you'll be home—why don't they let you come home at Christmas?—and you'll read these letters and know that I'm still being a twit. I hope you won't stop loving me.

What a dumb, rambling letter this is. I know you said you'd listen, but I'm sorry about boring you with my idiocy.

Now I must put on my best skirt and sweater and look sweet and demure and still sexy for Nick.

And when I see his eyes light up, I'll feel sweet and demure and VERY sexy.

And guilty as hell.

> Love,
> Confused Coz

22
CATHERINE

Ash Wednesday 1963
OLH

Dear Cousin,

I talked to Father Lyons, as you suggested, and he said pretty much the same thing you did. And I'm even more confused.

According to him, the best sign that we're doing what God wants us to do is that we're happy in it—not happy all the time, but more happy than unhappy. And if I don't feel happy at the prospect of entering in the autumn then I shouldn't do it.

And if God wants me, he insists, then it's up to God to make that real clear. It's not my problem. If I don't think things are clear, then I should commit my trust to God and wait.

I like that a lot. It puts all the responsibility on God and lets me enjoy life.

But I can't believe we were created merely to enjoy life. Oh, I don't say that you and Father Lyons are wrong and the nuns and Father Ed are right. I'm simply all mixed up.

So I'm going along with everyone. I'll accept what you and Father Lyons say and postpone any more thought about entering for another year. I certainly can't make the proper decision in my present frame of mind.

And I'll work in a tutoring program in an inner-city parish next summer, no matter what my parents say.

On the other hand, I'll try to have a good Lent and pray very, very hard and cool it with Nick.

And by the end of the summer, if I trust God enough and pray hard enough, I'll know. I'll just KNOW.

I don't have to tell Nick that I'm entering because that decision isn't final.

But I have told him that we're too serious about each other and that he has to finish law school, which is three years, and I have to finish college, which is also three years, and that if we keep on the way we are, we'll become a proximate occasion of sin for each other. I've convinced him that we should only see each other once a week during Lent and talk on the phone only twice a week and that we should both date others.

He won't have a hard time finding other girls. And, to my surprise, there are a lot of boys, many of them cute, who want to take me out.

I'm glad I've worked this out. It takes a load off my mind, at least for a while. But I don't have fun with other boys, not the way I do with Nick.

And I have this terrible guilty feeling that I'm letting God down.

Thanks for all the help, Coz. I wish I was as calm and collected about my vocation as you are about yours.

Love you,
Cath

23
CATHERINE

Ft. Lauderdale
Thursday in
Easter Week

Dear Blackie,

I'm sick. I have my first real, live hangover, the result of my
first real, live drunken binge—on beer, please. How much beer
does it take to acquire a hangover, Coz? Anyway I had a lot
more than that. And I also thought that the Florida sun was
just like our Grand Beach sun. Old Cathy doesn't burn, she just
tans, right? Wrong!

And I may be coming down with the flu.

And worst of all, I have terrible guilt feelings about my fight
on Holy Saturday with Nick the Ape-Man.

We do fight, you know. Or, rather, I try to fight with him
and he won't fight back, the bum.

Act One. Cathy announces that she's about to do something
that ranges anywhere from kind of silly to asinine. Act Two.
Nick says, Well, it's up to her, but maybe it isn't a good idea.
Act Three. Cathy says, Damn it all, she's not a slave and she
will do it too. Act Four. Nick says it's all right with him, but
has she thought of a, b, c, d? Of course she hasn't but she
won't admit it. Act Five. Cathy screams, shouts, stamps her
feet, and maybe even uses bad words. Of course, she hopes
Nick will laugh this off and say, Well, don't do it as a favor to
me. Instead, Act Six. Nick backs off, hurt and sullen. Cathy
screams some more and then goes and makes a fool of herself.

As you can guess, the subject of our Holy Saturday fight—in
back of St. Praxides' after services—was my sudden decision to
fly to Fort Lauderdale with Rosie and the crowd for Easter
vacation—to see if that's where the boys really are. And
reasons a, b, c, d are that Cathy is too innocent and naive for
the scene here and that lots of innocents like her become
victims of the predators.

An excellent line of reasoning, Coz, as I'm sure you know. I don't know word one about sex. I mean, I learned in school how the parts fit, but beyond that I'm at sea. Beneath all the innocence I think I may be a passionate person. After all, I do dote on painting bodies. But you have to go a long way down to find my "sensuality," as the nuns call it.

So I am a perfect victim. If I've escaped with my virginity, it isn't my fault.

And Nick was absolutely right. He even offered to come with me to keep me out of trouble. Can you imagine that? I called him several very vulgar names, right in the vestibule of St. Prax's, and stormed away.

And last night—or early this morning, I guess—when this med student from Columbia has my swimsuit off, top and bottom, and is using his medical training to do terrible but pleasant things to me and I'm more than half-drunk, I am wishing that good old Nick was along to protect the foolish virgin.

So I defend myself with my knee and flee the balding guy from Columbia while he rolls on the beach in pain. He called me some names I have never heard. Rosie hadn't heard them either.

Will I go back and apologize to Nick? Of course not. We'll never mention the subject again.

It isn't quite as bad here as the decline of the Roman empire. Not everyone is looking for quick sex, not even all the boys. Some of them are innocents too. And I've seen quite a few girl predators.

But it's a hell of a way to celebrate the Lord's resurrection, Cousin. And don't feel that the seminary does you any harm by keeping you away from Lauderdale at Easter.

Father Ed says we live in a pagan and godless time. We sure do. After this week, the novitiate will look awfully good next autumn.

I'm going to take some aspirin and find this cute boy from Notre Dame who is at least as innocent as I am and more sunburned. We'll hide in the shade and talk about art or music or something.

What can I do to make Nick fight back?

Love,
Chastened Cousin

<u>24</u>
CATHERINE

June 6, 1963
Chicago

Dear Blackie,

He's dead and you're not even home from the seminary.

My poor, wonderful, fat Santa Claus pope is dead. I can't believe it. I've cried all day. He looked so healthy when he held my hand a year ago and told me that I should be a wise woman. I knew he was an old man and had to die, but why so soon? Why did God take him away from us when his work was only beginning?

At least we still have the other John, the president. And thank God he's a young man.

I have to do something really important with my life, Blackie. That wonderful old man told me so and God must have told him to tell me.

I haven't paid much attention to the Vatican Council. I figured it was just a silly meeting of a lot of old cardinals and bishops. But the priests and nuns at Forty Holy Martyrs—where I'm training now for the tutoring program this summer—are very excited about it. Just think, Blackie, the church is going through one of the biggest changes in its history and you and I will be part of it. Father Lyons says that the Counter-Reformation is over and that the ecumenical age is starting. I don't know quite what that means, but I guess we can talk to Protestants now and that seems to be a good idea.

And the Mass will be in English and the birth-control teaching will change—doesn't matter to me; I want a big family just like the Ryans—and the church will become a democracy (again, says Father Lyons) and the laity will assume their rightful role in the church.

It's a wonderful time to be alive. Remember the quote from Christopher Fry that Father Ed quotes, "Thank God our time is now when the enterprise is exploration into God."

So I have to stop being a mediocrity and become good at something.

I started out this letter crying. And after I thought about what my Santa Claus pope means for you and me, I'm happy and all fired up again.

That's the kind of man he was, Blackie, dear.

I know. He and I were friends.

As you've doubtless guessed, I'm crying again.

Love you,
Cathy

25
CATHERINE

July 6
Forty Holy Martyrs
Rectory

Dear Blackie,

I don't see why they send you seminarians up to northern Wisconsin to watch over white orphans during the summer. I mean, I feel sorry for the orphans, but they live in a home where nuns take care of them all year round. The kids in this neighborhood need priests a lot more—and half of them are from families where the father isn't there. Besides, they are the kind of people you will work with after you're ordained.

Oh, well, what does poor dumb Cathy know about such things? I didn't even know there were places like Forty Holy Martyrs until a few weeks ago. How many times did I ride through this neighborhood on the Rock Island and not even realize that people live here, people like you and me, with feelings and fears, hopes, and hearts that can break?

I love it and I hate it. I love helping some of these poor kids to read a little better. And I hate, hate, hate that they are so poor and so neglected. Negroes are just like us, Blackie. Isn't that a stupid thing to say? But I guess I always thought they were different, that they had to be different to survive. It makes me angry and it also makes me wonder why I deserve to live in so much comfort when they live in so much poverty. Am I not in some way the cause of their poverty?

I don't understand these things at all. But I want to understand them and do something about them.

I felt very guilty about sneaking away to Grand Beach over the Fourth. These people have nowhere to go on the weekends but the hot, dirty and dangerous streets. No wonder there are so many juvenile delinquents.

But I was also glad to be back on the Beach with the sun and the sand and the water and the Ryans and, of course, NICHOLAS. All right, I was running away from the ugliness, but I'm such a shallow twit that I have to run away sometimes.

Nick is wonderful, better than ever. He's proud of his scholarship to Loyola and even prouder of his job with the law firm that your father got him. I think he's mostly stamping and filing things, but at last he's in his own world and you can see the self-respect shoot up like a skyrocket.

And he supports my work here. Everyone, my parents, even your family, is worried about me driving down into this neighborhood every day. Nick is worried too, poor dear, but he's also proud of me. And when Nick is proud of me I sail up to the highest clouds.

He finally managed to get up on one ski this weekend, wobbly as a baby trying to walk, but still he stayed up and even crossed the wake once before he wiped out.

It was great fun and there was only one thing wrong with

Grand Beach this Fourth of July. You weren't here.

And it will probably be my last Fourth of July here. Ever.

Miss you.
Love,
Cathy

26
CATHERINE

July 29
FHM Rectory

Dear Delightful Cousin,

You were wonderful last weekend. It was so good to see you again after almost a year. You're a powerful argument for a religious vocation, so happy and peaceful and content. Will I be that way a year from now if I enter in September?

Did you ever love someone the way I love Nick? Of course, you didn't. I know that you could and that if you were not a priest you'd make some lucky girl a wonderful husband, so long as she was quick enough to put you in your place when you needed it—like nine or ten times every day.

I know how you felt about Lisa. But you kept it a big secret and you recovered from her quickly.

I bet you've had all sorts of crushes on other girls too, but you've kept them to yourself because you're a sensible person and you're going to be a priest. I wish I were sensible.

One thing I learned at Lauderdale was how good Nick really is, despite his ridiculous religious doubts. I mean, he must want me as much as that dope from Columbia—more, because he has known me longer and loves me more. But he is so respectful and considerate.

Maybe too respectful. And I know you're going to say that Irish women are never satisfied.

Course not. We deserve the best.

But it is so easy to see us happily married. I imagine our wedding night being here at the Beach—the Ryan house, of course, fixed up special for the occasion, with no Ryans around. I won't know much more about lovemaking than I do now, but it will all be fine because he will be so strong and gentle.

And that's the way it will be always, except I will turn into a wildly passionate and very skillful lover.

And then I think, no, that will never happen. God wants me. And I cry a little. And then I think I shouldn't cry. I should be happy that God wants me.

I've talked a lot with Father Lyons, who is here this summer, especially after our YCS meetings. I know how much you respect him, so I listen very carefully. He says I shouldn't become a nun because I think the married state is inferior. Marriage is good and holy and not just for weak people. After all, it is a sacrament and the religious life isn't. You can serve God just as well as a wife and mother as you can as a nun.

I wonder if that's true. The nuns don't think so. And neither does Father Ed. But then I think of your mother and father, and now Helen, and I think of Mary Kate and her wonderful Joe and I'm not so sure.

And he says we shouldn't run to escape the secular world. God destines it for salvation too and we should live in it and love and save it by our love and the excellence of our lives and work. That is very exciting. It means I could be Mrs. Nick Curran and still be a great Catholic woman.

But then I ask him: Why have nuns and religious orders? He says that in God's kingdom there are many different houses and we're called to do different things and the best way we can tell what we're supposed to do is to find out what we like best and that's pretty much what God wants us to do.

He's a nice little man, a kind of smiling gnome, and I really like him. But he makes it all sound too easy. There's not enough suffering in his world. As Father Ed says, you find God's will only when you find the cross.

His parish is the next one over, by the way, and he has a terrific community organization which is campaigning for racial justice in housing. I'm going to distribute some pamphlets for him next Sunday at St. Prax's. You can imagine how my father and mother will like that.

Anyway I am really good with the kids. They all say I'm the

best tutor in the program. So it's not only white small persons who see a nutty small person like themselves when Crazy Cathy shows up. And I love it. So, even by Father Lyons's principles, I belong in a neighborhood like this one, teaching such small persons how to read and write and climb out of poverty. That ought to be enough fun for one life.

Nick is taking me to Ravinia tonight and I'm going to meet some of the partners in the firm and their wives. I must be on my good behavior and look my cutest. And keep my big mouth shut.

Well, Nick didn't say those things, of course. He wouldn't dare. And he knows that I never keep my mouth shut.

The music is Polish modern, Penderecki and that sort of thing. It was a mistake to let Nick find out about music. He not only knows more about it now than I do; he's acquired more refined tastes.

Bet I charm the partners and their wives even if I talk?

See you real soon.

Lots of love,
Cath

27
CATHERINE

August 14, 1963
Grand Beach

Dear Blackie,

Why am I writing this when you are only a block and a half away down the beach? I guess I'm afraid to tell you face to face, because I think you'll be mad at me.

And I don't want you to be mad at me, Coz, because I love you a lot.

I know you think I don't have a vocation. We went all

through it last weekend, didn't we? And your arguments are as reasonable as Father Lyons's. All right, I don't have to be a nun. I can serve God in the married state too. But what if I want to be a nun? What if I know in my heart that God wants me to be a nun? Then shouldn't I become one? You said that the only reason I wanted to enter was that I felt God would be disappointed in me if I didn't.

And Rosie's decision to enter next month had no effect on me. I think you're wrong—and not very nice—to say that she won't last six weeks. Rosie has lots of strength. And she's giving up that wonderful boy from Cal Tech she met at Lauderdale.

Rosie forced me to be honest with myself. I had about made up my mind to postpone until next year. But, as Rosie said to me, it won't be any easier next year. And we won't be any less attached to the world next year, either.

So for me it's now or never and it has to be now. I want to enter because I know God wants me.

Sure, I could stall for another year. Even finish college, but that would be putting off a decision, drifting through life without any goal, like I've always done, a ski boat run out of gas.

And lying to Nick. I mean even if I tell him that I'll probably enter after college, he'll still hang on and hope. I can't let him do that, can I?

So now is the time to act like a grown-up and decide.

I spent a lot of time talking to Father Ed last week. He doesn't disagree with you and Father Lyons, not really. From one point of view all states in life have equal value in God's eyes. But from another point of view there are degrees and grades. And the religious life with its vows of poverty and chastity and obedience is the most perfect way of being dedicated to God. Religious can fail every bit as much as married people can fail, but when they live up to their vows, they are the people who most please God.

And that's what I want to be: one of the ones who most pleases God. He has given me so much and I haven't given Him anything back yet. So now I'm going to give Him myself, not much but all I have.

Sometimes when I kneel in church praying, I know that God

loves me and will take care of me no matter what happens. I'm filled with peace and quiet and happiness. The whole world kind of comes together and I see my place in it and I know everything is going to be all right. How can I say "no" to a God like that?

And that's where Father Ed has been such a big help. He's made me realize that I would be saying "no" to God. I just can't do that, Blackie, even if you are mad at me.

Anyway, why can you have a vocation and I can't?

Father Ed is very concerned about me and with good reason, I think. He's afraid that I'm losing my nerve and my courage and that if I drift any longer I'll drift away from my vocation. I certainly lost my nerve after the second Mass last Sunday when the pastor ordered me out of the parking lot at St. Prax's.

I didn't have the courage to tell him that all the words in Father Ed's leaflets came from letters of popes and bishops. I am a gutless wonder and you know that too, Blackie.

So I've made up my mind and my decision is final. And, please, if you love me don't fight me. It's been terrible with Mom and Dad. He won't talk to me and she cries all the time. Last year she was proud to have a daughter with a vocation. This year she weeps that she will never be a grandmother.

I can't figure them out. Never could. But they won't stop me.

And Sister David Mark at the Mother House was very unhappy that I called so late. They have the largest entering class ever this year. Isn't that thrilling? I think she agreed to accept me mostly because she's convinced I'll be one of the first to leave.

I'll show her.

It will be hard to tell all the Ryans too, because I'm sure they will think, like you do, that I don't have the courage to be a nun. I guess I'll have to show them too. But don't you tell them, please, Blackie. I don't want the rumor to spread until I've had a chance to talk to Nick.

And that will be very difficult. I'll have to invest in a whole case of Kleenex.

Pray for me, I beg you, Coz. I will need all the prayers I can get.

Love,
Cathy

28
NICHOLAS

Catherine and I were sitting on the edge of the old pier the Sunday of the Labor Day weekend, under a blanket of warm and friendly stars, a little more than thirteen years ago—1963. It seems like yesterday, and yet, having read some of her letters now, I feel it could have been a thousand years ago.

It had been a very good summer for me. My law boards were over 800 and I could have gone to any law school in the country. But Loyola gave me a scholarship and Harvard was a long way from Catherine. And they liked me at the firm—indeed, they treated me almost as though I were a junior partner. Mr. Ryan's influence had done it, but I still felt at home in a way I never had at the brewery.

Catherine and I had settled down into what seemed a comfortable relationship. I thought she was growing up and becoming more of an adult every day, without losing any of the enthusiasm and vigor that made her so appealing. I worried a little that she wasn't receiving a good education in art at the Hill, but I thought I would not push that subject until her sophomore year was completed.

She needed another year away from home and I needed my first year of law school under my belt. Then perhaps she could come back to Chicago and attend the Art Institute. We might even be married after the second year of law school instead of after the third, though that was a radical and light-headed thought, one I had just begun permitting myself.

I had no idea of the turbulence that was raging inside her. No idea whatever. I don't think I had any feminist notions that long ago. It was probably just common sense that made me think that if my wife had a talent for painting she and I would both be happier if she developed that talent. And, again, it wasn't principles but common sense that made me feel that the more money she made from her painting the better.

She was magnificent the night at Ravinia with the men from the law firm and their wives—innocent, naive, charming and extremely well informed. When she lamented the weakness of the woodwinds in the second movement of the Bach, which was a peace offering after Penderecki, she convinced a number of skeptical Protestant senior partners that Irish blood did not necessarily make one musically illiterate.

My life seemed perfectly in order then. Law school, Catherine, the firm, success, happiness.

I didn't know how to handle her when she was flaky, although only after reading her letters did I realize how inept I was. Indeed, all I would have had to say was, "Do me a favor and stay away from Lauderdale."

Would she have abandoned her plans for the religious life if I had said, "Do me a favor and marry me instead?"

I haven't slept the last couple of nights from worry over that one. I'm afraid the answer is that she would have forgotten about the convent quickly and gratefully.

And be very much alive today.

She tossed her cigarette into the water. I lighted another one for her. She knew I didn't like her smoking. "I'll really give them up this semester," she said grimly.

"I hope so," I replied.

She grabbed my arm as if she'd been stung by a bee. "Nick!"

"What's wrong?" I put my arms around her. She was shaking like a leaf.

"Pray for me next week."

"I'm not sure I believe in prayers, Catherine."

"Please," she begged.

"Sure," I said lightly. "I'll address them to whom it may concern. Any special reason?"

"I'm entering the Third Order of St. Francis of Our Lady of the Hill," she whimpered.

My neatly ordered future came apart like a wall broken by a bulldozer. The carefully drawn fresco on the wall cracked, crumbled and fell into a million pieces. And then the bulldozer rolled on and crushed me too.

I had no doubt she meant what she said. Catherine's practical jokes were never of that sort and the trembling girl in my arms was not joking. I wanted to break her neck, throw her in the lake, put her over my knee and spank her as I'd done years earlier.

And the last might have worked, damnit.

As it was, I acted like a jilted lover.

"Do you think that is a wise idea, Catherine?"

She pulled out of my arms, spoiling for a fight.

"Why wouldn't it be wise?"

"Aren't you a little young to be throwing your life away?"

"Dedicating my life to God isn't throwing it away. Anyway, I won't take final vows for eight years. I'd be old enough by then to make a decision about marriage. Why not about being a bride of Christ?"

"I thought you loved me," I said stupidly.

"I do love you. I love you more than anyone else in the world. But I love God more. Jealous?"

"What point is there in being jealous of God? Why didn't you tell me before? Or is this a sudden decision?"

"I've been thinking about it for a long time. But I made up my mind about entering only . . . only this summer."

"Couldn't you have shared your thoughts with me earlier?"

"What difference would that have made?" she asked bitterly. "You wouldn't have understood then, either. You think it's one more flaky impulse of crazy Cathy."

"I didn't say that."

"You're thinking it."

"No, I'm not. . . . I suppose Rosie's impulsive decision to enter has had no effect at all on you?" I said sarcastically, although I knew that sarcasm was gasoline on the fire of Catherine's temper.

"I make my own decisions," she said hotly. "I don't care what you think, Nick." She stood up, dusted off her Bermuda shorts and began to stride off the pier. "I hoped you would understand. I'm sorry if you don't. But I have to live my own life."

I raced after her and grabbed one of her arms. She tried to shake free, but I wouldn't let go.

"I love you, Catherine. . . . I thought that someday we might marry."

She stopped struggling and, with her free hand, touched my face gently. "You're the most wonderful boy I've ever known, Nick," she said. "You deserve someone better than me. And you'll find someone too. Promise you'll forget about me. It won't be hard."

"I'll never forget you, Catherine," I said, trying to kiss her.

She responded with a quick movement of her lips against mine.

"Pray for me, Nick." And then she ran up to the Lake Drive and toward the Ryan house.

It was many years before I tried to forget her and by then it was much too late.

I sat on the pier again and listened to the locusts and the gentle slap of the lake against the beach. I peered intently into the heavy, starlit night, trying to organize my thoughts—like a good lawyer writing a brief. Most marriages did not seem to work. My father was an outcast in his own home the day after he and my mother moved into it. Catherine's mother and father rarely spoke to each other. Indeed, he rarely spoke to anyone. Up and down the beach there were many unhappy and disillusioned husbands and wives. So too in the Neighborhood and so too, I was beginning to discover, in the firm. Money, success, physical attractiveness—none of them seem to guarantee happiness in marriage. Perhaps it would never have worked between Catherine and me. We were oddly matched, even though we had seemed to complement each other. Certainly I had not understood her. I had not even tried to, or I would have sensed that something was on her mind. Looking back on that summer, I realize there were plenty of clues, if I had not been so completely focused on myself.

So maybe I was lucky to be free of her as she argued. But I wasn't persuaded. And even today I'm not persuaded. It could have been different.

I gave her plenty of time to tell the Ryans and then tiptoed back to the silent house and slept for a few hours. The next morning I found only Blackie on the porch eating breakfast and reading *The Spy Who Came In From The Cold*. In those days he and I had yet to become close friends, not yet bound together by our common concern over Catherine.

"Did she tell you?" I asked, pouring myself a cup of coffee.

"Yeah." He nodded glumly. "She told us."

"What do you think?"

"I don't know," he replied, the kind of answer I would never hear from him today. He buttered a piece of toast and covered it generously with raspberry jam. "Helen, among her many accomplishments, makes wonderful raspberry preserves."

Blackie and his beautiful stepmother had become close friends. She laughed every time he opened his mouth, behavior that delighted him enormously, even then.

"I think she's out of her mind," I said.

"It does not follow that she won't enter."

"Do you think she'll last?"

Blackie sighed. "The religious life is not for creeps, Nicholas. It's for strong, vital women. Catherine has the strength and the vitality all right. Whether she can contend with the people who seem to be in charge just now is another matter. And whether her talents might be put to better use elsewhere . . . " He shrugged and began working on another piece of toast.

"I think it's Rosie's influence." I began to whistle in the dark. "They'll both be out within a year."

"Rosie surely within six weeks," he agreed. "As for my cousin, don't underestimate her capacity for stubbornness once she has made up her mind."

"I don't," I said sadly.

I tried a long walk on the beach, hoping I wouldn't meet her, and then swam in the warm waters. I would love her always.

And law school lost all its luster. So did everything else in my life.

29
BLACKIE

"There were so many of them and they were so different," Marge Aimes said, tasting her drink. "We were frightened of them—honestly, Father John, we were. And then all the changes came and the chapters, each one undoing the work of the previous one. Now there doesn't seem to be anything left. I wonder what we should have saved from the old ways."

"Affection, happiness, love," I replied.

"There wasn't much of that, I'm afraid, in Sister David Mark's novitiate." She shook her head disconsolately.

"Nor in the Centro San Ysidoro, either," I added.

"Some of the women in Catherine's class are filled with those qualities today," she said. "They don't hate anyone."

"And they would have been just the same in the old ways."

"I think for them the new ways are better," she said. "Which is why maybe I ought to agree to run for the presidency of the community. It's ironic that my principal qualification is that I worked with Catherine, whom we expelled from the community only eight years ago."

"Would she have wanted you to run?"

"She would laugh and say, 'It sounds like fun, Marge. Do it.' Even at the end she never lost her sense of humor."

Nick had called me after his conversation with Joe McNally. Still proclaiming his belief in Ed Carny's sincerity, he told me that it appeared Ed had been running money for the Outfit and that Cath might have been the courier.

It would have been typical. She read every cheap spy novel that was

published when she was in high school. And she didn't like John Le
Carré because he made the world too complicated. Smuggle money?
Hell, yes, that sounds like fun.

I'd reiterated my position that I didn't question Ed's sincerity, only
his intelligence, and suggested that I attempt to pry more information
out of Margaret Aimes, who wanted to talk to me during a post-Thanks-
giving professional meeting in Chicago.

I took her to the top of the Hancock Center—where else does one
take a nun for a drink in 1976? I ordered my usual Jameson's straight up
and nodded with approval when she required a J&B and water. There
was a ground swell to make her the next head of the order, and she
wanted to consult with me as Cathy's next of kin, I suppose, about whether
she should.

Obviously she should. Marge had the common sense and the integrity to keep something of the tradition alive until the first stirrings of
a new kind of Religious Life begin.

And so we spent most of our time talking about Cathy. Marge, like
most others who had come under my saintly cousin's influence, wanted
to claim responsibility for her death.

"David Mark was a very stern novice master, Father John. My
principal task was to try to tone her down. She wanted to reject Catherine
when she was still a postulant. Now I think that might have been wise.
She'd still be alive today."

"Everyone wants to blame themselves, Marge." I signaled for a refill
of my Jameson's. She put her hand over her scotch. "Cathy was an adult
with her own free will. She chose for herself and she knew what the
consequences might be."

It was Joe Murphy's line. I didn't altogether believe it. Neither, as
a matter of fact, did he. It was true enough, but somehow not satisfying.

"I miss her so much." Marge's eyes watered.

"I don't think she'd like us mourning," I said with more piety than
I felt.

Damnit, Coz, why could you never see how much you meant to
people?

Marge called me Father John for reasons known only to her and
God. I responded by calling her Marge for reasons of pure perversity. If
she should win the election, I would still call her Marge, or possibly Ms.
President.

"David Mark had a breakdown and left the order in 1966, you know,"
she said, returning to Cathy's novitiate experience.

"I suppose she married a priest, has several children and is an ardent feminist."

"She married a monsignor"—she laughed—"has two children, I believe, and does not even go to church anymore."

Of course, novice mistresses marry monsignors these days. Who else?

"The Lord made them and the devil matched them," I said aloud, causing Marge to laugh again and agree to a second J&B and water.

I eased the subject back to San Ysidoro. "What was life like down there, Marge?"

"Not very exciting most of the time. The priests said Mass at the center and up in the *barrios*, Catherine and I dispensed pills and took care of sick people and pregnant women, the community organizers like Lorna tried to persuade the Indians and the peons to band together to seek their rights. Father Ed pushed his housing construction projects— which were tremendously effective. Some people taught catechism and offered adult education programs, all pretty standard missionary stuff."

"Doesn't sound revolutionary to me."

"In Costaguana at that time even dispensing pills and bringing the peasants together for meetings was revolutionary and dangerous. Then the real revolutionaries came out of the mountains and the rhetoric we'd been using forced us to put up or shut up. I never paid much attention to the Marxism and liberation theology. I was doing what nurses do. The people needed me, so I closed my eyes and ears and hung on till the paratroops threw all foreign missionaries out. And, of course, the coalition government won't let us back in."

"Were you that much of a threat?"

"I don't think we made any difference, to tell you the truth. The new government is more afraid of foreign missionaries being killed than it is of our stirring up another revolution."

"And the only ones who suffer are the people, who don't get the medicine."

She sighed unhappily. "I suppose you're right, Father John. But there was so much excitement at the *centro* when the guerrillas came out of the hills. We thought we were the vanguard of the people because we gave the revolutionaries food and told them where we thought the Federals were."

"And Catherine?"

"She was much more enthusiastic about the liberation rhetoric than I was, and more horrified by the guerrillas. But mostly she just worked.

She did more work than the rest of them put together. She had a clinic every morning in the old church in Río Secco at the railhead. She was so good as a nurse's aide that I trusted her judgments more than I did my own. And she kept the account books and taught catechism and led an adult education group and visited pregnant women in the *barrios*. That was what she was doing when she disappeared."

"And, of course, she traveled to the centers in other countries for Father Ed," I said lightly, trying to substantiate what Nick had heard from Joe McNally.

"Lorna didn't like that at all. We had a sensitivity session on the problem. It didn't seem fair that one person do all the traveling. But Father Ed insisted that it would impede the cause to duplicate responsibilities. He was always so sincere. . . ."

Another defender of Ed's sincerity.

"Of course. And he trusted Cathy to be his coordinator and he didn't trust Lorna."

She took another sip of her scotch and water. "I suppose you're right, but you must realize that Father Ed was in effect the provincial for seven centers all over the continent. The order had transferred ownership and responsibility for its missions to an independent board. And Ed was in charge of all the centers in the name of the Movement for a Just World. There was never enough money at San Ysidoro or anywhere else. And since so many people came to work with us who didn't have any skills, there were lots of mouths to feed. Ed was a wizard at raising money for all the centers. And Cathy visited each of them for him every couple of months. He raised the money and she balanced the books."

And smuggled out rich people's money in return for a cut, which helped to finance the "revolution."

Lots of people might want her dead.

"What happened to the books when she disappeared?"

"We burned them all before the paratroopers came."

It was four months after Catherine's disappearance that the new government politely but firmly bundled the foreign missionaries up and shipped them home. Almost anyone could have manipulated the books during that time. Better not ask too much.

"The other centers were pretty much like yours?"

"Some of them sounded more radical, but I think we were closer to an actual guerrilla army than any of them. Others may have had a little more money to give to the revolutionaries than we did, but no one had much money for anything."

Would Cathy's money, after the Mob took its cut, go for medicine or guns? Probably both.

"You wouldn't go back?"

"Not now," she said sadly. "I have too many doubts . . . but, Father John, you must not think that Catherine was unhappy in those final days. She seemed to have become much more self-possessed. She spent her free time in church praying, and she was the person who cheered the rest of us up when we were discouraged. The light went out of the mission, uh, I mean center, when she disappeared."

"I'm sure it did."

"She didn't have to die to be a saint, as far as I'm concerned." Margaret's eyes misted again.

At the end of your life, Cousin, maybe you finally grew up. I wonder if you gave yourself any credit.

"Did she talk about her parents' estate?"

"Only about it all going to the Movement when she died. I wonder if she had a premonition of death."

Or more likely she thought there was nothing left to live for.

We left the ninety-fifth floor of the Hancock Center and rode down and up elevators, like characters in a French comic film, until we found my car in the parking lot.

"What would you like to see in religious life, John?" she asked me as I drove down the circular ramp, a concrete corkscrew.

"It would be nice to have some sisters who didn't know all the answers. The ones who taught me in grammar school knew all the answers about religion. Sister David Mark and those like her knew all the answers about the religious life. And now sisters have all the answers about feminism and identifying with the poor and peace and justice. I would like, just once before I die, to hear a nun say, 'I don't know.' "

I called Nick after I dropped Marge off at the convent where she was staying.

"She was Ed's chief of staff and visited all the other centers regularly. If anyone was smuggling funds, it was she."

"I'm astonished. Why?"

"I think she was asking herself the same question when she disappeared. Nick, did she have any money of her own down there? Anything from the estate?"

Her principles had kept her from using her parents' money while she was alive, and she couldn't have had access to it until 1975 anyway. She locked the money out of her life. But what if, in an organization where money was in short supply, someone discovered that she had a secret fortune?

"No," he said. "Much of her money went to Roy in the divorce settlement. And she wouldn't take a penny from the estate, funds that I could have advanced to her under the terms of the will. She took her poverty seriously."

"Are you sure? Might there not have been a way she could get at some of it?"

"Well, there was the letter of credit. I requested First Chicago to establish a credit line for her in their correspondent bank in Sta. Marta. She objected, but I insisted that there be money there should she need it. In any case, it would be earning interest for the estate in Chicago until she withdrew it, so she finally agreed."

"How much?"

"Fifty thousand, as I remember."

I whistled. "Can you find out from your trust officer at First Chicago whether she ever used the credit line?"

"Sure. Do you think she was killed for that money?"

"People have been murdered for a lot less."

30 CATHERINE

September 5, 1963
OLH

Dear Blackie,

You don't smoke so you don't know what it's like to want a cigarette more than anything else in the world. I should have quit at the beginning of the summer, but like everything else I didn't have the willpower. Now it's driving me crazy. It almost takes my mind off all the other discomforts here.

Some of the postulants have smuggled cigarettes in. I'm sure Rosie—oops, I must call her by her right name, Sister Rosemarie—is smoking on the sly. I promise myself I won't ask for one, not even for a puff. I hope I have enough willpower for that.

The dormitory is curtained off into little alcoves, with a table (small), a chest for our personal things (smaller), a chair (hard) and a bed (harder). There is enough room to stand up in the alcove and nothing more. We have two tubs and three showers for eighty-five people—no, eighty-three, two have left already. Some of the girls are crying themselves to sleep as I write this before the lights go out. We'll be up at 5:00 in the morning and spend two and a half hours in the chapel on our knees before we eat breakfast. I thought I'd die of starvation this morning.

The windows rattle in the wind at night. The building is too hot now and I'm sure will be too cold in the winter. And it smells of cabbage, which is the favorite and possibly only vegetable of the community. Cabbage with all the life and flavor boiled out of it. Just like a good religious, as one of the kids said.

It's rough. It's supposed to be rough. How else can we be detached from our worldliness? I'm not afraid, as I was last year at the beginning of college. I know I can do it. I know I will be a better person. I know it's what God wants.

But I still wish I had a smoke.

Mother David Mark is the director of novices and Sister Martha is the assistant director. Mother is a thin woman, very beautiful, with shining blue eyes and an elegant voice. When she talks she moves her long slender fingers as if she were directing a chamber ensemble. She doesn't seem to smile much. Some of the wilder kids already are calling her the dragon lady.

I'm terrified of her.

Sister Martha, who is responsible for us postulants until we become novices next summer, is not so scary. In fact, she seems kind of uncertain about things. She has a solid, square face and kindly blue eyes, sort of a nice German-mother type. Sister Geraldine, who is next to me in chapel, says that we can probably win Sister Martha over to our side.

But we shouldn't be thinking about such things. We're here to learn Holy Obedience, not to manipulate our superiors.

I took notes on Mother's first conference with us. I'll

reconstruct it here since it will be a long time before you'll ever read these letters and the transcription will remind me of why I'm here. Here it is:

I wish I could say, young women, that you are raw material out of which we will mold sisters of the Third Order of St. Francis of Our Lady of the Hill. If that were the case our task would be relatively easy. In fact, however, you are deformed material. You have been corrupted and perverted by your lives in the world. In order to make you good sisters we will have to remake you. We will have to crush the hold the world has on you and break you of your corrupt and sinful habits.

It will not be easy. Most of you lack the docility for the work of destruction and reconstruction which is our task. You will leave us before the work is even properly begun. We will consign you to your fate in the world and pray that God will give you at least the grace of death-bed conversion so you will not spend all of eternity in hell. Others of you will attempt to compromise with sin and evil; you will pretend to be remade while clinging to your old worldliness. We will search you out and remove you so that your corruption will not spread like a contagious disease to others. Do not think you can escape our notice. Nothing that you do or think will escape our notice.

You have left the world behind young women—your friends, your family, your drinking and smoking, the boys with whom you may have sinned. All that is in your past. If we tolerate an occasional visit or letter from your family, that is for their sake and not for yours. I wish that you would come to realize that the community is now your family and discourage your earthly families from making any claims on you. If it were left to me there would be no family visits at all. They serve only to disrupt the order and discipline of community life.

We must wrest away from you all desires for and all memories of the pleasures and the pride and the possessions you have left behind. Whoever you were before, you are no one here, except a postulant who is grateful for our discipline. Whatever you had before you came, now you have only that which the community in its wisdom gives. And whatever pleasures you may have enjoyed, now your only pleasure will be to follow the wishes of your superiors.

Above all we must strip you of your own willfulness. From this moment on you are to do God's will. And God's will is revealed to you by your superiors, who have special graces from God to know what you should do. The Order of the House, the Holy Rule, the wishes of your superior, the routine of community life—these are to replace your own flawed and corrupt self-will. The ideal sister is that one who, after many years of work in a mission, is prepared to leave it at once and without regrets or questions when her superiors assign a new mission to her. You are to become docile tools for the service of the kingdom of God, who never question, never challenge, never hesitate and never think of disobedience. All your own self-seeking must be buried in the tomb before you are worthy to put on the Holy Habit, which will be the shroud you will wear to your grave. Your death to your old self begins now. You are preparing to die.

Because you hope that it is not too late to win forgiveness by living a life of total dedication to God, you have come here, young women, to get ready for your deaths. Pray for the grace of a happy death.

Brrr . . . chilling stuff, huh, Coz? But it's what I want. And I can do it, no matter how hard it will be. Pray for me.

Fondly,
Sister Catherine

31 CATHERINE

September 25, 1963
OLH

Dear Blackie,

I'm shook. Dear God, I'm shook.

Rosie's gone. You were right. She didn't last six weeks. In fact, it was only a little more than two weeks.

I was so groggy this morning that I didn't see her empty place in chapel till we were finished with morning prayers and meditation and Father had started Mass. I wish I could say I was practicing custody of the eyes, but at 5:30 in the morning the best I can do is keep my eyes open.

There are no good-byes here. If you want to leave, you tell Mother David Mark or Sister Martha and you are on your way within a half hour. You leave an empty place in chapel or at table for a day at the most. Then the rest of us move up and fill in your place and it is as though you were never here.

I went to pieces this morning. After breakfast I ran to Mother's office and complained. Rosie was my best friend. Why couldn't I say good-bye to her? We'd been together since first grade. Didn't that count for anything?

Mother looked at me coldly. "Candidly, Sister Catherine, you should thank God that your particular friend is gone. I had little hope for either of you. You both felt that your families' wealth entitled you to special privileges. You both are self-willed, selfish young women, do you understand?"

"Yes, Mother."

"I would have thought you were the weaker of the two. No matter. If you wish to follow your friend, you may do so. The doors are always open. We do not constrain you to stay. If you choose to stay, you must consider your friend dead. She has rejected God's grace. You may offer your prayers and sacrifices for her in the hope that God will grant her the grace of a death-bed conversion. Do you understand, Sister Catherine?"

"Yes, Mother."

She doesn't like me, Blackie. I guess I can't blame her. I'm a spoiled, rich flake. I'll show her eventually that I can be a good religious. But for now I'll have to suffer her dislike as one of my crosses.

We started on the wrong foot when I had my academic conference with her before school began—during the postulancy we take a full load of courses at the college.

"Against my better judgment, Sister Catherine," she said, "and on Sister Martha's advice, I am permitting you one course in art. I do not believe that any good comes from religious endangering their immortal souls with the temptations of the artist. Moreover, in your case, I am convinced that your petty little talent as a painter will be an excuse for your singularizing yourself for the rest of your life, unless we stamp it out now. Do you understand, Sister?"

I felt like someone had set off an earthquake. "Yes, Mother," I stammered.

"You have shown an aptitude for mathematics in high school, have you not?"

"I got good math marks, Mother, but I don't like it very much."

Wrong thing to say!

Her lips drew into a thin, firm line. "If you ever become a good religious, Sister Catherine, which I candidly doubt, you will understand that a religious does not have likes and dislikes. Her will is to do the Will of the One Who sent her. You will major in mathematics, not because you like it, but because the order needs math instructors and does not need art instructors. Do you understand, Sister?"

"Yes, Mother."

Rough? Oh, boy.

And I do enjoy my three hours a week in the art department up at the Hill. I'm the only postulant in the workshop and it's impossible to ignore the seculars—the other kids—completely, especially since a lot of them were in my classes last year.

It's like being out of the pressure cooker for a few minutes. And then I feel guilty for enjoying it and wonder if maybe I should give up the class because it brings out the worldliness in me.

Fifteen girls have left already, one more today after Rosie. If I can only hang on a little longer, I know it will be all right.

Pray for me, Blackie, PLEASE.

Fondly,
Sister Catherine

32
CATHERINE

October 21, 1963

Dear Blackie,

I saw Nick yesterday.

I didn't mean to, I didn't want to, I wish I hadn't seen him. And I'm glad I did.

I cried myself to sleep last night. And I've been crying off and on most of today. I mustn't let Davie or Martie see me, or they'll suspect something. We're supposed to report all unnecessary contacts with "seculars" to them and accept the penance they impose—eating a meal on your knees or saying an extra rosary or something like that.

I'm afraid if I told them about Nick, they'd send me home.

I hate to break any small part of the Holy Rule. As Mother says, if one breaks the least particle of the rule, one blasphemes against the whole rule.

But I want to stay, so I'm going to break the rule and not tell them that I talked to Nick.

I suppose that these letters to you break the rule too. We are permitted to keep a spiritual journal and I tell myself that this is my spiritual journal. But we're supposed to turn our journals over to Martie—Sister Martha—for her inspection. And I don't think I can show her these letters.

But I tell myself they are a way of letting off steam and that when I don't need them anymore I'll stop writing.

It's cheating, but I've always cheated.

It's funny, but I thought I'd never bump into Nick up here. I don't know why I had such a silly notion. He went to school down at St. Tony's. He had friends that are still there. He dated girls from the Hill when I insisted that we both should date others.

So it's perfectly natural that he would come up here for a football weekend and that he would be waiting for Jane Alabastro to take her over to the game when I was rushing back from the library where I'd been working on a history term paper.

It was a marvelous, golden Indian-summer day, like the paintings of Tuscany we saw in the Uffizi. I was late, as usual, and could see myself eating dinner on my knees again.

And I crashed into him like a billiard ball bouncing off a cushion.

"Catherine . . . "—him, picking me up off the ground.

"Big dumb lug."—me, giddy and giggly. "Ape-Man."

"You look wonderful, Catherine."—him, kind of holding my arms.

"Put on weight, ten pounds maybe, starchy food, call me Sister Catherine."—me, totally unglued and loving the strong feel of his hands.

"All right, you look wonderful, Sister Catherine."—him, kind and good and gorgeous, as always.

"How's law school?"—me, squirming out of his arms, picking up my books and preparing to run.

"Hard, but I love it."—him, drinking me in with his eyes. "How's the . . . the postulancy?"

"Hard, but I love it too, gotta run, late, bye."—me, rushing off and hating Jane Alabastro.

I haven't mentioned him in these letters, Blackie, because I thought that if I pretended to myself and to everyone else that he didn't exist, I would forget him.

But I haven't forgotten him. In a way, he's on my mind all the time, especially at night. What a fool I was not to break up a year ago. Just like cigarettes—it would have been easier to give him up before I entered than after. Too many things to give up at the same time.

Oh, I'm not going to bug out for Nick or for anyone else. But it hurts so damn much.

Touching him and being touched my him was like eating the ice cream they give us for dessert here once a week. I wolf it down in a couple of swallows and want more of it, want it every night for supper, can hardly wait till the next time, dream about the next round of ice cream.

Silly, stupid little worldling.

I dream about him at night too. I imagine that I will wake up and find myself in his arms. It's cold in my little alcove and I picture Nick hugging me and keeping me warm. It's a terribly sensual feeling and terribly nice.

And absolutely inappropriate for a religious. It's sexual hunger, that's what it is—to use a word that is never mentioned here. I want Nick's body. I want to hug it and play with it and love it and keep warm with it and give myself to it. I want to paint it too, even though I have given up my painting—yes, I withdrew from the class to protect my vocation.

And the name of that is temptation, terrible, terrible temptation to mortal sin.

Yet Nick didn't seem to be mortal sin yesterday when I collided with him. He seemed to be a good man, lonely and brave.

And the difference is that I am lonely and not brave.

Pray for me, good Coz, like you've never prayed before.

Fondly,
Sister Cathy

33
CATHERINE

November 23, 1963

Dear Blackie,

I'm in deep trouble. I was the one to bring back the news that the president is dead.

Most of our classes are over by one o'clock, and all the other kids are down here in the novitiate complex by one-thirty. I'm back in my art workshop because Mother—Mother Mary Emmanuel, the dear old woman who is the general of the order—insisted she wanted me to continue with the painting. I didn't think she even knew that I existed.

So just as I was leaving, one of the girls came into the

workshop and said they'd shot the president and he had died.

I ran back to the novitiate and burst in with the bad news. It was as if a tornado hit the place. We were crying and shouting and praying and pleading with Martie to let us listen to the radio.

Then Davie showed up, looking an avenging angel.

"Go to the chapel at once," she shouted. "I will not have the order of this house disrupted by worldlings!"

We went, out of habit, I guess, but sullen and resentful.

"It is unfortunate," she said, "that you had to learn of this event in so disorderly a fashion. I had not yet made up my mind whether it would be appropriate to tell you. It is, after all, part of the secular world, which you have given up."

I don't know how she thought she could hide it. We certainly would have found out in school the next day.

"Now that you know," she continued, "I suppose that it might be useful to pray for the repose of the man's soul. He led a wicked life, frequently not even making his Easter duty. He committed many terrible sins of the flesh. He died suddenly, with no time to make an act of perfect contrition. In all probability he is right now burning in the fires of hell. But God's mercy is limitless. It may be that He gave him time to make that act of contrition or that he made it on the plane flying to Dallas. Therefore, it is permissible to pray for the repose of his soul.

"And I'm sure you will want to offer special penance for him. Therefore I am suspending all recreation periods for the next week. And I will tolerate no groans or we will suspend them for two weeks. You may spend the recreation time in chapel and reflect on his sins and your disorderly behavior.

"And I want to see you privately at once, Sister Catherine."

She tore the hide off me for disrupting the order of the community with worldly news.

"But, Mother, he's the president," I protested.

"I am well aware of his political position, Sister. Since you cared for him so much, you will doubtless want to offer all your meals on your knees for the next week. Understand?"

"Yes, Mother."

The girls were furious. I thought there was going to be a rebellion last night, some of them were so bitter.

And then an odd thing happened. Word came down from Mother Mary Emmanuel that we were to have special funeral services for the president and a reflection period about what he meant to American Catholics. The recreations were all restored.

We think that some of the kids went to Mary Emmanuel or maybe Martie went up and saw her. Martie is a nurse and she knows a lot about emotional stress and what it can do to people.

Anyway, things have quieted down. I can't quite understand Davie. I mean I think she's consistent with her principles and I believe the principles, but are there no exceptions?

Maybe I reveal what a poor religious I am by even asking such a question.

There was so much trouble here that I haven't been able to digest the fact that he's dead. The pope and now the president. Only a year ago we were celebrating our two Johns and now they're both gone. I remember thinking when we lost my dear Italian Santa Claus that at least the president was young and would be with us for a long time.

Davie is right about one thing: We should all prepare to die, because we never know when death will come for us.

In my dreams last night it was Nick who was shot and I was sitting in the back of the car, holding his poor wounded head on my lap. The kids told me I screamed most of the night.

Oh, Blackie, I'm so sad.

Love,
Cathy

P.S. We just found out that we will go up to the Mother House to see the funeral mass on TV. Davie announced it like it was her idea.

And, oh, yes, the only thing that wasn't changed was my punishment. My knees are paying the price for my loud mouth.

34
CATHERINE

December 20, 1963
OLH

Dear Blackie,

Things are better, mostly better anyway. I've calmed down. I'm sleeping almost every night. And I don't cry much anymore. We've lost twenty-five of our band, but none in the last two weeks. Life is less hectic, not because the Order of the House has changed, but because I think I have changed a little bit.

Sister Martha has so much common sense. "Honestly, child," she said to me, "do you really expect to become the perfect religious in a few months? I've made a little progress in the fifteen years since I've entered and I have a long way to go. Can't you leave some room for God's grace?"

And I heaved a big sigh of relief, which has been with me ever since.

I keep eating like it's going out of style. I've had to let out my black skirt twice and my black cotton blouse is kind of tight. Sister Martha says it's a nervous reaction and I'll be all right in a few months.

"Maybe you can lose some weight during Lent, Cathy," she says.

And she doesn't call me Sister, either.

So I think maybe there are different ways to be a good religious and that Mother Mary Emmanuel has wisely put two totally different personalities in charge of us young people so that we'll learn about these different ways.

I also find a lot of peace in the chapel. Many times now I have had the feeling that I am loved and that I should trust that it will be all right.

Why do I have to suffer so much?

Why does anyone have to suffer? comes the reply.

What about Nick?

I'll take care of Nick and Blackie and everyone. Don't worry. Do you want me to stay here?

I want your love.

There's never any explicit direction in these moments.

I mean, Blackie, He knows He has my love wherever I am. I guess I have to figure out for myself what I should be doing.

The kids here divide up pretty much into three groups. We even have names for them: The wimps are those who are not strong enough to live the full discipline of the religious life. So they cheat. They don't ask for permissions. They smuggle in cigarettes and letters from their boyfriends and gin and newspapers and tampons (which we're not supposed to use) and they don't report rule violations, their own or others.

Why do they stay? I ask myself. Some of them say they want to be nuns but they don't buy all the shit (their word). Others say that other orders are changing and we're going to have to change too. And still others tell me that they don't give a damn about Davie or Martie and they just want to survive.

The simps, on the other hand, not only keep the rules themselves; they report others. They are always hanging around Davie and Martie and acting, well, simpish. Some of them even search other kids' rooms to find contraband. One of them turned over to Davie a letter from your sister Nancy, even though Martie had passed it. I got the letter back when Martie told Davie that it had come through proper channels, but I was in deep trouble again for a half hour or so. No one apologized, of course.

These girls argue that the religious life is serious and that those who cheat hurt everyone in the community. Maybe they're right. Maybe if I was a better religious I'd snitch too.

But somehow I don't think so.

For as you have probably guessed, good cousin, I am neither hot nor cold but lukewarm. So what else is new? I'm a limp.

What are limps? We keep most of the rules but not all of them and we ask permission most of the time and we report most of our faults and we don't snitch. We don't smuggle out letters and we don't complain when we get letters, like the last one from your stepmother, which have been cut into ribbons by Davie's scissors if she's the one who's reading the mail that day.

But we glance at contraband newspapers and we break the Great Silence and even raid the icebox late at night. I use tampons when I can get them, though I suppose sanitary napkins are better than the diapers they had to use in the old days. I let my hair down with the kids in the art workshop. I complain about Davie to some of my teachers, who don't like her much either. And I write these secret letters to you, which you may never see.

And who, you ask, thought up the simp/wimp/limp bit? You don't have to ask, do you?

A lot of what we do is hilariously funny, though Davie doesn't think anything is funny. Some of the kids say that my laughter keeps them going. Pretty thin motive if you ask me. And Davie accuses me of "levity," which isn't a good thing, I guess.

But if I don't laugh and make other people laugh, I'll cry and so will they. Laughter must be better than tears.

I suppose there will be changes in the years ahead. Somehow I hope they aren't too many. I like the tranquillity and order of our life. I like knowing that I'm doing God's will when I obey the rule and the wishes of my superiors. I like the routine that revolves around our life in chapel. I'm convinced that our prayers and meditations bring us into contact with the wisdom of the ages. I enjoy saying the rosary in common and the Little Office of the Blessed Mother.

I think I have the makings of a good religious—not a great religious, but a good one. I'm going to survive and adjust and become a new and wonderful woman. Only, as Martie says, I have to be more patient with myself.

But to tell you the truth, good Blackie, I don't think the God I encounter in the chapel is the same one that Davie talks to.

And that makes me wonder about a lot of things.

It looks like they're going to let me double up on courses next semester and go to summer school. That means that even though I will miss most of next year because we get only two credits in religion for our spiritual conferences when we're in canonical novitiate, I'll still graduate at the same time my freshmen class does, or maybe after a summer school session. That'll be kind of neat, won't it? The community has a terrible shortage of classroom teachers, so they are eager to rush us through if we want to be rushed. Oddly, Davie is all for that and Martie warns us not to push ourselves too hard.

I can hardly wait to be missioned out to a real parish and an actual classroom with live kids in it. Even if I'm teaching them trig, which I still hate.

Merry Christmas, Blackie. Pray for me.

Fondly,
Sister Cathy

35
CATHERINE

January 21, 1964
Infirmary

Dear Blackie,

You're at home now, and the Infirmarian, who is a wonderfully happy old woman with a thick Irish brogue, says she'll put all the letters to you in the mail. I know you're home on your midyear vacation. So you'll have all the news.

"You have to write to someone, dearie," says Sister Infirmarian (Violet Marie is her real name), "or you'll go crazy over at that madhouse. If you ask me, and I know you haven't, dearie, Davie Markie needs a long stay in a mental home. And herself running for mother general, if you want my opinion"— and she winks at me—"which I know you don't. Besides, a cousin who is a seminarian is about as safe as you can get, especially if he is such a dear boy like you say."

Points for you, John Blackwood. Sister Violet Marie thinks you're a dear boy.

Which you are, of course, wonderful Cousin. But I wouldn't put it that way myself. Typical Cath, I'd hide my feelings behind a wisecrack.

That's my most serious particular fault—I have so many of them that it's hard to find one to concentrate on—I'm a smartmouth. I said that to Davie a couple of weeks ago and she actually laughed at me.

"All communities benefit from a member who can make others laugh, child," she said to me. "It's not necessarily a fault."

That sort of surprised me. I mean she may not dislike me after all. And she can actually laugh. I wonder if being novice mistress is not harder on her than it is on us.

Superiors are humans too. What an interesting idea. I remember from what you said about the people at Mundelein that you have your doubts about their humanity. That's not very charitable, Cousin.

Anyway, what am I doing in the infirmary?

Well, I'm fine now and can hardly wait to get back to school. I don't want to pamper myself or exploit my illness.

I was very sick for a couple of days with a touch of walking pneumonia.

I've been dragging since Christmas, not sick and not well. Cold, cough, sniffles. (Doesn't affect my weight, darn it. The scale here says I have gained twenty pounds. I'm a balloon. And I look gross in the mirrors. We don't have any in the novitiate, of course.) I think maybe I've had a slight fever too.

And it's so cold in the dorm at night that I don't count sheep; I count chattering teeth.

Well, Davie doesn't believe in our pampering ourselves. So she told me to take a couple of aspirin and continue meeting my classes and taking my exams.

It was hard climbing up the Hill to the classrooms the last week or so. I thought it was all the extra pounds.

And then I collapsed after my trig exam (the last one, wouldn't you know), and they had to rush me from the classroom over to the infirmary, where Sister Violet Marie said I had a fever of 104.

The doctor came out from town and complained about novices overdoing it and gave me a lot of penicillin. He's a very old man and has taken care of us for years and years. He told me that in 1938 I would have died.

Thank goodness I didn't live in 1938.

But now I'm on the mend and enjoying the comfortable bed and the good food and sister Violet's endless happy chatter. I hope that when I'm an old nun I can be happy like that too.

The only trouble is that during the nights when I was out of it with the fever I had the most terrible dreams about Nick. I wonder when I'm going to be free of those dreams.

I suppose the new year had something to do with it. As you surely know, Nick and I committed a terrible sin after the New Year's Eve party when I was a sophomore. And that sin haunted my dreams when I was sick. Only it was much, much worse than in real life. We went much further in my dreams.

And while I was having the dreams, I was enjoying them so much. It was like my body was hungry for fire and consuming all the fire it could get.

Violet Marie tells me I shouldn't worry about the dreams. "If Himself is going to punish us for our dreams, dearie," she says, "we'll all go to hell."

But even when I am awake those feelings are attractive. I know they're terrible sins, but I can't dislike them.

I'm sure it's a result of the pneumonia and that I'll be all right when I return to the novitiate and the protection of Our Holy Rule.

Have a wonderful vacation and keep August 10th open. That's the day when I become a bride of Christ. I'll see you then.

God bless,
Cath

36

CATHERINE

March 1, 1964
OLH

Dear Blackie,

Do they tell you at the seminary about PF's—particular friendships?

Davie and Martie both harp on the subject all the time and I'm not quite sure what they mean. They seem to be saying that we shouldn't have close friends. Jesus did, both men and women, so I don't see why we who try to follow after Him shouldn't.

I was in trouble again the other day, kind of, because of a PF. Only I don't know what I did wrong because I don't understand what they mean. Davie said I had a "crush" on Sister Geraldine, who left us last week, and I haven't had a crush on anyone besides Nicky and Elvis Presley all my life.

We knew Gerry was leaving because she told us. A few of us even crept into the shower room for a smoke with her the night before she left, all of us shaking in the subzero cold. The community will never run out of money because of the heating bill at this convent. So it wasn't a surprise, like the time Rosie slipped away—and, by the way, I see her often at a distance in school, though we avoid each other. Too shy to risk asking all the questions we want to ask, I guess.

And I sneak weeds only once a month or so. Well, maybe twice a month.

Anyway, I was sad to see Gerry's place empty at lunch the next day. She was a leader of the wimps, but I think she would have made a good religious if she only had a little more perseverance. But you become accustomed to empty places.

I was surprised when Davie dragged me out of line after chapel tonight and said she wanted to talk to me privately.

"Were you disturbed by Sister Geraldine's departure, Sister?"

"Yes, Sister. I liked her a lot. I'll miss her."

Which was the truth but the wrong thing to say, I guess. A worried frown appeared on Mother's ivory face. She is so pale; honest, Blackie, I don't think she ever goes out in the sun.

"I am sorry to hear that, Sister. I was afraid that might be your reaction."

"Yes, Mother." Which really is the only safe response.

"You are a very pretty young woman for whom others naturally feel a strong attraction. Does that make you proud?"

Pride here is the worst of sins, though it doesn't beat sensuality by much.

"Yes, Mother. No, Mother," I answered as quickly as I could.

"I beg your pardon?" She raised one of her knife-thin eyebrows.

"Well"—I was now stumbling over the words—"I've been told I'm pretty, but no, I don't take any pride in it. Everything fades with time anyway."

"Indeed." She hesitated. "You seem to make close friends easily?"

It was both a question and an accusation.

"I'm an only child, Mother, so I've always had to look for friends outside the home."

"Friendships can be very dangerous, child."

"Yes, Mother." And then I couldn't keep my big mouth shut. "But . . . "

"But what?" she said imperiously.

"Jesus was friends with John the Apostle and Martha and Mary and Lazarus and . . . "

"I am not talking about those kinds of friendships, Sister." She was getting angry at me. "I'm talking about friendships with sensuality in them."

"Yes, Mother."

"Did you not think there was too much sensuality in your relationship with Sister Rosemarie and Sister Geraldine?"

"No, Mother." Whatever sensuality is—and I'm not sure—that wasn't what went on between Gerry or Rosie and me.

"How would you characterize those relationships?" she persisted grimly.

"Mischief," I said.

Mother's eyes bulged. "And what do you mean by that?"

"Well, like finding out the date of Sister Martha's birthday and giving her a cake."

"Hmmn . . . yes, well, I understand. Or at least I think I do. We must keep our bodies under the strictest safeguards, my child."

She could mean either do I put on my nightdress before I take off my underwear, which I do—well most of the time—or that I haven't lost enough weight. I tried the latter.

"I'm eating a lot less during Lent, Mother. I think I'm losing weight."

"Yes, I'm sure you are, Sister. I shall pray for you."

"Thank you, Mother."

So the next day I'm running up the Hill to class, late as usual, and I run by Martie, who is walking up to the Mother House for some meeting, I suppose. I stop and wait for her.

"May I speak with you, Sister?"

"Of course, Cathy." She smiles her warm, friendly smile.

"Aren't we supposed to have friends, Sister?" I'm old crazy Cath again, charging right in.

"Of course we have friends, dear. Whatever made you think not?"

"All the talk about PFs." I drop one of my notebooks and try to pick it up. "Particular friendships."

"Those are a special kind of friendship." She does the same long-frown bit. "We must be very careful of them, but that doesn't mean that ordinary friendships are to be avoided. On the contrary, we know that the great saints almost all had very warm friendships."

"Well, what's a PF, then, Sister? I'm confused."

"An, uh, unhealthy friendship, my dear."

"What's unhealthy?"

She hesitates and then finally just says it right out, "A friendship in which there is a strong sexual component."

That's the first time here that I've heard the word "sexual."

"Oh," I say, and we walk up the rest of the Hill in silence.

"Do you have any such friendships, Cathy?" she asked very gently at the top of the Hill.

"Only with boys, Sister." I must have sounded pretty woebegone because she laughed and so did I.

I don't know much about sex, Blackie. And I probably don't need to know much about it. But do they think I might have had a thing for Gerry's body like I do for Nick's? But that's crazy! I know that some women don't like men but only other women and vice versa. But me?

Well, if that's all they're worried about, I guess they don't have to worry about me. I don't have any dirty dreams about Gerry or Rosie. And Nick is still on my mind. Every night, strong as ever.

But I'm not quitting.

Anyway, pray for me.

Fondly,
Sister Catherine

37
CATHERINE

March 15, 1964
OLH

Oh, Blackie,

Am I in trouble!

And I hope you're not in trouble too. If they've done anything to hurt you, I'll personally blow this convent and everyone in it from here to the South Pole. I don't care about me. I'm used to eating supper on my knees, but you're an innocent victim.

I was called in to Davie last night and I could tell by the look on her face that this could be the end. I haven't done much wrong lately. It's Lent and I'm still a limp.

She reaches into the desk drawer and puts on her empty, shiny desk a box of tampons and my last letter to you.

"Sister, what is the meaning of this?" she asks me, as though they were dirty books.

"Those are tampons, Mother."

"I am not unaware of what they are. We do not use them here, Sister."

"Yes, Mother."

"Where did you get them?"

"From Gerry—uh, Sister Geraldine—Mother." Which is not the whole truth. I mean Sister Geraldine arranged the pipeline by which they come in.

"Feminine hygiene is not the issue, Sister," she says primly. "The issue is obedience. This is a flagrant violation of the will of the community."

I felt like asking what business of the community tampons are. But she'd say everything is the business of the community and anyway I know the letter is worse trouble.

"Yes, Mother," said I.

"And who is this Blackie person, Sister? A man?"

"My first cousin, Mother. We were born the same month and kind of raised together. I am an only child and he's been like a brother to me. It's a journal I keep, Mother; that's not against the Holy Rule, is it? I mean, I find it easier to keep a journal if I imagine someone reading it."

"And what has happened to the previous entries in this journal?"

"I tear them up, Mother."

Which is partly true, Blackie. I've torn up a lot of letters that I wrote when I was discouraged, especially about never receiving mail from Mom and Dad and their not coming on Visiting Sunday.

"I see." She's skeptical, of course, but she can't prove anything.

"He is a seminarian at Mundelein? And his name is, uh, Collins, like yours?"

"You're not going to hurt him?" I flare up.

"Answer my question, young woman, and answer it this minute or you'll be on the next bus to Chicago."

"Yes, Mother," I tell her. "I mean, yes, he's at Mundelein." I think she's bluffing. If they call Mundelein looking for a seminarian named Blackie Collins, they are going to be told there is no such animal and come back after me. Or if they find out your real name, they'll also blow a gasket at me. But if I hear nothing from them, then I'll know they've left you alone.

"And this Nick to whom you make reference in the letter?"

"He was my boyfriend, Mother."

"Do you write a journal to him?"

"No, Mother."

"Do you have any intercourse with him at all?"

Honest, Blackie, that's what she said. It was so hard not to giggle. I thought of our Lord suffering on the cross and kept a straight face.

"No, Mother, no letters either way. I saw him once up on the Hill on Saturday morning during the football season. He graduated from St. Anthony's last year."

"And?" I think she was impressed with my telling the truth. That was the idea, of course, but I WAS telling the truth.

"And I promptly excused myself and continued on my way to the convent, just as we are supposed to do with any contact with a secular on campus."

"How long is prompt in your time perceptions, Sister?" She leaned forward on the desk, like a hawk ready to pounce.

"Thirty seconds, Mother, three sentences. I think I can recall them. . . . "

"That won't be necessary." She waved her elegant hand.

The funny thing, Blackie, is that she said nothing about either particular friendships or my dreams about Nick or my "thing" for his body. I can't quite understand that.

Well, anyway. I'm going to be a real limp. I'll use their damn sanitary napkins as long as there are snitches to poke around my cabinet. But I don't think God cares in the least about such things. And, as you can see, I'm still writing to you. I'll mail them to Mary Kate and she can bring them to you on your Visiting Sunday. I'll sneak them out through Rosie.

She's in love with her guy from Cal Tech, the one she met last year at Lauderdale. And he loves her back, I guess. And she reports that Loyola won the NCAA championship this year in the last second of the game. I'm sure Nick was on cloud nine for weeks. You know what a basketball nut old Ape-Man is. It would have been fun to be at the game with him. Well, that's all the past, isn't it? According to Rosie, Nick has broken up with Jane Alabastro, which makes me a mixture of glad and sad. And I'm even sadder that I'm glad.

Maybe I'm compromising my ideals. Maybe I'm putting my will before the will of the community. Maybe I'll be more deeply motivated during the novitiate. But for now I'm going to continue to write.

At least till I find out if they did anything to you.

Love,
Dumb Cathy

<u>38</u>
CATHERINE

April 9, 1964
OLH

Dear Blackie,

Rosie gave me your letter this morning after history class. She brought it back with her when she returned from her Easter vacation, another orgy at Lauderdale. It was so good to hear from you. I laughed till my side hurt at your description of what happened to you when Davie Markie called your rector. Actually, you bum, the first time through the letter I wasn't sure that you were joking.

Anyway, I'm glad they didn't have the nerve to call Mundelein.

And I do appreciate your little lesson about homosexuality. I guess I didn't know very much about it. I'm glad that, as you certainly know, my problems are of the other kind.

Anyway, I'm glad you're going to be able to come to my reception in August. That will be a very happy day. I'm looking forward to the canonical year as a time to finally learn how to pray. And I'm so eager to don the Holy Habit and to become a member of the community.

As you can tell, the worst seems to be over at last. I'm

actually happy here now. Before, I told myself I was happy because I thought I should be happy. But now I don't have to force myself to say it.

The Holy Week liturgy was wonderful. I do so love the services, the color of the vestments, the candles, and the fire, and the water, and the Easter flowers after a purple Lent. I understand that the bishops want to put it in English because not many of the laity understand Latin. But I will miss the wonderful Latin plainsong melodies. Wouldn't it be better to teach everyone Latin? I hope I can study a little plainsong during the canonical year. The community will need lots of musicians as the liturgical changes are implemented.

And I've submitted my three names. The community most probably will select one of the three.

The first is Kathleen Mary, in honor of your mother and Mary Kate. There is a Sister Mary Kathleen, but they don't count name reversals anymore, because the community has grown so large.

The second is Edward John, in honor of your father and someone else whom I can't quite remember. And, of course, Father Ed is honored too. He's coming to the reception, by the way. I miss him so much.

The third name is Michael Nicholas and you can guess who that's for. I hope he comes. I sent him an invitation.

I would have used a parent's name, of course, but Mother David Mark says that neither Herbert nor Erin is a saint's name. I don't know whether they'll come to the reception.

A lot of talk about something that won't happen till August? I suppose so, but it gives me something to live for.

Pray hard for me, Blackie. I think I'm going to make it. And I can hardly wait to see you.

God bless you,
Sister Kathleen Mary

39
CATHERINE

May 20, 1964
OLH

Dear Blackie,
   If you promise not to show it to anyone, I'll let you read one of my poems.
   Promise? Cross your heart?

In a tiny moment of the night
When the moon smiles on the river
And warmly glows the red light
On the altar and in my heart

The world's clunking clatter
Seems far away and no matter
And my friend comes to me
That his love I might fully see

He does not tarry in the town
Nor pretend from me to hide
He does not hesitate at my lattice
But hurries to be at my side.

I want to take hurried flight
But there is no time to run
From the glorious sight
Of the exploding sun

Which sweeps into my self so weak
And tells me never fear
He not I is the one who seeks
And will be forever near.

Anyway, it's not all that good, though the composition teacher told me it had a nice lyricism to it. But it does describe how I often feel now, especially a couple of times in chapel when time just plain stood still.

Sister Martha (her real name, I found out, was Margaret Aimes and she was a great tennis player before she entered) found me in chapel one night long after I should have been in bed and said very quietly, "You need your sleep, Cathy, a lot more than God needs your prayer."

So I went quietly off to bed. God doesn't need our prayer, but He likes it.

They're afraid now that I'm going to turn into some kind of mystical nut. Cathy the Limp becomes spiritual freak. But they're wrong. I still can't meditate in the morning and have terrible distractions at Mass. I still dream about Nick and miss him awfully. I haven't changed a bit.

What happens is a gift. He came before I entered and I know He would keep coming if I should leave. The Community has nothing to do with it, except that it seems the best way to respond to Him.

Yet He never says anything about my vocation, as though it is a decision that is up to me and He'll swing with it either way.

Maybe next year I can read John of the Cross or Teresa of Ávila and find out what this is all about.

And I might even find a very wise confessor to discuss it with. But it seems too precious to share with someone who would not understand it.

So I share it with a wise cousin instead, who I know will understand.

You're so good to listen to me, Blackie. Someday when we're both old and gray in the service of the Lord, we can compare notes. I'd love to know what your problems have been.

You do have them, don't you?

God bless,
Cath

40
CATHERINE

July 4, 1964
OLH

Dear Blackie,

Only a month and a couple of days to reception. I'll put on Mary Kate's wedding dress and frilly underwear and white spikes and come into the chapel as a bride of Christ. And when the ceremony is over I'll be a member of the Community, a small and unimportant member perhaps, but still dedicated to the service of Christ my Bridegroom.

I wish I was happier about it. But I'm discouraged. Maybe it's the heat. It's been in the nineties all week and our black skirts and blouses are scratchy and smelly. As Sister Linda, one of the forty who have been accepted (four were rejected, so we're down to less than half of those who entered), said yesterday, it will be even worse when we put on the Holy Habit. I guess we'll get used to it like everyone else before us has.

And I miss the Beach. I've never been homesick for my house on Glenwood, but I am awfully homesick for all the fun on the weekend of the Fourth over where you guys are. I can give it up, sure, but I wish I didn't have to.

Which shows that after a long, hard year of being reshaped into someone who is good enough to be received, I am still the same old shallow flake.

I'm discouraged about the name thing too. I thought sure they'd give me Kathleen Mary. But they turned all three down, no reasons given. So I'm going to be Sister Mary Amabilis, instead. And because an old nun that they all loved who had that name just died. It represents an honored tradition in the community. But I don't think I'm really the Mary Lovable type.

I think they did it as a favor and an honor to me. I may not have become much of a religious, but both Davie and Martie like me now. So do the other kids. I'm kind of the leader of our band of soon-to-be novices.

141

"My Name is Cathy Collins and I'm the leader of the band. . . . "

What a wonderful parody I might write, if I wasn't so glum today.

I suppose you've guessed it. I'm broken-hearted because my parents won't come to the reception. I've wanted all my life to make them like me and I never seem to succeed. I had no idea they would react the way they have. My mother has given up all her private revelation things and joined the country club. And my father is talking about traveling around the world next month.

Why? I keep asking myself. When I was little and said I wanted to be a nun, Mom was pleased and Dad at least didn't seem to be displeased, though you could never tell what he was thinking. So I kind of took it for granted that they would be enthusiastic about my vocation. And I certainly expected they would recover from the shock quickly and be reconciled to my choice. But now they pretend I don't exist, that they don't have a daughter anymore.

All the other parents are coming, so it will be kind of hard. I can take it. But I wish they were pleased with me. One more failure.

And there's Nick. I wonder if I will ever recover from Nick.

Last Labor Day weekend if he had said to me, Don't enter and I will marry you after Christmas, I would have canceled the whole thing. And, you know, Blackie, if he should come up here on the day of my reception and say, Let's elope, I'd probably run away with him.

That would be shameful, wouldn't it? I do have a vocation, a canonical one now that the community has approved me for reception. And I'm still such a flutter-brained clown that I'd throw it all away to spend the rest of my life in his arms.

It probably wouldn't work. We're very different kinds of people. It might even be a solemn high disaster. And I won't walk out next month, not even if I could.

Please don't take this letter too seriously, Blackwood. I'm in a bad mood (and, yes, drat your impudence, it is my period). I'll be all right. Do pray for me, though, especially when we go on our prereception retreat. Would you believe, Father Ed is the retreat master.

And if you see Nick, invite him again to come. I would like to see him. Just one more time.

Love,
Cathy

41
MARY KATE

My father and Helen drove up the night before, seizing the opportunity to spend a night together in a motel, as they do at any pretext, God love them. Joe and I dumped the Brats with Nancy the next morning and picked up the Punk at the parish where he was teaching catechism.

Being from Boston, the Pirate is more of a traditionalist, which means both that he has had a lot of anticlerical anger to work through and that he tends to conservative piety—in his responses, not in his actual behavior.

"We are not going to a wake are we?" he asked as we proceeded in glum silence to the Hill.

"Depends," said the Punk.

"You disapprove of your cousin's vocation? Isn't it a great honor to be a bride of Christ?" said my husband, his Boston twang getting thicker as it always does when he's being pious.

"It's a nice image," said the Punk heavily, "and it makes a nice Gregorian melody." He hummed the "Veni Sponsa Christi" antiphon. "But it's only an image, and it's a terrible mistake to attempt to derive from it a complete theology and spirituality of the religious life."

"Ah," said Doctor Joseph Murphy. "Why?"

I hugged my man. "Joe, you're wonderful."

"The least I can do is be a straight man for my in-laws," he replied.

Blackie ignored our marital affection, just as he ignores our fights.

"Every Christian is invited to a nuptial-like relationship with God. Intimacy with Christ is a possibility for all of us, and indeed a possibility that is at the core of the Christian life. To claim it as a monopoly for the religious and indeed only for women religious is to ignore the basic premise of our faith. Some communities are already pulling away from the spirituality because they realize that it might be offensive."

"You're against the ceremony today, Punk?" I asked.

"No, it's a lovely ceremony, so long as it is not interpreted with fundamentalist rigidity, as, depend on it, Ed Carny will interpret it for us."

"But the big problem is not the ceremony, is it, Punk? You don't think Cathy should be a nun."

"I've been wrong before."

I ruffled his hair, a surefire way to make the Punk laugh. "Not recently."

He did indeed laugh. "You could say that, after all, no one is questioning my vocation. But neither does anyone think I'm running from something."

"She is?" said the Pirate. "From what?"

"Herself, most likely."

The ceremony started at nine o'clock, with a flourish on the organ that might be appropriate for a gathering of the Knights of the Round Table. Cath's band came in first, glowing and glittering in bridal dress. Then the novices, who are going to take one-year vows, and the juniors, who are going to take three-year vows. And then the older kids, who are going to take final or perpetual vows.

"Thirty-seven, I count," the Punk says. "Ed must have scared a few more away this last week."

The shrink in me doesn't like that word "perpetual."

Ed Carny preaches about brides of Christ. It's pretty icky, filled with far-out nuptial imagery. Because it's ninety-five outside the old chapel and at least twenty degrees warmer inside, sweat is pouring down Joe's lean face, which looks like he needs a shave five minutes after he puts the razor away. He leans over to me and whispers, "That may be the dirtiest sermon I've ever heard. I don't think they could put it in the mails. It makes me horny for my woman."

"Find her," I say, trying to stifle a giggle. Luxuriating on a wedding bed with Christ the bridegroom IS a little much. Ed is a wonderfully sincere fellow, but he gets carried away with his language, takes the images literally, just as the Punk argued.

Then the senile old bishop blesses the neat piles of religious habits in front of the altar and one by one the brides march up and take the black clothes in their arms, like they're carrying babies. They slowly process out the side door and down the stairs into the basement, as the choir sings "Veni Sponsa Christi" as if they are in the throes of love-making.

It is beautiful and at the same time drippy.

I know what happens down there because it was described so often to me in college. The happiest day of a nun's life, they said. I wonder.

The sponsor, in Cath's case, Sister Intemerata, the nun who taught her art the year before, takes the bride to her own little alcove. The bride then goes inside and removes her wedding dress and her fancy lingerie and puts on sensible underwear (bras are now permitted). She does it in such a way that I'm sure she's always modestly covered, though how that works escapes my imagination. I wonder if Cathy has written a love note to Jesus and put it in the bra of her wedding costume, as they used to. Somehow I think not.

Then the sponsor comes in and clothes her in the many layers of black that constitute the Holy Habit. Then the bride comes out of the alcove and her hair is cut, not shaved as we used to think, but cut very short. Since Cathy has short curly hair anyway, that's no great loss. Damned if I'd ever let anyone do it to my blond locks. Honey blond, in fact.

Then a cap is put on her head. She will wear one for the rest of her life. Hair, a woman's crowning glory, must never again be seen, even by the bridegroom, presumably, because she will wear a cap to bed at night.

Poor Cathy. I agree with the Punk. This is not for you.

I say some prayers to my mother, who I assume is watching this event with an enthusiasm matching that of the Punk.

Then the white veil is put on over the whole regalia. It will be replaced next year by the black veil and Sister Mary Amabilis will be indistinguishable from any other member of the order.

Then the band processes slowly back into the chapel.

It's very effective theater to give them their due. Beautiful young women in bridal garb leave the chapel. And little nuns in black habits come back in. Hardly a dry eye in the place. I'm crying. So is Helen, more than me. Dad pokes at his eyes, and even my Joe, who hardly knows her, is watering.

Only the Punk is staring straight ahead, looking like if he were pope, he would excommunicate the whole lot of them.

Sometimes I am very happy that the Punk will never be pope.

The ceremony goes on till almost noon and finally we are permitted to talk to Sister Mary Amabilis, OLH. She looks very pretty in her habit, the prettiest of them all, and I don't think I'm especially prejudiced.

"Damn Herbert," says Dad under his breath, one of the strongest denunciations of another human being I have ever heard from him.

Sister Mary Amabilis appears radiantly happy, serene and relaxed, unlike some of the other members of her band who are tense and awkward in their new robes. There's kisses for Helen and me and warm handshakes for the three men.

"Nick?" she says to Blackie.

He shakes his head. "He thought it better not to come."

She winces visibly, painfully. It was enough to break my heart. "Probably right," she agrees quickly.

And we discuss other things, children, school, future prospects. She still looks very happy. And then I remember the splendid Ado Annie fakery and wonder.

On the way home, Joe began the conversation again. "It is certainly an effective ceremony."

"I doubt that it has more than two or three years to run," the Punk responded. "Some of the orders are not doing it even this summer."

"What will they replace it with?" Joe asked.

"Something worse, you can depend on it," the Punk said somberly. "If you ask me, they're finished."

PART
THREE

42
BLACKIE

I received no letters from Cathy between the time of her reception thirteen years ago today and the end of her canonical novitiate a year later. She was completely cut off from the world, leaving the novitiate only to walk along the bank of the river for a half hour's "recreation" each day or a domestic work assignment at the Mother House up on the Hill. Her morning classes were in the novitiate building and her afternoon work was usually in that building too, as of course were her evening prayers. Most of the day was spent in silence, Great Silences and Little Silences and all kinds of damn-fool silences.

She read no books or newspapers and wrote and received only one letter a month, to and from her family. Since her parents did not reply to her dutiful monthly communications, she received no mail.

What bothers me about Uncle Herb and Aunt Erin this tenth day of August 1976 is that they were such moral infants that God probably let them off scot-free.

My cousin, meanwhile, was being "formed" into a proper member of her Community by techniques that were not invented by the Chinese and the North Koreans when they "brainwashed" American prisoners.

Am I too harsh? Solitude I celebrate. A year of prayer and reflection I endorse. Solitude and silence we don't have enough of in the noisy, talkative contemporary church.

But I can only use scatological language when I think of the novitiate of those days. Moreover, I used the same language then too.

Sometime after she finished the novitiate, and as I remember—though those tumultuous days blur—after she went on her first disastrous mission to Careyville and before our friendship was rent in 1969, Cathy mailed me some of her novitiate notes, "to fill in the blanks," she said. Whoever reads them will notice a change of tone and will perhaps agree with me that the difference is not merely because she did not intend them to be read by others.

Cathy was herself changing. No, that's not quite right. She was being changed.

I hesitate to include them with the rest of her diary. They do not recall my Cousin as I would like to remember her. Yet they are essential to understanding what came later. So on this hot summer day at Grand Beach, with an extra large ration of Mr. Jameson's elixir handy to moderate my distaste, I have decided to include them with my own notes at the beginning and the end.

Please keep in mind that the church was slipping into its own midsixties black hole when Cathy was received. In the brief period of five years—from, let us say, just after the death of John Kennedy to just after the death of his brother, Robert—the Bark of Peter sailed through the roughest seas since someone suggested that maybe it would be a good idea to find out if people were interested in Jesus beyond the walls of Jerusalem.

John Kennedy was buried in 1963 to the Latin liturgy. A few months later, on Septuagesima Sunday (which shortly afterward bit the dust as well), every altar in the land was turned around to face the people and the priest (soon to become president of the Eucharistic Community) said the sacred words of the Mass (soon to become the Eucharistic Assembly) in the language of the people—for the first time in a thousand years, give or take a few centuries, depending on your geography.

And a few months after Robert Kennedy was buried in 1968, our gloriously reigning supreme pontiff brought the era of papal-led reform to an end with his encyclical on birth control. Change continued, of course, but now it was out of control. The densely compacted energies and forces that had been created in the black hole blew up. American Catholicism became a supernova, an exploding fireball.

Even as Cathy was confessing sensuality on her knees in the novitiate's "Chapter of Faults" because she yearned for ice cream, a General Chapter of the community was taking place up on the Hill. In a bitter fight reform-minded forces were seizing control of the community and would abolish much of the nonsense that Cathy had to endure.

Although they didn't realize it, they were also signing the death warrant of their community.

My poor cousin emerged from her year of "formation," to be swept up in the crosscurrents and explosions of those black-hole years, utterly unprepared. She had been "formed" for a religious order and a church that no longer existed.

The church would never be the same.

Neither would Cathy.

43
SISTER MARY AMABILIS

November 2, 1964
Feast of All Souls

I do so like to reflect on death. The last moment of our life is the only important moment. It will seal our fate for all eternity. As we live, so shall we die. Mother says that we can be certain of a happy death if we live with death on our minds all our life.

It is not enough to make the nine First Fridays or the five First Saturdays, as I used to think. They are but tools to remind us of the certainty of death. But, like all our tools, they can become useless if we slacken our fervor and enthusiasm. The religious life is basically a preparation for death. Our Holy Habit is the shroud which will cover my already rotting body when I am buried in the earth from which I was made. The will of the Superior and the Holy Rule regulates my life in all its details so my mind and heart will be free to reflect on the shortness of life and the inevitability of death. Penance and mortification of self are an anticipation of death. Does not the very word "mortification" mean to make oneself dead?

Through Holy Poverty I will die to the lust of the eyes. I will cast aside all material possessions and live at the mercy of the community, so that I will never forget that I will die as bereft of material treasures as I was born.

Through Holy Chastity I will die to the lust of the flesh. By giving up earthly pleasures now, I will force myself to realize how transient are the joys of the world and permanent the torments of hell.

And through Holy Obedience I will die the most difficult death of all, death to the pride of life, death to my own stubborn will. I must become a docile instrument, devoid of self-regard and self-seeking, utterly at the disposal of God as he manifests his will for me through the voice of my superiors.

I see now that these things are possible for me, if only I love God enough and have the faith and the courage to force myself to overcome my bad habits and my deformed dispositions. I must make the most of this gloriously precious year to mold myself in the image of Jesus and Mary. All my superiors can do is help me. The work necessarily is my own.

And it would be so easy to fail. Even now the weakness of my own flesh, the temptations of the devil and the attractions of the world threaten to tear me away from my chosen path. I am such a worthless worm, fit for nothing but to be cast down the sewer.

Even today I had to confess at Chapter of Faults, on my knees and in a voice trembling with false pride, that I had once again desired chocolate ice cream even though I have promised that I will not eat any dessert until the canonical year ends. Mother was severe on me, as I deserved, indeed not as severe as I deserved. With self-indulgence comes self-seeking and then a whole host of demons rush back into the soul. From one small fault could come the tragic destruction of the opportunities of this year.

Despite my worries and despite the terrible sins I have committed during my life as a worldling, I am filled with serenity and peace. God will help me if only I do my part. I will gradually peel away all the layers of selfishness and pride and come to the core of my selfhood, which belongs only to Him and will be restless until it rests in Him.

Everything is really very simple. The choices are clear, the means are clear, the goal is clear, the price of failure is clear. I cannot take refuge in a plea of ignorance. Part of the grace of my vocation is to be confronted with the stark reality of life and death. I am not afraid of death anymore. I can watch the slow lingering death of nature in the autumn with joy because I know that I too will die just as nature dies and that then Christ my Bridegroom will come to take me home for eternal happiness.

Come, O blessed death, come and release me from the pain of life's struggle.

God is good. He wants me home in heaven. He wants me

in a special way because He has blessed me with the Unspeakably Precious Gift of a Religious Vocation.

But God is also just. He would not be true to Himself or to me if He did not impose stern rules for my response to his invitation. Only God can save me. Only I can damn myself.

And I am so afraid of my heinous sinful habits and my slothful weakness.

Dear God, please give me the strength I need. Don't let me be separated from You for all eternity.

Please!!!

44
SISTER MARY AMABILIS

Feast of St. Nicholas

It is bitter cold tonight. I will have to confess at Chapter of Faults tomorrow that I inwardly complained about the cold, even inwardly resented that the heat in our dormitory was not turned up when the cold spell hit us. As though I had the right to demand that the community spend its precious resources to keep a sensual worldling like me warm.

I will also have to confess that I took pride in the weight I have lost. The purpose of fasting is not to make my wicked and sin-crazed body look more attractive. We fast to discipline our bodies and bring them into the subjection of our souls. I will have a very thin body after a few days in the grave.

I must confess faintness of heart that Sister Joan Agnes returned to the world today. She was so filled with joy, or so it seemed to me, only a week ago. We have already lost eight members of our band. There are twenty-nine left out of eighty-five. I ask myself if I have any more right to God's grace than they did.

I wonder why she left?

And I will have to confess that flaky and worldly question.

Perhaps not. Perhaps I am making a long list of faults to confess so that by the very display of my evil nature I will seem to others to be good.

It is hard to tell. The tricks of Satan and of the flesh are so ingenious. And I am so ready to cooperate with them.

Perhaps I will deprive myself of the satisfaction of confessing that I wondered why Sister Joan Agnes left.

On a night like this I must remind myself of the sufferings of Mother Claire Reagan and the little band of followers who came from County Waterford 120 years ago, filled with faith and zeal and love for God's people. Big, strong, vigorous young women they were. Mother herself no older than Mary Kate, her band members my age or even younger.

There was no central heating in those winters, no electricity, no comfortable bed or warm blanket, no community to pay the bills for our training, no pious laity to provide our support, no doctor within 100 miles, no stone walls to cut the fierce winter winds.

Who am I to complain when I think of their generosity and courage?

Those poor young women must have known that they would never go home. They must have realized, as they drove in crude wagons over rough and dangerous roads, that they would never see their beloved Ireland or their families again. They were fully aware that they probably would not live to their thirty-fifth birthdays. Yet we read that they sang and told stories and danced through the long winter nights. And their letters are filled with lightness and laughter.

Dear God, help me to imitate their faith and generosity.

Would Mother be upset if I asked her why we don't sing and dance and tell stories? And why there is so little laughter in our community?

Only my stubborn pride would make me think of such a question.

I shall have to confess that at Chapter of Faults tomorrow. No, my list is too long already. I can save it for the next day.

Would I have their courage? Would I rush joyfully to the city when I heard that there was a cholera epidemic to care for the sick and the dying, knowing that I would probably die too?

Dear God, give me the grace to accept whatever death is your Holy Will for me.

Half of Mother Claire's first band died before they were twenty-five, from cholera or influenza. How unworthy I am to follow in the footsteps of such great women, martyrs as sure as if they had been thrown to the lions.

And how Mother Claire and the others grieved over their deaths. The letters home to Ireland break my heart.

Again my pride makes me wonder why they grieved. Mother David Mark says we should never grieve over death.

I will not think of that question anymore, lest I have yet another fault to confess.

I wonder where my parents are and what they are thinking. Is that a fault too? I don't think so. Dear God, protect them.

And on this feast protect the one whose name I dare not even think. Grant him the grace of contrition for the sins which in my weakness I led him to commit.

45
SISTER MARY AMABILIS

Christmas

Dearest Infant Jesus,
Make me as poor as your foster father
Make me as chaste as your holy mother
Make me as obedient as You were, even to the death of the cross
Make my heart sing as loud as the angels
Make me as docile as the shepherds
Make me as faithful as the wise men
Make me as prompt as Joseph
Make me as gentle as Mary
Make me as meek and mild as You Yourself.
Make me glow as the star of Bethlehem to reveal your love

Make me as selfless as the oxen in the cave
Make me as generous as the mule who carried You to the cave

Shower down on me the dew of heaven
Fill me with the light of the world
Take all that I am and have for Yourself
Bring me home to celebrate Christmas with You in heaven

Come O Wisdom and teach me truth
Come O Shepherd of Israel and save my faith
Come O Root of Jesse and make me flower
Come O Key of David and open my selfish heart
Come O Day Star and light my way
Come O Lord and wash me clean
Come O Emmanuel and be my God

And protect and bless this Christmas season my parents and
the Ryans and all my friends and [word here deleted].

46
SISTER MARY AMABILIS

Feast of the Epiphany

I talked to Sister Martha today about how hard it is to keep
the rules and to avoid pride over my humility in confessing
my violations of the rules.

I don't think Sister understood me.

She said, "Honey, can't you leave some room for God?"

"But, Sister," I replied, "God can't cleanse all the base
vileness from my mind and soul unless I cooperate."

"Can't He?" she asked, with a kind of mild reproof. "I thought He could do anything."

"But Father Radbert told us in theology class that God can't overcome the resistance of a soul steeped in sin."

"I'll let you in on a little secret, Cathy," she said, and smiled. "You're not steeped in sin."

"Oh, but I am, Sister, I am," I said. "I'm one of the worst sinners who ever lived."

She shook her head. "Now that is real pride."

Then I acted even prouder. "Anyway, my name is Sister Mary Amabilis now," I said. "I left that wretch Cathy behind on the day of my reception."

"What a shame," she said. "She was a very nice young woman." She laughed at me and I thought my heart would break because she didn't understand.

"I suppose I shouldn't tell you this, but the chapter has decided that we can resume our own names next summer if we wish."

I was horrified. "How terrible!"

"You don't want to be Catherine again?" She frowned a little.

"I'll never be anyone but Sister Mary Amabilis," I insisted. "She represents my new life. . . . Is the chapter going to destroy the Holy Rule? Will it leave us anything?"

Sister sighed. "The church has ordered an 'updating,' Sister, you know that. Pope John called it an aggiornamento. And he said that we should open the windows and let some fresh air in. We're going to change in order to remain the same."

"What would Mother Claire think?" I stuttered.

"Mother Claire was a great woman. She would have been one of the leaders in the chapter for letting in fresh air. We may have to suffer much because we drifted away from her spirit in the name of her word, but in the long run we'll be much better for it."

"I hope they don't take everything away from us," I said sadly.

"They won't, child. Now, how's your health? You look terribly thin."

"I'm fine, Sister. I've never felt healthier or happier."

"No stomach problems? We've had an ulcer epidemic it seems."

Three of the sisters have ulcers and I think some of those who left had stomach pains too.

"Just a little ache for chocolate ice cream now and then, Sister," I said, and both of us laughed. I was sure that the pain I feel in my stomach is what Mother says it is, my imagination.

"Now, about the rules," and she smiled that warm German-mother smile of hers that always makes me feel good. "The worst form of pride is to make keeping the rules an end in itself. Jesus will not judge us at the end by the rules but by our love for others. You don't want to tie yourself up in knots with a scrupulous conscience, do you?"

"I think I may have the most lax conscience in the world," I said, and we both laughed again. How can you be proud of a lax conscience? I can, I guess.

"Take it easy, Cathy," she said as I left her office. "Oops, I mean Sister Mary Amabilis."

And then I said something very stupid, which shows how little progress I have made since reception.

"You can call me anything you want."

So she does not understand my problems at all.

And I wish she didn't seem so happy about the changes that will be imposed on us. I'm afraid that they will make our salvation even more difficult to achieve.

If you want to call me home, gentle Lord, before the changes, it might not be a bad idea.

47
MARY KATE

"May I have some more ice cream?" the Punk said politely enough as he passed me his empty dish during his January vacation in 1965.

The Punk annoys the hell out of me because he can eat everything he wants and still look like a weasel.

"If you wipe the chocolate off your mouth first."

"Yes, ma'am."

"The boy wants more," my Joe said, imitating the beadle from *Oliver Twist*. "The boy wants more!"

I gave him two scoops, ruffled his hair and hugged him, which is standard treatment for the Punk.

"Do they feed you out there?" my Pirate said. "You've had two of everything tonight."

"Quality," said the Punk, lapping away at the chocolate like the puppy dog he is.

We had talked about the changes in the church through the whole meal, the Brats having been banished to bed or the TV room. The Punk, who had been reading all the theologians before the council, was unperturbed. His side was winning, though he had doubts that "our gloriously reigning supreme pontiff," as he always calls the pope, had the strength to control the whirlwind that had swept in through his predecessor's open window.

"How was lunch with Nick?" I asked, skirting the question that was most on both our minds.

"He is as insufferably legal as I am clerical," he replied, smacking his lips over a large swallow of ice cream. "Only he's serious. He's made law review next year and will probably be given an honors appointment to the Justice Department. I presume that means the U.S. attorney's office here, because his mother would never let him desert her by going to Washington. Poor guy, he should get away from everything."

We both knew who was included in everything.

"His religious problems?"

"He'll be all right." My brother shrugged. "I'm glad they're out in the open and he's thinking about them. Most people his age don't think they have the time to worry about God."

I didn't ask him if they'd talked about the most important topic. I'm sure they had.

"Do you think they'll change the birth control ban?" Joe asked, filling the silence as a good husband should. It was an academic question for the moment, because I was pregnant again—and had passed from resignation to delight.

It was also academic for the future because we had made up our minds. To wit: no more.

"The commission has given him a way out, I'm told. Whether he takes it or not remains to be seen. And as to your next question, Joseph, I don't think they'll drop the celibacy requirement. And even if they do, I'd make a poor choice for some girl, wouldn't I?"

We laughed, but I thought the girl would have to be pretty damn good to be good enough for my brother the Punk.

"And Cath?" I said finally, bringing the conversation around to the subject about which we were all worrying. "Rosie O'Gorman said at Christmas that she has seen her from a distance and she looks thin and haggard. A number of the girls have left with ulcers."

"I'm eating the extra ice cream for her." The Punk's spoon hesitated over the chocolate goo for a moment and then plunged in.

"I hope she doesn't ruin her health," I said softly, finally putting my fear on the table.

"It's altogether possible that she will, M.K.," Blackie said somberly. "Let's face it. Her mercurial temperament in that madhouse could turn inward and mess her up. Creeps."

"Explain to me again what you don't like about the nuns," my man said, half professional-shrink, half confused-Boston-Catholic.

"Let us assume, Joseph"—he considered asking for a third helping and reluctantly pushed the dish aside—"that you take your wife to the club for one of its major social events. And she wears old clothes that don't fit and are out of style and that make her look ridiculous among all the other women."

"Nothing fits now," I said, putting two more scoops in the dish.

"I'd be embarrassed," Joe admitted. "I mean, wouldn't people think that either I couldn't afford to buy her nice clothes or that I didn't care what she looked like?"

"Indeed, yes." The Punk hugged me this time, the huggingest punk I've ever known. "You want your bride to look sharp—or perhaps chic would be a better word—because how she looks reflects on who you are, and vice versa too, I suppose?"

"That's right," Joseph agreed enthusiastically, "I want my bride to look sharp."

"And not skinny or underfed?"

"Absolutely not!"

"That, I would imagine," my brother said triumphantly, "is how Christ feels too."

48
SISTER MARY AMABILIS

Palm Sunday 1965

I am worried that I will fail. If they don't want me in the community what will I do?

I am so weak and so proud and so sensual that they truly ought not take me. But if they don't want me, then my life will be wasted. I'll be nothing but a shallow flake until God comes along and demands an accounting.

I'm so proud of the community—a good pride, since it's not directed at me—and what it stands for. I want to be part of them. I want to devote my life to their apostolic work.

But I think they don't want me.

Mother has talked to me almost every night since I fainted in chapel. I wanted to tell her it was my period and nothing to worry about, but I haven't had a period in four months. Most of the other girls have the same problem. It's the body rebelling against the spirit.

She asked me about what I was eating and I told her the truth, but without yielding to pride. I've given up meat for Lent, of course, and also milk on my cereal, and eggs and butter.

"You look a little peaked, dear," she said thoughtfully. "Remember that, just as it is sensuality to eat too much, so it is pride not to eat enough."

"Oh, I'm eating plenty, Mother."

She made me promise to put milk on my cereal. But she didn't say how much. So I put a few drops on every morning now.

Then she talked to me for the longest time, about her college days, and how happy she was in the novitiate, and how hard it is to be a superior, and how unwise were many of the changes discussed by the chapter, and how much we'd lose if we tried to adjust to the world.

That night I thought she finally liked me and enjoyed talking to me. And when she put her hand on my forehead to see if I had a fever, I felt happy and peaceful, as if I were with my real mother, though I can't remember Mom ever doing that.

I do so admire her and want to be a good religious like her. I'll never be as holy as she is and would never dream of being mistress of novices or anything like that. But if I could only have some of her cool, self-possessed elegance, I would think I finally understood and lived the religious life.

So I want her to think I'm a good novice and on the way to being a good religious.

But afterward, when she talked to me almost every night, I became worried. The only reason a mistress of novices would be so relaxed with one of her sisters, it seems to me, is that she wants the sister to relax too and reveal her true self. Then she'll know for certain whether Sister should be professed at the end of the canonical year.

Mother must think that my true self is pretty bad. I am a much worse sinner and a much more proud and sensual worldling than she knows. I must hide what I am for a while longer so that I can finally discipline my rebellious body and will to measure up to the standards of the community.

I don't blame Mother. She's not exactly trying to trick me. It's her job to find out whether I'm worthy. Maybe I ought to tell her that I'm not worthy. I will confess to her in the summer if I don't change. I still have a little time, not much but a little. I must resolve to work harder, that's all.

Until then I'll continue to hide. Maybe someday when we're both old religious—she's only about ten years older than I am, I think—I can reveal my deception and we'll both laugh and agree that it was a holy hiding.

I must hide from Sister Martha too. She suspects that I have a bad case of scruples, which is utterly silly.

Me, scrupulous!

So I asked Mother tonight after the first few minutes if I could be excused to study for Father's theology exam tomorrow.

She said that I should run along. It wouldn't do to endanger my excellent grades.

As if I cared about grades. They're only one more temptation to pride.

VIRGIN AND MARTYR / 163

I thought that Mother looked kind of sad when I left. But
that must have been my imagination. Why would she enjoy
talking to me?

49
SISTER MARY AMABILIS

Good Friday 1965

Dear Suffering Lord Jesus,
   How great were your sufferings compared to mine. I can't
sleep at night on a comfortable bed. And your bed was the
hard wood of the cross. I feel a sharp pain in my stomach
occasionally and your chest was pierced with a lance,
making blood and water flow out. I'm so nervous and jumpy
that I can hardly stand still. And You were nailed to the cross
so that You couldn't move. I complain to myself about the
petty annoyances and inconveniences of life and You were
cruelly scourged with a hooked whip. My knees ache from
eating all my meals on them now and your whole body was a
solid mass of pain.
   I'm grateful to You for the many blessings of this year. I
have learned what it is to be a good religious, even if I am
not one yet. I understand my vocation and am eager to be
about your Heavenly Father's business in the community's
apostolic work. I am at peace with myself and the world. I'm
absolutely certain that my vocation is to follow you in special
dedication by making the Holy Vows of the religious life.
   And I've never been so happy before.
   You earned all of this for me by your ugly, painful death.
What can I give back to you, my gentle Lord? My poor life
isn't nearly enough. Help me to make something more of it
so that my gift in gratitude to you when I'm professed in
August will be less unworthy than it is now.
   And if it be thy will to call me home before my time, even

before my profession, then as You said to the Father in the Agony in the Garden, Thy will not mine be done.

Might I have cancer of the stomach? If I do, it is Thy will and I cheerfully accept it.

Sister Lorraine Iraneus, who was a novice long ago, back in the 1940s, died of cancer while still a novice and is now revered as a Saint by the whole community. Maybe she will be canonized someday. I have no right to dream of those things for myself. It's terrible pride to compare myself with her.

Should I confess it in chapter? I'm too tired to worry about that anymore. You love me despite my pride because You want me to eliminate it from my life.

Where was I? Oh, yes, if You do want me to die an ugly and painful death for you, Lord Jesus, I offer myself as an imperfect oblation, the sacrifice of a miserable worm.

As the soldiers did with You what they willed on Good Friday, so You do whatever You will with me. Your handmaiden is ready for sacrifice.

50
SISTER MARY AMABILIS

July 5

I'm scared stiff.

Not that I will die. I'm ready for that. But that they might postpone my profession because I'm sick.

Or, even worse, that I would have to drop out and do the whole canonical year over again.

It's only another month. I've made it through eleven months. I must hang on. The band is down to twenty-two members now, a quarter of those who entered. All of us look kind of thin and gaunt. Novitiate isn't supposed to be easy. Mother David Mark is concerned about us. Mother Mary

Emmanuel came down the Hill the other day to cheer us up.
I thought her talk was very funny and very worldly. It may be
a fault to make such a judgment about a woman who is
God's representative over me. I won't think about it.
Whenever I try to figure out what is a fault and what isn't my
stomach hurts worse.

Now that I know I'm too thin and my health could lead to
a decision that I do not belong in the religious life, I'm trying
to eat as much as I can. My confessor dispensed me from my
promise to give up ice cream. But, just my luck, we haven't
had it all this week.

I have no appetite. I force food into my mouth and down
into my stomach, but it doesn't always want to stay down. I
try not to let anyone hear me vomit, because my superiors
will think that ill health is a sign from God that I don't belong
here.

But, then, where would I belong?

I'm not the only one who is sick. This afternoon when I
was throwing up, Sister Christine Lucile was sick in the next
stall. Although it was the Minor Silence, we both laughed.

"Hang in, Cathy," she said to me, with a rueful grin.

"To the bitter end." I grinned back.

I wonder if I look as bad as she does.

That's a terrible sin of vanity. What does it matter what I
look like? My body will be rotting in the grave in a few years.

Maybe in a few months. Either it's all in my imagination—
one more excuse to pamper my rebellious body—or I do
have stomach cancer. I accept God's will.

Should I confess at chapter a sin of vanity, wondering
whether I looked as sick as Christine Lucile?

That would bring the house down. Everyone is terribly
giddy these days. I know. I'll confess that I wondered whether
I looked sick and not make any comparison. No, I better not.
Mother and Sister might think that is a sign from God that I'm
not strong enough to be a good religious.

It's almost over. Only four more weeks. Three weeks and
six days, actually. Dear God, help me to hang on.

51
BLACKIE

The next day Cathy collapsed, the victim of an ulcer and malnutrition, and was transported to the infirmary. Her condition was sufficiently serious that her parents were summoned. But my aunt and uncle were in Mallorca. So Joe and Mary Kate Murphy went to the Hill in their place, both brandishing their medical and psychiatric diplomas.

They found that she was down to ninety-one pounds and unable to keep solid foods in her stomach and that she had had no periods for nine months. Mary Kate wanted to bring her home that very day and Mother David Mark readily agreed.

"The poor child," she said, "simply does not have the stamina for the religious life."

Cathy dug in her heels. Only a month more was required to complete her canonical year. If she left, she would have to begin all over again. Mother Mary Emmanuel, the president of the order (her title had already been changed from mother general), proposed, over her novice mistress's strenuous objections, a compromise. Cathy would live in the infirmary until the doctor released her and participate in whatever activities down at the novitiate she herself thought feasible. Mother Mary Emmanuel bound her "under Holy Obedience" to make no strenuous demands on herself, a well-meaning gesture not unlike forbidding a salmon to spawn.

Mary Kate didn't like it. But she feared anorexia nervosa would develop if Cathy tried to do the canonical year again.

I believe her exact and typically Ryan expression was, "Better to get the horse manure behind her once and for all."

She only went along with Mother Mary Emmanuel's compromise, however, when that latter worthy agreed to bind Cathy to several dishes of chocolate ice cream every day.

Cath, she said, smiled at that, for the first time.

Mary Kate told me later that some of the other girls looked even sicker. Ironically, Cathy's band was the last to suffer a traditional canonical year. Mother David Mark was shipped out to Nebraska and her eventual monsignor the same week that Cathy began her final year in college, wearing the black veil of a nun who has taken her first vows of poverty, chastity and obedience and looking like an anemic scarecrow, with dull, hurt eyes.

At her reception she had been an enthusiastic and impressionable young woman, filled with generosity and idealism, open to direction and inspiration. At her profession, the enthusiasm, generosity and idealism were still there, but, I think, twisted ever so slightly out of kilter. Her youthful flexibility was gone and so too was much of her youthful common sense. Whether she had truly been formed in the image of Jesus and Mary is dubious. Rather, it seems to me, she was formed in the image of Mother David Mark.

And would be until shortly before her death.

Which we all now, in August 1976, seem to be living through again.

I trust that when the case of Mother David Mark, or whatever her name is now that she has a monsignor for a roommate, comes up, the Almighty will permit me a word for the prosecution. I do not wish her to burn in hell forever nor even to sizzle in purgatory (should there be fire in purgatory, which I very much doubt) until Judgment Day.

It will be sufficient for the Almighty to demand that she admit that she was wrong in what she did to Cathy and to other young women.

It won't happen. David Mark and her ilk would rather spend eternity in hell than admit they made a mistake.

52
NICHOLAS

The day after Thanksgiving Monica and I heard Bartoletti conduct *Traviata* at the Lyric with Tebaldi singing Violetta. Afterward we went to King Arthur's Pub for a nightcap before adjourning to my apartment for the weekend. I had insisted that it was my turn to do the cooking and entertaining. Monica, amused and skeptical, had agreed to go along with the experiment, so long as she had the right to demand one restaurant meal each day.

She removed her coat and pushed back her jacket in the pub, because, although it was frigid outside, the bar was hot and stuffy. Her wine-colored sweater outlined every line and contour of her lovely torso, and her long blond hair cascaded over her shoulders like a sparkling waterfall.

"Mustn't stare," she whispered in my ear, tightening her grip on my leg.

"You'd be furious if I didn't."

I had made up my mind to force the discussion of marriage during the course of the weekend. It was unconscionable to go on as we had. I didn't intend to tell her, however, that one of my reasons for insisting the festivities be at my place was that I didn't want to give Blackie her number and I felt I had to be available for his call during the weekend.

It was impossible to deceive her about what was on my mind.

"What, more on Cathy?" she asked casually, draining the bottom half of her glass of vodka and signaling to the waitress with a smile for a refill.

"Easy," I said. "I don't want you falling asleep on me as soon as we reach my lair."

"No chance. And answer my question."

"Monica, I . . ."

"I don't resent her, Nick," she assured me. "That would be ridiculous. But I'm fascinated and curious."

In summary, I told her that the trust manager at First Chicago reported that Cathy withdrew the entire fifty-thousand credit line in one fell swoop three days before she was arrested in Costaguana. Blackie was elated when I told him, as if he had already laid a finger on the killer. (I could picture Catherine striding up to the teller with her brisk, I'm-here-to-do-business walk and demanding fifty one-thousand-Yankee-dollar bills.)

"We hit pay dirt," Blackie said, his eyes shining, as we sat in my office looking over the withdrawal record. "If we can find out what happened to the money, we'll be a long way toward understanding what happened to her and why."

"Do we really want to know?" I asked wearily, suddenly tired of Catherine and the problems of her life.

"We really want to know," he said firmly. "There will be no peace till we know."

"All right, what do we do next?"

He asked if we had contacts at American Express and I told him that we did. Then he went into high gear. "Find out if Catherine purchased any traveler's checks from their office in Santa Marta between the time of her withdrawing the money and her disappearance—and include the month of November besides. If she did, find out where the checks were cashed and ask them to send us copies so we can check the signatures. We don't know when she may have been arrested first or where. Perhaps she was seized outside the country, drugged and taken back in. The traveler's checks will leave a trail. Or perhaps someone forged her name to the checks. If they did, they will have left a trail too."

The scents were pretty cold, but we agreed to follow them because there was nothing else to follow. The first check we turned up was a Costaguana draft. And the signature on it was a duplicate of Catherine's. Blackie asked me to check it out with a handwriting expert and I contacted one. His analysis would take several days.

"Would Blackie approve of me?" Monica asked as we rode in the cab to my apartment, after she and I had analyzed every detail of my story.

"I think so," I replied, as my hand touched the warm flesh under her sweater. "He kind of twinkled and smiled when I told him I was going to *Traviata*. He must have noticed the change in my personality and concluded that I have—"

"A good lay on the string," she finished for me.

"A close friendship," I corrected her.

Later, after we had made wonderful love, my conscience caught up with me. "I want to talk about marriage, Monica," I said.

An expression of shrewdness, mixed with regret, crossed her face. "Okay, but do you mind putting that pillow under my head?"

"As long as you don't try to slip away."

"Who's slipping? . . . Why do you want to talk marriage? Would I be any better a lay if I were your wife?"

"Yes."

" 'Fraid you'd say that. Lonely?"

"Yes."

"Want me around every night?"

"You bet."

"We could move in together."

"That's almost the same as marriage and doesn't have the advantage of commitment."

She sighed. "All the right answers. Look, I intend to marry again. When the right man comes along, I'll know who he is. I started out thinking you might be a good one-night stand—and I could even the score for what you did to me on the witness stand. Now I enjoy talking to you more than I enjoy screwing with you, and I enjoy that a lot, as I hope you just noticed." She touched my face. "You're a good man. I'd like coming home to your cooking every night."

I laughed and kissed her. "Consider it a formal proposal."

"That means the fun and games are over either way, doesn't it?" She looked very serious when she said it.

"They'd be over anyhow, Monica."

"Give me a little bit of time?" she said, biting her lip.

"As long as you want."

"It won't be long."

It had been relatively easy. One could not find a better woman with whom to spend the rest of one's life. I told myself I hoped she'd say yes.

And I waited for Blackie's call through the whole weekend.

It never came.

53
BLACKIE

"We made so many mistakes, Father John," Marge Aimes said sadly, brushing an unruly lock of hair away from her "good German-mother's" face. "We should not have let her combine her year as a junior sister with her final year of college. Joan Jerome, who was the new director of formation—the title *novice mistress* left with David Mark—was against it. She thought Catherine was still emotionally unstable. We should have kept around her for at least two more years."

"I suppose," I agreed, having failed in my two-hour probing in the Mother House—oops—Administrative Center visitors' room to elicit any more information about Cath's role as a courier.

"And her first mission was a disaster. No one was thinking about what might happen in Careyville. We were so busy with the Reform Chapter then."

"Indeed." If I wanted to learn more about Costaguana, I would have to listen to Marge's examination of conscience every time I talked to her.

"And her conflict with Martina Mary, that ought to have been mediated before the vote came up on the council. We were new in the use of Council procedures. It ought not to have been a vote, almost like a jury trial. Martina Mary was so persuasive. But that year we took all the powers away from the president only to give them back the following year. And Martina Mary and her group were voted off the Council after their term."

"And promptly left the order," I said. I had to sympathize with Margaret. She was blaming herself for stupid decisions that were not her responsibility. But she did so because, like me, she would have preferred a live Catherine to a dead martyr.

"Yes," she sighed. "That was ironic, wasn't it? In the meantime Catherine had gone to South America."

"Where you soon joined her." My only option now was candor, a strategy I dislike even with Germans. "Margaret, we have reason to believe that Cathy was smuggling currency out of the country for Ed Carny. We also know that before her disappearance she had withdrawn a substantial sum of her money from the Bank of Costaguana. Were there any signs of either at the center then?"

Margaret was startled. "No, she had returned only a month before from one of Father Ed's trips and would not have ordinarily gone on another till April or May. I don't know when she had a chance to go to Santa Marta to cash a check. I can't remember her leaving the center after she returned from that trip. And she didn't seem to be planning to travel when she took her bicycle up into the hills the day she disappeared."

"If she went to the Indian *barrio*."

"They told us they had seen her."

"Might they have been lying?"

"I'm not sure, Father John." She turned up the palms of her hands like a cardplayer holding a busted straight. "They were a very difficult group with which to communicate."

"I see. Were you the one who gathered her things together afterward?"

She nodded sadly. "A pathetic little collection of clothes and books and pictures. She traveled lightly at the end."

"This was when?"

"About two months after her disappearance. When we were pretty sure she was dead. Just before you and your sister and brother-in-law came. I took them home after the paratroops expelled us and sent them to Mary Kate."

Of course during those two months anyone could have rifled through her "pathetic little collection."

"And there was no sign of money?"

"Nothing at all, only the most inexpensive clothes."

Blind alley.

54
NICHOLAS

On Monday morning I was sated with Monica and depressed with my first phone call. The second call was from Blackie.

"Absolutely nothing. No traces of the money or any other possessions. I have the feeling I missed something, but I can't figure out what. Have you heard from American Express?"

"Just before you called. Nothing there either. No one named Catherine Collins or Catherine Collins Tuohy purchased traveler's checks in Santa Marta from September to April. And the handwriting expert took the signature along, but he thinks it's authentic."

"Try Pan American."

They were a harder nut to crack, but finally I found a lawyer who knew a lawyer. No Catherine Collins or Catherine Collins Tuohy had left Santa Marta that summer.

We were back to square one. And I reflected all day how the weekend with Monica reminded me of the weekend at Copacabana—in vehemence if not in anger.

For an answer from Monica I would not have to wait long.

55
CATHERINE

September 20, 1965
OLH

Dearest Cousin Blackie,

I'm not sure about a lot of the changes that greeted us when we came out of our canonical year. They yield too much to the flesh and to selfishness. But one I know I like is the freedom to write uncensored letters and to receive same. It's great to be able to write back and forth directly to you.

There's even a possibility that we'll have a long weekend off next summer to go home, but I'm not sure where home will be for me. I wonder if in the new church nuns can water-ski?

Anyway, it was so wonderful to see you the day I took my first Holy Vows. You looked grown-up and self-possessed and very clerical, with only the impish twinkle in your eye to tell me that you were still my Cousin Blackie and up to no good at all.

I wonder how your superiors cope with you.

I'm sorry I was so out of it that day. My body didn't have quite the perseverance my soul demanded. But I'm much better now. The stomach pains are almost gone and I'm on a mostly normal diet. I'm still kind of wobbly at times and sleep too much, but otherwise okay.

That's right: Sleep too much. Sister John Jerome, who is our new director of formation, insists that I have at least nine and a half hours sleep. And she rides herd on me too.

"I will not, young woman—repeat, not—tolerate any fuither damage to your health. You will do what you're told in that area of your life, or I will lock you up in your room and surround you with tons of chocolate and chocolate chip ice cream."

"And bonbons, John," I say to her. "Don't forget the bonbons."

The worldling in me likes the relaxed life: Minor Silence abolished, Great Silence reduced, only a few reportable rule violations, freedom to talk to the other kids (whom we no longer call "seculars") in my class, lunch with Rosie every couple of days (she's going to marry her Cal Tech guy this summer), my own name back. Television and newspapers every day, an occasional movie, the fun and laughter at our meals together (we have readings only at breakfast now), the joy that permeates the house under John Jerome.

But it's all too easy, Blackie, too relaxed, too worldly. It's not much different a life than that of the college seniors up on the Hill, especially those who aren't dating. Could it be that we're giving up everything too quickly?

I've seen drawings of the new habit that will be optional next summer. We'll look like airline hostesses with veils. I'm not sure that I want to look like that. Of course, I don't have to

174 / ANDREW M. GREELEY

wear the new clothes, but I'll seem kind of funny if I'm the
only young one who doesn't.

And we'll be uncovering our hair. My kinky curls aren't
much as a crowning glory. But I thought we had given up
concern about our physical appearance. And now we're right
back to the same old thing. The temptation to vanity and vain
comparison with others will be grave.

I learned that we should try to be different. Now the
Community seems to be saying that we should try to be like
everyone else.

In theology class we are studying *The Council, Reunion, and
Reform* by Hans Kung. He makes me angry. I admit that he's a
very smart man (and terribly cute too), but he's so young. And
he seems to understand nothing of the traditions of the past.
How does he dare imply that all the things we've been doing
for so many centuries are wrong?

On the other hand, it's nice to know that we can think of
Protestants as human beings. I mean, I didn't know any of
them in the Neighborhood or at the Beach, but I always
thought we were too harsh on them.

I can't complain that Cardinal Suennens is too young (though
he also is very cute). And he doesn't seem brash either. We're
hearing his book *The Nun in the World* at our breakfast
readings. He sounds very sensible and kindly. But he talks
about the world in a very different way from that of Mother
David Mark. I learned that the world is a dangerous place, to be
avoided whenever possible, and to be worked in as though we
were not part of it.

That seems to me to be reasonable. Whenever I hear "world"
I think of Lauderdale at Easter week. There was sin
triumphant, a place bad enough to make you want to spend the
rest of your life in a cloistered community.

But, according to the cardinal, the world is a place to love, to
respect, to learn from, to teach, to save. It sounds very exciting.
It also sounds very dangerous. The kids who are going through
their canonical year now can hardly believe what ours was like
(and one of the differences is that they can talk to us). I don't
suppose many of them will get ulcers.

But will they be as prepared as I am to deal with the dangers
and temptations of the world?

Speaking of which, what's with Nick? I'm over him now and I'd like to think of him as a friend, but I suppose that's not possible. I hope that someday he will forgive me for how cruelly I treated him. Could you tell him that, Blackie? I don't want to put you in an awkward position, so if you don't want to pass on my message, that's all right too.

But I hope he doesn't hate me.

I wonder whether he will have to go to Vietnam.

We see the war on TV every night. It's horrible. Especially the children. How can anyone do such things to children? Why are there wars, anyway? And why must American young men like Nick go across the ocean to fight in a country I never heard of before?

I feel kind of like a Rip van Winkle (I finally read that story in literature class this year). The canonical year was my Sleepy Hollow and the world into which I have returned seems at least twenty years different.

And after the first month, to tell you the truth, Blackwood, I don't think I like it very much.

A lifetime novitiate might be better than the confusions and temptations and uncertainties. I even find myself thinking seriously about the cloister. Our community is setting up a house of prayer in a lonely spot several miles down the river where you can live a full contemplative life. Right now that seems very appealing.

Don't get worried, dear Coz, I won't go there. No chocolate ice cream.

I'll be all right. Give me more time.

Lots of love,
Confused (again) Cath

56
CATHERINE

December 6, 1965

Dear Blackie,

Hooray! The doctor took me off the ulcer diet today and pronounced me as fit as a fiddle, a Stradivarius, he said, which I think was a compliment. Not exactly fat yet, but no longer looking like a concentration camp victim.

And much happier and more relaxed. I don't understand what is happening in the church, but I'm sure God and the Holy Spirit are protecting us. I will leave the worrying to them and concentrate on my own responsibilities—finishing college and preparing for my first mission in the fall. I'm so excited at the prospect of being in a classroom with real kids I can hardly wait. I hope I get eighth-graders. Do you remember our eighth grade? Wasn't it fun? It'll be great to be part of that fun again.

You asked in your letter about my painting. I'm not taking any courses this year. I'm sure the community wouldn't mind. You can study almost anything you want now. But they have more art teachers than they can shake a stick at. So I'm sticking to math.

Painting would cause me all kinds of trouble with pride and that I don't need.

Some of the kids from the art department are after me to take a course next semester, and I've walked over there to see what they're doing. The new nun there studied at the Art Institute and is very good, but it's not for me.

Father Roy Tuohy, whom I met in Rome with Sean Cronin, was here the other night for a lecture on "The Religious Life and the Vatican Council." He is even more handsome than he was then, but he certainly has changed his theology.

He made fun of a lot of things we used to do, Sister Mary Holy Water practicing custody of the eyes, confessing pride about humility at the Chapter of Faults, nunny glasses and nunny shoes; Sister Mary Kiss the Candle and her nine novenas every nine days; devotion to the Holy Founder's boot; claiming to be brides of Christ when everyone is the spouse of God.

The college kids, who came to the talk because they heard he was so gorgeous, thought it was hilarious. Some of the younger nuns did too. I saw a few of the old gals with tears in their eyes when they left.

But I can't disagree with his main thesis: sanctity is emotional maturity. The old religious formation kept us immature on the pretext that we would be saints, but actually deprived us of the freedom and maturity to make our own decisions. The holy person in reality is the one who is self-actualizing and self-fulfilled, capable of making her (he said "his") decisions in the light of her own values and commitments.

Obedience is a virtue only when there is harmony between the Holy Spirit working in us and the Holy Spirit working in the superior. Poverty is not an end or even a good in itself; it is a virtue only when it frees us for maturity and self-actualization. And chastity is a virtue that enables us to come to terms with our sexual energies instead of denying them.

I'm going to have to reflect on these ideas for a long time, but I am beginning to see daylight. And I'm so happy that our community is moving in the right direction.

You'll say the community saw daylight before I did.

We had our first sample of the new Holy Habit (we call it merely the habit now). Since I am kind of average size, Sister John Jerome asked me to model it for the others.

We'll look like airline hostesses with veils, but now I think that we'll look like cute airline hostesses with veils. Nuns will have legs again. Which may be hard on those who have ugly legs or let themselves become overweight (unlike your rag-and-bone cousin), but then, they don't have to wear it.

One of the kids said something strange to me afterward. "You look good in it, but that's why they had you model it. You'd look good in anything. It's not fair."

What's not fair? I wonder. The new habit or that I look good in it or that I look good in anything?

I don't think I acted vainly. I don't know why Sister was so upset.

Anyway, you must tell me what you think of Father Tuohy and of Hans Kung and Cardinal Suennens.

Love and Stuff,
Cath

P.S. What about Nick?

57
CATHERINE

January 19, 1966

Dear Blackie,

I am completely wound up, so excited that I couldn't sleep the last two nights. And it's not my ulcer either. It's Father Hans Kung!

I was kind of surprised that you weren't with the guys from Mundelein who came down to hear him at McCormick Place—after the nice things you said about him (and the terrible things about Father Tuohy. Blackie, really!). I know you can read his books, but the personality of a man is never fully revealed in his books.

He talked a long time and I didn't understand everything he said because I am not a theologian (yet). But the lecture was like a mystical experience. It was as if the whole of the Vatican Council and all the changes which have renewed and freed the church were packed into McCormick Place with that brilliant man, and the cheering, laughing crowd becoming the new church in miniature.

And his subject, "Honesty in the Church," was so perfect. Blackie, we have been terribly dishonest, to our own feelings, to what we knew was true, to what is the best in our tradition. We have lied, cheated, falsified, pretended—all in the name of obedience, or the good of the church or protecting the faithful from harm.

Well, that's all over now. We will speak the simple and

unvarnished truth, to one another, to the laity, and to our
superiors. And thank God we have priests like Father Kung
who will make the superiors listen.

We talked about nothing else in the bus on the way back to
the Hill. Everyone was sky high, laughing and joking, talking
and singing. We'd reached a turning point and everyone knew
it.

To be honest, and now I must try to be honest all the time,
not absolutely everyone liked Father Kung. A couple of nuns
said that he was just a popularizer and not half the theologian
that Rahner is. (I'm going to try to read him during the
summer, also Edward Schillebeeckx.) They said he makes a lot
of money on his books and lectures and that his greatest skill
is promoting himself. And they complain that he's a matinee
idol and not a scholar. Someone even said he was no better
than a Protestant.

These nuns wouldn't discuss what he said, they only wanted
to discuss him. I can't quite figure that out. Can you?

And also, still being honest, I don't like what you said about
Father Tuohy. He's not a cheap hack peddling other people's
ideas as his own. That's unlike you, Blackie. He's a good priest
trying to help us through these difficult and exciting times.

You're right about Nick. I shouldn't use you as a messenger.
I should tell him what I feel myself. The trouble is that I am
afraid that if I write to him, he'll write back and then I'll write
again and we'll both be in a lot of trouble.

We would have broken up eventually anyway. We are very
different people with different values and different goals in life.
But the way we broke up, all my fault, leaves this lingering
bittersweet memory that is bad for both of us.

It would be even worse to become involved again. And I
know my own weaknesses well enough to know that I could do
that very easily.

I guess I'll have to wait till I see him somewhere. Maybe in
Chicago this summer or at the Beach during my weekend at
home, which will be at the Ryan home since my parents are
touring the Orient.

Oh, I didn't tell you about the Institute. I have received
permission from Mother Mary Emmanuel to enroll in the
Summer Institute in Chicago for credit classes that will count
toward my degree. Instead of summer school here, it will be

summer school in Chicago. Is there any chance that you might be there too? I know you know everything, but it might be fun, like visiting the zoo to watch the animals!

Mother was delighted by my request. She said that she hoped I would want to continue the program after this summer at least to the master's level. In this time of transition, she told me, the community will have a deep need for trained professionals in the theological disciplines.

I've never heard Mother Emmanuel say "deep need" before.

But did you get the hint of "at least" the master's? Maybe I could go on for the doctorate? Wouldn't that be something? Doctor Cathy?

At last I'd be really good at something.

Lots of love,
Cathy

58
CATHERINE

Easter 1966

Dear Black One,

You're right, I didn't tell you about my shift to religious ed. I'm still majoring in math, but I have enough credits in that so I can take religious ed this summer and still graduate in August. It seems such a sensible thing to do, because of course I'll be teaching religion in my first mission, which will be grammar school, probably, and then even if I teach high school trig, I can still take some religion classes.

My "conversion" to rel ed was the result of a lecture by Brother Gabriel Moran. (Why are all the great new teachers cute, all except for that terrible sociologist fellow who says we're short on leaders and short on scholars? Every time he

gets in an argument he falls back on NUMBERS!) We haven't
been educating kids in religion; we have been indoctrinating
them. Remember that terrible Baltimore catechism? We didn't
know what half the words meant, but still we could repeat
them like a machine gun. And the act of contrition—we
thought that "heartily sorry" was either "hardly sorry" or
"partly sorry."

It was all memory, memory, memory without any attention
to content or thought. No wonder so many people have fallen
away from the church. Brother Gabriel says that values are
developed not by forcing young people to memorize words they
don't understand and in which they are not interested, but in
letting them talk, ventilate their problems, search for their own
values, discover and articulate the God within them.

That makes so much more sense, doesn't it? In fact, it is so
sensible that you wonder how we missed it for years.

I'm terribly excited about this new approach—but, then, I'm
terribly excited about everything in the new church and really
high that I'm going to be a part of it. Both of us will be part of
it, Blackie. That's why I hope you will be at the Institute this
summer too.

I was against all of the changes when I came out of the
canonical year last August, but I was tired then and sick and
the changes surprised me. But now I realize that, as Mother
Mary Emmanuel and Sister John Jerome say, the changes will
merely integrate the best of the past with the best of the new.

And, as Sister Martha argued last year, we have to change to
remain the same. I didn't believe her then but I do now. We are
not rejecting any of the truths I learned in the novitiate. We are
merely rephrasing them so that they mean more in the modern
world.

As for my health, I am absolutely fine. We can use the
swimming pool now and I swim every day. And of course we
have scales in the house and I'm almost what I weighed when I
entered three years ago—gosh, the time flies.

Anyway, I was a little overweight then.

Finally, Nick. I'm still wobbly on that one, dearest
Blackwood. I don't trust my own emotions. I'm not quite self-
actualized when Nicholas Broderick Curran is the subject.
Probably never will be. It's silly of me to think we can be

friends, but I don't want to be enemies, either. If I bump into him in Chicago or at the Beach, fine; if not, then I'll have to put it off till next summer, when I'll feel a little more steady.

I wish that I thought he wasn't waiting for me to leave. I'll never do that.

I hope I don't bump into him. He should be studying for the bar and he doesn't need any more distractions, does he?

See you soon. Easter Joy.

Love,
Doctor Cathy

59
BLACKIE

At the Summer Institute circus, Cathy was cast in the role of cotton candy—sweet, light and fluffy. And my worries about her grew more intense.

Mother Mary Emmanuel was dead right. The order and the church desperately needed trained professionals. But she was dead wrong in thinking the Summer Institute would provide them.

It wasn't her fault, nor the fault of those who administered the Institute. Few people in the church knew what a professional was or how one was trained. So they assumed that a couple of courses in summer school over a couple of summers produced the advanced training which was needed and wanted.

In fact, all that was accomplished was that vacuums were filled up. The quick answers, the simple theories, the ready-made programs of the Counter-Reformation and the Immigrant Church had been swept away, leaving room for new answers, new theories and new programs. But it was necessary that all of these be prepackaged, clear and easy to apply. There was no time to inquire too deeply, no time to contemplate complexity, no room for hesitation and doubt. The old certainties are gone; let us replace the old certainties at once with the new certainties so that we can get on with our work.

Religious education programs were revised or created from whole cloth for both dioceses and religious communities by men and women who had two years of summer school. Revised constitutions for orders like the OLH were put together by women with Master's degrees in theology, who claimed to be and were accepted as theologians of spirituality and who, I am sure, had never heard of, much less read, St. John of the Cross.

It was, not to put too fine an edge on the matter, half-assed.

The new rulers at Mundelein had no problem with my attending the Institute—mostly, I suspect, because they didn't like the people who ran it and took morose delectation (to resurrect a sin that I always thought was admirable) at the picture of my making their life miserable.

Who, me?

The Institute had not yet become the dating/mating market it would be the next year, when directors would serve for two of the three years of their term and then follow their students out of the priesthood and into the married state, mostly, if the truth be told, a married state with one of their more attractive students as a spouse.

As one director remarked, "I don't want to be the last man out of the priesthood."

You can imagine the wisdom and prudence that went into the selection of a man with such a vision of the Catholic heritage, to preside over a program of instruction that was supposed to provide the leaders and scholars for the updating on which we were all embarked.

The sexual lunacies would come later, though heaven knows the director paid his share of attention to Catherine even the first summer.

That year, the Institute was a relatively harmless tent show, a three-ring circus, a carnival, complete with clowns, trained animals, pitchmen, fakers and freaks. And the equivalent of hot dogs, popcorn, balloons and cotton candy.

Cathy, the light, frothy distraction of the circus, waltzed through its center rings and sideshows with glowing complexion and shining eyes, like Florence Nightingale in the hospitals of the Crimea. Dressed in the simple gray shift that had become the summer costume of the OLH nuns, with a short black veil and a plain cross around her delectable neck, Cath was a spring breeze of concern and laughter in the midst of the humid jungle of (half-assed) ideas and schemes. If you didn't understand what a traveling pitchman from Brussels was saying, well, you could always stare at her with dreamy eyes and fervent imagination and hope that you could talk to her during the coffee breaks or at mealtimes or at the recreation periods in the evening, which turned into teen-club dances for adolescent priests and nuns.

Mind you, I don't blame anyone for watching Cathy's every move. She was well worth watching—prettier than before she entered, transformed by the dedication that seemed to radiate through her transparent skin. The light loveliness of her body appeared to reveal the light loveliness of her soul.

And if you add "weight" to "light" you get the truth, but then she was a veritable Rocky Marciano compared to most of them.

She had changed in other ways too, small, subtle ways. The glow in her big brown eyes was a little more fixed, hinting at a trace of fanaticism; her spine was a trifle more rigid, suggesting a certain fixity of perspective, and her muscles were not merely firm but taut, revealing, perhaps, repressed anxiety.

In comparison with the rigidly anxious near fanatics who attended the tent show, she was flexible, relaxed, pragmatic. Yet she no longer laughed at goofiness the way she used to. And goofiness aplenty there was to laugh at.

I worried. The zealot was always there. She was Erin's daughter—and her aunt, my mother, had been a Communist in the thirties. But it required Sister David Mark to call forth the fanatic. And the plant was growing vigorously in the hothouse of the Summer Institute.

There was a lot of smoking and drinking and sitting around talking and getting to know one another and being honest and open and free—which, of course, meant actually putting on new masks, trying out new deceits, and experimenting with new forms of aggression. All doubtless sincere, but nonetheless dangerous because innocents were hurt, especially my innocent and radiant cousin.

A lot of them were forming "relationships," self-conscious friendships with someone of the same sex, or the opposite, which were supposed to be the basis for healthful intimacy in the new, open, honest and free church. For many fragile and timid people, kept in the emotional cocoon of the prepubescent, these informal workshops in interpersonal intimacy were the first steps out of lifelong shells. The steps were brave, I guess, but usually misguided and often self-destructive.

No one around had the sense to say that friendships are not formed self-consciously and interpersonal intimacy is difficult and dangerous. Not even the half-assed psychologists who were urging such relationships on the students. May they rot in the pit of purgatory for a very long time for that irresponsibility.

It was all, to be blunt about it, quite vomit-producing. And Cathy was the perfect victim again—in a clerical, summertime Fort Lauderdale.

So I attached myself to her like a modern-day Lancelot, with my wit the broadsword to decapitate pests. The word got around quickly enough that I was her cousin and a power to be dealt with, especially since I was the only one she danced with (the only one I would let her dance with, I may add). Several dozen men and perhaps a half-dozen women, with unperceived but ill-concealed desire stamped on their faces, asked me for an introduction to her.

I would sigh, pull out my notebook, write down their name and assign them a number, always over forty, and ask them to check back later to see how close their turn was.

No one ever did.

There were two kinds of pitchmen: the permanent ones, like Roy Tuohy, who were pure frauds, and the wandering ones, brought in from Brussels, Manila, Rome, Washington, Louvain, Tubingen, Lyons, Munich, Munster, San Francisco, Bonn, etc., etc. The Latin Americans had not yet exercised their monopoly rights, though there was much braying about the Third World from folks who had spent a few weeks somewhere in the tropics.

Some of the travelers made the Roy Tuohys of the Institute look like profound and original scholars. One seminar pitted a priest psychologist against a missionary returned from Africa in a discussion of the Lord's Prayer. The missionary had been amazed to find poverty in the Dark Continent (apparently no one had told him) and contended that the Lord's Prayer was a call to arms (the "kingdom" became the "revolution"). The psychologist, who had a hang-up on authority, insisted that the words "our Father" indicated an unhealthy dependency on God. Both, incidentally, were out of the priesthood and married within eighteen months.

Other pitchpersons were among the most distinguished Catholic thinkers of the last half-millennium, astonished by their new role as prophets and folk heroes and in most cases not happy with the role.

They would lecture profoundly on profound subjects, such as the nature of the church or the nature of the incarnation of Jesus or the meaning of the Eucharist, speaking in heavily accented English or in guttural Teutonic that would later be translated into obscure English. Most of the students would have understood no less if the translations had been omitted. And in any event they were not coming to learn from the folk hero (whom they could read if they were interested in his ideas) but to stare at him and worship. In the question periods, there was rarely communication between interrogator and respondent. The question usually could have been rephrased as either (1) How can I persuade my superior (bishop) that these changes are going to last? (2) Is there anything left to believe in? or (3) Why can't I fuck?

Since the words used in the question were not quite this clear, the foreign idea merchant would think that somehow his interrogator was referring to something that was in his talk and attempt to clarify for the stupid Americans.

It was great sport and there were always the teen-club sessions in the evening when the cult hero's personality, character and motivations could be torn apart.

To the end of her life Cathy never understood envy.

"Why were they so nasty about that man?" she asked as I was driving her home to the North Side convent to which she was assigned for the summer.

(I drove her home EVERY night, to deprive the predators who lived on campus of a post beer shot at her.)

The man in question was a gentle Frenchman whose field was Old Testament wisdom literature. He had said some wonderful things about the origins of Yahwehism in a more ancient wisdom tradition. Having read the great American Carmelite Roland Murphy, I knew about this, but it was one of the better and more original presentations in our cozy little Donnybrook. He was cut to ribbons at the "teen club," or "evening recreation" to give it its proper, if inaccurate, name.

"Because he is gifted and wise and famous," I said.

"Like the people who hate Father Kung?" she shook her head in dismay. "That's envy, isn't it?"

"You got it, Coz."

"How horrible. They want to destroy him because he's good. Like Jesus."

"Same principle. Clergy is full of it."

"Well," she sighed, "I'm glad no one envies me."

"Wrong, Coz. Half the nuns at the meeting are crazy with envy of you. You're the best-looking woman there. All the men defer to you; the most desirable of them, Ed and Roy, hang around you. You're bright and charming and fun. They hate your guts."

"What a terrible thing to say," she cried out, ready to burst into tears.

"What a true thing to say. They'll hate you all your life. Better that you know why. I think our friend Hans doesn't know that's why so many people despise him."

"I won't always be pretty," she said, trying to choke back the tears.

"Come on, Coz, remember me, Blackie? You don't need to be humble with me. You have Collins genes and you know what that means. You'll make that dress interesting for the next forty years."

"I don't want to," she said, sulking now.

"I wouldn't argue with God because he made you beautiful, if I were you."

We drove the rest of the way to the convent in silence.

After I stopped on the Jefferson Park street, reputedly cleaned by Polish matrons with toothbrushes before breakfast every morning, she ruffled my hair, an inveterate form of affection with the women in my family. "Thanks, Coz. Better that I should know about it."

"Better indeed."

But she never did understand the mentality of those who would destroy beauty and excellence. Even at the end, when she was finally their victim, she did not understand.

<u>60</u>
BLACKIE

Roy Tuohy, even in that summer of 1966, was conspicuous for two things, in my judgment. He was mean and he was a fraud. He was the kind of man who, for example, would be fifteen minutes late when you were supposed to pick him up somewhere and then climb in the car, blaming you for his tardiness and indeed lifting your culpability to the level of an example illustrating a general principle of what is wrong with the church.

"Your difficulty," he said decisively, "is typical of the irresponsible immaturity of the clergy. Mature people are precise. You were told to be driving in the opposite direction. That is why your car wasn't visible the first time I came out."

The worst thing about this rewriting of the history of the last fifteen minutes was that he had probably persuaded himself that it was true.

"Horse manure, Roy," I said, borrowing one of my favorite words from Mary Kate's vocabulary. "And if I hear one more word of it, I'll stop the car and you can walk to the Institute."

He left me alone after that, outside of class.

In class he was equally mean. No one of us was permitted to ask questions. It was not proper to interrupt the flow of a teacher's thought, as that wasted precious time and violated the gospel message of urgency as well as the principle of maturity, which said that mature people use time wisely and do not interrupt those wiser than themselves.

He could ask questions, however. They were always nasty and calculated to embarrass the students, especially the women who adored him, for reasons which to this day remain mysterious to me.

I imagined Roy as an Irish Dracula, lean, sallow, bloodlessly handsome, with a high forehead and slightly receding hairline, which seemed to give him small horns on the top of his head. He wore a tailor-made black suit and dark tie and lacked only the cape and the fangs to give Bela Lugosi a run for his money. Moreover, his voice was a nasal whine, the sort one would expect in a creature returned from the grave. And he treated students like his life depended on sucking their blood and draining away their vitality.

Mind you, I didn't like him. The younger nuns had a much more benign view. Roy, Cathy told me, was adorable.

Satan worship, I thought to myself.

One day he was working Cathy over about self-actualization: Had she worried about confessing too many faults in chapter?

"I suppose I did," she stumbled. "I didn't want to get credit for my humility."

"See?" he said to the class. "Is this not a classic example of my point? Your superiors inculcate this sort of immaturity to keep you immature and under their control. And you do not have the courage or the maturity to resist them. Isn't that true?"

"Yes, Father," Cathy agreed meekly.

"Maturity" was a word that appeared in at least a third of Roy's sentences. His course was entitled, "Christian Maturity, Self-Actualization, and the Gifts of the Holy Ghost," a surefire winner in those days. Like a lot of other fakers, Roy had retooled rapidly; that is to say, he read a book or two, lifted its key concepts and fitted them into a slightly modified traditional theology. It was just what the suckers, er, students, wanted.

His source was Abraham Maslow. His key theme—that superiors exercised social control by keeping clergy and religious immature—was unexceptionable and unoriginal. But he had read one psychology book and the students hadn't read any.

"What about you?" He gestured at me, not recalling my name.

"Me?" I said innocently, flipping my pages of Maslow (disguised by a false dust jacket).

"No one else," he sneered. "Are you afraid of being proud of your humility when confessing faults?"

"I'm not a religious, Father, so we don't have that hoary institution to jettison. But I'd like to read you a passage from your favorite author, Abraham Maslow, about professors who embarrass students."

The bell rang, as I had anticipated it would, and he was, he thought, saved by the bell. Actually I was, because there wasn't any such passage.

After class I waved the book under his nose. "You go after my cousin once more, you miserable son of a bitch, and I'll buy twenty copies of this book and distribute them to the class."

He left her alone. Later on I couldn't protect her from him.

61
BLACKIE

There was a time in that summer of 1966 when I felt sorry for Ed Carny.

He was forty years old and had been a priest for sixteen years. They had taken his school away from him, then his parish, then his community organization. He was reduced to being an assistant at a parish the order ran in the *barrio* and to working with knife-carrying teenagers. His hair was already turning white and the lines in his face were deepening. He still had his affluent friends on the South Side and was still adored by Irish women from eight to eighty. But his order treated him with open contempt.

And he did not deserve it. He was good at what he did, indeed one of the best. The order was not turned off by his male-locker-room piety and cheer, as I was; they were turned off by his success.

He was severely criticized for marching at Selma, and I suspect the favorable publicity he received in the national press for that action was the reason they took his parish away from him.

Then the Council came along and we were plunged into the black hole. They took away even his locker-room piety.

A lot of men his age quit, some to marry, some to remain in the priesthood but to ignore everything that was happening and work as little as possible.

Ed tried to update himself—worse luck for us as it turned out. He came to the Institute, as he himself put it, "to see if the old brain can be retooled."

But there was no way that a man with the following he had in Chicago could have been a simple student in summer school, even if he wanted to, and after a few days of adoration from the younger people present, I don't think he wanted to. So he became a kind of junior assistant scoutmaster in charge of emotional problems. And they were epidemic, perhaps because the most mixed-up people were the ones who wanted to attend the Summer Institute and get control of the black hole.

Ed had no qualifications to practice therapy, but he was great at the "get back in there and fight" line of exhortation. Behavior mod, I think they call it now.

And for some people, perhaps, it worked.

Cathy followed him around with the same adoring eyes with which the other men followed her around.

And Ed was constantly attentive to her.

Much to my dismay.

He also discovered Marxism.

Our seminar on Marx and Freud was in its own way the most spectacular of the freak shows. The leaders were a graduate student from a Canadian University and a Latin American theologian, the forerunner of the plague of Marxist theologians who would descend upon us in the seventies. The Canadian was a mousy little man with a drooping mustache who wanted to talk about symbolism in Freud and Jung. He had read them both. The Latin American was a bald scarecrow who wanted to talk about United Fruit, Anaconda, and Standard Oil and had never read Marx. Most of the group wanted to talk about sex, naturally enough, and the implications of Marx and Freud for clerical celibacy, a subject to which the two prophets had never turned their attention.

Ed Carny wanted to talk about power. He was the only one in the seminar, besides myself, who'd actually read Marx. The students at the Institute were not given much to reading. Ed, however, went home to his rectory and struggled through the pages of *Das Kapital*. (I had read both the prophets in high school, at considerable peril to my salvation, I was told.)

Ed understood enough of Marx to know about contradictions and the power that comes from exploiting contradictions.

"The leader who grasps the direction of the historical process that emerges from the dialectic of contradictions will be able to shape that process," he said very slowly one day, as though he had the key to something important. "So a priest who understands the dialectic in his community, who has a feel for the struggle between the contradictions, will be able to control the direction of emerging new order."

"That's brilliant, Father Ed," Cathy said kindly, trying to cheer her suffering hero.

"He becomes the leader in the class struggle," bellowed the theologian, "the way the church in Latin America must lead the class struggle against the multinationals and American imperialism."

"I don't think that's quite what Marx meant, Ed," I said. "The leader is more shaped by the process than shaping."

Ed nodded, not understanding what I had meant.

"Why do you think you understand Marx?" sneered the Latin American.

"His mother was a Communist for five years," Cathy observed proudly, defending another hero and a heroine too.

"Why was she a Communist?" Ed asked, as if he saw me for the first time, still not quite remembering who I was, much less that I had gone to his high school for four years.

"Because she wanted to help the poor," I replied.

"Interesting . . . interesting," he observed thoughtfully. "And why did she leave the Party?" the theologian eyed me suspiciously.

"The Hitler-Stalin pact made her face the historical lesson that Marxism never helps the poor."

We went off on another tirade, interrupted only once by the Canadian, who suggested that history had both a male and female component, both a dialectic and organic dynamic, both a conflictual and co-operative element.

He was absolutely right but much too sophisticated for those simpleminded days.

How could the childish nonsense of the Summer Institute be taken seriously? Especially by an intelligent young woman like my cousin?

Most priests and nuns are not very well educated. They are not trained in disciplined intelligence, careful reflection, precise expression and respect for the gray, complex nature of reality. Indeed, such qualities are thought to be unnecessary for virtue if not a serious obstacle to it. Take your typical priest or nun activist on television: Is he faced with a complex and painful social or human problem? He will respond with deep concern and great sincerity and a simple answer. The Vietnam war, for example, was the result of the multinationals' search for oil. Is she asked whether there might be another side to the question? Is it possible that there was a sincere desire on the part of American leadership to preserve a regime which for all its faults was better than what was to come afterward? She will repeat the same simple answer with greater sincerity and deeper concern. Is he quizzed on a subtle aspect of the situation? Might not the Khmer Rouge kill a lot of Cambodians, for example? The activist will change the response slightly and assert that we killed innocent Cambodian children with napalm. And when the Khmer Rouge killed a couple of million people, the activist was concerned about something else.

You ever hear the Berrigans talk about the Khmer Rouge genocide in Cambodia?

If pretty brown eyes filling with tears could have eliminated all the injustice in Latin America, my cousin would have done it three times over. But she was incapable of careful investigation of the historical and economic ramifications of such injustice and of serious thought about the implications of such an investigation. No one—besides Nick and myself—ever suggested to her that such investigation and thought were at all necessary and most of the people around her were convinced that investigation and thought were an escape from responsibility.

Some damn-fool Jesuits founded a nutcake house called the Center for Concern about that time. Concern was what was needed, you see, not competence or intelligence.

Cathy had enough concern for thirty such centers. She began to think only when it was too late. But typically she proved herself a clear thinker when she finally got around to it.

In those days we were not the only ones merchandising horse manure. On most college campuses, faculty members were insisting not only that they could learn morality from their students—an improbable but at least not totally irrational position—they were also contending that the students knew more about their own disciplines than the faculty did—a position which was utter lunacy.

We did our part to produce the Catherine Collinses and the Ed Carnys, but we had a hell of a lot of help.

Ed's reaction chilled me. He was working out the idea like a dog with a bone or a rat in a maze. It would take him time to translate it into his own terms. That day Ed found a substitute for his locker-room piety. He saw the wave of history and decided to climb on it. He had become a liberation theologian before the name.

I thought, in a tragic misreading of the future, that we would have little trouble keeping Cathy off that wave. That summer she would not even join the forty or so students who participated in a peace march.

Ed led them.

62
BLACKIE

"Of course I still love her," Nick said to me. "How could I not still love her?"

We were sipping beer on the porch at Grand Beach and watching the fireflies. It was 1966. Pat and I had dragged him off for a weekend at the lake, away from his law books and his witch of a mother (whose moaning about Nick's not working while he studied for the bar exam would have driven most people to murder). That Friday night Pat and a date and all the rest of the various Ryans were scattered about. My sister Eileen, she of the green eyes and the lovely voice (who was a law school classmate of Nick), and her husband, Red Kane the reporter, had not yet arrived at the Beach.

I had finally been cajoled into playing the go-between. "All she wants to know is whether you're angry at her. She feels she handled the leave-taking badly."

"Of course I'm not angry," he sputtered above his beer can. "She was in a terrible bind. And I was dumb. God, Blackie, I was so insensitive. I can't believe that I missed so much. . . . "

"She also hopes," I went on implacably with my message, "that someday it will be possible for you to be friends."

"I don't see why not," he said.

"Indeed. And the third point is that she hopes you will not wait for her to come out. She intends to stay."

"Isn't that my problem?" he snapped, showing a little of the anger that obsessed him when the subject was Cath.

"One for which she feels some responsibility."

"How long before she can't come out?"

"She's on a one-year temporary vow now. She'll renew it for three years next month. Then in August of '69 she will take solemn and perpetual vows."

Perpetual sounds like a long time. As it would soon turn out, it was a word that meant absolutely nothing.

"I can wait till then," he said grimly. "I probably wouldn't marry before that anyway. I'm not putting pressure on her, am I, by saying I'll wait that long?"

"Not unreasonable pressure."

He rose from his chair and paced the porch. The old timbers moaned softly beneath him.

"What do you think, Blackie?"

"Before the Council I think she would have stayed and been unhappy. Now it's all murky."

"I don't suppose I should do anything." He stared out at the placid lake, like a man waiting for a ship.

"That's up to you."

My cousin was edging toward zealotry. She had all the words—maturity, relevance, honesty, openness, trust, freedom, truth, multinationals, imperialism, greed, peace, justice. She used them readily and confidently, but they had not yet possessed her. In the journey from Mother David Mark to the Summer Institute, they were the *lingua franca* that made passage possible. They were not quite yet a new faith. They had not yet blazed out on her brain a road map for the rest of life.

On the contrary, she had a headache every night in the car going back to Jefferson Park. And she was buying cigarettes now, not borrowing them anymore.

The ideas were rushing around in her head like ice cream in a milk shake machine—and they had about as much constancy and substance. The dummies at the Institute were facile with the words because they didn't know what they meant. Cathy was smart, so she had to understand them. Immediately, of course. At once, if not before. Totally, if not perfectly.

Hence much anxiety and confusion. And many headaches.

She was still sufficiently wobbly that Nick might be able to sweep her off her feet.

"What's with her parents?" he demanded, letting his anger attack them, which was proper.

"Mad as ever. Her father hasn't changed the will much. A quarter million on her twenty-first birthday, which was in June, and the rest on their death, or when she's thirty-five, all tied up in neat trust funds. The only additional proviso is that she receives nothing so long as she is a nun—in which case, when she reaches thirty-five it all reverts to a list of rather unusual charities, most dealing with the protection of nonhuman animals. I could name them for you."

"Don't bother. She's fighting them too?"

"Perhaps not altogether consciously. Their position is that they simply have no daughter as long as she is a nun. And her implicit position is that she won't be browbeaten into submission by their withholding love. They never gave her much to begin with, so there is not much to withhold now."

"Where's she going next year?"

"Careyville, Illinois, to teach seventh grade."

"Where the hell is Careyville?"

"Just over the border into the nineteenth century."

"Maybe she ought to have a year under her belt, find out what it's really like to teach in a parish. It will be a lot different from a college environment."

"Certainly."

"Can you get out of these three-year vows at the end of one year?"

"It's not very difficult anymore."

In a short time you could get out of perpetual vows with a snap of a finger. So much for perpetuity.

"OK, I'll wait till next summer. . . . " He turned away from the lake and faced me. "Does that sound like a good idea, Blackie?"

"It does," I said.

And it did. Then.

"Don't tell her I said that."

I think that night we sealed her doom.

<u>63</u>
BLACKIE

I stopped the family Jaguar in front of her convent on the North Side. The Institute had just ended and she had been explaining to me with considerable excitement her lesson plans for an entirely different kind of seventh-grade religion course, combining Gabriel Moran's theory of extracting values from the young people themselves and the salvation-history theme.

It was gibberish, of course. Salvation history refers to the notion that there is a history of God's dealing with his people, beginning with creation and leading up to the present, and that you teach religion by concentrating on the major events in that history and showing their connections and similarities. Just the sort of notion that sounds breathtaking when spoken in French at a European institute. Needless to say, it will not play in Peoria. Or Careyville. Or Chicago. Or anywhere else, as far as that goes. Both words are guaranteed to turn off a classroom.

If one were to talk about God's love affair, one would say the same thing with much better audience appeal. But that is neither here nor there. I was sure Cathy's plan would be a huge success, because the seventh-graders in Careyville would fall in love with her if they were boys and identify with her if they were girls.

"And Nick?" she asked, changing the subject without warning.

I relayed his response. No, he was not angry at her. Yes, he thought they could be friends someday. And no, he would not stop waiting for her until after she had taken her perpetual vows.

"That's not fair," she said, with considerable acerbity.

"I beg pardon, Coz? I think it is fair. He is well within his rights in demanding that kind of proof from you, proof that you will persevere in your present plans."

"With God's grace I firmly intend to persevere," she said, falling back on the old piety.

"I told him you would say something like that. I don't think he will change his mind, Coz. Best to leave it that way."

"You don't think I have the guts to persevere," she said hotly.

I lit the cigarette with which she was fumbling, using the dashboard lighter.

"I think you have the will and/or the stubbornness to do anything you want." I put the lighter back into its plug, reaching for the right words. "The issue is one of mind, not of will, of deciding what is best for you. Once that decision is made, you surely have the willpower to follow it."

"The question is what is best for God," she insisted.

"What's best for you is best for God, Coz. You know that."

"I've already made up my mind." She snuffed out the cigarette after one puff.

"Even the Community does not think you have enough experience yet to make that an irrevocable decision. If they suspend judgment, why shouldn't Nick? Or any of us?"

"I suppose." Some of the stiffness went out of her shoulders, but not much.

"You've survived the novitiate. There can be no question of your fortitude. Now the operative virtue is prudence."

"A virtue for the immature," she said, quoting Roy Tuohy.

"To do the right thing at the right time?" I said mildly. "It seems that is the virtue of the very mature."

She leaned her head wearily on my shoulder. "You don't think much of us, do you, Coz?"

"I think it's too much too soon. We can't replace a culture that's at least five hundred years old in a few months. We have to proceed slowly, give it time, resist the temptation for the quick fix, the overnight update, the easy solution."

"We don't have enough time for that, Blackie."

She kissed me good night, the first time that summer.

So we finished the Institute. Cathy went off to some lake for a week of smoking and drinking and nonstop talking with a group of nuns. And I withdrew to the sane disorder of La Maison Ryan to sample my step-mother's raspberry preserves.

Cathy celebrated her subsequent weekend with us in a chain reaction of laughter and joy. She seemed relaxed and well. I worried a little less. Thereafter she went back to the Hill to take her three-year vows and then sallied forth cheerfully to her mission at St. Alphonsus Liguori Parish in Careyville, Illinois, with all the innocence of a first communicant embarking on a one-person exploration of the Gobi Desert when Genghis Khan and his horde were on the rampage.

August 25, 1966
Careyville

Dear Blackie,

This is the most wonderful place, a small town in the middle of the best farmland in the world. I've spent all my life in artificial settings—cities, summer resorts and college communities. I feel that out here I am close to the land, close to the people and close to God. In this small town with people whose roots are deep in the past and whose lives are linked to the processes of nature, I will live the way God intended us to live.

The convent is really two houses that were built right after the Civil War, with connecting passages on all three floors; it is sort of rickety and crowded. Some of the hallways and staircases don't lead anywhere and it could stand a good coat of paint both outside and in (the rectory was redecorated last year, but Sister says there is not enough money this year to paint the convent). I half expect to see a rundown ghost at the corner of a shaky old staircase, and there isn't much privacy. But the place is charming in its own way, an eccentric dowager whom you can't help liking because she's so cute.

The seventh-graders were on hand to help me unload my things and took me to the classroom. They are shy and gentle children, not hellions like we were at their age. They'll be wonderful students for my new religious-education lesson plan.

We're only two hours from Chicago, yet it is a completely different world—slower, more relaxed, more leisurely. It may be a little dull at times, but after the last three years I think a little dullness will be a good thing for me.

This is my first big challenge in the world outside, my first grown-up responsibility. I must meet the challenge as well as I can. I know that I'm young and inexperienced and will make stupid mistakes. I don't mind that. But I don't want to hurt anyone here because of my inexperience.

Pray hard that I do well, not perfectly but at least okay.

The terrible war goes on. There is a funeral Mass here next week for a boy from the town who was killed in Vietnam. But no one seems to have turned against the war yet.

I hope you have a good year at the seminary and learn all kinds of theology which will help you be a great priest.

God love you,
Cathy

65
CATHERINE

Labor Day Sunday
Careyville

Dear Blackie,

I met the two priests today and I have to admit that they kind of scare me. The pastor makes us count the money after Mass on Sundays. That really doesn't seem to be fair. We do it for nothing too. He says it's part of our parish responsibilities. The sisters don't like it, but Sister Martina Mary, our superior, says that Msgr. Wagner is an important man in the diocese and we must keep him happy if we do not want to offend the bishop.

We're cheap labor, American coolies, but I'm new and young and I don't want to start out on the wrong foot.

The monsignor is a huge man, in every direction. He can't be more than fifty, but he looks much older because he is bald and very fat, a kind of red-faced Humpty Dumpty. He must be six and a half feet tall and I would be surprised if he weighs less than 300 pounds.

His curate, Father Tierney, is in his middle thirties and has long, kind of ragged brown hair and hard, bloodshot eyes. He always seems to need a shave and speaks with a whine. I think he drinks too much.

I tried to be quiet and self-effacing, like a good young
religious. The monsignor does most of the talking. He lectures
us on the problems of the church and the parish and the
school. We nod our heads in agreement. Monsignor doesn't like
Father Hans Kung at all, although I don't think he's read the
books. And he denounces all the new scripture scholars, even
that divine Father Roland Murphy. How can anyone dislike
him?

He tells crude stories and we laugh. I bite my tongue and say
that he is the old church and I must not judge him by my new
standards. I even laugh sometimes, though they are not very
funny stories.

But, Blackie, he pretends that I don't exist. Sister Superior
didn't introduce me. I'll have to ask her why she didn't and
request she do it next time.

And I wish that Father Tierney would pretend I don't exist.
He asked me embarrassing questions about the Institute, kind
of hinting that everyone was sleeping with everyone else and
made derogatory remarks about what we learned there. He
looks at me in the most awful way. I suppose "leer" would be
an apt word for it.

I'm too sensitive, I guess. Father obviously has a drinking
problem and I should be charitable to him. But he makes me
feel like a whore.

I find it hard not to speak up when both of them ridicule the
changes. Monsignor assures us that the liturgy will be back in
Latin before Christmas. The bishop, who is about seventy-five,
heard that for certain from a friend who works in the Curia.
And then the pope will convene another council to undo all the
harm that has been done by the last one. Monsignor says that
this is absolutely certain.

You don't think this could happen, do you, Blackie? Sister
Martina Mary, who is on the council of the order and was a
delegate to the chapter, said afterward that she had heard the
same thing from her father, who is a Knight of Malta and a big
contributor to the church in their home city. Rome may even
order us to revoke the chapter and return to all the old forms.
She says that we would have no choice but to be good religious
and accept such a decision.

I don't know whether I could. Or even whether I should.

Pray, Blackie, that it doesn't happen. And pray that I am able to behave maturely on this first mission. I don't want to make trouble, but I won't be a patsy, either.

Love,
Cathy

66
CATHERINE

November 1
Careyville

Dear Blackie,

I hate it here, hate it, hate it.

I hate the nuns and the priests and the people. I hate everyone. Except the kids, of course. They're so nice.

You should see me with them, Blackie. You'd be amazed at how stern a disciplinarian I am. Steel-eyed, rock-jawed, Wyatt Earp-voiced Sister Catherine. They quiver in their boots. I merely raise an eyebrow and there's dead silence.

But they love me and I love them and we have a wonderful time. The classroom is an escape from everything else, even if I had to abandon my lesson plan and use the Baltimore Catechism.

There are only two kids in the class with whom I don't get along, both girls, both early developers, and both little whores if you ask me. Unfortunately, their fathers are poker-playing cronies of the pastor.

One of the girls told me, "We're going to get you, Sister Catherine. You just wait."

And they did. I was forbidden to teach anything but what is in the catechism, which was written in 1885. The bishop himself called Martina Mary with the order and she was furious with me. The problem is that I told them that the book of Genesis teaches religious truth and not necessarily literal history.

"The next thing you'll be teaching is evolution," she yelled at me.

"But, Sister, there are forms of evolution which Catholics can accept."

"Not in this school, there aren't."

She's not an old woman at all—in her early thirties, I think. She's the second youngest in the convent. All the others are over forty-five. But, Blackie, she's ugly as sin and sour and angry all the time. She's skinny and small and has hateful green eyes. When she's "incensed" (her word) at someone, she looks like a teenager playing the Wicked Witch of the West in a spur-of-the-moment Halloween sketch.

She was runner up to John Jerome in the election of our new president. She has a degree in theology from Catholic U and knows a lot about it, more than I do. And she's not against the changes. She thinks that we're moving too fast, and not listening to the experts. Sort of what you say, but she doesn't mean the same thing. Because by "expert" she means herself. I know that's uncharitable. But it's true.

Her family is extremely rich and she is always receiving gifts from them. I've heard the other sisters say that her bed is custom-made and that her underwear is elaborate and expensive.

Isn't that a terrible thing to gossip about?

So she's used to having her own way and sort of spoiled and she doesn't like me at all. And I don't like her, either.

"Those words, Sister," I said, "are taken directly from the 'Document on Revelation' of the Council."

"The Council is going to be revoked," she snapped.

"You can't revoke an Ecumenical Council," I said, trying to be calm and knowing I was right.

"You will not quote that document in a class in my school. I command you under Holy Obedience not to."

"You can't forbid me to quote from a conciliar decree," I stormed back at her. "Let's call Mother John Jerome and ask her."

Well, I won and lost. Johnny is in a tough position. After all, Martina Mary is the leader of the opposition on the council. But why did they send me, of all people, here?

I can, of course, quote conciliar documents. But I must teach the Baltimore Catechism in class, since classroom material is under her jurisdiction.

"All right," I shouted at Johnny. "I'll teach the catechism and I'll quote all the conciliar documents whenever they're relevant. I'll show the children how the church has changed."

Martina Mary was fit to be tied.

Because I had really won. And it runs in the genes, Blackwood—I love winning.

The kids didn't mind. I could be teaching from the New Testament in Greek and they wouldn't mind. I had to stop them from making life miserable for the two little whores. And then the latter came and apologized and thanked me for calling off the tigers.

So I'm friends with them now. I remember when I was a seventh-grade whore, so it's kind of easy.

I used to be embarrassed when kids swarmed all over me at the lake. Now I'm kind of glad they like me.

It wasn't the first fight I had with Martina Mary. The day before school started she commanded me to return to the old habit. I'm the only one here wearing the airline hostess thing. If I were as mean and ugly as Martina Mary I wouldn't wear it, either.

She said it was the will of the pastor that all sisters in his school wear traditional religious garb. The bishop has also mandated traditional dress for all the nuns in the diocese.

I know that at a lot of other convents the sisters don't pay any attention to the bishop.

"The chapter gave us the right to make our own decision, Sister," I said, kind of timidly, because I was new and I wasn't sure yet that she hated me.

"The chapter will be ordered to revoke that decision."

"Until it does, I'll wear the new habit." I was quiet and prim and very respectful.

Oh, hell, Blackwood. I was not. I was already spoiling for a fight.

"In this convent you'll do what I tell you," she says, going into her wicked-witch act.

"Only when the chapter or the council orders me to. Let's call the president and settle it now before school starts."

She didn't want to do that, because she knew that Johnny

would support me. But I insisted and I won. And she has never forgiven me and never will.

I lost that battle too, in a way. None of the sisters will talk to me, except when it's absolutely necessary. They talk about me at recreation like I was a puppy dog or an infant. But they won't talk to me. And Martina Mary says that they will not speak to me until I put the Holy Habit back on.

Take a typical recreation period after supper. We're sitting around darning socks or repairing clothes, the kind of things sisters do in recreation periods.

First Harpy: You'd think she'd have the decency to cover her legs.

Second Harpy: She has no shame. Showing off her body, and for seventh-grade boys.

First Harpy: No modesty, no sense. What do they teach them at the novitiate nowadays?

Second Harpy (giggling): Salvation history. Salvation through naked legs.

First Harpy: She won't last. She'll singularize herself out of the order.

Second Harpy: Couldn't do it soon enough to suit me.

Me (sobbing): You evil old women should never have been nuns in the first place. I hope that when I'm your age, I'm not a mean, hateful, envious bitch.

Exit Cathy in tears while the harpies cackle.

I know I shouldn't act that way. It doesn't help. But, do you know something, Blackie? I'm beginning to enjoy giving it back to them.

There were stories in the novitiate about houses where everyone was hateful. I didn't expect it to be like this. It's so small and petty and mean. Did we take vows of poverty and chastity and obedience merely to be nasty to one another?

I tried my best, but I couldn't compromise on principles, could I?

Well, I lasted through the novitiate and I guess I can last through a year here. But it will be only one year. And I won't leave any doubt in Johnny's mind about that.

Pray, Blackie, that I be patient and mature. It's so hard. And it's so silly.

Love,
Cathy

67
CATHERINE

December 6, 1966
Careyville

Dear Blackie,

Isn't the war ever going to end? I feel guilty that I'm not doing anything to stop it. But I'm so involved in my own little war here that I hardly have time to think about Vietnam.

Everything I do leads to a battle with Martina Mary. The last fight was about O antiphon posters (you know, the antiphon's a vespers the week before Christmas) which the kids made about Vietnam. Monsignor ordered them torn down. I refused. He came in at night and tore them down himself. I put them up the next day. Martina Mary called the Mother House this time.

"It ought not to be such a major issue, Catherine," Johnny says to me. "Surely you are flexible enough to adjust to the local situation."

"I will not have pro-Communist propaganda in my classrooms," Martina raged at her.

"It's not pro-Communist," I shout back. "And it's my classroom."

Johnny sighs. "Catherine, as a favor to me . . . "

"No, Mother. Not unless you order me to."

"I would certainly like it, Catherine, if you'd try to make a peaceful accommodation."

Then, Blackie, I blew up and said the most terrible things.

"You ought to be ashamed of yourself, Johnny. You ought not to compromise with evil. This is a shitty convent, filled with spiteful old women. The superior is a spoiled brat and you know it. If you were any kind of a leader you'd break it up tomorrow. It's a disgrace to the order. How do you expect to recruit any vocations if you let a bitch like her persecute young sisters?"

Martina sputters on the other phone.

Johnny doesn't say a word at first. Then she says, very quietly, "If you request a transfer, Catherine, I'm sure we could arrange it."

"Arrange nothing, goddamnit. I'm staying at my first mission to the bitter end. If you want me out of here you will have to transfer me."

"See how undocile she is?" Martina says, getting her tongue in gear.

"Why the fuck did you send me here in the first place? You knew she was a bitch and the others evil harpies!"

That's the first time in all my life I used that word. I didn't even really know it was in my vocabulary.

"Catherine," says John, utterly shocked.

I'm sobbing by now. "Are you afraid of her father's money and her father's friends?"

"That will do, Catherine. You're overwrought."

"Goddamn right I'm overwrought."

"Sister," she says to Martina, "I think we can leave the O antiphon posters up."

"Yes, Mother," she says triumphantly.

She'd won, you see, Blackie. She'd forced me to make an ass out of myself to the president.

But I've won too, because I've been honest and truthful to the president.

And she damn well better get used to hearing the truth.

Father Tierney worries me. Whenever he sees me, he whistles the old wolf call. I usually turn red and flustered.

"Don't pay any attention to him, Sister," says one of the ex-whores the other day in the schoolyard when he does it. "He's just a drunken bum. Everyone knows it."

I'm still sufficiently nunny to have a pious reply. "Don't talk that way about him, Jean. He's a priest and we should be respectful."

"A poor excuse for a priest."

The ex-whores are now virtuous virgins, going to Mass every morning and asking about how they can be nuns.

They have a crush on "Sister," which is all right, I guess. God knows I had them, though I wouldn't have used the word. I don't think their adoration will turn my head, not as long as I have to live with the harpies.

But how many girls will want to be nuns when they have memories of their seventh-grade teacher being humiliated by men like Father Tierney?

I examine my conscience, I really do, Blackie, to see what I am doing wrong. Should I sacrifice principle to get along? Or should I continue to be open and honest?

I don't know. Pray for me, please, that I may find the grace to be mature.

Sorrowfully,
Cathy

<u>68</u>
CATHERINE

January 6, 1967

Dear Blackie,

The last Christmas without a Christmas vacation. I could have used a few days away from here this year. But I'm surviving.

I don't know where I will go for Christmas next year. My parents certainly won't want me. And I hate to intrude on the Ryans and the Murphys all the time.

We were permitted to call home the Sunday after Christmas for three minutes (Martina talked to her father for half an hour). I took a deep breath, said a prayer, and called Mom and Dad. They hung up as soon as they found out who it was.

I should have expected it, but it still hurt.

Johnny put a personal note in her Christmas card which made me cry.

Dear Cathy,

If I was slow in responding to your angry words in our last phone conversation, the reason is that I feel very guilty. Your words and your anger are both justified. You ought never have been sent to St. Alphonsus Liguori. I hope you will accept my apology. And maybe even forgive me.

You're an extremely valuable member of the community. Some think that eventually you will sit in my chair, a mission I would not wish on my worst enemy.

By way of explanation, I can only say that we have paid very little attention to personnel matters. We have sent people to fill vacancies, without any concern for either the shape of the peg or the shape of the hole. This is a violation of charity and justice, and I'm sure Mother Claire would have been equally fiery if she knew we were doing it (I don't think she would have used your language, though her unexpurgated letters in our archives are occasionally quite salty). We are trying to establish a new personnel policy, emphasizing freedom of choice, but there are so many things to do and so little time. I can assure you that never again will you experience what is happening now.

I hope this reestablishes your faith in us and your affection for me.

In Our Lord,
Johnny

Well, Blackie, I sobbed and sobbed and sobbed. Such a nice lady. And I fired off a letter of gratitude and apology for my "salty" language.

Okay. BUT . . .

BUT what?

But why were we ever treated like cogs in a machine? And can they really stop? Are John Jerome and her allies strong enough to take the community away from people like Martina and will there be anything left when they do?

Oh, yes. I had it out with Father Tierney. Spectacularly. Not since Ado Annie have I put on such a show. I am ashamed of myself but not really.

It was at the parish Christmas party, a wonderful local custom. On the Feast of the Holy Innocents the parish has a party to which everyone is invited. They pay, of course, and Monsignor Wagner, the fat old slob, makes money out of it. But the people love it. This would be such a wonderful community if it had the right kind of leadership. Even as it is, the people kind of save the parish from the priests and nuns.

Most of them are not like Monsignor's poker partners. The parents of my kids are very nice to me. And I'm careful to spend more time with the women than with the men. Old prudent Cathy finally learning about sex.

So at the Christmas party I'm talking to some of the mothers of my kids—telling them about the chapter reforms—and sipping punch (I've already had two dishes of chocolate ice cream). Father Tierney walks by and makes with the wolf whistle. Some of the matrons are pretty cute too (note the proud "too"), but we all know who is the object.

So, quite calmly and deliberately, I give my red and green paper cup, half filled with punch, to a handy matron, walk across the room and slap his stupid face—hard.

My mothers applauded.

He cried, poor man, and left the party.

Monsignor saw what I did, but since he pretends, like my parents, that I don't exist, he could hardly take official note.

Martina says I've been excommunicated for striking a priest. I told her she was full of shit, that I was acting in self-defense.

I don't know, Blackie. I don't know. If I don't get out of here soon, I may end up an intolerable bitch.

Oh, I'll survive, but pray for me, please.

Lots of love,
Bitchy Cathy

<u>69</u>
CATHERINE

January 19, 1967
Careyville

Dear Blackie,

I'm scared.

Father Tierney tried to rape me last night. At least, that's what I think he had in mind. He was so drunk I can't be sure.

I had just finished correcting exams in my classroom—I simply skip evening recreation now. I packed up my briefcase and turned off the light in the classroom. I was feeling pretty good because my seventh-graders had done very well on the standardized tests, especially in math, so the community didn't waste its money on my math education.

I opened the door and stepped into the corridor, reaching along the wall for the corridor light switch.

I felt this terrible hand, cold and clammy, clutch mine, almost like a claw. I screamed but the walls of the school are so thick you couldn't hear a bomb explode—German monsignors build solid schools.

Then his arms closed around me like a vise. I smelled his vile breath and knew who it was. I was terrified. He's not a weak man. His mouth closed over my lips and he began to paw me. I felt sick and dirty and ugly, but I was too afraid to fight back. A voice in the back of my brain kept screaming, fight, fight, fight. But my muscles and nerves didn't seem to hear it.

He mumbled dirty words and then attacked my mouth again. I tried to push him away, but that only made him more determined. He pulled off the buttons on my blouse, and one of his claws squeezed my breast like it was a sponge soaked with water. The pain was terrible, but it broke the barrier between my brain and my muscles. I gave him the same treatment that I gave the bald medical student from Columbia, only even harder. The Columbia guy never hurt me.

He fell on the floor, screaming in agony.

And then—I'm almost ashamed to tell you this, Coz. And I'll never tell anyone else—I stood over him and said, "If you ever try that again, I won't just knee your balls, I'll cut them off."

Then, buttoning up my coat so no one would see my torn blouse, I went back to the convent.

Only when I was in my own room did I fall apart and sob hysterically. And there was no one to talk to. I couldn't talk to the sisters because they don't talk to me. And I couldn't call Mary Kate—my first thought—because Martina would eavesdrop. And if she found out, she'd blame me, I'm sure, for leading him on with my naked legs.

So I'll have to survive somehow. I almost fell apart at Mass when he put the host on my tongue. But I'm better now.

He didn't seem at all troubled by me at the altar rail. The poor man was probably so drunk that he doesn't remember what he did.

He's unhappy, Blackie, and he needs help. But, as much as I feel sorry for him, I am afraid for me.

And my breast is still sore. It will hurt for several more days.

What does he see in me that leads him to think I would want to make love with him? Maybe in a way it is my fault.

And I have to say this for the good old Holy Habit: Rapists have a lot more to fight their way through than they do now.

Maybe I should ask one of my friendly mothers if I can use their phone and call Johnny. I'm ready to get out of here now.

I want to run and run and run.

And I feel ugly and filthy.

I always end up, it seems, begging for prayers. Father Tuohy would say that shows an immature dependency relationship on God.

Right now I feel very immature and dependent.

> Love you,
> Cathy

70
CATHERINE

> January 24, 1967
> Careyville

Dear Blackie,

I'm much better now. Should I say, "thanks to you"? I haven't heard directly from you, but maybe I've heard indirectly.

Father Tierney is gone. The rectory cook told our cook that the bishop sent him to a hospital. That's where he belongs.

And I went right to the chapel and thanked God for helping me. Then I thought maybe I ought to thank a lot of other people. I remembered that Mary Kate went to school with Nora Reilly, who is now married to the brother of Monsignor

Cronin, the man who introduced me to the pope a thousand years ago. Monsignor Cronin is the cardinal's right-hand man, isn't he? It would take only six phone calls to send Father Tierney to the hospital. If my guess is right, thanks to all. I really mean it.

But, I ask myself, what if I were not a Chicagoan with clout?

I'm a young woman who has spent four years in a convent, in a small town without any friends, and with no access to outside help. I guess I have to admit that I'm naive and even innocent. But what do I do? And what if the man isn't drunk and is so much stronger than me that I can't bury my knee in his groin?

I could always run to the mother of one of my kids, but that would certainly create a parish scandal. I would have done it if I'd had to. But I don't think every young nun my age would have that kind of nerve.

Do men feel because they're a little stronger than us they can do anything they want to us? What a hellish thing it must have been to be a woman for most of our history. And even today there is a part of Father Tierney's personality, a demon maybe, which escapes when he is drunk, which thinks he can use me for his pleasure whether I want to or not.

That makes me very angry.

God, I'll be happy to get out of this hellhole.

Pray that I make it.

Love,
Cath

71
BLACKIE

I did not attend the Summer Institute in 1967, the summer of *Blow Up* and *Bonnie and Clyde*. Msgr. Cronin had other plans for me. And Mary Kate observed tartly that we ought to give Cathy a chance to take care of herself.

"She did rather well, all things considered, in Careyville, didn't she? Even knew when to call for help. And I bet she thought about that chain of phone calls before she wrote you."

My sibling, I'm sure, was correct on both counts.

I visited Cathy in her Jefferson Park convent before the Institute began. The light in her eyes had hardened. Now it was not only enthusiastic but angry, a hard, simmering glow. And her body was so rigid that you would expect it to break if anyone hit it a glancing blow.

Careyville was just what the program required if you wanted to produce a self-destructive zealot. She was not bitter yet. The glow in her was often replaced by the old laughing mischief. But bitterness was lurking like a virus ready to strike. Unless the community was careful, my cousin would be a tough, bitter zealot before she was thirty. One more bad experience would do it.

Mind you, she had plenty to be angry about. Careyville would have driven a less volatile personality to the brink of collapse. I was proud of the way Cathy had beaten back her enemies. She was a fighter and a survivor despite her innocence and fragility. I suppose most young women of her generation would have walked out of Careyville and the religious life under the circumstances.

I worried rather about the pattern of her life, a pattern that looked as if it were a design for self-destruction. Which it turned out to be.

I was at least confident that any horny priest who dared to be too fresh with her at the Institute would pay an adequate price for his audacity.

The Institute turned from "relevance" to "militancy" that year and from "renewing the church" to "identifying with the poor." And from talking about sexuality to doing something about it. The mass exodus had begun and the Institute crowd was leading the way.

I have often wondered how many passes Cathy had to fend off. At least it was not necessary for her to knee anyone in the groin.

Militancy was more important to her now than sex. There were demonstrations against the war and racism all summer. Ed organized them and Cathy marched in every one. The energies of Catholic enthusiasts, already partially frustrated by the church, and destined for more and far worse frustration the following summer, were turning away from the Institution and toward the rest of the world.

The causes, God knows, were good. The war was an abomination. But I feared that "doing something about the war" was more important than figuring out how one might best bring pressures to end it. Dan Berrigan was already condemning "politics" and demanding "liturgical gestures," a demand to which many were ready to respond. Some of them doubtless out of sound and healthy motives, and others because they were running from themselves and their own spiritual confusion.

As much as I loved her, I worried that Cathy, especially after the traumas of Careyville, might be numbered in the latter.

She was a spring of coiled tension at the end of the summer, when she came to spend a week with us at Grand Beach, though the years in the nunnery had harmed neither her figure nor her water-skiing skills. I opined that she was probably the first nun in history to water-ski in a bikini.

"And just let them try to report me," she said, lighting a cigarette as soon as she was inside the boat.

She was, however, happy with her assignment to a Hispanic parish in Chicago where her language skills would be useful. And by the time she left the madcap house of the Ryans she seemed a bit more at ease.

Collinses tended to be survivors. My mother had survived an interlude of manic zealotry in the thirties. But she had had my father.

"Does she remind you of anyone?" I asked him, as she strode fiercely out of the house late one evening for a walk on the beach.

He smiled. "Indeed she does. I was thinking the same thing."

"Mom was a survivor up to the end," I said.

"Collins women," he said, "are both fragile and tough. You can never tell what will happen to them. Until they die."

I never told him about my experience, which even questioned that proviso. Mary Kate wisely advised against it. As much as he loved Helen, he would always mourn for Katie Collins. As would we all.

As we now mourn for her niece, whose survival instincts, despite my hopefulness in the summer of 1967, were not quite so strong.

72
NICHOLAS

I knew who it was as soon as I saw the cigarette glowing in the dark. I had kidded myself that my few days of vacation with law school classmates at Michiana—across the creek from Grand Beach—were not timed with her visit to the Ryans. And I paid no attention to the throbbing in my temples when I saw her water-skiing from a distance.

And I needed the exercise that night—after thirty-six holes of golf at the Long Beach Country Club.

"Should you be smoking, Sister Catherine?" I asked, trying my best to sound playful.

She tossed the cigarette in the lake, a nun in short shorts alone on a beach, smoking a cigarette. It was, I supposed, an improvement.

"Nick!" She hugged me enthusiastically and briefly. She felt wonderful in my arms.

"Sorry if I scared you, Sister," I said, reminding myself that this was a consecrated virgin for whom I was so hungry.

"Drop the 'Sister' stuff." She laughed, a natural, happy laugh. "That was a postulant's mistaken zeal."

"Marching on a demonstration line is a mature religious's zeal?" I said, the most stupid sentence I had ever spoken.

She rose to the bait instantly. "Someone has to take a stand against napalming babies in the name of American imperialism."

"I often wonder why you protesters don't complain about the babies killed by the Viet Cong."

"I'm not Vietnamese," she replied tartly. "I'm American."

"And not responsible for the genocide that will occur if we turn the country over to the Communists?"

"I don't think that will happen."

"Then, like most demonstrators, you are ignorant of history. Thirty million peasants were killed in China after the revolution."

"A man who works for the National Council of Churches wrote an article saying that in the Great Proletarian Cultural Revolution, Chairman Mao is creating a new form of human nature which is more in keeping with the Gospel than is anything in modern Christianity."

"Do you really believe that bullshit?"

"Let's not fight, Nick."

"It seemed a good way to cover up my awkwardness."

We both laughed and the tension eased. I didn't like the war any more than she did, though I thought—and still do—that the protests would probably prolong it.

She took my hand, as she so often had before. "How are you?"

"Fine. Working hard at the U.S. attorney's office, learning the basics of trial practice the only way I can, in a courtroom."

"Happy?"

"More or less. Are you?"

"Usually."

"A rough year, from what the Ryans tell me."

"I survived. And learned. There is so much to be done."

"You'll be in Chicago next year?"

"Uh-huh. St. Retramnus."

"Do modern nuns occasionally have lunch with U.S. attorneys?"

"Sure do, especially when they need favors for their kids. I'll be working in a neighborhood with lots of street gangs—probably safer than Careyville at that."

"If I can help with any kid, don't hesitate to holler."

"You can count on it."

So we chatted and I walked with her to the steps of the Ryan house, far back from the water because the lake was so low that year.

She kissed my cheek and we said good night, both of us knowing that we would not be in touch with each other during the year.

Having read her letters, I now know that if I had carried her off that night, she would have come willingly.

Katie Collins had lived to bear children because she had Ed Ryan to help her. Catherine Collins died because she had Nick Curran to help her.

But we were both wrong on one count: We would meet each other again before twelve months were over.

In jail.

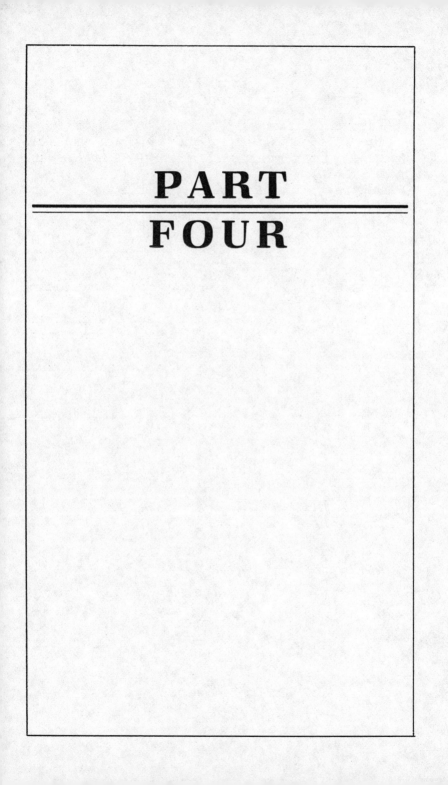

PART
FOUR

73
CATHERINE

September 16, 1967
St. Retramnus
Chicago

Dear Blackie,

You're back to the seminary for only two weeks and I miss you already. It was a good summer for me, both intellectually and spiritually, and the best part of all was my week with the Ryans. If I could spend the rest of my life as a sister with you guys, I'd have no problems at all.

And only three more years before you become Father Blackie. I can hardly wait. Are you counting the days? I am.

As for your flaky cousin, well, there's good news and bad news.

The bad news, first, to get it out of the way.

I went home the day before yesterday. I mean to my real home on Glenwood Drive. It was a typically impulsive Cathy trick. I drove the convent car out to 95th Street to have it serviced (for free, of course; there are still some advantages to being a nun). I was only two blocks away from home. I thought, What the hell, there's nothing to lose.

There was a lot to lose.

Mom answered the door. "Yes, Sister?" she said politely, with a big smile on her face, the wide-eyed, reverent one she reserves for priests and nuns.

"May I come in?"

"Certainly, Sister." Smile still in place.

It was only when I was inside that I realized she didn't recognize me.

"Sister Catherine, Mom."

For a fraction of a second her eyes lit up and she was almost ready to embrace me. I moved toward her and she stepped away. "We didn't know you were coming."

"I was in the neighborhood."

My father was sitting in the living room, reading—you guessed it—the *Wall Street Journal*.

They both were old, Blackie. They have become old persons in the four years since I saw them last. A twenty-two-year-old woman whose mother was almost forty when she was born ought not to be surprised that her parents are in their sixties.

But they looked older than that, brown and dried-up and breakable. In an instant I saw everything. They had counted on me for their old age and I had left them. But I didn't know they needed me and wanted me. They never said.

And now I could be home with them every weekend.

My father lowered the paper—his fingers were trembling, I think with age. His eyes glowed too and he came close to smiling. He stood up, the paper still in his hand. I thought he was coming toward me.

"Dad," I said, "I'm only twenty minutes away at the most now. I can come home for dinner every Sunday."

I think he took a step toward me. Then he turned and walked out of the room, a slow, discouraged, old man's walk, his *Wall Street Journal* clutched in his hand like a bent twig in the claw of an aging bird.

Mom started to cry. "You should never have come, Sister. Don't come again."

So I left, too numb, too stricken to weep.

They were both glad to see me, Blackie. I know they were. I think they were even proud of the way I look in my airline hostess habit (the sexy gray shift, as you call it, has been put away till next summer). They want me to come home for Sunday dinner. Nothing would make their last years happier.

I'm more sorry for them now than for me. I have survived all these years without them and am certainly not unhappy. I hate to say it, but I don't need them. They need me. I'm all they have and I could bring them joy.

They're trapped in their pride, not Davie Mark's pride, but real pride. They can't admit they made a mistake. They are not able to forgive me, even though they want to. And there's nothing I can do to help them. Enough. I hope I never let myself be trapped that way.

The good news is that St. Ret's is sensational. My first September letter has usually insisted that the new place is great. Then I have to take back my Pollyanna report. This year I waited till I was sure. It is as different from Careyville as night is from day. The convent was built before the Chicago fire and is impossible to keep clean. At the end of the day there is a layer of dust on everything. There's no air-conditioning system and the sisters tell me that the boiler is unreliable in the winter. The church hasn't had a coat of paint in ages. The school is dilapidated, the neighborhood dirty and dangerous. The teenagers are organized into gangs, and drugs are available on every street corner.

Why sensational? Because the priests and the sisters are a happy team, doing work they want to do. My seventh-graders in Careyville may have needed me a little, but for my seventh-graders here and the high school kids who come around in the evening, I am literally the difference between life and death. These people are God's own and I am privileged to serve them.

AND, they think I must be a Cuban because I speak Spanish so well. Maybe my dark skin helps. It's not so good to be a Cuban in a Mexican-American community, so I tell them very quickly that I'm plain old Irish.

I'll have to learn their accent so they won't make that mistake again.

I think I've finally found my place.

Happily,
Cathy

74
CATHERINE

November 4, 1967

Dear Blackie,

We had two funeral Masses this morning, two boys nineteen years old. One died in Vietnam, the other in a gang fight here in the neighborhood. I have been asking myself "Why?" all day long.

Father Ed preached at the Mass for the gang victim. He said that Luís was a victim of poverty caused by the American capitalistic system, which exploits the poor. And he remarked afterward to Father McMahon, our pastor, that one funeral was for a martyr to imperialism and the other for a martyr to capitalism. Father Mac, who is totally nonpolitical, laughed it off. He said one boy was killed by the Golden Kings and the other by a Russian-made rifle.

I don't understand enough about these things to know what to think. Why are these people so poor? We grew up in a neighborhood where street gangs existed only in *West Side Story*. Are we better human beings than these kids, boys killed in knife fights, girls pregnant at fifteen because they have been more or less raped? And why do they have to fight in Vietnam while we can escape by going to college or graduate school? Does God love us more than he loves them? Why am I rich while they are poor? Is my wealth the cause of their poverty?

I'm not sure, but I'm beginning to believe that Father Ed may be right. Maybe these people are poor because by keeping them poor we are able to be rich.

And if that is true, ought not the church do something about it?

Father Ed has been organizing peace demonstrations. His provincial made him stop and then backed off because there was so much support for Father Ed in the order. People are turning against the war. The Berrigans are challenging a lot of the rest of us to examine our consciences. I think the tide is changing in favor of Father Ed.

Which puts me on the spot. If he's right, then I'm wrong. I should be doing something about this hellish war too. If I don't work against the war, then am I not a cause of it? Am I not a war criminal as much as the president and the men around him?

Father Ed was sweet, as always, but he certainly gave me a lot to think about. "We must be on the cutting edge, Cath," he said. "Our vows give us the freedom and responsibility to do what others can't or won't do."

"But don't protests make a lot of people more sympathetic to the war? Don't they identify opposition to the war with radicals and hippies and haters of America?" I asked, repeating the arguments Nick used that night I saw him on the beach.

"Then that's on their consciences," he said. "They must answer to God for their consciences. We must answer for ours. How many more young men have to come home to St. Ret's in a coffin before you ask whether you're doing all you can to stop the killing?"

I can't picture myself on a picket line. Yet my uncle was killed in the Memorial Day massacre in 1937 and your mother was beaten by the police that same day. I remember that terrible scar she hid with her hair. Am I afraid to stand up for what I believe?

It's hard to know what to do. Should sisters demonstrate against the war? Many are doing so already. Does timidity prevent me from joining them?

Confused,
Cath

<u>75</u>
CATHERINE

December 6, 1967
Chicago

Dear Blackie,

The story in the *Sun Times* was terrible. The reporter misunderstood me, put words in my mouth, and twisted what I said.

I never said that the war was genocide. I'm not even sure what genocide is. And I didn't say that we were practicing nonviolence, like Gandhi. I have only the vaguest idea who Gandhi was and what he did. And I didn't mean that every sister ought to march in a protest against the war. I meant that I felt bound in conscience to do so. And all that silly stuff about my eyelashes and my dainty face and elegant hands. How irrelevant can you get?

I called Mother John Jerome as soon as I saw the story to try to explain. She wasn't angry with me, but she said that if I continued to follow my conscience on the war, there would be much opposition to me both in the community and out.

"Does that mean you want me to stop?" I asked her.

"No, Cathy. It means I want you to know what is likely to happen."

We've had a lot of hate calls at the convent and Father Mac had been deluged with them at the rectory. "Communist cunt" was one of the nicer things they said about me.

I can't comprehend it. All I'm saying is that I think the killing should stop. Doesn't a sister have the right to express her opinion on moral issues?

The other sisters here support me. They even admire me, which I can't understand. I haven't done anything except walk a couple of blocks to the Federal Building and say some dumb things to a reporter.

Father Mac doesn't approve or disapprove. "Do what you have to do, Brown Eyes. You'll always have a home here, regardless."

Regardless of what?

I hope I'm doing the right thing.

Love and prayers,
Cathy

76
CATHERINE

December 10

Dear Blackie,

I read Father Berrigan's poems before I went to his lecture, just as you suggested. They're lovely. A lot about death, but very beautiful.

And his talk was poetic too. Not so much a reasoned argument against the war as a string of images rallying us to cry out against the killing. I didn't know until I heard him that the American oil companies are behind the war because there are big oil reserves off the coast of Vietnam in the South China Sea.

Boys like Luís are being killed to put gasoline in our big cars. Ugh, how evil.

He is much angrier in his talks than he is in his poems, a thin little man, with burning eyes and a hurt face. I understand why there is so much anger in him. But why be angry at us, who came to hear him? Doesn't he know we are on his side? Maybe we are not dedicated enough.

He probably thinks that we ought to be resisting with our bodies the way he and his brother and their friends do. In our protest in front of the Federal Building I left when the policeman told us to leave. I don't think breaking the law helps to bring about peace. And the poor policeman was only doing his job. Father Ed and some of the others lay down on the ground. The police had to drag them out of the way and take them off to jail. I would have been terrified.

Father Berrigan says that we must disrupt the life of the nation to force America to its knees in penance. I wonder if he's right.

I know one thing for certain now. I'm going to oppose the war as best I can. We had another funeral today. One more Mexican-American boy who will not be coming home for Christmas ever again.

Pray for him, Blackie. And pray for me too.

All my love,
Cath

77
CATHERINE

Dear Blackie,

The man's face was as Irish as yours, red, full, blue-eyed, like a plump leprechaun. I was getting off my knees, preparing to be the dutiful citizen and obey the police. He knew I was leaving. I would not block the way into Holy Name Cathedral on New Year's Day. That would not help to end the war. A New Year's Eve prayer vigil for peace, yes; keeping people out of church on a Holy Day, no.

Then I saw the terrible hatred in his eyes. He wanted to hit me the way a man wants to have sex. "I'm moving, Officer," I said, scared half to death.

"Goddamn right you are, you fucking bitch." He grabbed me by the hair, pulling off the veil.

"Please, Officer, I'm leaving of my own free will."

"You're leaving because of this," and then he hit me in the stomach with his club.

The pain was terrible, like an elephant had stepped on me. I doubled up and collapsed on the sidewalk.

"Pull Sister over to the wagon," he yelled. "She wouldn't move when I told her to."

I would have walked to the paddy wagon if they'd let me, but my stomach hurt too much for me to get up before they dragged me.

That man deliberately hit me so I couldn't move and he'd have an excuse to arrest me.

The others were shouting and singing freedom songs and clapping for me. And all I was thinking was how badly I wanted to vomit.

Father Ed hugged me, jubilantly. "You're one of us now, Cathy. You know what the pigs are like. The TV camera got a perfect shot of him. It'll be on network news tonight—pig busts nun to start new year!"

I was barely able to walk into the Chicago Avenue station.

The cops—not all of them, but some of them—shouted terrible curses at us. The women were thrown into a cage with drunks and prostitutes, who said even worse things.

Part of me wanted to be understanding and forgiving like Christ on the cross. And part of me wanted to get the bastards. But I hurt too much and was too sick to do anything.

They kept us there all day because holiday court wasn't open. I did not even think of calling your father—I mean, I never needed a lawyer before. Helen saw what happened on TV and the Ryans showed up en masse—your father and Helen, and Joe and M.K.

Your father scared the daylights out of the captain in charge. He threatened to sue the police force and the city, said there was clear evidence on the TV film of unnecessary violence.

"What offends me, Danny," he said, "is that your officer was so dumb as to hit a nun in the stomach on network TV. Can't you teach your thugs to be more wary of the media? If you're going to brutalize nuns as a matter of policy, you'll need media-wise cops."

He was so neat, a handsome little man with white hair and clean-cut face, looking more like a priest than a lawyer. Except the eyes, those wonderful silver blue eyes that spit fire like a blast furnace.

"She shouldn't fucking have been there, Eddie. What's a nun doing in front of the cathedral anyway?"

"Praying, as the whole world saw on the TV tube. And exercising her constitutional right of free assembly. I'm going to tell Dick Daley that if he wants to play into the hands of the radicals, he's doing a fine job of it by permitting his police force to act like storm troopers. And I want that officer's name and badge number. From you. I can get it from the TV clips. But I want it from you. He's finished."

The captain didn't want to, but he gave him the man's name. Rafferty. How Irish can you get.

"Please, Uncle Ed," I said, remembering that I'm supposed to be a Christian. "I want to complain, but I don't want him fired. I'm sure he has a family. . . ."

And your father's eyes watered. You Ryans are such sentimentalists.

"Thank you, Sister," said the captain kind of grudgingly. "His wife and kids will appreciate it."

"Just in case you're too young to remember, Dan"—your

father's voice was cold as ice—"Sister's uncle was killed by Chicago police at Republic Steel in 1937. And her aunt, my late wife, was beaten almost to death by them. We have long memories about the Chicago Police Department."

"That won't happen again, Ed," the captain said nervously. "That was a long time ago."

"So I thought until today."

Mary Kate brought me over to Passavant Hospital. They took some X rays and gave me some pills. They wanted to keep me there, but Mary Kate said she'd take me home and watch me for a few days.

One day. I had to get back to my seventh-graders.

They cheered. "Kill the fuzz, S'ter," they shouted.

I gave them a good strong lecture about Christian charity. But I understood their feelings.

I'm so puzzled, Blackie. That man wanted to hit me. He enjoyed it. He was dumb to do it in front of a TV camera. The next time he'll be more careful. But he'll keep on hitting protesters because he likes it.

I wasn't attacking him. I wasn't resisting arrest. I wasn't interfering with traffic. I was doing what the police told me to do. Yet he hated me and wanted to hurt and humiliate me.

Why?

And so without even wanting to do it, I put my body on the line for peace. I'm a hippie nun now, according to the papers, and fair game for the pigs. A passive resister because I couldn't get off my knees quickly enough. And I didn't want to become that at all.

What's wrong with America, Blackie? Can't we even pray in public for peace? Your father says it's a crisis of generation and class, old against young, working class against middle class. I told him that sounds Marxist. He kissed my forehead and said he'd been married to one for a long time.

Maybe Ed saw it accurately long ago. We are a society that has become fatally ill from its own excesses.

I don't know what to do.

And my stomach still hurts.

Love,
Cathy

78
NICHOLAS

I paused in my reading of her letters after her New Year's Day arrest. What a fiendishly prophetic way to begin that terrible year of madness and stupidity and violence and murder. In retrospect I wished Daley had listened to Ed Ryan. I had been young enough to understand the protesters and cynical enough to distrust their leaders. But a first-year U.S. attorney does not tell the mayor of Chicago that he is about to make the worst mistake of his career.

I was scheduled for lunch with Monica. I didn't want to face the rest of 1968 in Cathy's life until that was over. Reading her letters to Blackie was a strange experience, like seeing an old movie a second time but from a different perspective and knowing that the unhappy ending would be the same. What would happen for the rest of the year was fated, locked in, inevitable.

Yet with hindsight I don't know what could have been done to protect her.

My boss and I both wanted to prosecute the cop with the billy club. "Frigging bastard hit a nun," he exploded. "For the frigging fun of it. Get Ed Ryan on the phone."

But Ed went along with Cathy.

"Is it like 1937, really, Mr. Ryan?" I asked him.

"History never repeats itself exactly," he said in his wonderfully gentle voice. "This one could be worse."

I put the bulky folder in my desk, locked the drawer and walked briskly through the last-week-in-November snow flurries to the University Club.

As soon as I saw her blond head and shimmering gray dress at the far end of the room, I knew I was going to be served my walking papers.

"You don't even have to say it," I began, kissing her cheek.

"Sorry." With the wonderful freedom of women to be emotional, she permitted herself a few moments of tears.

Then, having dabbed at her eyes with a tissue and repaired her face briefly with a compact, she launched into her explanation, most of which I could have told her without hearing it.

"It's not you, Nicky; I mean, you're spectacular in every way a woman could ask. Not pushy enough maybe, but that's curable. I'd never be unhappy with you. And you'd never be unhappy with me. Still . . ."

"Too many ghosts."

She nodded sadly. "Not that it's wrong. You have to keep alive your hope. She's entitled to that. I'd like to have known her. . . . I hope someday that I will know her."

"There's no chance," I said quickly.

"You don't believe that," she replied.

I wanted to make love with her after lunch. She would agree if I asked.

"One chance in a million. I don't know why I cling to it."

"Because you loved her, that's why. There will come a time when you'll know you should give up. You have to follow your instincts."

"Do you have your eye on someone else?" I tried to sound light.

"No such luck," she replied with a laugh. "I'll be on the lookout for someone, however. You've sold me on marriage again."

"If we find definite proof that Cathy's dead . . ."

"I'm not going to wait for that, Nick. It would be morbid."

She had not slammed the door shut. There was still room, still time.

We didn't make love after lunch. I didn't suggest the possibility. It hurt like hell. And it would continue to hurt. But she had been a good friend. With any luck she might remain one. She had taught me a lot about women. Almost as much as I was learning from the letters I was reading.

From both sources I was also learning about myself.

More than I wanted to know.

79
CATHERINE

April 1, 1968

Dear Blackie,

Sometimes I don't know why you guys put up with me. All these months I've been worrying about protest and nonviolence and Gandhi and Father Berrigan and I've forgotten that I'm from an Irish Catholic political family and our country is a place where politics can be made to work.

We were busy marching on protest lines and passing out leaflets and being brutalized so the TV camera could show the world what pigs Americans are. And a senator from Minnesota, with a few college kids to help, managed to force the President of the United States to withdraw from the race by running even against him in New Hampshire.

"Abe Lincoln said," remarked Father Mac, after we'd seen Mr. Johnson humbled on television, "there is no successful appeal from the ballot to the bullet. Are you going to work for McCarthy in Illinois, Brown Eyes?"

"Would you mind if I did?" I'd replied. I hadn't even thought about door-to-door politics.

"It would be good for you. There are other ways to change national policy besides liturgical displays."

I thought for a minute. "I'll work for McCarthy, unless Bob Kennedy runs. I'll ask Paul Cronin to help me get a part-time job. I'll keep up with my classes. . . ."

"He'll run, all right," Father Mac said, with his big Texas-cowhand grin. "And with people like you working for him, he'll win."

So I called your father and he called Paul and I'll be at the Kennedy headquarters as soon as it opens the day after tomorrow. John Jerome said, "More power to you, honey. Bring home a winner."

I phoned Father Ed, but he doesn't believe priests should take part in political campaigns. He'll keep up the protests.

I'm so excited that I can hardly contain myself. Camelot all over again.

But, to tell you the truth, I felt sorry for President Johnson. He looked tired and beaten. He is not, I think, a very nice man. Still, he did wonderful things for the black people before the war. And I'm sure he's sincere and honest and means well.

How is it, Blackie, that good people do bad things? That our best possible intentions lead to evil results? It's enough to make me believe there really is a devil after all, even if theologians like Father Tuohy say it's a form of regression to childhood fantasies.

And I wonder too about my own enthusiasm for Senator Kennedy. I want him to win. I want the war to end. But might all our good intentions end up doing something terrible? I suppose I'm the only one thinking that. When the president announced that he would not seek reelection, everyone in the room applauded. So did I. And I remembered how we all had cheered in the recreation room at OLH four years ago when he was elected.

It's strange and confusing, but thank God we have a country where you can still do things peacefully.

Pray that we win.

Love,
Cathy

80
CATHERINE

April 6, 1968

Dear Blackie,

It's like a nightmare, Coz. Thank God you're not here. There's a truck thing—Father Mac says it's an armored personnel carrier—at the next corner. And paratroopers with loaded guns and fixed bayonets everywhere. Chicago is an occupied city, two divisions of soldiers to put down an uprising in which scores of people have been killed.

All in the name of a man who was an American Gandhi.

Why did the black people do it? Doctor King was a great man and they should be angry. But, Blackie, they destroyed the stores in their own neighborhoods. Where will they shop? And they've burned the buildings of their own neighbors. Where will those neighbors live?

And what you read in the papers or see on TV about the people who are killed doesn't really tell you that almost all of them are black, shot by the police or shot accidentally by one another. Not only is Doctor King dead but so are hundreds of black boys, some of whom were just innocent bystanders.

Of course, Crazy Cathy had to see what happened. I put on the old Holy Habit, thinking I might be a little safer, and went down to Thirty-ninth Street, which is only a few blocks away. It was like a scene from Dante's inferno: fire sirens screaming like wounded and confused animals, smoke and fire belching from some of the stores, firemen fighting through showers of rocks to try to put out the blazes, the sick-making smell of tear gas, blue lights whirling over the squad cars, black teenagers throwing stones at the police (many of whom are black too), policemen grabbing a few kids coming out of a TV store and hustling them over to the paddy wagon, girls screaming obscenities at the police.

Everyone out of their mind.

Gunshots sound like firecrackers, did you know that?

God, Blackie, I wish I were in Rome with you.

"What are you doing here, S'ter?" a black sergeant asked. In the blue light, he looked like a cute witch doctor, and an exhausted witch doctor whose magic hadn't worked.

"Praying, sergeant. Is there anything else I can do?"

"No, S'ter. It really isn't safe here you know. What school you at, S'ter?"

"St. Ret's."

"Sure enough? My kids go to St. Columbanus. You s'ters teach him good discipline. I hope they don't grow up to do anything like this."

"They have something to be angry at, Sergeant."

"Doctor King wouldn't like this, no way. Now, you go home, S'ter. Nothing you can do here. Wait a minute, I'll have one of my men drive you home. Pray for us, S'ter."

"What were you doing here, S'ter?" asked the young white cop—he was cute too—who drove me back to the convent in a squad car with the blue light flicking ghostly glows in all directions around us.

"I thought maybe I could help," I said softly, wondering whether he had a billy club.

"The worst is over, I think," he said wearily, tilting his blue helmet to the back of his head. "When the troops arrive that should end it. We need them only to give us cops some sleep."

"How long have you been here, Officer?" I asked in my sweetest nun voice.

He rubbed his hand over his forehead. "I don't know. Forty-eight hours, I guess. We're tired and nervous and gun-happy. And scared shit—stiff, 'scuse me, S'ter. And my wife, she's expecting our first kid, she hears these rumors about cops being killed and she's a nervous wreck. It's a madhouse, S'ter. Pray for us."

As he drove away, I heard more fire sirens and the putt-putt of gunfire.

I spent the night in church praying, Blackie, for cops and kids and soldiers and white and black and for me too. Because I'm scared stiff too.

When will it end?

> I miss you,
> Cathy

81
CATHERINE

May 4, 1968

Dear Blackie,

The senator is an astonishing man. I rode with his party through Gary and East Chicago and Hammond and all those places today. We have been working for him in the cold and the rain, getting ready for the Indiana primary. And I guess because I'm a young nun and look good on TV, they wanted me close to him.

It doesn't embarrass me anymore. If it helps us win, what do I care what nuns like Martina Mary are saying. (She and her group have complained to Johnny, but Johnny is standing by me.)

The senator looked awfully tired, like he hadn't slept in a thousand years. But he had a big grin for me. "With you pulling for us, S'ter, we can't lose."

"And with her collecting signatures too," said Paul Cronin. "She had the biggest take in Lake County, Bob."

"Great, Sister, just great." He shook hands with me and grinned again. Almost like shaking hands with my Santa Claus pope a couple of lifetimes ago.

I think he's surprised by the reaction of the people to him, blacks and white, young and old. And it seems to make him, well, kind of more sensitive and fragile.

"I've never seen anything like it, Paul," he said once to Mr. Cronin. "Who do they think I am?"

"The man who will lead us out of darkness."

"God, I hope I can live up to what they expect."

I'm not sure anyone can, but isn't it remarkable that he can be humble when the crowds are going wild over him?

"Pray for us, S'ter," he said. "For me and my family."

I wanted to hug him but that wouldn't have been prudent. "I sure will, Senator," I said.

We just have to win, Blackie. We just have to. Everything depends on it. Pray for us that we do.

I'm tired and wet and cold, but I feel that I'm doing something truly important for God and for the country and for peace.

> Love,
> Cathy

82
CATHERINE

June 10, 1968

Dear Blackie,

I'm sorry I haven't written. I know you'll be home from Rome in a few days and we can talk then. I'm skipping the Institute this summer to work on the campaign. John Jerome said that it was fine.

We're all numb, moving around like zombies or sleepwalkers. The funeral service in the chapel at Quigley was lovely. Very Catholic, grief and hope. The flags of Camelot will dance again.

But not this year. Your father says that Senator Humphrey will win if he breaks with the president and promises to end the war. But how can he break with the president? And will he really end the war? I'm sure he'll be nominated, but I still have to work for Senator McCarthy, if they'll have me. And I suppose they will. The sexy little nun.

I'm too worn out and heartbroken to care what anyone says. I was asleep last Wednesday morning, sure that we'd won in California. Sister Freddy woke me up.

"They've killed him. They've killed Kennedy."

For a moment I thought I was back in the novitiate and the president had been shot. Then I knew what she meant and couldn't believe it. I ran down to the rec room and turned on the TV just in time to hear the announcement that he was dead.

I had to rush to the bathroom and vomit. Then I dashed over to church, still in my pajamas and robe, for Father Mac's mass. He was crying as hard as I was.

Why? Why? Why?

Why are we at the mercy of madmen and lunatics? Why are our best men killed at the precise time they seem likely to lead us out of darkness?

What's wrong with us, Blackie? How has our country become so sick? Is God punishing us for our sins? Have all our wealth and our waste and our greed brought heaven's vengeance down on our heads? I feel that when all of this is over, I'll want to go to a cloistered convent for the rest of my life. If there is anything left at all.

Some people are saying we won't survive another tragedy. Your dad disagrees. But he thinks there are going to be more tragedies before it all stops.

Hurry home, Blackie, and explain it to me.

We were all crying at the Mass at Quigley, for him and for ourselves. For the lost hope, the fractured promise. Someone quoted what Mr. Moynihan said when the president was killed. "If you're Irish you know the world will push you around. We thought he had more time. So did he. We may laugh again, but we'll never be young again."

I'm almost twenty-four, which isn't very old. Sure I'll laugh, as soon as I see your lovable face. But I will never be young again.

Love,
Cathy

P.S. Father Ed may have been right after all. Maybe our country is so sick that nothing will work anymore. Traditional politics may have failed. Perhaps we need to be brought to our knees.

83
BLACKIE

Catherine was not bitter when I saw her the night of my return from the seminary in Rome. Hollow-cheeked and grim-faced, but more hurt than angry or bitter. Still, I worried. She was, it seemed to me, close to despair. And despair is a convenient conduit from anger to bitterness. Before the summer was over she would take it.

There were no answers to her questions, then or now, more than eight years later. The forces of hell certainly seemed to have been unleashed on American society. The devil concept is a useful model sometimes, especially when the demonic results of human behavior so exceed the individual malice of those involved. Oswald, Ray, Sirhan—three trivial men who worked incredible destruction.

The world has always been that way. Not much of an answer for a twenty-three-year-old nun who was already a disillusioned idealist and who, like most of her generation, had no knowledge of anything that had happened in human history before 1953.

She dragged me to a lecture at the Institute by that consummate fraud Roy Tuohy on "The Politics of Violence in the Christian Tradition." Roy had expanded his reading list. Now he used three authors as his source material: Fannon, Marcuse, and Cleaver. Jesus was a political revolutionary, a dissenter who believed in violence as the purifying force by which society would be renewed. Witness his treatment of the moneylenders. And was he not executed for preaching sedition against Rome?

No one asked Roy if the point of the Scriptures wasn't that this was a trumped-up charge. No one dared to ask Roy anything.

With savage sarcasm, he dismissed the Kennedy campaign. Only the most naive would have expected that a man whose brother was the first Vietnam war criminal would really have the courage to end that conflict. Those who displayed their immaturity (Roy never gave up old words, he just added new ones) by their enthusiasm for Kennedy did not understand that the weaknesses of American society precluded any solution to its problems by electoral politics. Only on the streets and the barricades could the evil of Amerika be brought down.

Cheers from the crowd of clerics, none of whom could have built a barricade much less mounted one.

He must also have bought a copy of the sayings of Chairman Mao, who was busy disposing of a million or so of his people in the Cultural Revolution at that time. For his concluding theme was that "Morality, like political power, grows out of the barrel of a gun!"

Loud applause from the adoring nuns and priests, none of whom had ever touched a gun. Nor would Roy for that matter.

"You think he's wrong, don't you?" Cathy said as we walked down Michigan Avenue in the early summer twilight.

"There is room in the tradition for his theme. The last time the church embraced it was when it proclaimed the Crusades. Kill a Moslem for Jesus. The historians are currently not very approving of that era."

"But how else can you stop the war?"

"When good does evil," I said, "to prevent evil, it becomes indistinguishable from what it is opposing."

"Is that Blackie or someone else?"

"T. S. Eliot, more or less."

"What's wrong with our country, Blackie?"

"It's in a mess. It's been there before. This is, after all, the human condition, Coz."

"But we've tried everything. Violent revolution is the only course open to us."

Michigan Avenue on a gentle summer evening is a Garden of Eden, a sexual paradise, swarming with attractive young people of both sexes, filled with the promise of life yet to be born. And my sweet-figured, pretty-faced cousin in the short veil and the gray shift is gently talking about violent revolution.

Goddamn Roy Tuohy, I thought.

"What right do you have to expect success, Coz? Where was it ordained that our generation, alone of all those which has ever lived, has the right to success the first time out? I don't like the war, but bad wars have been fought before and opposed before. No one has ever claimed before that his opposition to the war gives him a claim on instant success in ending it."

"Maybe our generation is purer than any of the others. Maybe we are the beginning of a new age. Maybe we're the first one to understand what love means."

How do you talk about the complexities of history or imperfections of the human condition to someone who thinks, or perhaps I should say feels, that way?

"Because you have LSD and marijuana and open sex and the Beatles and girls can say dirty words?"

"Pot isn't anything. I've smoked it a couple of times. I'd rather have chocolate ice cream."

"An excellent idea." I steered her into an ice cream joint and we disposed of two triple-scoop cones.

"I'm still afraid," she said, licking the chocolate delicately off her lips, "that violence may be the only way."

"Perhaps, Coz. However, be honest about it. You cannot dig the Berrigans and Thomas Merton, God be good to him, on peace and Roy and Chairman Mao on violence. If one theory is right, the other is wrong."

She didn't understand what I was saying. In her confused and aching head it was all jumbled together. From demure poster-carrying to the barrel of a gun was a simple and logical progression. Of course that was an era when the *New York Review of Books* carried a recipe for a Molotov cocktail on its cover. Cath was not the only fouled-up person in the land.

"I think the young people who are coming here to disrupt the convention in August are doing what saints would do," she said. She finished her last dab of ice cream. "I wish I had the courage to join them."

"You're not?" I said with considerable relief.

"No, I'm not that brave. I'm going to try politics one more time."

"Has it occurred to you, Coz—have some more, M.K. says you're still too thin . . . yes, two more triple dips, triple. The young man thinks we're odd."

She was grinning for the first time all evening. "Has what occurred to me?"

"The demonstrators will win votes for Nixon. The more craziness there is on TV in August, the more likely he, tricky Dicky, will beat Humphrey."

"What difference does it make? They're both the same. Anyway Hubert Horseface Humphrey is a war criminal."

"He will end the war long before Nixon would."

She shook her head in strong disagreement. "The American oil companies won't let him end it. McCarthy is our only hope."

That was before the senator saw no problem with the Russian takeover in Czechoslovakia. I'm not sure it would have made any difference. Cathy had no idea where that country was or why it might have mattered.

So I began to worry a good deal more about her.

Not nearly enough, as it turned out.

84
NICHOLAS

The morning after I was dumped by Monica, I had a thoroughly satisfying court appearance. A high-class ambulance chaser was branching out, taking on plagiarism suits. A writer was being harassed by a nut who claimed that the writer had stolen her story. Normally the insurance company would have bought her off and the ambulance chaser would have pocketed a big hunk of the blackmail money.

And insurance premiums for writers would go up just as insurance premiums for doctors. I persuaded the publisher to fight it and won that morning on a motion for a summary judgment. Lucky at law, unlucky— God, how unlucky—at love. But the victory kept me going to lunch, which is a couple hours less than a victory usually carries me.

After lunch I went back to my office to continue the diary. I felt rotten. I would miss Monica physically. After a long period when I was almost as celibate as Blackie, I had learned to expect and enjoy good sex and lots of it. But I missed her more emotionally. There was no one for whom I could save up stories and experiences to laugh about.

No one to call on the phone and display my skills in the cause of the good guys against ambulance chasers and other bad guys. I thought of calling her anyway, so desperately did I want to share my triumph with someone who was not a lawyer. And who was a woman.

But I told myself that if I carried two torches I would not have a free hand to carry my briefcase.

Momentarily, I put my hand on the phone to call her and then thought better of it. Not fair to her.

"A Doctor Tuohy to see you, Mr. Curran," said my secretary.

Not a man high on my list of people I wanted to see.

"Send him in."

Tuohy had not been treated kindly by the years. He was in his early forties and looked ten years older. Marriage to a wife far richer than Catherine had provided him with the resources to eat at Washington's most expensive restaurants and the status to wolf down hors d'oeuvres at its most fashionable cocktail parties. He was thirty pounds overweight and had lost most of his hair. His once thinly handsome face was now equipped with multiple chins—Bela Lugosi become Sidney Greenstreet.

"I've been lecturing at the university on religion and economic freedom," he announced.

In Chicago when people say "the university" they mean the University of Chicago, and that is the implication he meant to convey. In fact—I checked after he left—he had lectured at De Paul. Like Michael Novak, who had swung from left to right in a few years, Tuohy was now a New Conservative, a staff member of the Freedom Center in Washington. As Blackie would have put it, he'd abandoned Franz Fannon for Milton Friedman.

"That's nice," I said in reply. "I hope no one asked you about your lectures in 1968 in favor of violent overthrow of the government."

"I came about my wife's will," he said, dismissing my crack as beneath his notice.

"Former wife," I corrected him, happy at the thought that here was yet another bad guy to rout. Two in one day.

"That is not the point," he responded. "I accepted a divorce settlement that was inappropriately small. My attorneys tell me I have some claim on the inheritance."

"You ought to hire better attorneys."

I had not been involved in the divorce trial, in which Catherine had not contested his charge of desertion. But I knew that the settlement had taken most of the money she'd received in trust on her twenty-first birthday and which became hers as soon as she left the order.

"Oh?" His eyes, peering out behind thick glasses, became hard. Pig eyes, I thought, except that was hardly fair to pigs.

"Legally, you can't claim a penny." Shooting down Tuohy was like potting away at ducks in a gallery. I ought to have been ashamed of myself.

"Morally, I believe I can. And I have come to serve notice on you that I propose to do so."

"That doesn't interest me. Save it for probate. As far as I'm concerned, there is no legal proof of her death. You may be able to win some hush money from the beneficiaries, who do not want the inheritance tied up in long litigation. That's between you and them."

"Would you want it to be known that your precious martyr was smuggling money out of Costaguana to Swiss banks?" he sneered. "That would ruin her image as a saint of the revolution. It was rich people's money, don't forget."

"I doubt that very much, Roy," I said serenely, clenching my fists.

"I have friends in certain government agencies who have confirmed for me that she made such trips under the name of Angela Carson. I fully intend to see that such information is revealed if my claims in justice are not honored."

"I don't think you will," I said.

"And why not, may I ask?"

"A number of reasons. Catherine may not have chosen to fight your divorce suit. But I have here"—and I pulled from my desk Blackie's letters—"correspondence from her describing the circumstances of her marriage to you, in rich detail. Moreover"—I returned the folder to its hiding place—"I have also considerable information about your, ah, habits in Washington, information that neither your wife nor the Freedom Center would find savory."

"You filthy bastard!" he yelled, an aged and overweight grizzly backed into a corner.

"Get out, Tuohy. You make me sick."

He left.

There were no details of their marriage in Catherine's letters. I had not put private detectives on him. But I had disposed of Tuohy and felt better about life. Scratch two bad guys.

So much better, in fact, that it was late afternoon before it dawned on me that we had important new information. I phoned Blackie.

"Your friend Roy Tuohy paid me a visit this afternoon. . . ."

"Ah. I trust you've had time to sanitize your office."

"He claims that his pals in the government knew of Catherine's trips to Miami."

"That would not be unusual, would it?"

"And that the name she used was Angela Carson."

"So. They faked an identity for her. Stupid of us not to have thought of that." He began to hum "The Whistling Gypsy," an Irish folk tune that he hums when he's thinking intently.

"Can we run with that?"

"Of course, we can. Go back to your friends at American Express. I think I must pay another visit to the Hill. This is too important to leave to the phone. I'll be in touch."

And before I could respond, Blackie had hung up.

85
BLACKIE

St. Ret's was a good place. Larry McMahon was a fine pastor, and the nuns, most of them not much older than Cathy, were there because they wanted to be there.

I dropped in several times in the evening that terrible summer of 1968 to see how Cathy was surviving the campaign. She wasn't, it seemed. Her shoulders were slumped and her eyes dull. She knew that the cause of righteousness would certainly lose. McCarthy and McGovern together could not keep Hubert Humphrey from the nomination.

She perked up only when there was gossip from the Institute. Marrying and giving in marriage was now almost a daily event. Some sisters from her community, who were attending the Institute, lived at St. Ret's during the summer. They were distinctly in the marriage market.

The conversations about who had resigned, who had written for dispensation, who had received a rescript from Rome, whose engagement had been broken off, and whose new marriages were already in trouble sounded like what I imagined the conversations in a sorority house to be during the last semester in senior year in those days when you were déclassé if you didn't have a diamond as you walked down the aisle for your diploma.

But since most of these women were in their thirties, their regression to adolescence had about it a touch of the grotesque. A punishment on the church for having kept them emotional adolescents for so long. Sad to report, Catherine oohed and aahed and giggled with the rest of them.

"They're bearing their own witness against the irrelevance and oppression in the church, Blackie," she said to me, reproach in her big brown eyes when I made fun of the superannuated adolescents. "I'm not following after them. But I have to respect their freedom and admire their courage."

"Courage to violate a lifelong commitment?"

"They didn't understand what it meant when they made the commitment."

A valid point. The church did its best to protect them from as much knowledge as possible of what it might mean.

"Did you?" I said, more nastily than I meant.

"I'm not backing down on my promise. You know that. Besides, if church leaders see they are losing their best people, they will have to change the rules and permit priests to marry."

"But only marry nuns."

"Blackie!"

"All right. Still, I think it is self-serving for those who are climbing off the ship to say that they are the best and that those of us who remain are only the rats without enough talent to leave."

"You're not a priest yet. You can still quit."

"A proposal, Coz?"

And that made her laugh again.

It was not unthinkable in principle. First-cousin marriages are possible with dispensations for Catholics, though most American states don't permit them. But Cathy and I had been quasi-siblings for so many years that the incest taboo had long since descended on us. If that had not been so, Nicholas would have had strenuous competition. Not that I would have performed any better. The role of a cousin/confidant is much less vulnerable than that of a suitor.

Don't think I wouldn't have liked it.

There was no laughing at St. Ret's the night after the encyclical letter *Humanae Vitae* of our gloriously reigning sovereign pontiff was issued.

The group was gathered in Mac's TV room, as usual, morose and angry.

"Why did he do it, Blackie?" my cousin asked in a woebegone voice. "You said he was looking for a way out."

"And was afraid of it when they gave him one. For the last six months the best we could have hoped for was no document. When I left in June that was still a forty/sixty chance, even though the rough draft had been written. Be glad, at least, he cut the lines about infallibility."

"Are we antisex or something?" Mac asked. "Don't we believe that married people should sleep with each other?"

"Sex has nothing to do with it. Power is the name of the game. The Curia sees change as a threat to their power. They persuaded the pope to think that a change would be a weakening of his power. They overplayed their hand. They didn't want the encyclical, either. But they manipulated the pope's conscience a little too much."

"People will leave by the millions," said the associate pastor, Father Mike O'Toole.

"I think they'll ignore it by the millions. They do already," I rejoined.

"What an awful man he is," Cathy said. "I wish my Santa Claus pope had lived long enough to make the change. Everyone dies too soon. Does he really think married people will stop sleeping in the same bed?"

"He might. The Curia people will say that we must take human weakness into account and be very sympathetic to the pastoral problems of married people. That means business as usual. It will be a crisis only in this country and the British Isles."

"Where we're too honest to accept that dodge," she said bitterly.

"They would say too inflexible."

"That man is as bad as Lyndon Johnson and Hubert Humphrey." She shook her head in disbelief. "And we expected so much of him."

"The church sucks," said one of the Institute students.

On that night her judgment was a widespread opinion among the clergy and religious who had been riding the crest of the post-conciliar enthusiasm. They had come up against the hard wall of Curial intransigence and papal isolation from reality. They had already been disillusioned by the bishops' heavy-handed attempts to bank down the fires of enthusiasm and the Curial wheelings and dealings to cancel the effects of the Council. But they had counted on the pope.

Now they realized that the future was in their hands, not his. They could stay and continue the battle or give up and find a spouse, hoping that if the departures were massive enough the pope and the Curia would back down. They knew not their enemy.

The black hole had become a supernova.

And Catherine was right in the middle of it.

86
BLACKIE

"Can you recall Cathy ever suggesting that there might be a place in the Center or somewhere around it where she could hide something valuable if necessary?"

We were in Margaret's office at the Mother House now. Apparently I was sufficiently trusted to be admitted into the office of the vice-president and putative next president of the Order of Our Lady of the Hill. Margaret may have been a new nun and a survivor. Nonetheless her office was as pin-neat as any mother superior's office in the early fifties. And no Polish matrons with toothbrushes to sweep the floor either.

"No, Blackie." She wrinkled her forehead. "I can't recall any hint. There was no place in the Center to hide anything. It was pretty primitive."

So I was Blackie now? Indeed. Well, Marge would hold a remnant together until the new forms emerged. More power to her.

"Perhaps somewhere else, Sister? Maybe in one of the *barrios*. Or in Río Secco."

She looked at me strangely. "Río Secco . . . I do remember . . . She loved the old church. No resident priest had been there for twenty years. The people kept it up. But like everything else there, it was an indifferent job. And after sweeping it, they would perform pagan rites out front. Toward the end, Catherine used to pray there for a half hour every day."

"Go on," I said impatiently.

"One day—oh, it must have been six months before she disappeared, their autumn, our spring—she took me into the crypt of the church. I didn't even know it existed. There was a rusty old gate behind the main altar, and a slippery staircase down to the crypt. It was dusty and moldy and smelled of death. I was frightened, but Cathy said that they couldn't hurt us. There were maybe twenty-five tombs, on either side of the wall, like in the catacombs. Stone caskets with barely discernible names and dates. One was from 1610."

" 'Look at this one,' Cathy said, heaving a stone cover off one of the caskets. 'Isn't it amazing?'

" 'I'm not sure I want to,' I said nervously.

" 'Don't be afraid, Margaret. It's empty. There's no one here. Maybe never has been.' "

"Can you remember the name on the casket?"

"Don Alfonso something or the other. Cathy said it reminded her of her first mission, so the name sticks in my mind."

A long shot, but perhaps not unreasonable. In the church in Río Secco at the railhead, in the crypt, an empty stone casket of a certain Don Alfonso. Was it, I wondered, still empty?

"That's very interesting, Sister. It could be a big help."

"Do you think she's in it, Blackie?" Her good German-mom's face turned pale.

"I doubt it," I replied, feeling less confident than I sounded. "At least we have somewhere to look for another clue."

"We have to know, don't we?"

"There will be no peace for any of us till we do. Now let me ask you another question. Did you ever hear Cathy mention someone named Angela?"

Marge's eyes widened in surprise. "Now, how would you know about that?"

"She did talk about Angela?"

"Yes. I had forgotten all about the incident until this moment. . . ."

"When was it?"

"I don't remember exactly. Is it important?"

"Tremendously."

"Then let me concentrate. It wasn't immediately before she disappeared. But it was certainly after her last trip out of the country. Is that a help?"

"Indeed it is. Now, what were the circumstances?"

"One afternoon we came back early from the clinic. We found Lorna poking around our room. She had taken a suitcase from under Cathy's bed and was trying to pick the lock on it. That was Lorna. She was supposed to be an Alinsky-trained community organizer, but she spent most of her time spying on the rest of us."

"A simp?"

Marge smiled faintly. "A terrible woman, but she had Father Ed's ear. Cathy hit the ceiling, called her vile and said she'd break her arm if she ever caught her doing that again, and warned her that if she dared bring it up at our sensitivity sessions, she'd make them choose between the two of them—one would stay and the other leave. For a change, Lorna was intimidated."

"I would imagine. What did Cathy do with the suitcase?"

"It was a small one, carry-on luggage. The next day she took it with her to the clinic in the basket of her bike. She said something like 'I'm going to protect my friend Angela from that sneaky bitch.' She patted the case like she really had another woman inside it."

"In a way she might have."

I tried to call Nick from the Mother House. He was in court. So I drove back to Chicago and phoned him from a booth on the toll road. He had a long trip ahead of him.

87
NICHOLAS

The year 1968 was a hard one for me. I was scarcely out of law school and totally inexperienced in the practice of law. Ordinarily I would have handled minor trials in the United States Court for the Northern District of Illinois. But this was no ordinary year. So I was involved in riots, police brutality, protests, bomb threats, sit-ins, rumors about terrorists and other such entertainments.

If one did not live through that era, one cannot understand how frayed were everyone's nerves, and how anxious we were about the next unexpected explosion. It was easy after the convention disorders for an outsider to analyze the mistakes. But we were all under the gun, or so it seemed. We were tired, frazzled, frightened and confused. We had to make instant, instinctive decisions, and our instincts had been dulled if not shattered by what went before.

Some of the young people who came to Chicago wanted to work for the candidates. Some wanted to protest the war. And some wanted to disrupt the convention and tear the city apart so that they could engage in "revolutionary action" on worldwide TV.

As to the motives of the "revolutionaries," some thought it was fun, some loved being media celebrities, some were getting even with their parents, and some were perhaps serious radical revolutionaries who wanted to overthrow American society.

One of them wrote a wild article, which the *Village Voice* carried on its front page the week after the convention, about "revolution sweeping the streets of Chicago." It was sweeping only two or three streets and it was a funny kind of revolution in which everyone packed up and went home on the weekend.

But it felt to the kid who wrote it like a revolution. And at that point all that mattered was how you felt.

The revolutionaries dominated the week. Because we let them. Because we drove everyone else into their arms. The various law enforcement agencies in Chicago knew what the Abby Hoffman/Renie Davis/ Jerry Rubin/Tom Hayden crowd were up to and we let them get away with it. We did everything we possibly could to give them success on a silver platter.

To this day I'm not sure why. We were "frigging angry" at them. And we let our anger get in the way of our common sense. We learned, however, from our mistakes. Some genius thought of giving personality tests to cops. Then they only used "happy cops" to police the later demonstrations. It worked. Incidentally, I checked Rafferty's test—the bum who clubbed Catherine. He flunked with flying colors.

The media made it more difficult for us. They were on the side of the punks and against us. The sainted Walter Cronkite arrived on Sunday night and began attacking us: The electrician's strike, which impeded the TV links into the amphitheater, was a trick of Mayor Daley to make the media's work more difficult. It was part of Daley's attempt to censor American freedom of expression. That was not true, and a little investigation would have proved it untrue. But Cronkite and the rest of them weren't interested in truth. They were interested, as the national media usually are when they come to Chicago, in doing us in.

Cronkite lied about us every night of the week, until he had what he thought was the chance of his career, an interview with Daley. At last the great Walter would reveal the shanty Irish mayor for the dummy he was.

It was one of Daley's finest hours, about the only one that week, and Cronkite's worst hour. The sainted Walter made a fool of himself.

He was later booed at a CBS cocktail party. Da Mare had run all over him. I still relish that interview. There isn't much else to remember with any satisfaction.

There were a number of incidents early in the week in which network TV crews faked scenes of police brutality to make the evening news because their assignment was to get footage of such things. If there isn't any news, then you create it. Later in the week they didn't have to fake anything.

It was argued in defense of the cops that they were exhausted, that they had excrement thrown on them all week, that they had been called every vile name in the language by kids whose parents made four or five times as much a year as the cops did, that they were shocked by the filth and the promiscuity and that they too did not know what was happening to America and were frightened.

All of which is true. Yet police discipline did break down. The Mayor and the police brass permitted it to break down. And we in the prosecuting agencies did not try very hard to prevent it.

In the midst of this Cathy was savaged.

I like to think sometimes that the water of Lake Michigan was poisoned with a secret chemical which made all of us mad. For that terrible night in front of the Hilton seemed to be a nightmare dreamed up by a malicious and drunken God.

Blackie claimed the name of the poison was Original Sin.

Police with clubs, guardsmen with bayonets, tear gas, mace, shit and urine; bearded, beaded, and pot-smoking kids; TV crews; frightened politicians; eager reporters; a maelstrom of angry people seething and screaming at one another. It was not one mob but many, all blaming the others for the coming apart of America.

I saw the police charge from the door of the Hilton, on my assignment of watching for violations of civil rights. When the cops finally broke ranks and charged the punks, there was a sense of tremendous relief and exhilaration all along the street. The TV crews had their pictures, the revolutionaries had their martyrdom, the reporters had their stories, the politicians had their cause, and the police had their fun.

To my credit I vomited on the spot, but maybe only because of the smell of the gas and not because of disgust with myself and everyone else.

It was an orgasm on Michigan Avenue, a sick release of enormous energies, a rape that temporarily satisfied everyone.

And then, when the TV crews had enough footage for the morning news programs, they packed up and went home. And so did everyone else.

Except the law enforcement types.

I walked over to police headquarters at Eleventh and State. Two national guardsmen with bayonets stopped me at the corner of Eleventh and Michigan, nice kids who had kept their discipline because they weren't tired.

They had no right to stop me, but I showed them my ID.

"Nice job," I said. "You guys kept your cool."

"My brother was on the other side," said one of the kids. "It's a fucking, mixed-up mess."

And a cop with a battered blue helmet, looking like he had just screwed a woman, came running at me with a can of mace in his hand and a look of pure ecstasy in his eyes. I was clean-shaven and short-haired, but I was young and that was enough.

"Where you going, you fucking punk?" he shouted, holding the mace two inches from my eyes.

"Before you fire that, Officer, I ought to tell you that I am an assistant United States attorney." I flipped my ID at him.

Grudgingly he lowered the mace.

"Where's your name plate, officer?" I demanded.

"The fuckers tore it off."

Of course, they had not. The police took the name cards off themselves before they charged.

"Let me see your badge."

"I fucking won't." He turned and lumbered away.

I found out later who he was and made a complaint. It didn't do much good. We indicted some of them, but no jury in Chicago would convict police for bashing the protesters, maybe no jury in the country. The media said that we didn't try to convict them. We did try, but it was a waste of time.

I read somewhere that the Michigan election research team reported that half of those Americans who were doves, who favored immediate withdrawal from Vietnam, thought the Chicago police used the right amount of force and a quarter more thought they didn't use enough force. It didn't matter. We'd still lost.

As I walked into the brilliantly lighted madhouse at Eleventh and State, looking like a set for a film instead of a real police headquarters, I was certain that Nixon would win and God knows what other collective orgasms would occur on our city streets.

252 / ANDREW M. GREELEY

Sandy McBride, a classmate who worked for the State's attorney's office, rushed up to me, a short little Irish firebrand who could just as easily have been on the other side.

"Hey, Nick," he yelled, "I have a dilly. Tell me what you think. I got to make an immediate decision."

"What now?" I said with something like despair.

"Some cops said that the kids in McCarthy's headquarters were dropping bags of urine. They went up there and worked them over pretty good and dragged them in. Should I hold them?"

"The cops?"

"No, the Clean-Gene kids?"

"Are you crazy, Sandy? Hold them for what? You won't even be able to find the cops who hauled them in tomorrow morning. How can you prosecute without arresting officers? The McCarthy kids don't do that kind of thing. Get them out of here before the cameras show up."

"Yeah, that's what I thought. No records or nothing."

"Nothing. Get rid of them."

It was only after I had reassured Sandy that I remembered Catherine had been working in the McCarthy office.

"Wait a minute, Sandy. Where are they?"

"Up on three. You want to come along?"

I ran up the stairs leaving him far behind.

She was sitting in the corner, quiet and withdrawn. Her veil was gone, her habit torn. Blood was trickling down from her hair across her face, she was bent over in pain, holding her right arm like it might be dislocated or broken. An ugly lump was swelling over her left eye.

I called Ed Ryan from a phone on the wall. "Nick. Eleventh and State. They got her again. Bring Mary Kate. For the love of God, hurry."

Then I went over to her and knelt on the floor next to her. I put my arm around her back, being careful not to brush the injured arm.

"It's all right, Catherine. The Ryans are on their way. No one is going to hurt you again. There aren't going to be any charges. We'll try to find the police who did this and see that they are punished."

She slowly and painfully swiveled her head so she could look at me. She was numb and disoriented, a victim of shock as well as the beating.

Why do they always go after the beautiful ones?

She didn't seem to recognize me. Her glorious brown eyes seemed to move in and out of focus.

"Nick," I said.

Then she recognized me. And her face twisted in a grimace of hatred.

"Fucking pig," she shouted, and she spat in my face.

88
BLACKIE

The cameras found her coming out of the emergency room of Passavant the next morning, her head bandaged, her arm in a sling, a patch of plaster over her black eye. Her dress was pinned back together. Somehow she had found a veil. Even as a victim, Cathy was stunning on camera.

She was filled with painkilling medication and disoriented from the assault. But she knew what she was doing. Oh, she knew exactly what she was doing. My cousin had learned the media game.

Dad and Mary Kate tried to hustle her into Joe's waiting car. Politely but firmly she shook them off and walked to the camera.

"What happened, Sister?" asked the reporter eagerly, wondering doubtless how BIG a raise this scoop would earn.

"I was working in Senator McCarthy's headquarters at the Conrad Hilton. Chicago police officers rushed into the room and began beating us. They said we had thrown bags of . . . of filth out the window at them."

"Did you?"

She made a rueful face. Even more lovely. "Of course not. It doesn't matter to the Chicago police. All young people are proper targets for them, whether they are Yippies or McCarthy staff."

"Will you try to prosecute the police?"

"There is no justice in Chicago."

"Will your superiors be angry at you for being arrested?"

"I had to follow my conscience."

"What does this tell you about America, Sister?"

"It tells me that America is the kind of country where police beat young people for working peacefully in a political campaign."

Ah, Cousin, you have all the right words.

"Is the country evil, Sister?"

"It is as bad as Nazi Germany. Amerika has been committing genocide in Vietnam and against its own Blacks and Browns. Now it is committing genocide against its own young people. God will bring Amerika to its knees to punish us for our wealth, our arrogance and our cruelty."

"Will you continue to be involved in the campaign, Sister?"

By now he thought he might win a prize for the footage.

Her lip curled in contempt, pretty, dainty, nunnish contempt, as if she were talking to a seventh-grade boy caught reading dirty magazines in the cloak room.

"Electoral politics has failed in America. Those of us who believe in peace and justice must take to the streets."

89
NICHOLAS

There were no letters from her that summer. She was seeing Blackie every weekend and a few nights a week besides. But as I sat in my office, hunched over her correspondence, I recalled those awful days. The memories were as vivid as the incidents themselves had been. I saw the blood trickling down her tearstained face, felt the spittle, heard her hate-filled words.

The phone rang. I looked at my watch. Six o'clock. Time had slipped away while I nursed my memories.

"Nick? Blackie. Can you make a long trip tomorrow?"

"If I have to. Where?"

"Costaguana. Pan Am has a 6:00 P.M. flight to Río. Change there tomorrow for Santa Marta. Be on it. I'll drive you to the airport."

"What's up?" I grabbed for a pencil and paper.

"Catherine may have had a hiding place in the crypt of the church at Río Secco Annunciata. There is an iron gate at the back of the main altar, coffins in a catacomb at the foot of the stairs. There is one purporting to contain the mortal remains of a certain Don Alfonso something or other. However, it is, or was, empty. Moreover, Catherine apparently brought 'Angela,' or a carry-on bag carrying Angela, to the church and may have hid it there."

"Find out what is in the coffin?"

"Exactly."

"Will it be Catherine?"

"That would free us all, wouldn't it?"

"It sure would. Still, I hope not."

"So do I. Have you heard from American Express yet?"

"No, I'll have my secretary keep after them."

"Good enough. See you in the morning."

I packed the letters in my briefcase. What better place to finish them than on a flight to Costaguana.

90
NICHOLAS

The convention was over and both the protesters and the media had left. We were busy preparing the indictments, from which eventually there would come not a single conviction. The week before Labor Day I took the weekend off and went to Michiana. Saturday night I walked through the woods to Grand Beach to see who was at the Ryans'.

I had heard from Ed Ryan that Catherine had gone home to the Mother House to work out her future with the head of the order. There seemed to be general agreement that she ought to leave Chicago for a time.

So I did not expect her to be in the Ryan place.

But I hoped she would be.

And she was.

I walked in the door—it was always open and in the summer no one bothered with the bell—and Cathy was sitting in the living room, smoking and reading *The Wretched of the Earth*.

She was wearing shorts and a T-shirt. Her arm was still in a sling but the bandages on her head and face had been reduced to small pieces of plaster.

She stood up when she saw me, finger still in the book. She looked exhausted and confused, but thank God not angry at me.

"Catherine," I said tentatively.

"Nick," she replied with equal caution.

And then we found ourselves in each other's arms.

At first it was merely renewed friendship. Then quickly it became much more. I knew little about women then. But I knew enough that this woman's body was asking, pleading, demanding that I love her. Careful to avoid her injured arm, I caressed her as gently as I could and she caressed back.

Our lips pressed together. Our mouths worked avidly as if we were trying to devour each other and become one person. Our moist tongues touched, teased, tantalized. My hands fell to her firm, delicious rear end and pulled her even closer. Then, holding her tightly with one hand, I explored her bare breasts with the other. She was soft, full, warm. And mine.

Together we swam to the brink of the waterfall and then turned back. I'm sure if I had insisted we would have gone on. We stopped, detached ourselves and retreated to chairs at the opposite sides of the room, both of us breathing heavily.

"Well," she said. "That's one way to end a fight. I'll get you some lemonade."

When she came back, her eyes were sparkling with their old mischief, but I knew that she was shaken by our embrace as least as much as I was.

"No sand, please."

"Ha! Wait till you see what I put in it."

"Not poison, I hope."

"A narcotic."

Not LSD, as I feared for a moment, but plain old gin.

"I was not myself that night, Nick," she said quietly as we sipped our gin and lemonade.

"I know that. Who was?"

As close to an apology as Catherine was able to come.

"A nightmare. Let's not argue about whether America is sick or not. I don't want to argue with you tonight."

"Nor I, Catherine, with you. Let's stipulate that it has enormous problems and let it go at that."

"I'm not sure what stipulate means"—she laughed an old-fashioned, hearty Catherine laugh—"but I agree."

"What will you be doing next year?" I crossed my legs and settled down for a pleasant evening's conversation.

"Sister John Jerome, our president, has missioned me to go away to school, to New York, as a matter of fact. I'll be studying theology. She gave me a choice of a number of different missions and graduate work seemed to be the best. I'm looking forward to it."

"It's probably wise to get out of Chicago for a while."

She bit her lip thoughtfully. "I suppose so." She smiled ruefully. "I've had my problems here. But St. Ret's was such a grand place. It was more fun than anything since grammar school. I guess they have enough difficulties without being saddled with me."

"Did they want you to leave?"

"If they didn't," she said impatiently, "they should have. And you?"

"I'll stay on with the U.S. attorney for a couple of more years and then go back to the firm. I can have a place there anytime. Trial work, I guess. I'm good in a courtroom."

"I'm sure you are. You'll be working on the stuff from the riots."

"Full-time and extra time and double time."

"You sound like it is a waste of time."

"Probably will be. I don't think anyone can be convicted on either side."

She nodded, either agreeing with me or at least understanding what I meant.

I realized that we were in different worlds. Catherine no longer believed in the American system. She didn't think our law or our politics worked anymore. Maybe she was right.

"You're still waiting till next year?" she resumed.

"You're still going to be a nun?"

"More determined than ever." Her chin jutted upward. "And we're in different worlds now, Nick."

A precise echo of my own thoughts. Our embrace suggested that it might not matter, but I did not want to discuss that.

"I believe in peace and justice as much as you do, Catherine. I don't want to argue with you and I won't. I concede your good faith and I hope you concede mine."

I saw the beginning of a flow of words from Fannon and Marcuse form on her lips. Then the flow stopped, to be replaced by a wicked Catherine giggle. "I'll stipulate that."

Then a horde of Ryans, all ages and sizes, streamed in, hardly pausing to notice the strange tête-à-tête, and the party began in earnest.

She kissed me lightly on the lips when I left. "It was good to see you, Nick," she said.

"Same here. I'll be back next summer."

"Fair enough."

Blackie insists that nothing could have developed from those circumstances. Maybe he's right. He usually is. But he didn't hold her in his arms and feel the pressure of her soft young body against his.

I would remember that embrace, the cool elegance of her bare legs and the outline of her breasts against the thin shirt, for many years. I still remember them.

That was eight years ago. I didn't see her the following summer. I did not see her again till shortly before she died.

My cousin and I were fated to drift apart. I went back to Rome and she to New York. We had come out of the black hole aimed in different directions. We would correspond intermittently until our friendship disintegrated completely. But there was little left to talk about. The longer the time after we were expelled from the black hole, the further away the velocities of our movement carried us.

I did not miss her as much as Nick did. But I missed her and still do. I take some consolation from the thought that we began to curve in on one another toward the end.

She went off to Assembly Theological School, where Roy Tuohy had won for himself a distinguished chair in Roman Catholic studies. Assembly was one of the great theological institutions of the land. But the nitwit who was its president in those days ordained that no one would beat it and him to the cutting edge. Therefore, it was to become the "Seminary of the Oppressed." Its chairs would be evenly divided among blacks, women and the Third World. To which he shortly added gays and lesbians.

Most of the internationally renowned scholars on the faculty were shamed by guilt feelings into accepting this change. Those who didn't locked themselves into their offices and continued their work, much as St. Augustine finished _The City of God_ while the Visigoths attacked the city walls.

At Assembly, the generic Visigothic theology went something as follows: I am a Visigoth and hence a member of an oppressed group. I speak for the million people of my group. I theologize out of our experience of oppression. We are a holy people because of our oppression and indeed the only holy people. All other peoples have no right to claim holiness or even Christianity. They must listen to our theological pronouncements on their knees and abase themselves for what their ancestors or their society have done to us poor Visigoths.

So it went. It was a good way to earn a living and even to become a celebrity. No one besides clergymen and other scholars took them seriously. But the theological academy is a cozy pond in which to be a big fish.

There were a few minor questions of data and logic. Like who is holier, a black or a woman? The answer, as ought to have been obvious, is a black woman.

And as for St. Paul's passing reference to the fact that in the church there was neither male nor female, Greek nor Roman, Jew nor gentile, St. Paul ceased to be an important figure at Assembly; and as a Jewish male, a member of a group which was overrepresented in the university world, he would not have been eligible for a faculty appointment.

If he had established his tent-making shop on the fringes of the academic enclave of which Assembly was a part and the shop was trashed during one of the riots, it would have been whispered that everyone knew now the Jewish merchants exploited the poor blacks.

And if his Boss had shown up not carrying the Kalashnikov rifle with which he was pictured in Assembly's favorite form of socialist realism in religious art, he would have been sent packing too.

For Assembly had become the school not merely of the oppressed but of the revolutionary.

Needless to say, no one on the faculty or in the student body would have known one end of a Kalashnikov from the other.

It was a situation made to order for Roy Tuohy. To become a highly paid, tenured faculty member at Assembly (which provided clergymen for upper-middle- to upper-class suburban parishes), he need not have a publication record, he need not have read many books, he need not even have had a single original or serious idea. If one had the proper revolutionary credentials, one was welcome.

As a card-carrying revolutionary Catholic, Roy was a shoe-in after Dan Berrigan turned down the appointment.

It was into such an environment Cathy was going, away from the Ryans, away from Nick, away from the support of her religious order— save for the nuns in the convent in which she lived, most of whom probably disapproved of her attending Assembly.

We must, I tell parents, permit children to make their own mistakes and not require that they repeat ours. So too with beloved cousins.

I drove her to the airport the day she left for New York. We chatted merrily, as though it was merely one more ride to O'Hare. Both of us knew what was happening. Neither of us knew how to discuss it, even how to articulate it. It was the end of a long love affair, and in a way it would be a relief.

We kissed and she boarded the 727.

I never spoke with her again.

92
CATHERINE

December 6, 1968
NYC

Dear Blackie,

I feel terribly guilty about not writing before. The work at Assembly is very hard, especially since the reactionaries on the faculty will not agree with the curriculum reform we have demanded. They insist on irrelevant required courses about things like church history and medieval religious art and wisdom literature. Some of us want to strike for a change, but others, afraid of the jobs they want after ordination, won't join us. Finks.

So I take the shit courses and write the shit term papers. The community expects me to earn my degree. Roy says that it is immature for me to permit the community to control my life in this fashion. I suppose he is right, as always. But I have never felt closer to the community and I want to be responsible to them.

John Jerome could not have been nicer. She told me that they are proud of me and only hope that I don't get myself seriously hurt. Isn't that strange, Blackie? Two years ago I was in trouble for wearing the new habit and now I'm a heroine because I'm an antiwar activist.

I don't wear the habit anymore save at the demonstrations, where it has sign value. A number of us have talked about this very seriously and we feel that the habit is a barrier to our relationships with others—remember when we called them "seculars"? A uniform is a mark of distinction and, indeed, class prestige, which interferes with the commonality of our basic humanity. The first day I came to class in skirt and blouse I was delighted to see how all the barriers melted away.

And ashamed that I had been responsible for the barriers.

There were some complaints from the old bitches in the convent where I stay, but they are irrelevant.

I have been in four demonstrations and plan to go to
Washington for the counter-inaugural. I suspect I'll have to
spend a night or two in the District of Columbia jails. They
can't be any worse than the jails in this shit house called New
York City.

I do love you, Blackie, darling—I'll always love you. I know
that we are drifting apart and I wish it were not so. But I must
be true to my principles and convictions. I hope we can stay
friends. My reason for not writing you before is that I feel it is
very difficult to share with you all I have learned about myself
and the world and God. You will certainly disagree. You're so
much smarter than I am and so much funnier, you always win
the arguments. You don't make fun of me, and if I ask you, I'm
sure you won't make fun of my ideas, either. Still, I'll know
you're laughing and that makes it difficult to be open and
honest and free.

And you don't like or respect Roy. I think he is one of the
great men of our era, greater even than Thomas Merton or Dan
Berrigan. It is irrelevant that he has published only one thin
book and a few articles. How many books did Jesus publish?

He's my mentor and he's going to direct my doctoral
dissertation on the theology of oppressed women in the
Catholic church. So please try to think kindly of him. He's
been an enormous help to me in adjusting to this very
interesting but quite different (for me) world.

That's right, my dissertation. I will be Doctor Cathy after all.
Most of what Father Lyons said was shit, but he was right
about the need to be good at something. I feel very strongly
that I will not be self-fulfilled until I have achieved professional
excellence, and in a subject area, oppression, that is politically
relevant.

John Jerome wrote me that after I make my final vows next
summer, I can come back here and stay as long as I want to
finish my degree work. I don't want to spend too much time on
it. Even a revolutionary school like Assembly seems at times to
be irrelevant.

Speaking of final vows, as always, there is the question of
Nick. You only lifted an eyebrow when you saw us talking last
summer. We were at the very edge of lovemaking, Blackie. I'm
sure you saw it in both our faces.

It happened so suddenly that neither one of us realized what we were doing. I don't believe anymore that it would be a sin for two people who honestly love one another to express their love by fucking. I'm sure, however, that Nick would not agree. He would have wanted to marry me. And I love him so much I might have consented. Now, with my consciousness slowly being raised, I think I would be strong enough to resist him.

Most men are male-chauvinist pigs, rapists determined to keep women subject for their own pleasure and for economic gain. But Nick isn't. He is good and sweet and kind and always will be.

I can't argue with him about waiting for another year. But you must prepare him, if you write to him, for disappointment. I am absolutely determined to stay in the community. Religious orders are one of the few bases available to us revolutionary women to fight back against oppression and chauvinism.

I'm afraid that you will be angry at me when you read this letter, Blackie. Please don't be. I hope never to lose you.

> All my love,
> Cathy

93
CATHERINE

January 25, 1969

Dear Blackie,

It was wonderful for you to reply so quickly. I'm glad we're still friends and that I can talk freely to you. What a nutmeg I was to think differently.

Richard M. Nixon is now president of the United States. Amerika at last has the kind of leader who reflects to the world all the putrid corruption in our country. I'm sure that the war will go on for four more years. But if Hubert the Horseface had been elected, he probably would have stopped the war and the revolutionary pressures would go out of American society. As it is, we will certainly have a revolution, probably a bloody one, according to Roy, by 1972. Then there will be a new era of peace and justice.

I did think seriously about your comment on "check-signing power" in the church. Women do have more of that power in the church than in any other human organization. And have had for a long time. A Marxist like me has to recognize that kind of power. But as Roy says, that is merely a trick of the real power structure in the church, the all-male hierarchy, to deceive women into thinking they have power. So what looks like respect for the independence of women is in fact a particularly nasty manipulative trick.

I spent only one night in the D.C. jail during the counter-inaugural. I thought Irish cops were the worst until I was pushed around by redneck pigs in D.C. But none of them tried to bust my gut or my head.

I've been experimenting a little with heroin. Roy says we must be open to all the experiences of the poor and the oppressed. It doesn't do a thing for me. Neither did pot, if you remember. I guess I'm strictly an Irish beer-type.

If we are to follow in the path of Jesus, Blackie, we must identify with the poor and the oppressed. We must be in the vanguard of the battle against genocide and imperialism and racism and sexism and classism. We must fight against the multinationals, the oil companies, Dow and Kennicot and General Motors. We must be the advocates of God's poor people, encouraging them, leading them, joining them, following them.

In the class war we must be on the side of the weaker class and against the stronger class. The rich and the middle class are the enemies of the poor and the workers and they are therefore our enemies. The church should abandon all its ministry to the affluent and concentrate on supporting the cause of the poor. We must preach in the name of Jesus the Liberator, Jesus the Revolutionary. If we fail to do that, then we fail to follow Jesus.

The Latin American theologians have done wonderful work

on the theme of liberation in the Gospels. Jesus was a man of the poor. He lived and worked with and for the poor. He organized them. He marched on Jerusalem with them. He challenged the corrupt power structures of his day and demanded freedom and justice for his followers. And he was arrested on the charge of sedition and executed because he was a revolutionary leader.

As Roy says, from the point of view of the ruling class, Jesus was indeed guilty as charged. Camillo Torres, the priest who died fighting with the guerrillas, indeed guilty. The Berrigans are indeed guilty. In an unjust society, the structures of injustice necessitate that those who are the advocates of justice be judged guilty of breaking the laws.

Roy has also taught me that the resurrection of Jesus is irrelevant to a theology of liberation. It is death that matters. For a death in the name of the cause of human liberation is a resurrection in itself. If we wish to follow Jesus—and I always have and still do—we must be prepared to die in the ranks of the revolutionary vanguard.

I wonder how long I can justify the academic life. While I am living comfortably and eating well, the poor become poorer and the rich richer. Did you know, Blackie, that Americans are only six percent of the world's people and consume a third of its raw materials? Most of the Third World countries have been forced into a relationship of economic dependence on us. Our greed for coffee keeps Brazil and Colombia in oppression; our lust for fruit eats up the lives of Central American workers; we take cocoa from Ghana, bauxite (I'm not sure what that is) from the Caribbean islands, copper from Chile, tin from Bolivia, silver and copper from Costaguana. And what do we give back to them? Our killer automobiles, our disease-carrying packaged milk, our stomach-rotting Coca-Cola, our tawdry films and TV series, our cheap pornographic magazines, our guns and our bombs, our CIA training in torture, our silly computers and our deluxe hotels, in which pig-fat American tourists broil themselves under the sun.

The garbage from one American family would feed a hundred Indian families. Half the world goes hungry every night. Millions of sweet little children, whom their mothers love even more than American mothers love their children, bloat up and die of starvation every year.

And we have become a nation of fat, overstuffed pigs.

I'm sorry for shouting, Blackie. I feel so goddamn guilty because I live in Amerika, the land of blueberry jelly, apple pie and genocide.

But, no matter what, I still love you.

Always and ever,
Cathy

<u>94</u>
CATHERINE

April 12, 1969

Dear Blackie,

I'm tired and confused. Easter was a dud for me this year. It all seems so irrelevant to the sufferings of the poor people with whom we must identify. And I become so angry when I see a fat fart of a priest slouch around the altar. He knows that he belongs there by right because he is a man, no matter how dumb. And I could preside over the liturgy so much more gracefully and preach so much better, but I can't do it because I'm a woman.

I now believe that I am called to the priesthood. Why not? You and I were born the same month. You always wanted to be a priest and I never even considered it. I was brainwashed into thinking that because I am a woman I am not good enough to be a priest, not even to want to be a priest.

I don't see how I can continue under the domination of an all-male clergy, every one of whom is deliberately to blame for my oppression.

Whenever I think of that injustice, it makes me so mad that I want to swear.

Not that it would do any good. The fat-pig priest would merely pat me on the head and say, "A pretty young woman like you, Sister, shouldn't use such naughty words."

Shit.

According to Roy, it would be immature of me to leave the community, because I would lose my revolutionary base. The so-called sign value of being a religious is a chauvinist invention that can be turned against the pigs in the all-male hierarchy. A sister revolutionary makes a much greater impact in the mass media than does a woman revolutionary who is not a sister.

The only valid criterion of truth in a revolutionary situation is praxis. What works is true. And I certainly know from the experience of my own praxis that a sister revolutionary sends a more powerful message.

And I'm tired, more tired than I have ever been in my life. I stay up to three o'clock every morning at the books and am up at seven to attend my consciousness-raising session, and then back to class for another day of irrelevancies, broken only by Roy's sensitivity training group before lunch (where I really have learned to be in touch with my own emotions and to understand the impression of myself I convey to others). After class our Third World study group meets until seven o'clock. Those poor people are so angry. We have to let them be mad at us so they can be angry at someone.

And I'm smoking too much and drinking too much coffee and guzzling too much beer. I never thought I would have to worry about calories again. I have no desire to use my body to gratify male-pig fantasies. But it is important, as Roy says (and he's very stern about my physical appearance), that I have the right image for the media. In our sick Amerika, a fat young nun does not attract nearly as much attention as a slender young nun.

I'm doing a lot of work for Roy, typing, collecting his notes, helping him put together his new book, which will cause a sensation. I learn more at the typing desk in his office than I do in all my classes put together.

I suppose you've noticed I don't attend Mass every day. There is no time to pray, Blackie. Roy says our best prayers, indeed our only valid prayers, are the prayers of our life in revolutionary meetings and on the streets.

I still believe in formal worship, but I can no longer participate in a liturgy performed by an all-male priesthood. On Sundays I attend a Eucharistic banquet conducted by one of the other sisters at Assembly. We permit only women to participate and it is a celebration of joy and love and anticipation.

Someday soon there will be women priests in the church. There will have to be because of the shortage all over the world. But that doesn't help us now when we need Eucharist with our sisters, so we support one another in the struggle against male-chauvinist oppression.

Yet I'm not sure of anything anymore, Blackie. I feel sometimes that I'm nothing more than a machine responding to the demands of others, demands from the outside and demands that I have internalized in my crowded, aching head. If only I could take off a little time to rest and relax and maybe swim. But I don't see how I can do that. I must finish my work this summer, I have so much to catch up on and I have to take the required shit courses in Greek and Hebrew. And, of course, Roy needs my help to finish his book. The pig publishers threaten to cancel our contract unless the book is delivered in the fall. They won't accept the obvious truth that in a revolutionary period leaders cannot be held to the obligations of a piece of paper.

But in Amerika, they can reclaim their advance, another form of capitalist oppression.

Still I wish I could take time off this summer and sit down to talk to you like we did long ago.

As ever,
Cathy

95
CATHERINE

June 15, 1969

Dear Blackie,

I'm in a quandary. Again.

Father Ed visited me in New York last week, on his way to Latin America. We had a couple of drinks in a black bar near here. The people were so friendly once we told them that we were a priest and nun and that he was on his way to the Third World.

He has a sensational new assignment. He has been made provincial over all his order's missions in Latin America, with instructions to reorganize them so that they are in the vanguard of the struggle for liberation. Many inexperienced priests and sisters went down there in the early sixties when my Santa Claus pope called for help in Latin America. Some came home sick, some were co-opted by the power elites, and some were radicalized. Father Ed wants to organize the radicals into a new kind of missionary center in which the church identifies completely and totally with the poor against their class enemies.

It's a terribly exciting idea. He wants me to come with him and be his helper. I'd love to go. I'm so tired of all the academic shit. What is more irrelevant than a Ph.D. anyway? Ed looks around at the expensive buildings and the elaborate classrooms and the overstuffed chairs in the faculty lounge and says with his wonderful blunt Christian wisdom, "Is this what the Gospel is about, Catherine? Is this the most relevant thing you can do for Jesus and the poor? Read books and take tests and write a dissertation? How many souls have been saved, how many people have been freed by dissertations?"

And he needs me. You know how disorganized the poor man is. I could be the difference between success or failure in a situation where one man is forced to coordinate the work of liberation in seven countries.

But Roy needs me too. He'll never finish his book if I go to Costaguana. Action is important, as he says, but only if it's the revolutionary praxis that tests the validity of ideas. You must have the ideas first. Ed is in a certain sense betraying the cause by charging into a revolutionary situation without having clearly articulated the contradictions inherent in the situation. Moreover, he has been co-opted by the power structure in the church, which wants him out of the United States so that he will no longer be a voice for peace.

And Father Ed is very hard on young people. I told him my belief that we must learn from them because they are the beginning of a new age, the first generation to live in the future and not in the past. It has been hard for me to sympathize with the drugs and the dirt and the nudity and the free sex and the wild rock music that makes poor Elvis seem so tame. But I have come to see that the Woodstock generation, or the generation of Aquarius, the Beatles' generation, is much more Christian than I am. It has the simplicity and the clarity of St. Francis and will change the world not by doing anything but by being themselves.

Father Ed replies that they're irrelevant middle-class poseurs who lack the discipline for authentic revolution. There are no rock festivals in the Third World.

America is sick. It is an oppressive, violent, shallow, one-dimensional society, which is living off the poor people of the world. But how does one change our country? We need a revolution. But what kind of revolution? The revolution of rock festivals or the revolution of political liberation? Will we be saved by our own young people, who live for the future and not the past, who reject by their lives the capitalist values that are destroying us? Or will we be saved by the poor people of the Third World, who will sweep across the earth and force us to abandon our injustice and exploitation?

When I try to sort it out, I end up with a terrible headache.

It reminds me of the discussions we had in college religion class about what St. Thomas said concerning the conflict between thought and action. It's been so long ago that I can't remember the answer, but I think he chose both.

Which is no help for me.

I wish you were here to advise me what to do. Each work

would be an important contribution to the revolutionary cause. And each man needs me so much.

It's like trying to decide between Nick and the community when I was about to enter.

I know what advice you would give, Blackie. St. Thomas said both and you would say neither.

And that, of course, would not help at all.

But that doesn't mean I don't love you. I still do and always will.

                                        Love,
                                        Cathy

96
SISTER JOHN JEROME

                                        July 1, 1969

Dear Sister Catherine,

I regret that I must inform you that the council was not able to reach an agreement authorizing me to reply affirmatively to your petition to make your solemn and perpetual vows next month. You may of course renew your present temporary vows for three more years and reapply for profession three years from now.

This is in no sense a reflection on you but rather the result of a decision on the part of the council that an applicant for profession ought to have time for mature reflection before making so critical a decision in her life.

I am looking forward to seeing you here at the Administrative Center at the end of the month for the retreat which will precede your renewal of vows.

                                        Faithfully in Our Lord,
                                        Sister John Jerome OLH
                                        President

97

SISTER JOHN JEROME

Dear Cathy,

I tried all day yesterday to reach you by phone. Sister said you were at a demonstration somewhere. So I am putting this note in with my formal letter, by way of explanation, hoping that it will soften the disappointment. Please call me on my private number any time of the day or night so we can discuss this matter further.

I'll be blunt with you, Cathy, as you have always been with me. It was Martina Mary and her clique on the council. You are not the only one to whom this has been done. They are trying to rewrite the chapter so that it is stamped with their interpretation. Some of the older sisters on the council, while not agreeing with them on most points, are uneasy about the activism of the younger sisters. The three-year renewal was a compromise to gain their support. I know you don't believe in compromises, but I had no choice.

In fact, there will be fury in the whole community over this decision. Martina Mary is a curiously blind person when it comes to such matters. She expects to be supported because she has willed that everyone agrees with her. She and her friends will be defeated in the council election next year and will no longer plague us. I can promise you that if you reapply for profession next summer there will be no difficulty.

As you know, the mother general used to make these decisions herself. And usually they were the right ones. Now the council must make them on my recommendation. This year we had a fight on every single candidate, an example, I fear, of well-intentioned democracy run wild that will be repeated often in the church in years ahead.

It's difficult to restructure overnight, Cathy, and I hope and pray you'll give us a chance to correct this horrible injustice.

You can imagine the nature of Martina's objections. Although I myself do not always accept the wisdom or the prudence of what you do and say, I respect your freedom to act, as I hope you respect my freedom not to agree with you all the time.

But while I may at times question both the prudence and the wisdom of your activities, I have no question at all about you, Cathy. I made the strongest possible recommendation for your profession and I will make it again next summer. You are a fine religious now and will mature into an even better one in years to come.

We need you, Cathy. We want you. We love you.

In Xto,
Johnny

98
CATHERINE

July 5, 1969

Dear Blackie,

I guess this letter says it all. I've cried for three days. And I've let my own emotions interfere with my work for Roy, which is a terribly immature thing to do.

They don't want me, Blackie. After all the years and all the work and all the effort, they don't want me. They let a tight-assed little bitch like Martina Mary do me in.

I'm broken-hearted. I've failed at so many other things in life; now I have failed at this too. I must be a truly terrible person to fail at everything. I suppose God is punishing me and I deserve to be punished. Will I ever amount to anything?

I called Johnny immediately (I was in jail again) and demanded a full explanation. I'll only mention some of it. I was blamed for trying to seduce Father Tierney. I was accused of seeking publicity in front of the cathedral when the pig hit me in the stomach. I was blamed for throwing the piss on the police in front of the Hilton. I was charged with being Roy's mistress. Can you imagine that, Blackie? He's never put a hand on me. They said I am responsible for Father Ed's becoming a Communist.

On and on and on.

I sobbed through most of the conversation. Johnny tried to calm me down, but I don't want to be calmed down. They screwed me. And she helped them. She is so damn proud of her political skills. She wouldn't stand up for principle. She's the Hubert Horseface of the order.

I suppose the sensible thing to do is to swallow my anger and return to the Hill and renew the vow for three years.

Except what would that do to poor Nick?

And there is the principle involved. I was tried, convicted and condemned by a court without ever being given a chance to testify on my own behalf or challenge my accusers.

It's a fluke, Johnny says; it won't happen again. But an institution that is so structurally deformed that it permits something like this to happen once will permit something equally unjust later on.

And I can't consult with Roy because he is away on a week's vacation, poor man. His doctor insisted he take a few days off. I can't even phone him because the yacht he is on doesn't have a phone.

I finally caught up with Father Ed. His advice was to make the three-year vow, forget about it and come to Costaguana where no one gives a damn about such things.

Can you imagine that, Blackie? Father Ed actually said "damn."

I'll let you know what happens.

I wish you were here instead of in Europe.

>   All my love,
>   Cathy

P.S. I made up my mind. I enclose a copy of my letter. You may not admire the decision, Blackwood, but I think you'll like the style.

99
CATHERINE

July 6, 1969
New York

Dear Sister John Jerome:
Fuck you and the whole order.

Cordially,
Catherine Collins

100
CATHERINE

August 14, 1969

Dear Blackie,
I'm going to be married!
Roy and I have talked about it for the last month. We have
agreed that we have compatible values and interests and that
we will be happy together. I will participate fully in all his
theological work and hence be an integral part of the creation
of revolutionary ideas that can be tested by revolutionary
praxis. He will continue at Assembly. I have already made a
down payment on a house in Riverdale, which is only a brief
commuter ride from Assembly but a very lovely neighborhood,
much like St. Prax's.
You see, when I left the community last month all that
money from the family came to me. I'm happy that I will be
able to put it to good use.
We will be married in Central Park on Labor Day. Father

McGovern, a married classmate of Roy's, will officiate at the ceremony. We won't have time for a honeymoon, because we must finish the book by October 15, at the very latest. The editor is demanding many stupid changes.

As you probably have guessed, Roy is not applying for a dispensation from his promise of celibacy. To do so would be to acknowledge the arbitrary and oppressive power of the Curia over the lives of priests. Those who apply for dispensations are the cause of their continuing power. If every priest who wanted to marry simply did so and paid no attention to the pope, all priests would soon be free of oppression by Rome.

Moreover, he is still a priest, even by the old theology. He may no longer have official approval from the ruling class in the Vatican to exercise his ministry, but what does that matter? He still will stand on the leading edge of revolutionary Catholic thought.

I will consider my marriage valid in the sight of God and will be proud to be the wife of a priest. Eventually priests will be able to marry. Why should Roy and I wait till we're too old to enjoy life together and to have children?

And I so want children.

I'm very calm and serene in this decision, Blackie. It is not the result of immature romantic infatuation. It is rather the outcome of sophisticated discussion and reflection. We are two adults who wish to share our lives, our work, and our visions. To better share, I will withdraw from graduate work, which makes such heavy demands on my time as to preclude the sharing to which we are both totally committed. It will be a relief to escape from all the shit courses anyway.

I know that you will not approve. I plead that you give Roy and me time to demonstrate to you by the happiness of our common life that we are choosing the wisest and most mature option available to us.

It is a terrible imposition, but I hope you can come home from Europe for my marriage. You're the only brother I have.

Please come, Blackie, please.

Love,
Coz

101
BLACKIE

August 20, 1969
Salt Hill
County Galway

Dear Cathy,

I cannot come.

And because I love you so much I will be candid as to why. I would not mind breaking a thousand summer vacations for you. Nor is the problem Roy. He is your choice and I must respect any choice you make.

But I cannot be part of contempt for the church.

No one who is unhappy in the priesthood should be constrained to be a priest. When a man has served for a period of time and wishes to withdraw from the active ministry, then I say let him go forth with dignity and honor and gratitude.

As to whether priests ought to be permitted to marry, that is a question on which I have mixed emotions, but it is not pertinent. They are not permitted to marry at the present time. If dispensations were impossible or extremely rare, then I would not fault a man who married. And I agree with you that God wouldn't, either. However, again, this is not the case.

Dispensations are easy to obtain. The process is mildly annoying, not nearly so bothersome as the annulment process for married people. (I admit the parallel is not perfect.) To refuse even to attempt to obtain a dispensation seems to me deliberately and self-consciously contemptuous of the church.

I am no defender of the abuses of power by those in church authority. I reserve the right to criticize as Paul criticized Peter, "to his face." But I can't be contemptuous of the church. It may not be much as a church now, but it's the only one I have.

I respect your right to make your decision in the name of your principles. I must ask the same of you.

As well as your forgiveness. I wish there was another way.

I love you, Catherine. Since the first day I was aware that

there was another creature in the playpen, like me and yet not quite like me, I have loved you. I can't imagine ever not loving you.

Again, please forgive me.

All my love,
Blackie

P.S. (after much hesitation) God in heaven, Cathy, don't do it! Wait. Give yourself time for reflection. Just a little more time. Talk to Mary Kate. Get her advice, but don't do it.

102 **CATHERINE**

August 30, 1969
New York

Blackie,
Goddamn you to hell, you miserable fucking asshole.

Cathy

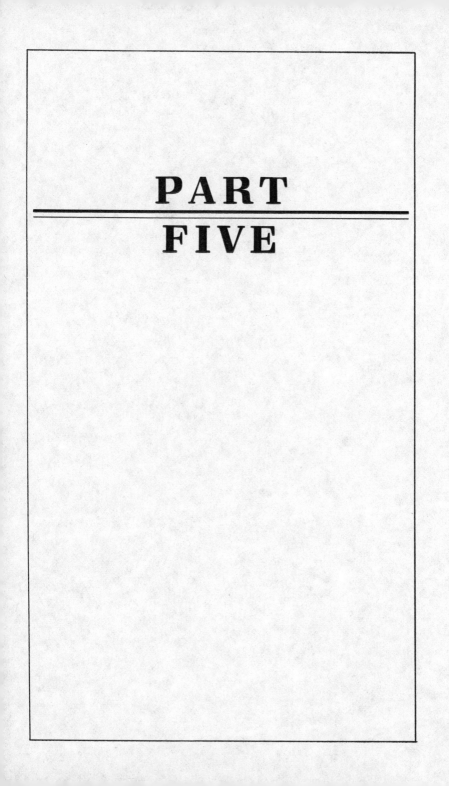

PART
FIVE

103
MARY KATE

"Tell me again why men hate beautiful women?" I asked Joe from Boston as our 727 climbed into the gray twilight sky over Manhattan Island and with dogged determination rushed toward an incoming line of thundershowers.

"Not all men," he replied slowly, slipping his arm around my shoulders. "I've been known to rather enjoy a beautiful woman on occasion."

"Chauvinist," I said, snuggling contentedly in his arm. "But, okay, why do SOME men—no one here present, surely—need to punish beautiful women? I can sniff them when they come into my office. Either they will humiliate me or they'll quit therapy. What ails them?"

"They see their own anima reflected in the woman's attractiveness and are terrified at the hint of their own feminine beauty."

"Cut the Jungian crap," I insisted. Oddly enough for a Boston Irishman, Joe is a follower of Carl Gustav while I am, of course, a classic Freudian, trained at the institute. Sig 'em, Sigmund!

"A woman is a threat to their masculinity because her sex appeal makes them dependent on her for the fulfillment of their needs," my Pirate said with a sigh, resigned to speaking in Freudian categories when I permitted shop talk. "Beauty in woman is enormous power. You brutalize, humiliate and degrade a beautiful woman so that she won't unman you. You demean her lest she consume you. Our new in-law, Roy, gets his jollies out of enslaving women like Cathy because he is afraid that if he does not, she will overwhelm him. If I were in his boots I might do the same." He tightened his grip on my shoulder.

"The hell you would."

Our mean aluminum machine bucked and swayed like a troubled rhino. Nonetheless, a cabin attendant appeared to take our orders for two vodka martinis, standard airplane medication. Joe did not let her charms go unnoticed.

"You wouldn't humiliate that one, would you?" I sniffed.

"You noticed her too? Do you think Roy is a homosexual?"

"My guess," I said thoughtfully, "is that he is mostly neuter. Power is more important to him than sex. Dominating a woman is more pleasurable than fucking her. Terrible mistake."

I was not disturbed by the cabin attendant or indeed by all the cabin attendants in the world. Not only was I a better traveling companion than any of them, I was also a better lay. Especially, because of some strange reason of my psychology and physiology, after an airplane ride.

"I can only agree," the Pirate said in his best professional-colleague manner. "I don't know that I approve of Blackie's boycott, but that wedding was like a visit to an institution for delusional schizophrenics."

Knowing what I had in mind as, damn him, he always does, Joe's hand slipped down my arm so that his fingers were resting lightly against my breast, tentatively enough so that he could fold them away when yonder cabin attendant returned.

I would call Nancy from O'Hare and take her up on her offer of watching the Brats till Sunday night. Monday morning even. There was something so marvelously healthy about good old-fashioned heterosexual lust after Catherine's wedding.

Imagine, if you will, a marriage ceremony in which the groom was the main focus of attention, instead of the bride. And imagine such a horror show enacted in Central Park under a hot sun and a hazy blue sky, with balloons, banners and dancing boys in leotards (no dancing girls, please note), a bearded, long-haired celebrant dressed in gold watered silk, readings from Mao, Marcuse, Norman O. Brown and, of course, Roy Tuohy.

Neither God nor Jesus made it into the ceremony, though the celebrant had arranged his mane and his beard so that he looked like Jesus. Indeed, the deity was not mentioned even in the various freedom and revolutionary songs that were bellowed at strategic points in the ceremony—causing, as far as I could see, no alarm to the agents of capitalist repression from the New York City police force who were watching from a distance with only mild curiosity. Perhaps they thought it was the crowd from the Harvard *Lampoon* doing a parody of the Roman Catholic Mass.

But if God wasn't mentioned, there was certainly a considerable celebration of Roy Tuohy. He was resplendent in monastic robes, cardinal red in color, tied with a gold cord, in which he plunged his hands repeatedly during his forty-five-minute homily, not as if he were controlling his passions but rather to certify the dignity and thoughtfulness of a great man making an important speech (largely composed of citations of his own works). His long beard was speckled with white—artificially, I suspected—to confirm the impression of a prophetic wise man, a character straight out of the book of Ecclesiastes.

"We stand here today as partisans of the new humanity, as Christian revolutionaries beginning the construction of a new and better world, as men and women unafraid of the repression by either the political or the religious establishments. We repudiate them. We challenge them. We defy them. Our revolt against their oppressive authority, symbolized in today's ceremony, is the first step in the birth of a new Christianity. They will say that one more priest has proven that he should never have been a priest in the first place. We say that one priest has the courage to stand up and tell them that their age is over and ours has begun."

Loud applause from the congregation.

"Horse manure," I said aloud.

Secure now that the cabin attendant and her colleagues were tied down by seat belts like the rest of us, Joe continued his delicious remote foreplay. "In spades, you should excuse the mixed metaphor."

"If you keep that up," I protested, "I will not survive to the room at the O'Hare Hilton you're going to get for us the minute we escape from this mean trimotored machine."

Roy favored us with a second address over the wine and cheese—cheap domestic wine and stale cheese—after the "liturgy." In measured cadences, he told us about freedom and maturity, oppression and child-ishness, Cuba and the Vatican, Vietnam and the oil companies, without a single mention of his bride.

This was not particularly surprising because she was hardly men-tioned in the ceremony. The whole show was devoted to the celebration of Roy Tuohy, with only minor reference to the fact that it was a marriage ceremony. Cathy wore a brown homespun dress and a long veil, both concealing the reality that women's bodies are somewhat different from men's bodies. Any wedding that needed to hide Cathy's superb figure, I thought, was sufficiently sick to call for the immediate institutionalization of all involved.

The climax, you should excuse the expression, came when Cathy proposed a toast to her new husband in a timid and anxious voice: "To my new partner, one of the great revolutionary thinkers and leaders of our era!"

Multiply compounded and blended horse manure.

"I've finally found a purpose and a destiny for my life," she mur-mured softly when I embraced her—a hell of a reason for embarking on marriage's problematic seas.

Roy disdained my embrace, the pig.

I might not have minded so much if I had thought there was any possibility of good sex for her. She needed that desperately, unless I misread all the signs of middle-twenties penis hunger. But not from Roy Tuohy, who was a classic autoerotic.

What had happened to my fun-loving, vital, pretty cousin/sister? I tried being angry at her parents, at the novitiate, at dumb, gorgeous Nick, even at the Punk, who should have done SOMETHING. It didn't work. I ended up being angry at Roy Tuohy. And at Cathy herself.

"Did you have the impression that we witnessed a ceremony in which a man married himself?" I asked my consulting shrink, who, because we had passed through the storm and were not bound by the seat-belt sign, had temporarily ceased his importunities.

I'd seen enough problems in my practice to know that no marriage is perfect. Most don't work as well as they might. And a lot don't work at all. You shoot for box cars when you cast the dice on your wedding day. Joe and I have had our problems, occasionally great big, spectacular shanty-Irish shouting and screaming problems (you can guess which of us does the shouting and screaming). But with each passing year we enjoy each other more in bed (inventing new and pleasantly unspeakable things to do to each other), laugh more at each other's jokes, and are more unhappy in even short interludes of separation.

And Joe, Jungian from Boston or not, was so sensitive and gentle with me that it broke my heart that I was not good enough for him.

At a minimum, Cathy was entitled to that. No way she would have it.

"With his own image of himself," he said, twisting a bit as my fingers touched his thigh—what is sauce for the Jungian is sauce for the Freudian. "How long do you think it will last?"

"With most women no more than six months. Cathy is different. She is stubborn enough to hang on for a long time."

I was now so eager for the reassertion of human passion—screwing my man, if you wish—that I pondered the stories about couples making it in the washrooms of airplanes. It struck me as being anatomically difficult if not impossible, but what sort of a scientist is it that will not seek evidence? Alas, the seat belts went back on. Dear God, please protect Cathy and bring her home safe to us.

"Any more than two years and she will spend the rest of her life in custodial care." My Pirate shook his head sadly. "He's already pushed her pretty close to the brink. I thought the red robes were appropriate. All he needs is the pitchfork and the horns."

104
CATHERINE

April 15, 1970
Riverdale

You miserable son of a bitch, how dare you invite me to your ordination and first Mass?

If you had any courage you would refuse ordination and lead a movement to persuade the other cowards that only when all young men refuse ordination will the oppressive celibacy rule be abandoned. Those who accept ordination, as Roy says, under the present tyrannical conditions, are morally responsible for the continuation of the tyranny.

Since you are not involved in solving the problem, you become the problem.

You ought to be ashamed of yourself.

Catherine

105
BLACKIE

I had not expected Cath to come to my ordination. Indeed, I had grown resigned to her disappearing from our lives. In the years after, the birth-control encyclical caused the black hole to explode; priests and nuns were running for secure cover, some in marriage, some in the pursuit of the annual ideological fads, some in drugs and drink (a lot in drink, to tell you the truth), and some in desperate attempts to resurrect the old order.

There were new heroes every six months. The Roy Tuohy wedding was celebrated in the *National Catholic Reporter* with a full-page spread of pictures, and the National Federation of Priests' Councils unanimously resolved that he was to be supported and praised and demanded that he be returned to the active priesthood. It was an odd resolution, as Roy had never been much interested in saying Mass or preaching for an ordinary Sunday congregation.

Heroes and heroines came and went; even the Berrigans began to fade when it was revealed that Father Phil and Sister Liz had been living in a common-law marriage (fornicating, my patron, Bishop Sean Cronin, called it). Roy Tuohy's public role as a hero was brief. The fads at Assembly still dominated the marketplace, but after the celebration of Norman O. Brown's polymorphous perversity at his wedding, Roy withdrew into silence. One of my friends from the New York clergy reported that Roy now felt that great men should speak in public only rarely and then with the utmost solemnity.

My guess was that he was searching for a replacement for Norman Brown, for another book to define the next fad.

Moreover, Roy knew in his heart that he wasn't very good at theology. He had skated just ahead of the pack for a long time. Now the pack was filling up with some gifted thinkers, most of whom would be caricatured by the ideology of unreason, but a few of whom would actually make something intelligent out of it.

Roy was silent because he had nothing new to say and was afraid that if he said something old he would be punished with a fate worse than death—derided as out-of-date and a has-been. So he was busy searching for a new gimmick, one which would take him out of the old race and put him in a new one.

And enjoying the good life with Cathy's money.

Dear God in heaven, what could we have done to save her?

There was only one class of priests and nuns who were permanently barred from hero/heroine status in those days—the ones who hung on and did their work, and did not want or need or perhaps wouldn't accept the latest security blanket. And they, of course, were part of the problem, weren't they?

Cath had found her security blanket in Roy Tuohy, the same sort of protection from the uncertainties of life that her mother had sought in devotion to the Fatima letters a decade and a half earlier. At least her name disappeared from the lists of religious and ex-religious who were dragged off to jail at the weekly demonstrations around the country. There was not a word about her in the accounts of the Cambodia and Kent State protests the year I was ordained.

Sometimes I consoled myself with the thought that Roy was probably marginally better than Ed Carny.

Which showed how much I knew.

106
NICHOLAS

You fly to Santa Marta, the capital of the Republic of Costaguana, through Río. And there were two ways to Río, an overnight flight from either New York or Miami. I went to New York early in the morning to consult with the Consul General of Costaguana, who attended Harvard Law School with one of the senior partners in our firm. He spoke on the phone to Don Oswaldo DeGrazia, the minister of justice in the coalition government, and assured me that the minister would be most happy to see me.

I was sure that the poor man would be anything but happy to see me, but would do so because his administration's relationships with the United States were so important to its survival and I was presumably a man of influence. I don't know much Spanish, but I think that the consul general spoke of me as a potential member of the United States Senate.

Once I wanted that. Now, since I could not share it with Catherine, I was repelled by the thought of public office.

That night at six I boarded Pan Am 201, nonstop to Río. I flew coach, despite Blackie's insistence that Catherine would want me to fly in comfort, and slept fitfully as the 747 cut through the night skies to Brazil. My only entertainment was a joust with Kevin Rabbit, the "peace and justice" guru of the American Catholic church, whom I had met at a Council of Foreign Relations seminar. A tall, glowing-eyed zealot, Rabbit assured me that he was opposed to Marxism but that a country had the right to choose its own economic and social system and that the United States should not try to interfere with those countries which had chosen Marxism.

I asked him what those countries were. It seemed to me that Marxism had always been imposed by the morality that grows out of the mouth of a gun, either a gun of the Red army or a gun of a revolutionary elite. He praised the accomplishments of Cuba, particularly in health and education. I responded that even before Castro, Cuba had the highest literacy rate and the best educational system in Latin America. Rabbit, almost a caricature of Blackie's picture of the "new priest," replied with a quote from a papal encyclical.

"When did the people of Cuba choose Marxism?" I demanded hotly.

"When they accepted the revolution," he replied serenely.

"At bayonet point. Is that what the pope and the church mean by freedom of choice nowadays?"

"Some Latin American Catholics argue that civil liberties must not become an obsession when they stand in the way of the cause of social justice," he replied. Another carefully memorized answer, like a Catholic street preacher arguing, when I was a kid, against the validity of Anglican orders.

"And did the people of Germany have the right to choose Nazism, which they did in a free election, by the way? Should the United States have tolerated such a choice?"

"That's different," he said smoothly.

"I'm going to Costaguana to look for the body of a woman who died because she listened to shitheads like you!" I exploded.

Rabbit faded away, a wraithlike assembly of clichés, a ghost who ceased to exist when you exorcised him with a challenge for which there was no slick, hollow answer.

Blackie would have said that I had tried to transfer my feeling of responsibility for Catherine to a helpless and harmless bureaucrat.

It was summer in Brazil, and Río International, despite its air-conditioning, felt like a Turkish bath in which the heating unit has gone out of control. I yearned for the sands of Copacabana and the pool on the top of the Palace Hotel.

But there was no time and too many memories of my encounter there with Catherine the year before she disappeared—confused, angry, bittersweet memories of which I would never be able to make sense.

I had been waiting for her, one way or another, since 1962—fourteen years. No one ought to wait that long. But the decade and a half had been cut into smaller segments—the two years of postulancy and novitiate, after which I was convinced she would leave the religious life. Then the three years till her final vows. And the interlude with Roy, which I knew would end. Then her three-year promise to serve in Costaguana, which was finished when she disappeared. Finally the last two years of waiting for proof of her death.

An obsession? I guess it was. But knowing that I was obsessed, perhaps with a dream woman and almost certainly with a dead one, did not lessen the hold she still had on me.

What would I find in the church at Río Secco? One of two things, either Catherine's body or the Angela disguise. Either one should free me from my obsession.

The flight to Costaguana was delayed, and it was late in the afternoon before the weary old 707 lifted itself out of Río International and banked over the giant statue of Christ that overlooks the bay.

I was hot, dirty and tired. Yet I was still able to pray to the One for Whom Catherine had tried to be a bride.

I began with a prayer that at the end of my search I would find liberation from the obsession which had haunted me for so many years. And I ended praying that Catherine might still be alive.

And that we could begin again.

107
CATHERINE

June 1, 1971
Riverdale

Dear Blackie,

Already a year in the priesthood. I wonder if you're happy? I suppose you are. You manage always to be happy. I heard from someone that you're doing parish work and studying the classics and running errands for Sean Cronin. I suppose in a year or two the bishop will be running errands for you, poor man.

I miss you all. Please write.

All my love,
Cathy

108
MARY KATE

I was in no mood for problems when the Punk appeared with Cathy's letter. I mean personal problems. The professional ones I leave in the office. My life-cycle crisis was that I was getting old. My husband, the shrink, was decidedly unsympathetic. "If you didn't want to have a daughter graduate from grammar school when you're thirty-seven," he said briskly, "you shouldn't have seduced a resident the first year you were in medical school."

I made some tasteless remark about horny residents. Tasteless and, as we both knew, quite dishonest. I decided I wanted Joe the first time I saw him in the hospital, looking dreadfully wise and competent. Mind you, he didn't resist much.

But the end result of my youthful lust was that my Caitlin was graduating from St. Prax's and I had graduated, myself, only yesterday. Or the day before. She was a willowy blond with fresh young breasts, a sweet smile and an even temper that was utterly out of place in our family. But she had the glint in her eyes, the sort of glint that makes the Punk special. It was a fragile glint still, a young imp not quite sure that she should be as impish as she wants. But kind of willing to risk it. I didn't want to hurt her by revealing my envy of her youth.

So I was in no mood for Catherine's letter.

"A *cri de coeur*," he said, as I considered the two short paragraphs.

"Don't talk dirty," I replied, trying to concentrate on Cathy's crisis of passage instead of my own.

"She wants help."

"Sure she does. It's a cry from her heart. You ought to fly down there and visit her."

"I think you should be the visitor," the Punk said, not being one to beat around the bush. "She needs a woman's help now."

"How do you know?" I demanded dubiously.

"She won't let down her hair with me. The intimate part of the marriage isn't working. And she'll share that only with another woman."

"You mean the fucking is lousy?"

"I mean that there probably isn't any. And not much else, either, save for bolstering Roy's galaxy-sized ego. She might try to pretend with me. Not with you."

He was perfectly correct, of course.

"Why didn't she write to me, then?"

"She half-wants you to come and is half-afraid that you will."

"That's not a good prognosis for therapy," I said, mentally thinking of which Brats would go to Helen and which to Nancy. Caitlin is still too young to take care of them and their father when I bound around the country.

Another year or two, though, and she will be left in charge. Assistant matriarch. All right, it is useful to have a teenage daughter.

"We're a long way from therapy, M.K. This is strictly a rescue mission."

"Get her the hell out of there?"

"The sooner the better."

Joe usually groans when I bound around. This time he was enthusiastic, eliminating my last excuse.

"This may be her last chance, Mary Kate. Don't blow it."

"Thanks for the professional confidence." I kissed him and hurried down the jetway to the waiting 727.

I didn't recognize her when she opened the door of her palace in Riverdale. The woman in the doorway was fat and slovenly, no makeup on her unhappy face, her hair ratty and unwashed, her cheap housedress wrinkled and unattractive. Cathy at forty maybe, but not at twenty-six. I was tempted to retreat at once to my rented red Chevy, in which I had hoped to pack her luggage when it came time for us to settle with the hotel and split.

Damn the bastard.

At first she hesitated, like I was selling encyclopedias instead of salvation. Then she broke down and hugged me, tears streaming down her face.

She made herbal tea and I let her show me the house and talk. She had dropped out of everything, because their mutual commitment to Roy's work was the only thing that really mattered for the present.

"It's a masterpiece, M.K.," she said devoutly. "It will be as important to the future as was *The City of God* or the *Summa*. We have to finish it before they take the advance back."

Horse manure, I thought to myself.

She was writing the book, it turned out. Roy dictated his ideas in "rough form." She wrote them down, recast them in readable English, submitted them to him for review, and then rewrote them again—sometimes five or six drafts—until he was satisfied.

"He has a very precise and demanding intellect," she said piously. "But the work is so important that I don't mind our having had to let everything else slip until it is finished."

Roy had married himself a housekeeper, a financial angel, a secretary, an editor, and probably a thinker too. Nice work if you can get it.

I raised my first point. "How's the sex?"

"It's all right," she said listlessly. "We're both so busy. . . . It doesn't seem important."

"A couple of times a month?" I said, knowing it was less.

"Some months." She looked away in embarrassment. She didn't want to talk about it. And, on the other hand, she wanted desperately to talk about it. "The sex is mostly my fault. I . . . I'm not able to be very attractive for Roy. And we have so many other things that bring us satisfaction. . . ."

"The marriage was consummated?" I demanded.

"More or less," she replied miserably.

"Is he a homosexual?" I asked bluntly.

"That's not a term we find acceptable," she said firmly. "There is room among sophisticated people for a wide variety of sexual relationships. If Roy has other intense friendships, I have no right to be possessive of him. Ours is a totally free and open marriage."

"He has a lover at school?" I said, pushing on relentlessly.

"Yes, we're quite open about it, a young, black assistant professor from the West Indies. It is a very enlightened relationship, based on mutual commitment to the oppressed peoples of the Third World. He and Roy are working on a book together."

"You mean he's writing it for Roy the way you're writing this masterpiece."

"Please, Mary Kate," she said hotly. "Try to understand what an open marriage is."

"Oh, I understand all right. Open for him and closed for you."

"That's not fair." She was close to throwing me out of the house.

Okay, Mary Kate, go for broke.

"Do you want to know what I think, Cath?"

"I'm not sure I do." Very stern and aloof.

"Then why did you write the Punk and tell him to send me here?"

"I didn't. . . . " She grinned faintly, a hint of the old hoyden. "All right, I do want to know what you think."

"I think"—a deep breath as I sailed off the high dive—"that you've become a slave to a man who hates women and who enjoys degrading them. He has taken away your freedom, your good looks, your mind, your ability to think for yourself, your sexuality, your money, your career, your politics, your selfhood and made you an extension of his own autoerotic ego."

The explosion I expected did not happen.

"I can see how you would think that," she said mildly. "But it really isn't true."

"Oh, yes, it is. And you know that it is. And you wanted to hear me say it to confirm what you suspect."

"I don't know what to think anymore." She shook her head in confusion. "I can't seem to think for myself."

I had an idea, a risky and dangerous idea. But I had to try it. My Jungian roommate had diagnosed the situation perfectly. If we didn't rescue her now, she was institutional material.

"The key to it is his need to degrade and punish beautiful women. . . . "

"That's Freudian ideology," she snapped at me. "Roy is unfailingly kind to women."

Aha, she was falling into my trap.

"You will admit that for a broken-down old mother of a grammar school graduate, I retain some sexual appeal."

"Caitlin graduating?" She smiled enthusiastically. "How wonderful! Where is she going to high school? . . . All right, I won't change the subject. You're a knockout, M.K., and you know it."

"A fading knockout," I said with totally false humility. "Now, I predict that if I wait here till your husband comes home, he will be vicious and cruel to me. Oh, he won't lay a hand on me. But you watch how he acts and what he says. And remember he's been doing that to you for years and is eating into the core of your personality."

"He won't do that at all," she said confidently. "But let's see what happens. It will refute your ideology."

Poor Roy couldn't help himself. I had worn a white wrap dress with a broad sash which said "sex" in very large letters. His fear took over before his reason could grasp that he had been set up.

"You didn't say that your cousin would be visiting us, Catherine," he snapped at her as soon as she had reintroduced us.

"It was a surprise visit," she said meekly.

"The affluent and the idle can afford surprises. Those of us with responsibilities must adhere to our schedules. It is typical of your class, with all due respect, Mrs. Murphy, not to respect the value of other people's time."

"Doctor Murphy," I said crisply.

"Ah, yes." His smile was genial, like Basil Rathbone's as Sir Guy in the old Robin Hood movie, but his eyes were hard and frightened. "The Freudian. Tell me, Doctor Murphy, have you ever cured anyone?"

My Boston Irish bed partner will tell you that beneath the hard shell I am an extremely vulnerable woman. He damn well better tell you that, anyway. However, I am able to cope with the nasties most of the time. So this time I chose not to cope and let myself be vulnerable out in the open.

"I try. . . . "

"Do you have no problems of conscience accepting . . . what? Fifty dollars an hour several days a week from patients for three, four, even five years? Do you not feel that it is exploitation?"

"Cheaper than kidney surgery and maybe more important."

"Ah, yes." He smiled again, this time more malevolently. "But after kidney surgery, the patient is healed. In the case of psychoanalysis, there is never a cure, is there? At most an improvement. Do you not feel sometimes that you are a social parasite?"

There were many smart-assed replies to choose from, but I had put on my vulnerable persona. "We are aware of our weaknesses and limitations . . . "

"Weaknesses and limitations?" he snorted, stroking his beard. "I would say rather complete moral and intellectual bankruptcy."

Cath was listening quietly, pensively, her face expressionless.

"We can help only some people," I stammered, waiting for the tears, which were forming. "But I do think we help them a lot."

"Help them? Rather, you reduce them to a state of total dependency, of permanent immaturity, in which they become a gold mine for you, a source of income which you will never let out of your claws. Does that not strike you as parasitism?"

I had hit it rich. The more vulnerable a beautiful woman, the more uncontrollable Roy's rage against her. His mother must have been a real ball-buster.

"I don't think so," I said, now making visible efforts to hold back the tears.

They were real enough, God knows. But they were for Cathy.

"Nor do I find it morally acceptable that it is the wealthy you exploit. Your so-called science merely facilitates their adjustment to the oppressive order of capitalist society, does it not? Are you not parasites living off parasites?"

The tears were flowing like Niagara by now. Cathy was implacable, like she was watching an Albee play on television.

"We do our best to diminish the suffering in the world," I said through my tears.

"At the price of creating more suffering," he sneered triumphantly. "It is not to be wondered at that you feel free to intrude on our work without warning. Your conscience has been deadened by your life of exploitation. You are not involved in the solution to the problem. You are part of the problem."

It was all I could do not to go after that cliché.

"We try—" I stumbled.

"DOCTOR Murphy," he fairly crowed. "You would be much better advised to spend your time with your children. That way you would only injure a few lives instead of many."

He was in trouble before that line, but it was the one that did him in. If I had not pulled Catherine off him, she would have clawed his eyes out. Her fury was speechless, but not soundless. She screamed like a banshee pouncing on a damned soul.

And poor Roy wasn't worth sending to hell.

She took him completely by surprise. He tried ineffectually to brush her off and ended up pinned to the ground while she pounded lumps on him, all the while wailing like the aforementioned banshee.

I let her blacken his eye before I pulled her off.

Roy gathered together the shreds of his dignity and retreated toward the door. "When you come to your senses, Catherine, and are ready to seek my forgiveness, I will be at the faculty club. You may call me there, but not after seven."

"With your goddamn faggot lover," she screamed, at last finding words to express her anger. Even then, however, the words were aimed at the lover and not at Roy.

"You and the horse you rode in on," I hollered after him, no longer the vulnerable shrink with the clear complexion, blond hair and bedroom-blue eyes.

We packed some of her clothes, dressed her in a suit, which was much too tight, and gathered up a few precious items, including, of course, her Pope John rosaries.

On which we prayed as we got the hell out of there and back to La Guardia in my rented car. We took a couple of wrong turns and ended up in a place with the odd name of Rye. But finally, after wandering across a number of mean suspension-bridge machines, we managed to navigate into La Guardia.

Cathy had no money, but my credit cards still worked. We were wait-listed for two flights and missed them, because I would not let her travel without me.

Somewhere in the vicinity of Cleveland, Ohio, we both began to laugh. I ordered two vodka martinis and we drank to each other's health. Cathy struck up a conversation with the cabin attendant and advised her about returning to college. The three children who were on the plane crowded around her and one rode to O'Hare on Cathy's lap.

In the taxi from the airport she chattered about seeing the Punk again, after all these years. "He isn't mad at me, is he?"

"The Punk doesn't hold grudges," I said, lying through my teeth.

"He does too. Does he have a grudge against me?"

"The day after the pope becomes a Baptist will the Punk hold a grudge against you."

It would take a lot of work for a very competent shrink, woman rather than man, I thought, but for Cathy the worst was over. She was coming home where she belonged.

And I could not have been more completely mistaken.

109
CATHERINE

July 4, 1971
OLH

Dearest, Darling Cousin Blackie (aka The Punk),

You can tell Bishop Sean Cronin that I don't care how cute he is or how effective a congressman his brother is or how absolutely gorgeous his sister-in-law is, I will find it hard to forgive him for sending you off to Poland the day before I came home.

I'm sure you're stirring up revolution there.

But I'll be so happy to see you at Grand Beach when Labor Day rolls around.

I'm here at the Mother House putting myself kind of tentatively back together, praying and fasting (to peel the layers of fat off my bod) and trying to figure out how I could have been so dumb.

I'm not doing any of these things very seriously—except the fasting, which is absolutely critical if I ever want to put on a swimsuit again and be seen on the same beach with the Ryan clan. M.K. says I should go into intensive therapy in the fall, but she approves of me spending a few weeks here first, to get over the worst of the last couple of years.

It seems like a terrible dream even now. I can hardly believe that it was all real. I'm not planning on contesting the divorce. Let him have the house and whatever else he wants. I'm happy that it's over, and I never want to see him again.

And I've already lost ten pounds.

Johnny Jerome has been so loving to me that you wouldn't believe it. How can a sick, vicious bitch like me be loved by tons of wonderful people? Martina Mary and her crowd were beaten at the last election and have left the order. Martina has already married a stockbroker, could you believe? And, despite all the wicked ugly things I said to them, Johnny and the others are treating me like a long-lost daughter.

Not that I'm necessarily going to rejoin the community. Putting my life in order with a really good shrink (M.K. says a woman, and I think she's right) comes before everything else. And Johnny says that while I'm always welcome back, she wouldn't readmit me unless I go through the therapy first.

I'm scared of it and looking forward to it. Kind of like taking off your clothes and finding out what's really under them.

Now, no cheap cracks from you, Coz. Remember you're a priest. And you owe me a first blessing.

M.K. was spectacular that day in Riverdale. God, Blackie, what an incredible broad she is.

I think I may return to painting in the fall too. M.K. says I need something else besides head-shrinking to keep me occupied.

You wonder about Nick, of course. Oh, Blackwood, dearest, so do I. Why hasn't he rushed up here to see me? I suppose that if he did, he wouldn't be Nick, would he?

M.K. went over to see my parents, at my request. Now that

I'm no longer a nun I thought they might talk to me again. But I guess I'll never be able to please them. Now they're angry at me because I left the community. And because I left my husband. M.K. didn't give me the gory details, but I can imagine—Mom babbling about irresponsibility and Dad limping out of the room, his *Wall Street Journal* hanging from a thin old hand.

Obviously that is a big item on my shrink agenda.

I haven't changed, Blackie, dearest. I still believe that we must identify with the poor and the oppressed. I'm still sick when I think about this terrible war. I still feel guilty for being rich while other people are poor. I want to be involved in the McGovern campaign next year. We have to throw that horrible man out of the White House.

But I've learned one thing in the last few years—with your sister forcing me to see it: If I don't pull my own act together, I will be no good to anyone or any cause.

I want always to be a radical, but a radical because of my convictions and not because of my neuroses.

Of which I have more than a few. Fortunately I also have good and loyal friends who take care of me.

Father Ed Carny will be here in a few weeks, back from his incredible work in Latin America. He has completely turned around the missionary apostolate down there. Instead of making converts to North American Catholicism, he is organizing the poor to fight for their own liberation.

When I think of people like him, I realize there is still hope for the church and for the poor people of the world.

And now I MUST go swim a mile. I do it every day. To make my body taut and trim and svelte and sleek again. For you and for the Ryans and for myself too. That may be false consciousness, but I'll work it out in the fall with my shrink.

And for Nick too, the S.O.B.

Oh, Blackie, I can hardly wait to see you again. Labor Day seems so long away. I DO love you. Pray for me.

All my love,
Cathy

110

NICHOLAS

I began the last file of letters on the flight from Río to Santa Marta. Where was I that summer when she retreated to the Hill, to pull herself back together and to discipline her body into shape so that she would be attractive to me?

I was in Chicago, waiting. Not for her to take the first step, Lord knows. But giving her time to sort herself out. Good old sensible, reliable Nick, not rushing in where angels fear to tread.

I was adjusting to the luxuries of private practice, escorting innocent, braless young women—it was that era—to concerts at Ravinia and ignoring their hints that, while they were radical feminists, they would still be willing to go to bed with me.

I was nervous and uneasy about Catherine. My hopes that we would get together again were sky high. But I didn't know who she was anymore and I did not want to seem to pick her up on the rebound.

It would have been easy to sit down with Mary Kate Murphy and ask her what I should do. Maybe I didn't because I was afraid that she'd tell me that courtship with someone like me was precisely what Catherine needed.

Why did I hesitate?

Monica was quite blunt about it. "You were so accustomed to being in love with an obsession that you felt more comfortable with it than you would with the possibility of loving a real woman."

As I cleared customs at Santa Marta, I realized how right Monica was. When I did have a chance with the real Catherine at Copacabana, I blew the opportunity sky high.

A young officer greeted me outside the customs hall. The minister of justice had personally sent him to greet me. He was so sorry that the plane was late. My reservation at the Santa Marta Intercontinental had been held for me.

They were trying hard to please, as if courtesy and efficiency could replace a dead woman.

Yes, I would have blown the chance that summer just as I had blown it at the Copacabana. Yet I was at Grand Beach on the Labor Day weekend, ready to begin again if she would give me a chance.

By then it was too late.

111
BLACKIE

I was groggy from talking English to Poles who responded in French and from jet fatigue when I walked into Mary Kate's crying fit on the Friday of the Labor Day weekend. Dad and Helen were still in San Diego, and Joe had the audacity to be away at a Jungian meeting when his bride needed him. So consolation was provided by Caitlin, an expert at coping with her mother's occasional but fierce weeping binges.

Caitlin was already taller than her mother and easily the most ravishing of the Ryan/Collins/Murphy tribal confederation, a fact of which my sister was simultaneously inordinately proud and inordinately displeased. Caitlin, alas, showed distinct signs of sanity, an unacceptable condition for the women of the clan. We all had hopes that with maturity and good example such a propensity would disappear.

I raised a weary eyebrow for an explanation.

"Oh, Crazy Cousin Cathy went off to South America to work for Father Carny," Caitlin, dressed in the required summer uniform for her age group of a string bikini, said calmly. "And Mom blames herself instead of realizing that poor Cathy is still searching for a surrogate father."

You see what I mean by the tendency to sanity.

"When?" I asked, seeking a chair and wondering if Caitlin could console an uncle as well as a mother.

"She left the Hill Tuesday," sniffed my sibling. "She called from the Miami airport an hour ago to say that she had no right to indulge herself in psychiatric treatment as long as there were people in the world who were starving to death."

My finger itched for Ed Carny's esophagus. "Indeed."

"And it's all my fault," wailed Mary Kate, nestling in her daughter's competent arms. "I should never have let her go back to that place."

"Cathy is an adult," I said heavily. "And Ed would have found her anyway."

The first statement was of dubious truth. The second, sadly, was all too true.

I manufactured the required vodka and tonic for my sibling, produced a can of Tab for her daughter and decided to resist the temptation to dilute my Jameson's with ice. It was, after all, the beginning of the Labor Day weekend. And they do not sell John J's nectar in Poland.

"She has to make up for all the time she wasted with Roy," M.K. declared, "who was a reactionary pretending to be a radical. Her own life and her own happiness are unimportant compared to the suffering of the poor and the wretched. The purpose of life is not to seek happiness for yourself but to lose yourself in the service of the poor and the wretched."

"Crap," said Caitlin decisively.

"And how long is this loss of self to persist?" I asked.

Mary Kate dabbed at her eyes with a tissue that mysteriously appeared in her hands without any visible assistance from Caitlin.

"Three years. She promised she'd be back in three years and go into therapy then. She must do something worthwhile with her life before she tries to find out who she is."

"Felt her feet growing cold at the prospect of all that self-revelation, and Ed came along with the right excuse to escape it."

Mary Kate nodded, drinking generously from the vodka and tonic. "Too much tonic," she protested.

"To quote your daughter, crap."

"And she's going where?" Caitlin inquired.

"Put my golf clubs away, will you, hon? Thanks for the shoulder when the old lady needs it. . . . Some crazy place I never heard of. Costaguana?"

The Republic of Costaguana was a country they had trouble with even at the Secretariat of State in Rome. The cardinal archbishop of Santa Marta was a throwback to the days of Mussolini. He was a strong supporter of the "anti-Communist" government, which was a particularly nasty and crooked bunch of military tinhorns, the kind who come into power to fight a nonexistent communist threat and then by their stupidity and cruelty create that to which they are allegedly opposed.

And, believe me, the boys in the papal diplomatic service can live with almost any kind of tinhorn dictator. That the junta in Santa Marta and the cardinal there dismayed them was no small accomplishment.

"I see," I said, though even in my most depressed moments that weekend I could not have seen.

"All the common sense she had a month ago vanished." M.K. frowned at her drink. "The horse manure was back, as though it had never been shoveled away. Purpose, sacrifice, oppression, freedom, the wretched of the earth, liberation."

"Nice words."

"But meaningless on her lips. Running away to the nunnery again to please Daddy and Mommy and God."

"And to make up for her own worthlessness," I added sourly.

"Crap, to quote my daughter."

We both laughed, hollowly.

"I knew I should have gone up there last week." The weeping binge was about to return. "She's such an easy target for a wild-eyed visionary."

"Martyr complex."

"And I'm to blame." Tears welled up in her self-described bedroom-blue eyes.

"Cut it, Sis," I ordered. "You know better than that. No shrink is responsible for a patient's folly."

"I'm her sister," she sniffled, in control now.

"All the more reason to grant her fundamental freedom," I said, lapsing into jargon for the sake of the moment.

"But I am my sister's keeper," she protested.

"Don't quote scripture at me, woman. You didn't kill anyone, like Abel killed Cain. You did your best. That's all that can be asked."

Neither of us believed that, of course.

Nor did Nick, who showed up for my Mass in the Ryan parlor dressed in an absurd blue blazer and white flannel slacks—as if he were a yachtsman, for the love of heaven.

If Cathy had been there she would have been wide-eyed with admiration. Drat the girl. How could she have been so stupid?

Nick arrived after I had started Mass. His eyes roamed the room, looking for her. Joe Murphy, who had returned in time to protect his marriage from the permanent dissolution with which it was supposedly allegedly threatened, squared his shoulders during the Gloria and whispered into Nick's ear.

Every trace of joy and hope sagged out of his life.

The poor fool would, naturally, wait out another three years.

And a lot longer.

112
CATHERINE

October 13, 1971
San Ysidoro
Costaguana

Dear Blackie,

I feel terribly guilty about leaving before you came home. It has been so many years and I did want to see you. But I knew that God was calling me through Father Ed and that I could regain my self-respect and a purpose for my life here. If I hadn't accepted the invitation I would never have been able to forgive myself.

I won't pretend that this is an easy task. Half the time I'm scared silly and most of the other half I'm in culture shock. I thought I knew what poverty was like from my year at St. Ret's. Oh, Blackie, darling, the people there are rich beyond the imagination of the peons who work on the *campo* and live like gods compared to the Indians in the hills around us.

The dirt, the smell, the hopelessness, the ugly wounds, the squalid mud and stick huts, the bloated bellies of little children, the faces of women who are my age and look like they're sixty—they are all so bad that for the first few weeks I was sleeping fourteen hours a day.

The smell is horrendous—excrement, sweat, disease, filth of every kind. But all that would be bearable, if the rich capitalists in Santa Marta would leave the peons and the Indians a little dignity. Yet their greed cannot even spare that. And, of course, they are working for the American multinationals and the CIA.

The soldiers, who are led by American-trained officers, kill, maim, rape, destroy at their pleasure. No one dares to stop them. When their jeeps race through a *barrio* killing any child or animal that gets in the way, the people hide their daughters and their few possessions. If they find out the army is coming, they flee the *barrio* beforehand.

And if the jeeps stop, everyone in the village must fall on

303

their knees. I was in a little *barrio* the other day and, arrogant American that I am, I didn't kneel. I was knocked in the head by a military policeman, and I think I would have been raped if Margaret had not shouted at them that I was an American nun. So I was only kicked a few more times.

That's what American imperialism looks like in the Republic of Costaguana.

Margaret Aimes, Sister Margaret, who used to be Sister Martha when I was in the novitiate, saved my life probably that day and saves my sanity every day. I don't think she is much of a revolutionary, like the rest of us. But she's a good nurse and is training me to be a nurse's aide. Typical of my useless life, I have no skills at all to help people here or to contribute to the revolution.

From the safe distance of North America, Blackie, it's easy to be relaxed and dispassionate about the revolution. But here you see that there is no other option. Even if the revolutionaries are Marxists—and many of them are—a Communist government could not be any worse than what we have now. We at San Ysidoro are fortunate that the revolutionaries will tolerate our help. We must persuade the people, who have been terrified and degraded, that they can stand up and fight for themselves if they band together under the leadership of the revolution.

They're good people. Once you get to know them you realize that they are human like us, with as much pride and hope for themselves and their families as we have. They have been browbeaten for so long that they have no confidence in their own strength and power. We must raise their consciousness and lead them into the revolution, which will liberate them, make them free, the way God intended them to be.

But it's hard work, hard and discouraging. The junta is powerful. The peasants are poor and weak. And the revolutionaries have only a few outmoded weapons.

I know what M.K. and you and all my friends at home think of this new vocation of mine. You would approve of it, however, if you could see how bad life is for the ordinary people of Costaguana and realize that we Americans are responsible.

Here at San Ysidoro there is no doubt that we Christians must be on the side of the poor. And if we have become allies

of the Communists, the reason is that they are the only other
ones on the side of the poor.

I do love you and I do miss you. Please try to understand
how important what I am doing is to the suffering people of
Costaguana.

Love,
Cathy

113
CATHERINE

San Ysidoro
February 4, 1972

Dear Blackie,

It is unbearably hot here. Can you imagine, I didn't even
realize the seasons are reversed down here? February is like our
August. I don't quite understand how it happens, but geography
always gave me a headache. Remember all the cartoons I drew
during geography class at St. Prax's?

How long ago that seems.

I've been sick off and on, nothing serious. Stomach problems,
which make me weary all the time, but are not nearly as
threatening to life and limb as are the military police. They
made a sweep through the center last week, kept us all at
gunpoint while they searched for revolutionaries.

Father Ed told them we were hiding no one. But they were
certain the revolutionaries had been here. As far as I know,
there have been only a few visitors who might be part of the
movement.

We stood in the sun all day long before they left. I collapsed,
but they wouldn't let anyone pick me up or give me a drink of
water.

I'm better now. At least I don't have to worry about being

fat. No one in Costaguana, outside of the wealthy capitalists in the cities by the coast, is fat.

Lorna, who is a nun and an Industrial Areas Foundation community organizer from Buffalo, says we should arm ourselves. If the military police are convinced that we are part of the revolution, they will come to rape and kill us.

Margaret thinks that if we have the guns, then the junta will be justified in charging we are part of the armed revolution. I'd be afraid to fire a gun. But how can you have a revolution unless some people have guns? As Father Ed said at our last sensitivity session, Christians must not turn away from violence in the cause of defending the oppressed.

So I suppose there will be guns. And I'll have to learn to fire one.

I'm still a drag on the community, as Lorna points out at every one of our sensitivity sessions. I have no skills, I am in poor health, and my zeal for the revolution remains to be proven. But I'm good at one thing anyway. I can already speak Spanish like the peons on the *campo* and I'm learning some of the Indian dialect. You should see the looks on their faces when I talk to them in their own languages. First of all they're frightened, then they're flattered, then they are enormously pleased. When they are pleased, they laugh—both the peons who are part Indian and the tribes who are full-blooded Indians. Now they laugh whenever they see me.

The way kids used to laugh at me on the beach.

I hope I get my health back soon. There is much work to do. Margaret now depends on me as her nurse's aide. I can't let her down.

On these hot nights I dream of summers at Grand Beach. It seems millions of miles away, instead of only thousands. And it's covered with snow now too, I suppose. At least I've grown mature enough to admit to myself that I miss it and all of you. I'll not try to pretend I like it here. Actually I hate the heat and the sickness and the poverty and the fear.

But here is where I belong, on the side of the poor.

Pray for me.

Love,
Cathy

114
CATHERINE

November 15, 1972
San Ysidoro

Dear Blackie,

It hardly seems possible that I've been here for more than a year. We learned the other day that Nixon was reelected—we don't have radios; they're incompatible with service to the poor.

Once I would have thought that was a disaster. Now I realize that it doesn't make any difference. McGovern would have been as much a tool of the multinationals as Nixon is. America will only change when there is a world revolution, when the poor peoples of the Third World throw off the chains of their bondage and sweep across the world like the winnowing fan in St. John's gospel, burning and destroying everything in their path.

My health is much better now and I'm a fully accepted member of the community. Father Ed even has me doing some special work about which I can't write. It's interesting and fun. I hate to use the word "fun," because it makes me sound so frivolous and we have no time for frivolity when a revolution is in progress. I am repeatedly confronted in our sensitivity meetings with my frivolity and the charge is certainly fair.

I laugh too much. Especially with the Indians in the *barrios*. And my laughter probably is a form of manipulation and does not contribute to the raising of their consciousness. Still, they like to see me laugh, and every time I am with them and try not to laugh, they joke and clown around and won't let me tend to their aches and pains till I laugh with them.

What sweet, wonderful people.

There is a revolutionary offensive underway now, before the rainy season sets in. Their strategy, the way Father Ed explains it, is to disrupt the economy of the country. In China, Mao and his brave brothers proved by their raids and ambushes that there was no safety or security in areas which they did not protect. If there is enough violence and enough unrest, the people will finally be driven into the hands of the revolution.

So bridges are blown up, trains derailed, buses destroyed, fields burned just before harvest time.

Some of us don't like to call it terrorism, but as Father Ed tells me, that's the way Ireland won its freedom from England, and the people here have as much right to their freedom as the Irish did. I wish I knew more Irish history. My blood runs cold every time I hear of violence. I'm afraid to sleep at night when I hear the sound of explosions or gunfire in the distance. And we hear it now almost every night.

I bet you'd never guess who won the marksmanship prize. That's right, old kooky Cathy turns out to be a dead-eye with a great big ugly forty-five that she can hardly lift.

One of the revolutionary militia—he lives in Rio Secco but he comes up here to maintain contact with the guerrillas—has instructed us in the use of weapons. Margaret says we are asking for trouble and exercised her absolute freedom of conscience to refuse instruction.

I don't have that kind of courage, and anyway, I'm not sure. So I'm the one who ends up with the Lenin prize for the best revolutionary sharpshooter.

Father Ed does not permit weapons at any of the other centers. But here, because the phase of active revolution is already upon us, it is essential that we arm. Just like the Minutemen in 1775.

I'm sure I could never shoot the ugly automatic thing at anyone.

Blackie, I'm worried. I'm not sure I'll ever come home. Danger is with us all the time now. Some of the others say they are accustomed to it, and hardly notice when they see a jeep coming down the highway or a revolutionary patrol scurrying through the bush. I'm not used to it, however. And I'm such a coward that I never will adjust to the possibility of dying violently and without warning any hour of the day or night.

Maybe I'm an alarmist. But if I have to lay down my life for the people, know that I do so willingly, even if I am scared stiff.

And know too that I love you and all the family.

God bless,
Cath

115
CATHERINE

March 17, 1973
San Ysidoro

Dear Blackie,

The revolution has won a great victory today, a kind of St. Patrick's Day celebration.

The San Tome silver mine was blown up by a heroic band of revolutionaries who gave their lives for the destruction of this ancient bulwark of imperialist oppression. It will be months, perhaps years, before the mine can be opened again. This is a devastating blow to the economy of Costaguana, one from which the nation will not recover, perhaps, for years. It's the biggest success for the revolution yet.

Some miners died in the explosion. The papers in Río Secco say more than three hundred, all of them Indians, who are the only ones poor enough to be willing to work in the mines.

That is a terrible tragedy. Yet they are, in truth, martyrs for the revolution. Their lives were not much better than death anyway. The actual responsibility for their deaths lies not with the revolution but, if we correctly interpret the necessary dialectic of our struggle, with American imperialism, which has been sucking the blood of the miners of San Tome for almost a hundred years.

As Marcuse says, there are some circumstances in which the hope of freedom and happiness for future generations justifies the violations of freedom and rights and even life, so long as the end is present in the action. We kill, when we have to, not out of hatred, but out of love and with a sense of repentance.

The victory is especially sweet, because the mine is the property of Don Felipé Gould, who is the "strong man" of the junta and the head of the military police. He will have less of his own money to pay the torturers and murderers who staff his private death camp at Esmeralda.

I don't know when I've felt so hopeful for our cause.

Fondly,
Cath

116
BLACKIE

My letters to Catherine were very cautious. I wrote mostly about family because that did not seem controversial. I mentioned in passing that I had helped Lisa out of a bad marriage and a drug problem and into a good marriage and a promising film career. Cath alone knew how far gone I had been on Lisa in high school, but I wanted to make it easy for her not to comment, because I thought that by then she viewed Lisa as a parasite.

And I avoided remarks about international economics, save for an occasional observation about the LDCs (Lesser Developed Countries), a term which she had never heard, which had caught up with the West in life expectancy, literacy and infant-survival rates. Even though they were stretched out on a continuum of political freedom from Costa Rica to South Korea, none of them needed bloody revolution or Russian/Chinese-style authoritarianism to eliminate the worst effects of poverty.

It was a waste. Cathy didn't know where Singapore and Taiwan were, probably not even Costa Rica. And none of Father Ed's disciples was concerned about the technicalities of public health, for example.

The revolution would solve all problems. And any problem that did not point to the revolution was a distraction from it.

Where did a sweet young woman who made Indians laugh learn the drivel about murdering with love and repentance? By this time the drivel flowing from the liberation theologians had reached flood tide. I have on my desk almost two score books, most published by Maryknoll, which will keep the world supplied with more than its quota of drivel for much of the next millennium. Or, to change the metaphor, if these books were biodegradable, they would fertilize the truck gardens of the whole world for several years.

They are characterized by the following: A fierce hatred of the United States. An innocence of the complexities of international economics. A bland assumption that Marxism has been validated as a solution to social problems. A poverty of serious theological reflection. And the pretense that no Marxist society exists anywhere in the world by which Marxist "praxis" (their word, if you say "practice" you are horribly out of fashion) could be evaluated.

Their basic argument was as follows. Christians must be committed to the elimination of social injustice; Marxism eliminates social injustice; therefore, Christians must be Marxists.

The major premise was unassailable. But the minor premise was not self-evident, save to them, and the logic of the conclusion not compelling, save to them. (What if there were alternative cures for injustice?)

The San Ysidorians, except for Ed, did not read these books. They were too busy identifying with the poor to read anything. But I can see him, dead tired, late at night, his face locked in a deep frown, pouring over them by kerosene lantern, painfully searching for passages he could quote, as he used to search from Abbot Marmion and Dom Hubert Van Zeller for quotes in his high-school retreats. He'd jot the quotes down on index cards and commit them to memory. Thus my cousin's frequently empty head would be filled with distilled drivel.

I remonstrated with my Lord Cronin as to why the Vatican went after conservative thinkers like Hans Kung and let the flaming lunatics of liberation theology go undisturbed.

"They have dirty fingernails, stringy hair and bad breath," he said. "And are read only by Americans who go to meetings and vote resolutions and by one another. They are not handsome Swiss authors of best-sellers."

"Kung is a threat to their monopoly of power and the Communists with clerical collars are not?"

"They don't wear collars," my Lord replied. "And the church has survived worse. They're not very important."

"Yet they are partly responsible for the death of the woman I loved above all others."

Cronin paused, not accustomed to such emotion from me.

Finally he replied, "Fuck the bastards, Blackie."

117
CATHERINE

May 1, 1973
San Ysidoro

Dear Blackie,

I feel unclean, as if I had met and been leered at by the devil himself.

The wife of the first secretary at the American embassy in Santa Marta was a classmate of mine at the Hill. I didn't know Jeanie very well, but she seemed nice enough and smart enough. She invited me to an embassy party some time ago. I didn't want to go because the embassy is a nest of CIA vipers that is mainly responsible for the setbacks of the First Revolutionary Offensive.

Father Ed said that I ought to attend the party, if only to see what our enemies are thinking and saying.

They are not thinking or saying much, because no one likes the ambassador, whose only qualification for the job was a large campaign contribution to Nixon, and everyone is afraid that he might ruin their careers. He is the only one who thinks that pig will survive the "Watergate scandal," whatever that is. I can't imagine a less interesting question, but that's all the people at the embassy discuss. There is a revolution here in which they seem to be totally uninterested. After a visit to the American embassy I am tempted to believe that the enemies of the revolution will do all our work for us.

Jeanie was candid about the invitation. After the article

about me in the *New York Times*, the ambassador wants to take credit for winning me back to the "American cause."

Honest, Blackie, I hated the interview. But Ed insisted. I'm a famous person back home because of all the trivial protest activity. As if that mattered.

"I don't know what you're trying to prove out there, Catherine," Jeanie said. "God knows those people are poor, but the Marxists will not improve their situation any. No, I don't want to argue about it. I merely want to warn you what old Idiot Ass is up to. I'm sure you can take care of yourself."

She really wanted me to make a fool out of him. And it wasn't hard because he is a stupid man, even if he is a Knight of Malta, and expected a naive and pious nun. No one seems to have figured out that I was thrown out of the community and never went back. But just to make certain, she lent me a white strapless gown that converted me into a dazzling young adventuress. I haven't paid much attention to how I looked since I came down here and was astonished to see the femme fatale in the mirror.

But before the night was over I wished I had worn my wedding dress from Central Park. Then I wouldn't have attracted the attention of major (or *comandante*, as they call him here) Felipé Gould, the head of the military police.

He's blond and handsome, a reflection of the English background of his family a hundred years ago, and speaks with a perfect Oxford accent because that's where he studied (Jeanie says he flunked out).

He was talking to the cardinal archbishop, his cousin, when I saw him. The cardinal is a vile little runt, with a wicked, tiny face, like an evil elf. If Felipé's eyes light up at the thought of torture, the cardinal's glow at the thought of gold and silver.

The ambassador introduced me to both of them as "one of our brave young American missionaries." The cardinal favored me with a lecture about the unemployment caused by the San Tome explosion.

I ignored him, for fear that I would tell him what a greedy little ghoul he was.

"You are a nurse?" the *comandante* asked, leisurely devouring me with his eyes.

"A nurse's aide."

He kissed my hand reverently. "And much more beautiful than one would expect from the article in the *New York Times*. What a pity you North American women have to be concerned about politics."

A typical sample of Latin machismo but said in a tone of voice that made the words sound like an invitation to unspeakable vices that would end in death.

"And what a shame you South American men are not concerned about poverty and misery in your own country," I fired back.

"Ah, *señorita*, that is the woman of the interview. But you say your words with such charm. Surely you must realize that if there were no poverty here, lovely women like you would not come to aid our poor. And then we would be a very underdeveloped nation, would we not?"

Honestly, Blackie, I was scared stiff all the way back here on the train. And cried in Marge's arms till I calmed down.

He wanted me, Blackie. Not just to sleep with, although that would be bad enough. But to torture slowly to death.

Jeanie told me not to be ridiculous. He wouldn't dare touch an American. I'm not sure about that.

So there's one more terror to keep me awake at night. Not only will I see images of the silver miners dying of suffocation, I'll see Don Felipé Gould coming after me with the riding whip he always carries.

Please pray hard for me.

Cath

118
MARY KATE

The Pirate and I had a monumental fight after Blackie showed me the letter about Don Felipé What's-his-face.

I was busy packing for my flight to Santa Marta when Joe came home from Little Company of Mary.

"You're being very unprofessional," he said, leaning against the bedroom door, looking especially sexy with the silver streaks in his hair.

"Fuck professionalism."

"You wouldn't do it with a client."

"She's a sister, not a client. I've got to protect her from that sadistic madman."

"What if she doesn't want to be protected?"

"I'll drag her home."

"What if she won't come?"

"Fucking coward."

"Does Blackie think she'll come home?"

I hadn't considered that. "I'm going," I said. "The matter is settled."

"You did in Roy because she wanted to leave him. Is there any evidence in her letters that she wants to come home?"

"She'll come home," I screamed, making up in noise what I lacked in conviction.

"The trouble with you and Blackie," he said in that damn consulting-room tone of his, "is that you blame everyone for her plight but Catherine—her parents, yourselves, the nuns, Roy, Father Ed, the liberation theologians. Don't you think you owe her the respect of acknowledging that she is a free agent?"

"She doesn't know what freedom is," I yelled, slamming shut my suitcase, which immediately popped open again because I had packed twice as many clothes as it could hold.

"What would you say to a client who made that argument?" he asked, very softly.

"Fuck off," I replied, slamming the lid again.

"My turn for supper, I guess. What kind of wine do you want?"

He departed the room very quietly.

Our wedding night had been pure farce. Practicing psychiatrists we both might have been (well, I was a first-year resident), but we knew only the theories. Having to choose between a nightmare and a comedy, we opted for comedy. We were not really tuned, either. Sooner or later sex must become comic. Better sooner. Poor Cathy never had any laughs with Roy. Or Nick.

Or anyone.

We drank some of our precious Niersteiner Eiswein, which even wine-hating Caitlin likes. The Pirate knew I needed good wine after the humiliation of unpacking.

He was right, of course, about my lunatic scheme. Yet when we went to Santa Marta on our futile search for her body, he suffered more than Blackie or I.

119
NICHOLAS

Don Oswaldo DeGrazia, the minister of justice for the Republic of Costaguana, reminded me of an Italian tailor on 83rd Street who was a close friend of my father, a skinny little man with almost no hair on the top of his head and a large mustache, which he nervously smoothed when he talked.

Like the tailor, DeGrazia was extremely intelligent. Unlike him, he was also very well educated—Notre Dame and Michigan Law.

His voice was soft and resigned. He had been exiled twice, once by the last elected government, when it outlawed his Christian Democratic party, and once by the junta. His credentials as a man of integrity and rectitude were impeccable. It was said, according to my notes, that he was the only civilian politician that the paratroopers who controlled the country trusted completely.

"You know something of the sad history of our country, Mr. Curran?" he asked with a self-deprecating wave of his hand.

"Something."

"Perhaps you would permit me a brief summary? Good. We are not poor in Costaguana. There is much poverty, but that is not because we lack resources—copper, silver, grain, beef, perhaps even some oil off the coast of Azuera. Our problem is one of a political economy that is as weak as a man without a spine. We have a long tradition of democratic elections, a nice chess game between the clericalist Conservatives and the anticlerical Liberals. These old dons played the game well for many years and made some social progress with the wealth that was left over. I will not exaggerate the progress, but I will not minimize it either. By 1955 we were reaching a point at which we might have brought the death rate down to European standards in another ten years. Gradualism, if you will?"

"I have not come here to judge your country, sir."

"We are not quite as rich as Argentina, so our failures are not as bad as the Argentine miracle of failure. Yet there seems to be something in our culture that dooms us, like the Argentines, to an endlessly repeated cycle of political and economic failures." He spread his hands on the vast, cluttered desk and shrugged again, as if realizing that I was not interested in the puzzle of Latin American failures. "In any event, my generation graduated from college confident that we would bring our country into the twentieth century. Some of us founded the Christian Democrats as an alternative to the reactionaries in the Conservative party. Others formed the Social Democrats as an alternative to the Liberals. The old dons were lazy and did not take us seriously. Besides, our country had a tradition of respect for civil liberties. We almost won an election. The dons ordered us out of the country. I myself believe that we would have won the next election because the dons were too incompetent to steal it from us."

"What went wrong?" I saw behind him the stately plaza of the Seventeenth of June, a date from the revolutionary past. The architect who had designed the government buildings of Santa Marta had Paris and Vienna in mind and had done an impressive job of creating the same atmosphere of stately buildings and broad plazas. Earlier I had mentally ridiculed such pretensions. Now, listening to this intense little man, I realized that there were dedicated intellectuals who did stand for a tradition that might be worth respecting and saving. At another time I might have been fascinated. Now I was only concerned about the tomb of Don Alfonso in the church of Río Secco.

"Some of our younger friends abandoned their faith in democracy and went underground. They became terrorists, middle-class urban terrorists, rather better than our old rural guerrillas because they were so much more intelligent and better educated. They argued that if they created enough havoc the military would step in, impose an intolerable tyranny, and drive the people into the arms of the well-to-do urban guerrillas. They were right in every respect but the last. I cannot speak for other countries, only for my own. But here the Marxists have never had popular support."

"And one junta replaced another, each one more repressive?"

"Precisely. Counterterrorism, if it is ruthless enough, is an excellent antidote to terrorism—if you believe, as I happen not to believe, that the killing of the innocent and the naive is an acceptable price for destroying a threat to society. A government which is willing to dispose of twenty thousand people to eliminate a few thousand terrorists will succeed. Before you denounce us, Mr. Curran, you should realize that the juntas did exactly what their enemies were doing, only more efficiently. They followed the same methods many Americans find acceptable if they are pursued by left-wing revolutionaries."

"Catherine wasn't a terrorist," I said, trying to hold back my anger.

"Of course not," he said, his eyelids drooping sadly. "Yet she talked of violent revolution. Sedition is a crime in your country too, isn't it?"

"We don't butcher people on suspicion of sedition!" I shouted.

"I am not defending them, Mr. Curran." He slumped even lower in his chair. "I am only trying to explain the mentality which comes to believe that a Felipé Gould is an acceptable alternative. Actually, the Marxists were never a serious threat, as they may have been in other countries. Our army was too professional to lose a guerrilla war. Indeed, the paratroopers revolted against the last junta because they suspected, with every reason, I assure you, that it was deliberately losing an occasional skirmish to enhance the Communist threat. That and the Esmeralda, of course. . . . "

His voice trailed off as he touched on a subject he wished he could avoid.

"And then they permitted an election, much to everyone's surprise, and you and the Social Democrats rule in an uncertain and tenuous coalition." I spoke with some impatience because I wished to discuss the Esmeralda and be done with it.

"And would you believe that only last spring a worldwide group of Catholic scholars denounced us and endorsed the Marxists as true freedom fighters?" His voice rose slightly, hinting at great bitterness. "The resolution was proposed by a French fool who spent two days here. Two days and he knows enough to condemn a democratically elected government. His group endorsed the Tupamaros in Uruguay in 1970. The Tupamaros destroyed Uruguayan democracy. Do the Catholic scholars of the world want to root out our fragile plant of freedom? . . . but I tire you with my complaints. . . . "

"I have a friend who is a priest. He would say that theologians don't deliver precincts."

"But they do stir up unrest among young and uneducated clerics. However, that is enough about our problems." He laughed softly and continued to talk about his problems. As a member of the Council on Foreign Relations committee on Latin America, I ought to have listened carefully.

"The paratroopers are earnest young men. They flirted with socialism for a few months and then decided to give parliamentary democracy another chance. It is our last chance, but I think the strange alliance of young officers and middle-aged Social Democrats and Christian Democrats has an outside chance." He paused and frowned. "If only the world and the United States give us a chance."

"Which the latter is not likely to do until you placate it over the expulsion of the missionaries."

He shrugged, just like the man on 83rd Street trying to explain an improperly pressed uniform to my father. "The paratroopers are stern men. The missionaries were cooperating with the Marxists. I argued that they were doing little harm. And my *capitán*—the paratrooper who watches over me—said that such slovenliness was responsible for the problems of our republic. So the missionaries went. I will say this for my *capitán* and his colleagues, they are becoming more politically flexible."

Or I wouldn't even have been permitted in the country.

"Were the missionaries really irrelevant?"

He played with his fountain pen and then decided to tell me the truth. "Only outside the country as an object of media attention did they have any impact. Here they had no effect. In Brazil it was different. There the church was stronger, the military regime much less vicious and the church leadership tough and resourceful. Here"—he shrugged wearily—"the church has been lazy for many years and the hierarehy feared only the Communists. Our own priests, with a few exceptions, did not care, and the missionaries were make-believe guerrillas. I cannot speak for other Latin American countries. Here it was the politics of gesture and television interview."

"For which some of them were tortured to death," I said angrily.

Don Oswaldo sighed. "You are more than just her lawyer, *señor*, if you will permit me. Were you a lover?"

I was not sure what the nights in Brazil made me. "I loved her, Don Oswaldo."

"She is dead, Mr. Curran. I know you do not wish her money to go to that foolish priest and his coterie. And as a lawyer, I would not trust his witnesses, but she is dead. You will only hurt yourself by hoping that she is not."

"No records, no body. . . . "

"Twenty thousand such cases." He gestured toward massive file cabinets. "When the paratroopers seized Esmeralda and killed Gould, they searched for records. There were virtually none. He covered his tracks by his own inefficiency."

"Some prisoners were released, were they not? And others escaped. Could she not have slipped away unnoticed?"

"It is true"—he nodded sadly—"that some were permitted to escape, but only when it suited Gould's damnable purposes or his devilish whims.

But if she did escape, where is she now? Why has she not come forward? It is not wise to keep alive hope, *señor*, not wise."

She might be so badly mutilated that she was afraid to come forward, a chilling thought that had plagued me on the trip down from the States. I didn't want to raise that possibility with him. Better that he not know about Angela.

"Is he certainly dead then?"

"Of course." DeGrazia searched through a stack of files and came up with a photo. It looked like the pictures in the press and like the man Catherine had described in her letter. Except that his eyes were closed, one side of his face was smashed and the chest of his smart uniform was covered with blood.

"Your paras are not above torture, either?"

"He was killed by the first bullet. The rest was rage."

We were both silent. "Take the picture," he said.

And not knowing quite why, I took it.

Don Oswaldo searched through another stack of files. "Mrs. Tuohy, or Miss Collins, as you prefer, was arrested on the last day of October. We have a record of the arrest from the police station at Rincon—taken into custody by the first platoon of the military police, Gould's own bodyguard, and held for questioning. That is all. Four months later she was not in the prison camp at Esmeralda when the paratroopers captured it—just as Gould was about to dismember a woman. Some of those who were freed remembered her. One thought she had been sent to Punto Malo, where Gould had a villa overlooking the rocks. In all probability, Mr. Curran, that is where she died. And her body was thrown on the rocks beneath to drift out to sea and be consumed by sharks. I am being candid, because you will suffer false hopes if I am not candid. I hardly need tell you what this information would do to our country if it were made public in America."

"Goddamn your country," I exploded.

"Many times I have said the same, Mr. Curran." He bowed his head. Then, as if he were making a decision, he raised his face toward mine, his dark brown eyes infinitely sad. "Pray that she died quickly, Mr. Curran, and is now home with God in heaven."

"How can I pray for that?" I demanded hotly.

He removed another picture from his file, a woman naked to the waist, arms crossed to protect her breasts, eyes averted. On her haunches hung a tattered dress. She was kneeling, patiently waiting for more torture. Her body was torn and bruised, her face swollen.

"Mrs. Tuohy?" he asked delicately.

"I don't know," I replied honestly. "Perhaps, probably."

My world leaped into movement. The cheerful colors in the plaza outside his window whirled around like a spinning top. The gaily dressed young women seemed to be standing on the clouds. I put my head on his desk, and hung on to it, trying to slow down the dizzying spiral that had taken possession of the planet. I straightened up again and took the tumbler of cognac from Don Oswaldo's tiny hand.

"You think I am cruel, Mr. Curran?"

"I understand your intentions."

"My niece, my sister's only child, and two of my cousins died in Esmeralda. They were totally innocent of anything but their relationship to me. Believe me, I know how you feel. And, believe me, we must leave the dead in peace."

"I believe you," I said, feeling sorry for this gallant little man. But I still had to know what was in the tomb in the church of Río Secco.

"I can help you a little in your trial," he said sorrowfully. "I have asked my staff to prepare a dossier on the two witnesses. I think you may find it useful. It will be ready when you return from your visits to Esmeralda and Río Secco, if you still wish to . . . "

"I do," I said flatly. I didn't give a damn about Esmeralda, but Blackie had pointed out that I might stir up suspicions if I went to Río Secco and up to San Ysidoro without visiting the shrine the paratroopers had created at the abandoned barracks.

"Of course," he sighed. "I understand . . . do you wish this picture, Mr. Curran? Truthfully, we found it in a collection at Punto Malo. While she has been hurt, she has not been mutilated. . . . It is to be hoped that she was near the end when the picture was taken."

I glanced at it again. It was Cathy all right. I wished that Gould were still alive so I could have killed him. And I prayed that Catherine had died quickly.

"No thanks, Mr. Minister. I have other memories I would rather treasure."

"Of course," he said sympathetically. He extended his hand hesitantly, not sure that I would take it. I shook it warmly and felt even more sorry for him than for myself.

But I was still going to Río Secco and to the empty tomb in the crypt.

120
BLACKIE

Cathy's parents departed this world in a far more spectacular fashion than they had lived in it. On a clear crisp morning in June of 1973, a gas main ruptured beneath their house. The fumes probably would have seeped through their air-conditioning system and smothered them in any case. But something caused a spark and the explosion blew off the roof, tore apart the first and second floors, caved in the walls and sent the bodies of my aunt and uncle, now in a number of separate pieces, in the general direction of Alpha Centauri.

A more dramatic leave-taking than they deserved.

My father made the funeral arrangements with his usual calm, though in his eyes I saw pain for the lingering end of his generation. The women of the clan wept because that's what they did at funerals and wakes. Even Caitlin.

And I preached on the infinity of God's mercy and love, both of which I would have been prepared to deny the evil old wretches, but as Mary Kate says, thank God I'm not God.

Catherine was not there. We received a cable which said bluntly, "Unable to attend funeral. Catherine."

The clan was shocked. Erin and Herbert Collins did not deserve a bit of Cathy's attention. But it was in her nature to try. I noted the words carefully. She did not say that she would not attend but that she could not. Perhaps she was afraid that she would not be permitted to return to Costaguana. Or perhaps that damnable moron was tying her down with his envy-ridden sensitivity brainwash.

I thought of flying to Santa Marta myself and trying my fingers around Ed's windpipe. To make sure they were the right size. But Cathy's next letter prevented such direct revolutionary action against the revolutionaries.

I still should have gone. If only Nick and I were somehow combined into one person.

121
CATHERINE

June 30, 1973
San Ysidoro

Dear Coz,

Does everyone think I'm horrible for not coming to the funeral? Actually I kind of wanted to come. I suppose having failed them in life, it is only appropriate that I let them down in death too.

But the sensitivity group argued that the fact that I was the daughter of a wealthy family gave me no more rights than anyone else. Many poor people are not able to attend funerals at home because they have no money. It would be oppressive of me to spend the money on a frivolous and sentimental plane ride when it could and should be spent on the weapons our movement so badly needs.

I might have argued that the money was not going to be spent on anything for a long time.

But I'm tired and sick again and discouraged by our slow progress and by the poverty and by the smell, to which I will never acclimate. And my parents' death hit me hard. I wanted to be alone up in the hills with my bike and my Indians and not talk to anyone at the *centro* or in Chicago.

I did love my parents and I will pray for them every night for the rest of my life, as I have every night since I can remember. On my Pope John rosary.

I have only one left, by the way. I gave the rest to the Indians, who know all about him, even if they think he is a lesser God to whom to offer their incense—which is a drug that knocks them out.

I couldn't face home right now.

I am worried, however, about all the money. Your father wrote that when the taxes are paid, I'll have seven million dollars. That's kind of funny for a woman who has finally overcome her distaste for an outhouse.

I talked to Father Ed about it privately, because I knew some of the others—Lorna and Father Luís, particularly—would give me a very hard time. I asked him if I could meet with a lawyer to make my own will, in case I fall off my bike coming down a hill in the rain or encounter some other and more violent misfortune.

He was very sympathetic, as he always is, and told me that on one of my special jobs for him I could meet a lawyer anywhere I wanted in Latin America.

That's fine with me. I can take care of my responsibilities and not face Chicago, for which I am not ready now. And may never be.

Would you ask your father if he could arrange it so that Nick becomes my executor, not my parents' but mine. When the money comes out of probate, he can look after it. And if I should die, I can trust him to do what I want with it.

I realize that this may seem kind of creepy. But I don't know anyone else and I don't want your father to be caught in cross-pressures again. Nick will do what he is told, even if he doesn't like it and I'm sure he won't.

Does it sound strange, Blackie, that I want to do it properly for my mom and dad? They never approved of me while they were alive and I'm sure they would have been terribly unhappy if they knew what I intend to do with the money. But at least I can try to be responsible in the way I do it.

And maybe now they think a little better of me.

> Give my love to everyone,
> Cath

122
BLACKIE

"They'll screw," said Mary Kate with her characteristic shyness and reserve.

"Will it help?" asked my sister Eileen, her green eyes flashing. She knew of course that at our house all questions are rhetorical.

"No, they won't," my father interjected mildly.

"I think they will, darling," said Helen gently, so unlike Katie Ryan in everything save for what really mattered.

"See?" insisted my sister. "And Helen is the only lady in the house."

The Ryans and the Murphys and the Kanes were in the parlor at the Beach on a sunny December afternoon, after another painful tragedy for the Chicago Bears. However, there was still joy in Mudville because the fighting Irish, led by Joe Theisman, had a shot at the national title if they could win on January first. Somewhere in the country, Red Kane observed, the Rosary was still being said. New Year's Day turned the subject to the fact that Nick would not be available to pray for God's team on New Year's Day because he was venturing to Río.

"Caitlin is a lady," I said irrelevantly, "despite all the good example she receives from her family."

"You don't think they'll screw?" Mary Kate demanded.

"I don't think it makes any difference," I said sadly.

"And I agree," Joe Murphy added. "How can a mild-mannered organization Democrat like Nick Curran tame a revolutionary firebrand, in or out of bed? And even in the Palace Hotel, or whatever the hell it's called, on Copacabana Beach?"

"I should be taken there on a trip," M.K. said, shifting her line of attack.

"Oh, he could tame her all right." I ignored my sibling, who does not need to go to Brazil to stir up the lights in her husband's eyes. "That's not the question. The issue is whether he will. The quicksilver mists will be all over Río, but Nick isn't ready yet."

"When will he be ready, Blackie?" asked my stepmother, the only one on the porch who engages in normal conversational practices.

"I don't know if he ever will be, Hel, but the day after that will be the only chance Cathy is likely to have for the rest of her life."

"That's putting a heavy burden on him," M.K. said, remembering that she was an internationally famed psychiatrist, specializing in marriage therapy.

And it was. Poor Nick, who had never been out of the country, was terrified by the prospect of his pilgrimage to Río. We had to help obtain a passport, negotiate with travel agents (I insisted on deluxe all the way, as a technique for testing the patience of Erin and Herbert in whatever part of the hereafter they had been assigned), check the climatic conditions and even select his wardrobe for him—the latter, most serious obligation, depriving my sister of a day with her clients and Caitlin of a day at school.

Never had a man gone to a romantic assignation with more style and less confidence. Poor Nick, he seemed to think that the long weekend in Río was strictly a matter of legal obligation.

Mind you, Cathy was concerned about her inheritance, which obviously she intended to hand over to Ed Carny and his pack of loonies and nutcakes, winning from him approval she never received from her father.

And she knew Nick would scream bloody murder but do what she wanted.

She was also lonesome, homesick and worn out. She wanted to see her man, even if she didn't quite understand that, and Nick was still, after all these years, her man.

As for sexual intercourse, the odds against it seemed to be pretty short. Two frustrated and lonely people who had always loved each other, on the beach at Río? Who's kidding whom?

On the other hand, Nick had not been exactly a flaming comet in his pursuit.

The real issue is whether he would pack her up and bring her home with him, which is what deep down she wanted, as she always had.

I could not see that happening. So it was likely to be a hateful, hurtful mess.

"Do you think she has a premonition of death?" Helen asked as twilight turned to dusk and the air in the parlor turned chill.

"Cath isn't the premonition type, is she?" Eileen asked.

"She doesn't need a premonition," I contended. "She's in a dangerous country playing a dangerous game. It's only prudent to put her affairs in order."

"I'll let the pun escape without notice," Dad said with a chuckle. "And with the observation that it will be the first display of prudence in her young life."

The hyper-prudent and the hypo-prudent encounter each other in Río. Of such encounters stories are made, occasionally comedies, and often tragedies.

As it turned out, the quicksilver mists were quicker than either of them. Not enough perhaps to save her life, but enough to give her existence some purpose and intelligence in its final moments.

123
NICHOLAS

I don't know what I was expecting when Catherine appeared at the doorway of the poolside terrace of the Copacabana Palace. But the young woman who paused at the entrance to the dining area glanced quickly around, saw me, smiled briefly and strode briskly in my direction was a heart-stopping surprise.

So was all São Sebastião do Río de Janeiro—St. Sebastian's of the River of January, much less romantic in English than in Portuguese. I had never been out of the United States before. And my adventures in my native land had been business trips to New York and Washington and one quick visit to San Francisco, which had been shrouded in fog.

I had not slept on the flight from New York to Río. Excitements of various kinds plagued my imagination with both promise and premonition. I was dead tired by the time I arrived in my room, overlooking the middle of the beach, but not so tired as to escape the multicolored charms of Río—water, mountains, sky, modern buildings, and crowds of people all swarming together to create what I would have considered overdone if it were a movie set—one of the few places in the world, I guess, that looks better in the flesh than in picture postcards. My only previous experience with the city was the film *Black Orpheus*, about the carnival. I refused to believe that such a complex and intricate jewel was possible.

But here it was, fresh and new with the smell of midsummer in the air, almost fresh enough and new enough to erase the stench of the *favelas*, or shanty towns, that ring the city and encroach even on the edge of the highway from International Airport (on Governor's Island) to downtown Río.

One look at those places was enough to confirm my conviction that Catherine had a valid cause. Valid or not, however, I resolved not to fight with her, not this time.

I had hardly put my bag on the bed and begun to unpack it when the phone rang.

"Tired, darling? Breakfast or lunch or brunch on the pool terrace in ten minutes?"

"My client calls and I come," I said with a laugh.

The phone clicked. Message delivered. She sounded light, airy and quite businesslike.

And when she walked across the terrace toward me, she looked like an international model out of the pages of Vogue, a bronzed, dark beauty in a light blue suit with a blue-and-white-striped blouse. Confident, self-possessed, sophisticated, obviously she had made good use of the money I had sent her for the trip.

Not my image of a missionary or a revolutionary.

"You are as beautiful as ever, Nickie," she said, kissing my cheek as I rose, stupefied, to greet her. "You improve with age."

"I think someone has stolen my opening lines," I said, holding her shoulders firmly in my hands. She did not try to pull away, but permitted me to admire her, indeed seemed to enjoy my admiration.

She grinned like the mischief-loving Ariel I used to worship. "And deliberately too. Go on: Say them anyway. I'll lap it up."

"You sure as hell beat Sugarloaf Mountain."

We both laughed enthusiastically and then five years disappeared. It was as if we had never been separated.

In the back of my head I wondered as we clowned through lunch why she was so flawlessly dressed and impeccably made up. I knew so little about women even then. She was dressed for me, and actress that she was, she played the sophisticated-international-model role for me too. Doubtless she had exercised and dieted (eating either more or less depending on the state of her health) for me. I was her man and she wanted to please me.

Only once in the course of the meal, in which I drank a form of high-performance engine fuel called a *batida* and consumed a delicious mixture of fish, rice, and coconut milk called *vatapa* (both ordered by Catherine), did a frown of worry mar her piquant face.

"Too much luxury, Nick, when so many people are poor."

"Can I recite my lines now?"

She smiled affectionately. "Sure."

"I've seen the *favelas* on the way in. I imagine they're the green wood. I don't doubt the justice of your cause, Catherine, as much as I may disagree with you on the best means to advance the cause. But I won't argue with you. And the Ryans insisted that you consider this hotel necessary medication."

She touched my hand. "I'll stipulate that, Counselor."

For a second I saw tired eyes and a weary face. Behind the makeup and the charm there were sickness, discouragement and exhaustion. But the next second the actress had reasserted herself and I forgot until I was flying home that moment of terrifying revelation.

"Is your room all right?" I asked lamely.

"Room?" Her big brown eyes widened even more. "You mean you put me in a suite and only gave yourself a room? I disapprove, Counselor."

"Blackie," I said, "dealt with the travel agent. For him the best suite in the Copacabana would be barely good enough for his cousin the princess."

"I like being a princess." She laughed again and I laughed with her. We had negotiated the first bank of shoals.

"Come for a walk on the beach or do you need a nap?"

"I can nap next week. What's the beach like?"

"Clean, hot, crowded, overrun with volleyball players, and filled with the most gorgeous male bodies in the world."

"No female bodies?" I asked.

"I'll leave that to your judgment. See you in ten minutes."

There was one heart-stopping female body waiting for me in front of the Palace ten minutes later, clad in minimal patches of red fabric and an ingenious collection of strings and knots that would have shocked even Mary Kate Murphy, who had advanced views about female beachwear.

"Do you mind if I gape?" I asked.

"I believe that is the goal. It's called a *tanga*, and in anything more I'd be overdressed by the standards of this place, as you are, by the way, darling. We must buy you appropriate shorts this afternoon."

Only on the sorrowful flight back to New York would I wonder about her body tan. It didn't come off in the water so either it was very good makeup or she had found a place somewhere in Costaguana to sunbathe. For me, as I now realize.

Copacabana dazzled you with its loveliness, if you had time to notice the beach. In the endless cultural conflict about which part of the female anatomy is the most to be admired, Brazil had obviously opted for the rear end—as you could tell by noticing how even the five-year-olds walked. Logically, then, the *tanga* left very little of a neatly turned posterior to the imagination.

"I think you missed one tawny beauty about a quarter mile back," she taunted me, as we emerged from the surf, which was too strong to swim in. Her own posterior was, incidentally, quite neatly turned, a fact of which she was by no means unaware.

"You looked like you were making mental sketches for paintings," I retorted.

"Aren't the men breathtaking? I could stay here forever. Funny you should mention paintings. I haven't thought about that in years."

"Good excuse for boy watching, oops, man watching."

An extra big breaker knocked her off her feet.

"Watch the waves some of the time," I said, dragging her to her feet. "They're more dangerous than the men."

"Play in the surf." She giggled. "Swim in the pools."

We walked farther down the beach. Periodically she insisted on anointing me with suntan oil. "Can't have my counselor roasted alive by the sun," she insisted.

Her touch was feather-light and paralyzing.

Without warning it was too much for me—sun, surf, sand, sleepiness, gorgeous bodies all around, and Catherine. I took her in my arms and kissed her, repeatedly and fiercely. At first she went through indifferent motions of resistance. Then her body and her lips responded to mine and indeed took charge of our passion. We twisted and swayed, as if we were blown by a strong wind.

Her breath smelled of *batida* and hot dog, her skin was slippery with suntan oil—which she administered herself—and her virtually nude body was a bundle of soft, supple, yielding delights. I was within an instant of wrestling her to the beach.

"You're not going to rape me in public, are you?" she said shakily as we paused.

"That seems a very good idea," I said, returning to my attack.

"Maybe we should both dive into the water, though I don't think it's cold enough," she said during the next interlude.

I released her. "The Arctic would not be cold enough."

We nonetheless dived in, ducked the breakers, and played and splashed.

"I don't know, Nickie," she joshed as we walked back down the beach. "A *tanga* shouldn't have that effect on a grown man."

"Ha," I said happily. "How would you have reacted if I had dragged you down on the sand?"

"Fought like hell," she said firmly.

On the way back—it was too hot to turn the rock corner at the end of the beach and walk down Ipanema—she explained to me that the votive candles on the beach were in preparation for New Year's Eve. At midnight the people of Río would offer gifts to Imanjeia, the African goddess of the waters, who was also, in the blend of Catholicism and Macumba (kind of like good Voodoo), which is the national religion of the country, Santa Barbara and the Blessed Mother.

We swam in the pool on top of the Palace, drank another *batida* and agreed to meet in an hour for dinner. "Bring your papers and let's get them out of the way," she said.

As I left the elevator on my floor, she said: "At first."

Only under the shower did I realize that she was referring to her comment about resisting my fantasy attack. On the whole, it was the most suggestive remark a woman had ever made to me.

Thereafter, I donned my formal jacket, as required by the best restaurant in the hotel, and brought my briefcase. Catherine brought herself in a white gown, with tiny straps around her neck, various ingenious slits and openings and no room or need for a bra.

She could run through millions of dollars on clothes alone if she had a chance.

"Can I say you're gorgeous without being accused of chauvinism?" I asked.

"You'd better," she said, blushing.

How long since anyone had complimented her on her beauty? What the hell was this lovely, sexy, gifted woman doing in a mission station in the mountains of Costaguana?

Serving the least of the brothers and sisters, and I could not criticize that.

But wasn't there room for both parts of her personality in her life? Couldn't she swing her pert little, mostly uncovered ass down the best beaches in the world and still work in the mountains?

It's a question I did not raise. I'm sure that her colleagues at San Ysidoro would have instantly ridiculed it. Yet I thought then, and still think, that she could have done both and would have been a better missionary if she had honored all elements of herself.

But now I sound like the Doctors Murphy.

The legal problems went smoothly. Catherine wanted the money invested in "sound" securities and watched over "prudently"—two words I had never before heard on her lips. All of it was to be willed to the Movement for a Just World, as Ed Carny called his reconstituted mission province.

"No arguments on that, Nick?" She cocked a pugnacious eyebrow.

"Do I disappoint you?"

"A little. I was hoping for a fight." She touched my hand in a quick gesture of affection that never would become routine. "Thank you for understanding."

"I'm not sure I do understand," I said, adjusting my reading glasses, "but I respect your wishes and your decision." I hesitated and then asked a stupid question. "Do you mind if I ask a personal question?"

Her hand was still on mine. "Has anyone told you how cute you are in reading glasses?"

I felt my face grow warm. "Not till now."

"The question?"

"Huh, oh, the personal question. I had kind of fallen asleep in a soft brown sea. . . . " She removed her hand and blushed again, a lot of blushing tonight. "Why don't you give the money to the Movement now? Do you want the right to change your mind?"

She drummed on the table with a spoon and signaled the waiter for another *batida*. "I trust Ed," she said finally. "I don't trust some of the others. It may sound dramatic, Nick, but any of us could die at any time. I figure I should exercise responsible stewardship while I can. After that"—she shrugged her lovely bare shoulders—"it's up to God."

"Fair enough."

Catherine might still need years of therapy, but she had grown up in some respects. I thought briefly about the old RAF movies—pilots partying one night and going out to die the next day. Catherine was on the firing line, a foolish firing line perhaps. Or maybe not. But brave she certainly was.

We came close to a fight only when I insisted on a letter of credit for her in a bank in Santa Marta—"go-to-hell money," as it was called by girls who brought enough money to get home in case they told their date to go to hell.

"I don't need it," she insisted. "I'll never leave till my work is done. Do you think I'm a quitter? It's a waste of money."

"There is no money involved," I tried to explain again, making a huge effort to control my impatience. "The credit line merely gives you the right to call on your money in Chicago should you need it. It's a contingency fund, that's all."

"What contingency?" she demanded, her eyes now dark and angry underground lakes.

"Any contingency. It's the nature of contingencies that you can't anticipate them beforehand."

"I don't want it."

"Then get a new lawyer."

Her lips became a thin, taut line. Then she relaxed. "I don't want a new lawyer."

"Then let me establish the credit line."

"Yes, Ape-Man. Anything you say."

Rarely did I win a test of wills with Catherine. It felt good to win this one.

Later we danced and drank coffee and cognac and danced again, this time cheek to cheek. Invitation exuded from every inch of her.

We rode the elevator silently to her suite and both entered together by unspoken agreement. Her suite was both opulent and decadent, like the rooms reserved in days gone by for the assignations of the emperor of Brazil. It took only one quick movement to strip off her gown and hold her, naked except for a transparent panty, in my arms. And then both our demons took control.

We were intoxicated with *batidas*, sun, loneliness and desire. The pent-up passions of twenty years erupted savagely, violently, harshly. Catherine was not quite a virgin, thanks to Roy Tuohy, but utterly without normal sexual experience. And I was only a little better prepared for lovemaking. So there was not much love, only angry and at times cruel passion. We both wanted to give each other more, I think, but did not know how.

Catherine yielded at first and then froze on the couch in the parlor of her suite, after I had torn off the affronting panty.

"Do you want me to stop?" I asked, gritting my teeth for self-control.

"Finish what you started," she said hatefully.

And I did, ineptly.

But there was too much hunger in us for it to end there. Later, stretched out on the lounge underneath the stars above her veranda, Catherine found pleasure, more from her own efforts than from mine.

There was little gentleness or affection in what we did, only hard, bitter need and clawing, scratching animal energy.

And she was so very beautiful, a spectacular womanly body, yearning for reassurance and tenderness. My mind, such as it was, wanted to respond to her yearnings, but my body was unskilled and had not the time to learn.

We had both caused each other too much pain to learn the arts of love in a weekend.

So we spent the weekend on sex, everywhere we could and as often as we could. In her suite, in my room, in a car, on the beach, even in a secluded mountain nook overlooking the city. We rarely spoke to each other. We ate, we drank, we swam and we used each other's bodies.

Was there love there? Could it, with time, have become love— again or perhaps for the first time?

Who knows?

But during the New Year's holiday we went through the motions of love. And I was the aggressor only some of the time.

Ariel she was occasionally, ordering another *batida*, shoving a hot dog into my mouth, ducking me in the pool, pushing me into a wave.

But there was no merriment in her voracious sex. And most of the time she was brittle and jumpy.

But we came close to an argument only on New Year's Eve afternoon when, lying on a blanket on the beach, I stared too long at a particularly luscious teenager in a particularly scanty assembly of strings, knots and cloth.

"You're objectifying her," she snapped, "treating her like a thing, a sex object to be used and discarded."

"I'm only admiring her good looks," I replied mildly. "I wouldn't use her, much less discard her. A man would be a fool. . . . "

"You'd like to rape her," she insisted.

"I'd like to make love with her," I defended myself. "But however wild my fantasies might be, I would never frighten or hurt her."

"All men are rapists," she said sharply, and launched on a long diatribe against male exploitation of women.

I outflanked her by agreeing with most of what she said. She wasn't satisfied with my refusal to fight.

"You'd never permit your wife to have a career of her own," she shouted.

"I certainly would," I argued.

"And what if she made more money than you did?"

"I'd retire and enjoy life."

"You wouldn't take care of the children."

"I'd love to. But if my wife made more money than I did—assuming I could find someone to marry me—she could afford to hire help for me and I could loll around the house eating bonbons and making love to the milkwoman."

She frowned, uncertain about my seriousness. "I don't believe the bonbon and milk-person part, but I think you really might let your wife support you."

"Sure would," I said truthfully. "There's a strong lazy streak in me."

She ended the argument by leaning over toward my end of the blanket and kissing me with a hunger that forced us to retreat to the red walls and dark drapes of her suite.

I bit my tongue in time and did not suggest that she might be the rapist instead of me.

An hour before midnight we walked the beach, now jammed with white-clothed men and women, some of them preparing seriously for a religious rite—dancing and humming around little shrines shaped like ships—and others swaying with eager expectation of a great celebration. I felt I had walked into a scene from *Black Orpheus*. The sound of the samba drums (not exactly samba, Catherine insisted), the thousands of lighted candles planted in the beach, the cheerful tension in the crowd— all combined to remind me of a mixture of Midnight Mass, St. Patrick's Day and a parish carnival.

"Half-Christian, half-pagan, and a one-hundred-percent celebration," Catherine murmured, leaning against my arm. "We Americans should be able to celebrate so easily. . . . Let's go to my balcony and watch midnight from there."

I wondered how much they celebrated at San Ysidoro, but did not spoil the magic of the night by asking her.

At midnight Copacabana (Our Lady of Copacabana, according to Catherine, who must have studied a travel book, so she could be tour guide as well as lover) exploded. The white-clad crowds surged to the water, eager to see if their small gifts of mirrors, half-empty bottles of beer and tiny packets of food would be accepted by the goddess. The drums beat at fever pitch, skyrockets colored the sky, firecrackers popped like machine guns, enthusiastic currents raced up and down the beach like sparks from a loose trolley wire, everyone seemed to be dancing.

Deeply moved and not quite understanding why, Catherine and I clung to one another like frightened children.

"Paganism," I murmured defensively.

"But it could be in honor of Mary the Star of the Sea," she replied, her voice muffled by my chest. "Let's pray that she'll protect us this year."

So we said the Hail Mary together and then, perhaps blasphemously, collapsed into one another's arms. For the first time our love was sweet and tender.

We were cheating, of course. On God, on our ideologies, on our life commitments. We knew it too. Our bodies carried one passionate message. The back of our brains said something else. There was too much dishonesty for affection to mix with lust and turn it into love.

And in the farthest recess of my brain I knew, even then, that we were in a race with death.

I guess Mary the Star of the Sea didn't hear our prayer. We lost the race.

124
MARY KATE

"Do you think she might still be alive, Punk?" I asked my sibling, favoring him with my sternest come-clean-to-mama-shrink look.

Joe and some of the Brats were returning from South Bend to Grand Beach, dragging their asses after the annual ritual slaughter of the Fighting Irish by the perfidious Trojans. Caitlin, who had her eyes set on the Golden Dome (making me proud that she was smart enough to get in and envious that the damn male-chauvinist pigs would not take me when I was her age), would be unbearably morose, a trait inherited from her father.

While we watched the sun disappear behind the Chicago haze and awaited the return of the mourners to Grand Beach, the Punk had explained the reason for Nick's trip to Costaguana.

The thought of him speeding again through Río where they had made love well if not wisely, to search for her corrupted body in an old tomb in a moth-eaten church on the high plains was enough to make shivers run relays up and down my spine. I silenced A Chorus Line on the stereo and faced my brother firmly.

He ducked the question. "At least he's not here to respond to those morons from the National Federation of Priests' Councils," he sighed.

That worthy group—a kind of priests' union—had passed a unanimous resolution censuring Nick for refusing to release the "inheritance of a saint" to those poor people for whom it was intended.

"How do they get away with it? What's Nick supposed to do? Break the law?"

"The Hegelian hogwash in their resolution about critiquing the legal system covers that. These days all you have to do is say you're engaged in a critique and the rules of logic and reason are repealed."

"Idiots. They claim they identify with the poor because that gives them moral superiority and then they can say any damn-fool, asinine thing they want. They all need five years of analysis, but not on my couch," I said with some feeling. "They'd make me an anticlerical."

"There was another resolution which didn't pass," he said wearily. "It called for priests to improve the quality of their preaching. They tabled it when one of their leaders reminded them that they were ministers to the whole world and not just to their parishes."

"I think I'll let the Christmas collection basket pass me by this year. And you haven't answered my question. Do you believe there is a ghost of a chance that she's still alive?"

"How could she be?" he asked sadly, filling my martini glass—had to protect some of the pitcher from my returning Pirate, who becomes quite uncontrollable when the alma mater does its death-wish thing.

"Didn't that reporter tell us that some people escaped from Esmeralda?"

"Where would she have been for the last two years?"

"Being Angela Carson."

"Why?"

"Maybe she was tired of Catherine Collins," I said kind of tentatively. Perhaps my sister/cousin got tired of careening down that highway and traded in on a new-model car—and new-model road too.

"Do you think that likely?" He peered over the top of his own tumbler, looking far too unhappy to be my Punk.

"Clinically," I said, using my favorite adverb to hide blue-skying, "it's not impossible. And remember, Punk, she could be tough and resourceful when she wanted. You don't survive a childhood like hers without an extra quota of resiliency, at least a standard deviation above the mean."

"Remember the med student at Lauderdale?"

"Indeed, I do. And the priest that tried to rape her at what's-that-awful-place?"

We were both giggling—even though I was only on my second and the Punk had barely touched his first mildly diluted vodka.

Cath was with us momentarily, the tough little clown who could make narrow escapes the material for slapstick comedy. For a few dreamy seconds, she was out walking the beach in the short, late autumn afternoon. Or riding back from Domesville with Joe and the Brats. Any minute now she would come in, her face flushed with vitality, pour herself a modest-sized martini and console us with the enthusiastic assurance that Notre Dame would easily be number one next year.

The last time Nick had gone to Latin America was the year they won the championship. Three long years earlier. Cath should have been here with us watching that New Year's Eve game, screaming with delight at Theisman's end-zone pass.

But she was not with us then and she was not with us now. Our illusion was fading.

"If anyone could do it, it would be Cath," I insisted.

"Only no one did it," he said as the illusion vanished.

"I know," I agreed. "What will he find in that awful tomb place, Blackie?"

"Angela Carson, I suppose."

125
NICHOLAS

On New Year's morning we tumbled into an interlude of tenderness.

At Catherine's insistence we hurled ourselves into the pool almost as soon as the sun rose. We were sitting on her balcony, towels wrapped around our waists, eating croissants and drinking orange juice and tea.

I saw her gazing up at the sun-soaked hills, a pensive frown on her forehead. Thinking of the poor people in the *favelas*, of course.

So I gave my lecture about Brazil, gleaned from a couple of Council on Foreign Relations seminars. A hundred and twenty million people. Rapid economic growth. Soon to be the eighth industrial nation in the world. Nation of immigrants—Germans, Italians, even Japanese (largest settlement outside Japan itself). Hardworking people, identify strongly with the United States, our friends throughout history. Helped us in the war. Economic miracle. But perilous future. Vulnerable to increase in oil prices resulting from the Yom Kippur war two months ago. Vast resources of Amazon, but no Homestead Act to open up the wilderness to ordinary people. Concentration of wealth. Perhaps the land wasn't meant for farming anyway. Good land in the northeast, but prone to multiyear droughts. Hydroelectric development and irrigation might help. Inefficient government-owned businesses. Danger of enormous explosion in its debt to American and European banks. Political oppression. Death squads. Growing middle class. But half the country, particularly in the northeast—Recife, Fortaleza—in poverty. An industrial nation with its own internal Third World. A toss-up whether the miracle would continue. But how else increase the national wealth so that sharing with the poor would make any difference. No easy answers.

It was a fairly impressive lecture, especially as I was distracted throughout by Catherine's deliciously bare breasts, taunting my memories of the New Year's party in 1960. She knew, I had no doubt, that she was a distraction and reveled in it. But she listened carefully to what I said, her brown eyes thoughtful, her head cocked at an angle that hinted bafflement.

"Did you learn all that about Latin America just because I was down here?" she asked, the hint of an impish smile on her lips.

"Partly," I admitted, my face hot again. "It doesn't make a bit of difference to those people up there on the hills."

"But you at least know something about the problems. I don't know anything. I rush around like a nut. How can I tell whether I'm doing any good?"

It was a confession of ideological disillusion that I hardly expected. She was looking at knotted fingers now. I took her hand.

"You're helping people, anyway," I said lamely, well aware that we were briefly on opposite sides of the question. "That's more than I'm doing."

"Only my poor Indians . . . Oh, Nick, they are so wonderful. Sensational sense of humor. Did I tell you . . . . "

And so my poor Catherine told me about her Indians. Or, rather, she acted out incidents in which at one moment she was herself and then a whole cast of Indian characters. All the time clinging to my hand.

As best I could tell, the Indian wit was childlike in the extreme. But I laughed through the whole narrative, captivated by the half-naked comedienne whose only goal was to entertain and delight me.

In the pursuit of which goal she was totally successful.

And then the sunlight was gone and the clouds were back.

"And my jokes with them are no more pertinent to changing their lives," she said bitterly, "than your lecture was to the people in the *favelas*."

"You make them laugh," I said, touching her breast as gently as I could. "Maybe that's what God wants from you."

She arched her head back and bit her lips, partly in despair over human misery and partly in pleasure. "Oh, Nick!"

"Oh, Catherine!" I cried, my trembling fingers brushing her skin, as I edged into ecstasy.

And so we were kind and good to each other for the only completely honest minutes of the holiday, healing with now infinitely sensitive bodies the pain of our common uncertainty and fear.

The mood was soon lost. The violence of angry passion exorcised our transient sympathy. It was, God forgive me, spectacular passion.

That Sunday night I lay in bed with Catherine sleeping in my arms, wondering what sort of afterglow behavior might have been appropriate for such a female tiger. Below us the Atlantic Ocean pounded Copacabana solidly. The fragrance of her hair blotted out the brine of the ocean. Her back was as smooth as expensive linen and her hard brown nipples were like precious stones set in ivory.

In time, I would learn how to respond to her. I was a reasonably quick study at everything else. I could figure out Catherine's sexual rhythms and needs with a little practice. And it would be an interesting and amusing experience. I knew one fact already. My love was a furiously passionate woman.

Passion and death. It was the Fatima letter that had scared her into vehement sex after the 1960 New Year's Eve party. Was it now the fear of death in a prison camp in Costaguana?

If she needed passion desperately, she also needed affection more desperately. Her family had provided her with very little. And I had not, so far, done much better. I could learn that too. But I would need time.

And time I did not have. Tomorrow I would board the 747 for New York and she would leave for Santa Marta on a battered old 707. Perhaps Ape-Man should drag Jane by the hair of her head onto Pan Am flight 202.

I strengthened my grip on her. That is precisely what Ape-Man would do.

But in the cold light of early morning, Ape-Man lost his nerve and changed his mind.

And Jane, icy and somber, became a bitch.

"I hope you enjoyed yourself," she said bitterly as we rode in the limo out to Governor's Island. "Had a nice holiday of fucking."

She was now wearing jeans and a blouse, the lay missionary, the hardened woman revolutionary returning to combat. I imagined RAF music in the background.

"I thought it was love, Catherine," I said defensively.

"Love," she replied with a sardonic laugh. "What does a male-chauvinist pig like you know about love? You had a woman to fuck and you fucked her, without any consideration for her own needs or emotions."

There was enough truth in what she said to unnerve me. "It takes time, Catherine," I pleaded. "No one learns a lover's needs in a few nights."

"And you're an expert on such things, I suppose?"

"Not really. I try. . . . "

"To men like you, a woman is an object to be used and discarded. You don't know, you can never comprehend, the meaning of mutual sharing and love."

"I don't think that's either true or fair," I said, my own temper rising. She had used me as much as I had used her.

"You're a fine one to talk about fairness," she said derisively.

"Catherine, I do love you." I tried to put my arm around her.

She pushed me away. "Don't you dare touch me. I will not be exploited anymore."

So Ape-Man lost all thought of dragging Jane onto his 747 and tried to make peace with her so they wouldn't part enemies.

He failed.

There was no kiss, no handshake, no farewell when her plane was called. She nodded stiffly and walked across the lounge to the jetway.

And at the last moment she turned and lifted her hand in a tentative wave, her face woebegone, her eyes filling with tears, a child leaving her parents behind. I waved back.

She smiled through her tears and disappeared into the jetway. It was a sad, final image. But I prefer it to that of the tormented woman in the Esmeralda barracks.

126
CATHERINE

All Saints Day 1973
San Ysidoro

Dear Blackie,

The revolutionaries raided a *barrio* near us the day before yesterday. There was a firefight with the local militia and some men were killed on both sides. We hid a couple of wounded revolutionaries. One of them died. It was the first time I have seen a man die of gunshot wounds. It was horrible.

The guerrillas took the other wounded man away this morning, just before the military police came to search us.

They made us stand in the rain all day. They did not find our guns, which are hidden in a cave near here. I don't know what use they are in the cave. We could not have obtained them in time if the police were planning to kill us today.

I suppose you have heard all the gory details of our weekend in Río from Nick. He is the kind of *Playboy* lover who couldn't resist bragging about his exploits in love. I was a fool to permit him to get away with it. What happened serves me right. I don't know what I ever saw in him. At least he's out of my system. Permanently. I suppose a weekend of chauvinist exploitation is a small price to pay for that.

The present revolutionary offensive will fail too, I fear. The odds are so heavily against us. The burned buses and blown-up bridges will provide the junta with excuses for even worse oppression. That is supposed to drive the people into the arms of the revolution. But so far it seems only to turn them against us. The tide of history will ensure the success of our struggle for liberation, but it may take a long time.

Many of the people here think that by next year there will be a revolutionary government in Santa Marta and the junta members will be dead and buried. I wish I was so confident.

Give my love to all.

Fondly,
Cathy

127
CATHERINE

Christmas Day
1973

Dear Blackie,
   Merry Christmas and a Happy New Year to you and everyone.

Would you ever do for me the most tremendous favor?

There's no reason why you should have saved my letters from the last ten—no, eleven—years. But, knowing you, I'm sure you did. Would you send them to me, please? No, better yet, make copies and send the copies.

That's a stupid instruction, isn't it? Of course, you'd send copies. And the leopards in the zoo haven't changed their spots yet, have they?

Love and peace,
Cathy

128
CATHERINE

January 20, 1974
San Ysidoro

Dear Blackie,

Wow, I mean, like really wow!

Anyway, thanks for sending them. I read them instantly and then reread them five times. I've burned them now. I don't want anyone here snooping around them.

It's like looking at yourself naked in a mirror and seeing all the warts and blemishes and splotches. I am really a quite ugly person.

But kind of interesting for all of that.

A terrible prig, a fanatic, and sometimes sort of sweet.

I'll digest it all while I am riding my bike under the summer sun. Then I'll write to you again.

All my love,
Cath

129
NICHOLAS

We drove out of Santa Marta in a brilliantly polished military command car, across the *campo* and up into the hills toward the barracks-turned-shrine of Esmeralda. The Higuerota Mountains, where Catherine's Indians lived, only farther north, loomed in front of us, seemingly quite close, though still dozens of miles away, according to Capitán Ramírez, my guide. Beyond, far in the distance, were the year-round snowcaps of the Sierra. In the mountain valleys between, many of them dense with rain forests, the guerrillas had hidden until the paratroopers routed them.

"There are still a few of them," said the *capitán*, who was the officer who "supervised" the Ministry of Justice. "And there will always be some of them so long as they can obtain Libyan and Cuban weapons and American mass-media publicity."

"Forget it, Capitán," I said coldly. "American publicity never won a single battle. If your regime persuades the people of this country that there can be some social justice here, a couple of score of bandits won't make any difference."

The *capitán*, a smart, handsome man with the required trim mustache, considered me speculatively.

"You will actually run for the Senate of the United States someday?"

"Will you run for president of the Republic of Costaguana someday?"

He laughed and extended a strong, firm hand. "So there will be no—how do you say it?—bullcrap between us?"

"Fine, Capitán. We understand each other."

The neatly whitewashed barracks of Esmeralda were surprisingly small. There was no reason they should have been big. No more than a battalion had ever been stationed there.

And the courtyard where the executions had taken place was no bigger than a school playground, a square of white buildings that looked bland and harmless. The floor of the yard was now planted with grass. Floral bouquets were strewn about, like toys left in a child's room. Two women with shawls on their heads and three men in dark gray suits were kneeling in fervent prayer.

Capitán Ramírez knelt himself and made a large sign of the cross. I joined him.

It did not seem possible that my Catherine's last view before she died was of these quiet walls. Perhaps she had been pushed over the cliffs at Punto Malo. I strove for emotion but could find none, neither pain nor sorrow nor hate nor love. Only blankness. I prayed, without much feeling and without much intent. I guess I prayed for Catherine and myself.

"You loved her, Señor Curran?"

"Yes, I did, desperately, hopelessly."

"I loved a woman who died here, a nurse. She committed no crime. There were no charges against her. She was one of Comandante Gould's random victims."

He spoke without any trace of emotion. The place left him flat too.

"You killed Gould, Pedro?" I asked.

"Yes, Nicholas, I killed him. I would have saved him for trial, but he was drawing a gun on me. He was a crack shot. . . . "

"I wished you had saved some of him for me."

"I understand. But he was a demented man, of course."

"Of course."

130
CATHERINE

March 20, 1974
San Ysidoro

Dear Blackie,

It's been a long time since my last letter because I've had to do a lot of thinking. There's more yet to be done, but I can give you a kind of interim report.

It started with Nicky last spring (our time) in Río. I came back here furious at him, a male-chauvinist pig who used and exploited me like I was a *Playboy* centerfold.

Except I know better. Nick is a dear, good man. So I had a lot of talking out to do with Marge. It's a strange feeling at first to discuss your love affairs, well, singular, love affair, with your former mistress of postulants.

She made me see that I seduced Nick. I went to Río determined to have sex with him and by damn I had it. In spades. When your sweet little cousin turns wanton, Blackie, she does so with a vengeance. Even surprises herself.

I don't suppose it surprises you. You always knew I wasn't the postulant type.

Anyway, Nick has always been an obsession with me. I have never escaped from my childhood crush on him. All these years he has been lurking in my brain. Whenever I think about him, my head pounds, my blood rushes fast, my hands tremble and I feel my face grow warm.

And if I had not entered the community we would have certainly broken up before I graduated from college. I am still in love, not with a real man, but with a teenage illusion.

Nothing happened in Río, Blackie, to cure me of my illusion or my obsession. I miss him more than ever. But now at least I am sensible enough to know that it is an obsession and that I tricked myself and exploited poor, dear Nick.

And I was totally unaware of what I was doing. Or, more exactly, I deceived myself about what I was doing. And then I covered up—continued to deceive myself—by having a furious fight with him and blaming him for everything, poor innocent galoot.

Actually Nick was very sweet. If I had given him the tiniest bit of help he would have been a wonderful lover. He was kind and I was a bitch. In the midst of all the violence and anger there was love, hints of ecstasy in the middle of a swamp of hateful passion. And it was his love for me. I'm quite incapable of loving anyone.

Then it occurred to me to wonder how many other times in my life I played games with the emotions of other people and deceived myself. That's why I wanted to see the letters.

And the verdict, your honor, is that my whole life has been self-deception. My vocations and my causes and my enthusiasms were all tricks I played on myself and on others.

Marge says I must not be too hard on myself, but it's difficult not to be hard on the little bitch who wrote those letters. I've played sick games all my life. I should have done what Mary Kate wanted and gone into full-time, all-day, all-night, all-week therapy after the nuttiness with Roy went on the rocks. Instead, I ran off here on one more crusade.

I don't know what follows, Blackie, dearest. I'm good at what I do here now. I speak the languages, I tend the sick, I heal the suffering. I laugh with the Indians. I don't make much of a contribution to the revolution, but I think that's going to be delayed for a long time. Perhaps I'm wrong about it, however. If I leave here, there will be no one else to help the Indians up in the *barrios* and the peons who come to our clinic in Río Secco.

I must think these things out. I have time, fortunately. My three years are up in August. By then I will decide.

Please keep all these things to yourself. I don't want to stir up anyone's hope without grounds. The work I'm doing here is the best thing I've ever done in my life. Maybe I should continue with it. And maybe I shouldn't. I do believe we should identify with the poor. But maybe I ought to identify with myself too.

And I don't know what that means.

And I'm not sure that Catherine Collins is worth identifying with.

My letters may be infrequent, Coz. That's not because I don't care about you or the rest of the clan. Or about Nick. But I think our mail is read here. And I have to take the opportunity to slip this in the mailbox when I'm somewhere else.

Pray for me like you've never prayed for anyone before.

> All, all my love,
> Cath

P.S. I reread the letter and argued with myself that I do too love Nick. But I don't, Cousin, darling. I'm too much of a mess to love anyone.

131
CATHERINE

Dear Blackie,

I can't tell you where I am or why I'm here. But I do know about the Watergate impeachment. I'm astonished. Could any other country in the world dispose of a crooked president so easily?

Anyway, I'm still uncertain, still hesitant. I will stay after the end of my three-year promise because I haven't figured everything out yet. I certainly do not want to hurt Father Ed, who depends on me more every day. I will decide before the first of the year, I promise.

I have never been able to drive from my mind the explosion of the mine at San Tome. How is it different from what Felipé Gould does in his prison in Esmeralda? We justify it because it is in the name of the revolution. The end justifies the means. When I think of the cheap rationalizations in my letter to you, I'm horrified. If I were the wife of one of those miners, it would make no difference to me that he died in the name of the revolution. Nor would I be any less sad to know that he was killed in a spirit of repentance and for the happiness of future generations.

When we who are on the side of justice approve of terrorism, are we any different from those who practice terrorism on the side of injustice?

I would not dare ask that question in San Ysidoro. But I can ask it in my own heart. Am I partially responsible for the death of those poor men who suffocated in the mine? Am I not on the side of those who did it? Don't I support them by working at the *centro*? Have not I defended revolutionary terrorism to the journalists and TV men who come to the *centro* to interview me?

What right do I have to approve of the death of any innocent?

And I have terrible nightmares that Nick was one of the miners. I've never mentioned them to you before because I was embarrassed by them. But I've dreamed such things since I first heard of the explosion.

Maybe Lorna is right. Maybe I will always be a shallow, middle-class romantic.

But maybe Lorna is a rigid bitch too.

It's all chaos and confusion in my head now, Blackie. But I think I see some daylight ahead of me.

All my love,
Cath

132
CATHERINE

August 15, 1974
San Ysidoro

Dear Blackie,

Two bad incidents on this third anniversary of my promise to become an advocate of the poor here in Costaguana.

Father Ed is terribly upset with me because I won't renew my promise. I told him I needed time to think. He says that in the cause of the revolution there is no time to think, that I am considering my own puny and unimportant emotions when the world is marching toward historic liberation.

And he is right, I guess. If I go home to nurse my confused psyche, the poor Indians in the hills won't have anyone to replace me. On the other hand, how much do I have left to give them? I'm tired and terribly depressed. And I'm not sure about the revolution at all.

I told Father Ed that the most I could do was three more months, till November 15. Then I would make a firm decision either way. He was very pleased. My revolutionary conscience had reasserted itself as a result of our confrontation. Or so he thought. The poor man is even more tired than I am. I keep thinking of the line from Joseph Conrad—"Mr. Kurtz, he dead." Is Father Carny dead the same way?

Am I?

Then today I was returning on the bus from Santa Marta. I collect my bike in Río Secco and ride up here. Anyway, sitting next to me on the bus was a young woman from Río Secco who attends the university. I talked freely with her about the revolution, because I thought that all students supported it.

But she was bitterly opposed, not only to the revolutionaries but to us.

"Why cannot you North Americans leave us alone? Why must we be exploited by both your capitalists and your Marxists? Why do you impose on us your revolution, just as you imposed on us your religion? Oh, yes, the poor come to your clinic in front of the church. And behind your backs they are afraid that you will bring the guerrillas down from the mountains to destroy our town, just as you used to try to destroy our religion with yours."

"We try to serve the poor and be their advocates," I said, surprised by her vehemence.

"Who asked you to be our advocates?" she spit back at me. "Can't we be free to be our own advocates? Who voted for you?"

"It's our task to raise the consciousness of the poor," I argued, and realized for the first time how patronizing that sounds.

"Ha," she said bitterly, "and is it not the essence of imperialism to assume that your consciousness is superior to ours, just like your religion and your economics? Why can't you leave us alone? Why must you bring death and destruction to us? Why must you ruin our crops and blow up our mines and bridges and murder our children in school buses?"

"We support the revolution in the name of liberation," I said.

"Who have you ever liberated, *señora*? Have you even liberated yourself from your own foolish messiah's complex?"

A fair question, huh, Blackwood? And no good answer.

She calmed down and really was a very sweet little thing. She hates the junta as much as we do. But she hates the revolution every bit as much. And blames both on America.

So I'm confused. But if Elena—the girl's name—is right, then
Father Ed and the rest of us are wrong.

Soon, Blackie, soon it will all be over.

Pray real hard for me.

Love,
Cathy

133
NICHOLAS

I rode in the bus to Río Secco, repeating Catherine's ride. Foolishly
I looked for a young woman on the bus who might be Elena, but saw
no youthful intellectual. It was the middle of their summer and the sun
was blistering hot, but Río Secco is in the hills and there was a mildly
refreshing breeze. Nonetheless, I took off my jacket and carried it over
my arm, a very North American thing to do.

I was sure that my friend Pedro was having me followed, as much
for my own protection as to keep an eye on me. He was a smart young
man and was not altogether convinced about my motives for the trip.

A battered Ford from the early fifties was waiting at the bus terminal—a withered sun shield with holes in it next to the railhead from
Tonoro, down on the coast 100 miles south of Santa Marta. The taxi
had been ordered beforehand by the travel bureau in Santa Marta. We
bumped up the hilly road to San Ysidoro, ten rough miles. Catherine
rode it on her bike every day, rain or shine, summer and winter. Flaky
she may have been but also marvelously brave. I wonder if anyone else
besides Marge Aimes really did anything for the poor whom they were
supposed to be advocating.

The plan, carefully laid out with Blackie, who has a superb gift for
intrigue, was that I would stay only a brief time at San Ysidoro and then
return to Río Secco an hour before the bus was scheduled to return to
Santa Marta. That would give me time to explore the crypt in the old
church.

It was very much on my mind as we struggled up to San Ysidoro.

What would I find there—the Angela identity? Catherine's body, now nothing more than a skeleton?

I was not much interested in the remains of San Ysidoro. Only the chapel and one of the buildings, an assembly-hall kind of place, were still standing. There were traces on the ground of ruins of the dormitory, once of a high school for Indian boys and then of Father Ed's revolutionaries, and of the school building where the adult education and sensitivity programs were held. I wondered where the target range had been where Catherine had won her Lenin prize.

It was an utterly trivial ruin, an empty chapel with a few broken candles and fractured stained-glass windows and a crumbling auditorium occupied only by rats and scorpions. Unlike the old church down in Río Secco, which had been built for the centuries, the relics of the American missionaries had been built for a few years, a decade or two at the most.

Throw them away and buy new ones.

How could a man possibly think that such a *centro* would contribute to the sweep of history's wave, even a man as sincere and well intentioned as Father Ed?

Just as in Esmeralda, I felt no sense of Catherine's presence, only awe that she could have lived in such a barren and uncomfortable place for so long. How did you do it, my darling? What demons and what angels kept you here?

I had not met any of her laughing Indians, however. If there was any monument to Catherine's life, it was not the statue at the Hill but the memory of that secret Indian laughter, which stirred her out of her revolutionary seriousness despite herself.

I told the taxi driver to return to Río Secco. He was reluctant. There was much time for the bus. I offered to drive myself, by force if necessary, and he understood my point. The car that waited beyond the Hill followed along at a discreet distance. Don Pedro was taking no chances.

Soon I would be at the end of the chase. Would I find the neat bag with Angela locked in it? Or would I find all that remained of Catherine? Or would I find anything at all?

134
CATHERINE

October 28
San Ysidoro

Dear Blackie,

The agonizing is over. I'm coming home. I haven't told Father Ed yet, but I suspect he knows. And I'm not sure of the date. Right after the fifteenth of next month, when my three-month promise expires. I have kept the faith in that promise anyway.

I have not decided about the revolution yet, not chosen between Father Ed and Elena, as I described the choice to you in my last letter. Maybe I'll never be able to decide.

I have nothing more to give to the people here, especially my wonderful laughing Indians. I'm empty, Blackie, drained, spent. Maybe after I straighten out my life I can come back and help my Indians again. But I can't promise that now. I will commit the next three years of my life to Catherine and find out who she is really and what makes her tick.

And I'm dying to see all of you, Blackwood. I can hardly wait to come home.

See you soon.

Love to all,
Coz

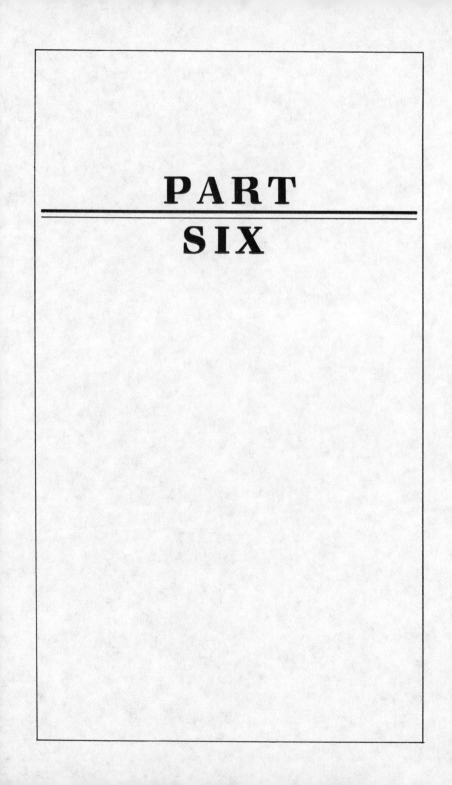

PART
SIX

135
NICHOLAS

The sun was sinking toward the distant Sierra when I paid the taxi driver in front of the church in Río Secco. A cool breeze forced me to put my jacket back on. Some peons were kneeling in front of the church executing rites with fire and little bundles of paper to deities that God alone could sort out. I steered around them.

My heart pounding, I knelt on the earthen floor of the old building, praying in the dim candlelight and the dusty mist, for what I wasn't sure.

Her last words, in the final letter, which was in my jacket pocket, had been "see you soon." Two days later she disappeared. No, my darling, you did not see any of us soon.

I had rightly calculated that Don Pedro's man would respect the privacy of my prayers. Glancing over my shoulder after what seemed to be an eternity but according to my watch was only five minutes, I picked my way up to the main altar, ignoring the disapproving stare of, I think, St. Joseph.

Behind the altar it was almost completely dark. I removed my miniature flashlight and flipped the switch. It barely cut through the gloom.

There seemed to be no creaking iron gate. Was the crypt itself a fantasy? Catherine might have imagined something like it, but not good, solid Marge Aimes.

I felt along the cold marble of the altar and finally touched something that seemed like iron. I examined it with my tiny light and, sure enough, there was a grating, so closely fit to the altar that one would hardly be aware of its existence, if one did not know it was there.

It was elegant and delicate ironwork at that. There must have been a wealthy *hacienda* here sometime in the past.

I pushed hard against the grate. It would not move. I pushed again, now breaking out in a sweat despite the chill of the church. What the hell, had someone locked it?

I inspected the interface of the grill with the marble. No sign of a lock. Then I had a brilliant insight. Pull it, you dummy. There's no reason under heaven why gates to crypts should all open inward.

It swung toward me, not easily and not silently—squeaky, as Marge had said it was. I wondered if Don Pedro's man was in church. What would he think if he could not find me in the gloom and then heard a loud rattling behind the altar?

To hell with him.

I picked my way carefully down the stairs, dusty, old and worn. The dry, discouraged smell of long-ago death permeated the cavern. My light made little impression on the gloom. Damn fool. What kind of an agent would you make? Not even sense enough to buy a powerful flashlight.

Bending over, I began to explore each of the stone coffins for the name of "Don Alfonso." I made the circuit, first one side and then the other, of the low corridor. No Don Alfonso.

I tried again, cursing the dim flashlight and my trembling fingers. Again nothing. What was wrong with me? This had to be the place. And there was a coffin in every niche.

Then it dawned on me that the nameplate might be on the top of the coffin. I explored again, feeling in the dark for a plate or a carving and then examining it with my flashlight.

Finally I felt a slight depression on the top of one of the caskets. I flipped the light on; its batteries were waning.

Sure enough. "Don Alfonso Rodrigo . . . " The last name had vanished, which is why Marge didn't remember it.

I put the light back into my pocket and shoved against the coffin cover. It moved slightly. What had ever persuaded Catherine to open it? A ghoulishness I would not have expected in her.

I shoved again and it slowly surrendered to my pressure. One last push and it swung open, as if someone long ago had designed it to do just that, someone who wanted to use feigned death as an escape.

I fumbled in my pocket for the light. My mouth was dry, my head thumping. What would I find?

There was nothing in the tomb, no trace of either Angela or Catherine. Only an empty stone box. Hardly believing my eyes, I examined the inside, inch by inch, with the now fading flashlight.

Nothing. No one and nothing.

What did an empty tomb mean?

136
BLACKIE

"What does an empty tomb mean?" I said to Nick. "It means that someone has stolen Angela, that's what it means."

We were sitting in Nick's office. He was a wreck. Pan Am 202 arrives in New York at 6:20 in the morning. He grabbed a cab at Kennedy and caught the 9:00 American to Chicago from La Guardia. At 11:00 he was in the office—tired, battered, discouraged and, for the first time, looking old. We had to bring this mad quest for my dead cousin to an end soon if there was going to be anything salvaged of his life.

"Who would do that?" he said wearily.

"Almost anyone. I assume that the inside of the casket was covered with dust?"

"No." He paused, trying to remember. "It wasn't exactly clean, but the layer of dust was thin compared to the rest of the crypt."

"And no stench of a recent corpse?"

"I don't think so. . . . "

I hummed "The Whistling Gypsy," a sign to Nick and others that I was thinking. So Angela had been there, but not Catherine, at least not dead. "Have you heard from your friend at Amex?"

He reached for his phone and punched a number. Obviously he had memorized it.

"I see," he said, his face freezing. "Yes, that's very interesting. No, I won't reveal my source. I understand it's very sensitive. Yes, I'd appreciate that very much. Call me back as soon as you find out."

"Angela bought traveler's checks in Río?"

"Uh-huh," he said. "A couple of days before Catherine's final letter."

My stomach did several interesting flip-flops. "He's checking to see if they were cashed?"

Nick nodded. "Fifty checks, in denominations of $100. Identified herself with an American Express card. Five thousand dollars. I can't think straight anymore, Blackie. What does it mean?"

"It means that whoever kidnapped Angela took her money."

"Why would Catherine have purchased checks under an assumed name? That doesn't make sense."

"We don't know that she did. All we know is that someone who found Angela, one way or another, bought the checks. That's all we know, Nick."

"But assuming it was Catherine . . . "

"We can't assume that . . . but she might have wanted to fool the authorities. Or perhaps she knew from past experience that Angela had an easy time with the airport police. Or maybe she was hiding from the people at the *centro*. Remember that she didn't trust them. Or maybe it was a just in case . . . There are still four hundred and fifty hundred-dollar bills unaccounted for. When will we hear from your source?"

"Tomorrow at the earliest."

137
NICHOLAS

I thought I would not be able to sleep that night. I played with the notion of calling Monica and reporting. But what had I to report? My obsession with Catherine was alive and well, even if she were not. And now there was another obsession—Angela Carson. Who was she? What was she? And where was she?

Most important, perhaps: Was she?

Exhaustion caught up and I slept twelve hours. I was late in arriving at the office, a phenomenon that shook my secretary's sanity to its roots.

"The man from American Express called," she said in a shattered voice.

"Get him back, please. Sorry I'm late."

"Not at all, Mr. Curran."

I talked to him briefly and then dialed Blackie. He wasn't at the rectory or at school. I found him at Bishop Cronin's office.

"Angela Carson used her traveler's checks in Florida, at the Key Biscayne Inn during January and February of 1975. Nothing since then."

There was uncharacteristic silence at the other end of the call.

"Ready for another plane ride, Nick?"

"We don't have any choice, do we?"

"None whatever."

138
BLACKIE

The manager of the Biscayne Inn, a slender, handsome man whose bland face, restrained courtesy and faint English accent made me think of Jeeves, was elaborately cordial. "We will do everything we can to cooperate, Mr. Curran, Father Ryan. Of course, it was two years ago. . . . "

He had every reason to be cordial. The hotel corporation's law firm was the most distinguished in Miami. And, if Nick's firm was not the most famous of the Chicago law factories, it was certainly the most solid.

Solid and reliable, just like Nick.

So a couple of phone calls were made and we were sitting in his office, watching the white breakers roll gently up on the beach under a benign December sun. The Biscayne Inn was not one of your gigantic Miami Beach convention hotels trying desperately to cling to both its sand and its recollections of past glories when the beautiful people came to Miami in the winter, instead of European tourists in the summer on cut-rate tours.

Rather it was a medium-size, self-confident and very discreet place to which the important people came when they wanted sun and peace closer to New York or Washington than the west coast of Mexico or the north coast of Venezuela. And important people are delighted not to have the beautiful people around.

Angela Carson, whoever she was, had good taste. And, I thought unhopefully, more knowledge of posh watering places than one could have expected from Cathy.

"A woman named Angela Carson did indeed check in here in January of 1975." He ran a pen down a page in a leather-bound record book. "She was rather fortunate. At that time of the year we normally do not have any vacant rooms. However, there was a cancellation just before she arrived and we were able to find her a nice oceanside room. Let me see, she identified herself with an American Express card, but paid every week with traveler's checks, two-hundred-dollar denominations."

It was our knowledge of the checks that had brought us to the Biscayne Inn in the first place.

"May I see her signature, sir?" Nick asked.

"Of course," he said affably, passing the binder across his big oak desk to Nick.

I peered over Nick's shoulder. "It's Angela's signature all right, like the one on the checks for the airplane ticket."

"And here's our copy of the final bill, when she checked out four weeks later. It appears to me, though I am hardly an expert, to be the same signature."

It was a good deal more self-confident signature. Angela was more self-possessed when she left than when she came to the Biscayne Inn.

"And no forwarding address?" Nick examined the signature carefully.

"None, sir. We don't usually insist."

"Mind if I copy the AE number?"

"Not at all." The man hesitated. "We, uh, we have no notations that she was at all an undesirable guest. You'll note that she took most of her meals in her room. Many women come here for a bit of peace and quiet. We do our best to provide it for them."

"You were not the manager then?"

"No, sir, I was working in San Francisco at the time." He slid a sheet of bonded notepaper across his desk, which was as empty as an ornamental conference table. "I have examined our records to see what employees might have been in contact with Miss Carson. The maid who serviced her room and the bellman who brought most of her meals have both left us for New York. However, the housekeeper, the doorman and the maître d' are still on our staff. If you wish, I can ask them to have a word with us?"

Indeed we wished.

The housekeeper was an attractive Cuban woman in her late thirties who nervously played with her wedding ring as she talked to us.

"Let me try to remember, *señores*; Room 423. Not last January and February, but the year before. Yes, of course, there was a young woman. Quite pretty, as I remember. Nice to the staff, but quiet and reserved. She wore dark glasses and, I think, heavy makeup."

Nick showed her four pictures of Cathy.

"I cannot say for certain, *señor*. I do not think so. As I remember, she had blond hair. But there are so many guests. . . . "

The maître d' could not remember any such visitor at all. But as he told us in a Parisian accent, which was possibly authentic, "We have so many beautiful women at the inn. This one is very beautiful indeed. But I do not recall her."

"I'm glad there is room for beautiful women in the inn," I said, drawing no laughter for my scriptural reference.

But the doorman, a little Irish cop from New York, who had fled to warmer climes, thought he remembered an attractive blond who had taken a cab each day in midmorning for a couple of weeks and returned in early afternoon.

"That could be the one"—he considered Cathy's pictures carefully— "though this one is a brunette." He put his hand over Cathy's hair. "It's a nice face, very nice. But not special, ya know what I mean? I'm not sure that even if the one in the picture had blond hair I could swear that this was the one."

"Dark skin, almost gypsy?" said Nick hopefully.

The New Yorker shook his head. "Light skin, I think. Course, ya can't tell with makeup."

"Your best guess is that the guest is not the woman in this picture?" Nick tried to keep his voice level.

"What can I tell ya?" He shrugged. "I'd hate to have to testify in court."

"I don't think that will be necessary."

Later in the parlor between our two rooms—I argued vigorously that Cathy would not want her estate to scrimp on our travel expenses—Nick was dejected.

"American Express says that it is the number of a gold card taken out of service four years ago after a theft. And it was not issued to Angela Carson. There have been no charges to the account since then. Useful for identification, but risky for anything else—just the sort of thing that someone forging credentials would normally have available."

"As phony as her address on the hotel register."

"Right. It is a reasonable enough East Eighty-ninth Street address, but it doesn't happen to exist in New York."

"A woman can dye her hair or wear a wig and she can change her complexion with makeup."

"And she might have been visiting a doctor over in Miami . . . but we're kidding ourselves, Blackie. It's not Catherine. Why would she pretend to be someone else?"

"Maybe because the Movement needed a martyr and she didn't want to die."

"And was never arrested?" He looked sadly out the open balcony window at the ocean, doubtless dreaming of Grand Beach. "It's a dizzy enough project for her. Like one of her old practical jokes. But I can't see Catherine engaging in deliberate deception. And, remember, she wanted to change her will. If she was disillusioned with the Movement, why would she agree to be a pseudomartyr for them?"

"I hadn't forgotten."

We spent the next three days talking to security men, taxi drivers, storekeepers and doctors and found not a single clue. One taxi driver thought he recognized her but could not remember where he had driven her or exactly when. I thought I sniffed something odd at Mercy Hospital, which is just south of the Rickenbacker Causeway on the mainland. But it might have been merely that I was looking for something odd, figuring that Cathy would surely have chosen a Catholic hospital, especially if it was only a few minutes' drive from her hideaway on the key.

If, of course, Angela and Cathy were the same person. And my doubts on that possibility were increasing every hour.

We had a portrait made of Cathy with blond hair and that did not stir any memories of recognition. We even asked the Dade County police if they would dust her hotel registration card. They looked at us dubiously, but they too had been told to cooperate. There were a lot of prints on the card, most of them blurred and none matching the set of Cathy's prints we'd borrowed from the Chicago Police Department. And the FBI had no record of any of the prints that the Miami people were able to tease off the card.

"Dead end," I said as we walked the moonlit beach on the night of December 4, listening to the reflective pounding of the surf against the sand.

"I went to the very top this time. Never mind what I mean by that. Anyway, they admitted they didn't tell me the whole truth when I went to Washington a couple of weeks ago. I chewed the hell out of them for telling a goof like Tuohy, who had no right or need to know, and not telling me. They confirmed what he said. The FBI was aware that a number of people were bringing in currency from Costaguana and handing it over to Outfit couriers for transfer out of the country. They kept an eye on it because, while there were no violations of American laws, Costaguana was a hot subject then. One of the couriers was a woman who went by the name of Angela Carson, who they had reason to believe was Catherine Collins Tuohy from Centro San Ysidoro. The deliveries stopped after Catherine disappeared. They continued to watch for her for a few months and then stopped when it seemed that the whole operation had been terminated."

"And the color of Ms. Carson's hair?"

"Brown," he said sadly.

"And we still don't want to launch a nationwide search for fear that we will stir up the Outfit."

He nodded his head. "We may have asked too many questions as it is." He polished his reading glasses thoughtfully. "It's so damn hard to balance all the factors. If the woman is Catherine, we want to protect her. If it is someone who has taken her money—and you don't have to tell me again that such is probably the case—we need not worry about protecting her. So we tie our hands in search of a probable thief in order to protect an improbable Catherine."

Indeed she was always improbable.

"So we fly back to O'Hare?"

Nick placed his glasses on a table at the edge of the pool and rubbed his tired eyes. "No, goddamn it, we stay here as long as we can until we come up with another angle. I don't know what such an angle would be, though. I'm at a dead end."

"Go get some sleep," I said, pleased that he had not quit yet. "Maybe the new angle will be revealed in a dream."

He laughed and started to walk toward the door leading from the pool to the main part of the hotel. "Coming along?"

"No, I want to study the moon for a bit."

He shrugged and left me alone.

I did not, however, pay much attention to the moon. Rather I devoted my attention to systematic speculation of a sort that is impossible for an empiricist trained in the Anglo-Saxon legal tradition. Trailing after Nick as he played the Sherlock Holmes game interfered with such speculation, especially as, God forgive me, I had cast myself in the Holmes role and Nick as Watson.

The speculation took me to some very interesting places. It was all completely theoretical, of course, but consistent with what we knew.

I went back to our suite, made sure that Nick was asleep in his room and then called the rectory in Chicago, knowing that my good pastor would be awake watching reruns from "Twelve O'Clock High." He provided me with the list of names and phone numbers, without even asking why I wanted them.

He knew me too well.

The next morning after breakfast, while a determined but disconsolate Nick drove across the causeway to talk once more to the Miami police, I purchased a map of Florida in the hotel gift shop and began to make my phone calls. Everyone was polite, but no one had that for which I was looking.

The gift shop did not offer maps of other states. Why think of someplace else when you were in Florida? So I went to a service station, smiled politely and said some words in Spanish to the young man in charge and came back with maps of Alabama, Georgia, South Carolina, Mississippi and Louisiana.

I made two more calls to no avail and paused to consider that, however internally consistent my speculation was, it had no basis in reality other than certain assumptions that depended on a more basic assumption, which was highly improbable.

Nonetheless, I called another number, in area code 205.

Astonishingly, they had exactly what I was looking for.

My hand was shaking and I was perspiring heavily when I hung up. It did not follow that because I had found what I was looking for, the basic assumption was true.

But it hadn't been disproven, either.

My pocket flight-guide said that Eastern had connections to our destination through Atlanta. Everything south of the Ohio River connected through Atlanta. I almost made reservations for that evening. Then I noticed that the date was December 5. No, one must wait till the Feast of St. Nicholas.

And give my Nicholas time to push whatever insights he might still have with the Dade County authorities.

We would leave late in the morning for Atlanta. I would not tell him why. Now that we were so close to the end of the trail, I would spare him the further agony of wondering what we would find.

I called back my number and asked for the name of a high-quality motel or hotel in the area. I was told that the "Stars and Bars" was very close and rated four stars from Shell. I apologized to my ancestors who fought with the First Illinois in the Civil War and made the reservation, telling myself again that Cathy's estate would not be bankrupt by providing us with comfortable beds.

My hand continued to shake for another quarter of an hour. I too was afraid of what we would find at the end of the trail.

"Why are we going to Mobile?" I demanded again as the DC-9 lifted out of the rain of the congested Atlanta airport.

"A long, long shot, Nicholas. Indulge me." He hummed "The Whistling Gypsy" for the eighth time that day. I think in his heart of hearts, John Blackwood Curran identifies with the hero of that ballad.

So I indulged him. Blackie loves the mysterious and there is no way you can pry him open when he wants to keep something secret. Moreover, he was obviously trying to protect me from worry. I was certain that somehow he had found evidence that Angela was not Catherine but did not want to crush my faint hopes until he was absolutely sure.

So I listened quietly while he lectured on my patron saint.

"The most important wonder worker in Christian history, and the most popular nonbiblical figure that we have ever known. So what do we do with him? Under the aegis of our presently gloriously reigning supreme pontiff, we throw him out of the calendar."

"Why did we do that?" I asked, knowing my lines by now.

"For the idiotic reason that he didn't exist."

"How did all the wonders get worked, then?" I asked.

"An interesting question. But then how do all the Christmas presents get delivered?"

"By parents."

"Precisely. In any event, he started out as a substitute for Poseidon, the god of the sea, whose feast, as you doubtless recollect from your liberal education at St. Anthony's, is also today. A church seems to have been built at the seaport of Mrya to seek protection from the winter storms which begin to be severe in the Eastern Mediterranean at this time of the year. Who the Nicholas was after whom the church was named we haven't the foggiest. And the stories about the bishop who was martyred are legends that appeared many centuries after the alleged fourth-century fact. Nonetheless . . ."

"Nicholas was killed too? I guess I should have known that from Santa Claus's red robes?"

What was I doing talking about Santa Claus when I was beside myself with grief over Catherine—and still desperately hoping she was not a martyr.

"Of course not," Blackie said impatiently. "Those are bishop's robes that the good Claus wears. He was a martyr in the sense that he was tortured for his faith, but apparently was too stubborn to renounce it and too stubborn to die. So they sent him back to Mrya, battered and bent, but not beaten. And he promptly became the local surrogate for Poseidon. This is all legend of course."

"Of course." Despite my worry, I couldn't help but laugh. Blackie was patently trying to keep my mind occupied and doing a good job of it.

"He then was given charge of working wonders at sea. Since a fair number of sailors do survive bad storms, it was natural that he would receive credit for it. And the merchants whose goods were saved became, needless to say, very grateful. Then it developed that Nicholas had once thrown three bags of gold over a wall to provide some young women with dowries, bags of gold which are even today honored in the three gold balls over pawnshops."

"Really?"

"Oh, yes. One thing leads to another, as it does in these cases, and the good saint became in rapid order, as the centuries go, patron of bankers, thieves, scholars, small children and New York City, as well as merchants, sailors, pawnbrokers and unmarried young women. A wandering thaumaturge, so to speak."

"Indeed."

"Precisely. A bunch of crusaders had the impression that he didn't want to remain in Mryian any longer and wanted rather to have his bones lie in the cathedral in his honor at Bari in southern Italy. So they facilitated this movement by, uh, stealing the bones and transporting them to Bari, where he was received amid universal rejoicing."

"But if he didn't exist, how could he have bones?"

"Bodies are a dime a dozen in ancient cathedrals," Blackie said impatiently. "Doubtless the good burghers of Mryian turned one of their available bodies over to the wandering Mafiosi and thought themselves to be lucky to escape worse havoc. There have been, needless to say, many miracles at the tomb of this unknown Mryian. Then, in his role as patron of little children, he was deputed to preside over the winter-festival custom of exchanging gifts in Northern Europe, particularly Holland and the Germanic states. From Holland he journeyed to New Amsterdam, where he became the patron of the Dutch in a society of St.

Nicholas, against whom it was necessary for later arrivals to set up, in honor of an equally imaginary American Indian chief, the Society of St. Tammany, an institution which was still later to fall into the hands of our fellow ethnics in an ironic historical twist."

"Yes, indeed. I wish I were a miracle worker, like my patron."

Blackie looked at me curiously. "Who knows what opportunities may lurk? Well, to continue, a pious Anglican in that city named Clement Moore wrote for his six children in 1822 (he would later have three more) some delightful if not exactly prize-winning verse called "A Visit from St. Nicholas," tying together some of the old Germanic and Dutch customs with an assist from the writing of Washington Irving. Then Thomas Nast immortalized the old man in a collection of splendid drawings and Santa Claus, redone in New York, spread to the rest of the world, somewhat ahead of Coca-Cola, though he only returned to Europe in his present Americanized version just before and just after the Second World War."

"Remarkable," I said as the landing gear was lowered. The rain in Atlanta had missed Mobile. I had a brief view of the bay as we came in for our approach.

"Quite. A wonder worker with bishop's robes and a beard and an American accent representing God's love for little children all over the world. And the damn fools in Rome have to demythologize him just when the story was getting good."

"Does my name impose any obligations on me for miracles?"

"Who can tell about saints?" he replied. "Especially when they are only legends."

"Can I have some credit for the storm missing Mobile?"

"You might," Blackie said, considering me carefully, "make an appropriate Poseidon."

He had ordered a Hertz Ford Thunderbird for us and inquired of the young woman at the Hertz counter the direction to the Stars and Bars Motel. As we walked away from the counter, he softly hummed "The Battle Hymn of the Republic," pleased as punch that he was now Holmes and I Watson.

Mobile manages to mix Old South and New South with more charm than most southern cities. Even the new suburbs between the airport and the town seemed to have a gracefully worn look about them which suggested the easy charm of a lovely aristocratic matron. Although it was December, the grass and the trees were still green—which for a Middle Westerner is enough to suggest a leisurely and pleasant existence.

Our rooms at the motel were large and comfortable, the walls lined with prints of the Battle of Mobile Bay as seen from the Confederate side. Blackie turned his promptly to the wall and told me that we should meet in the lobby in fifteen minutes.

I changed to sport jacket and slacks, hardly knowing what to expect, and tucked my briefcase with the documents of the Collins estate under my arm. Blackie was wound up tight, and somehow that seemed to me to suggest the hope, the possibility of good news.

"Where to?" I asked when he joined me a quarter hour later in the car, clad in full clerical attire.

"We take the first left turn, drive past the golf course and turn right at the entrance to St. Peter's College."

A guard waved us down at the college entrance, saw Blackie's collar, smiled and signaled us to proceed. St. Peter's had the same mix of buildings as any other Catholic liberal arts college in the country; the center of it, however, was not a log cabin or an old stone chapel or a Gothic castle or a New England manor, but an antebellum Southern mansion with a vast, wooden front porch.

"Frenchmen's Bend," he said, as I drove by it looking for a place to park. "It requires only Burl Ives on a rocking chair."

The students strolling around the campus seemed to be relaxed and easygoing, the girls in spring dresses and shorts, the boys carrying golf clubs.

"Nice, discreet country-club atmosphere and relaxed admission standards if you can afford the tuition," I said, speculating about the quality of the school. "Makes one want to go through college again."

"It's bad enough to be young once," Blackie replied. "Ah, there's a parking spot."

We walked under an avenue of weeping willow trees toward the mansion which looked like it had been designed for a Faulkner novel. Blackie stopped to ask directions from a honey-blond student with glorious legs. I didn't hear his question, but her response was to point toward the old home.

He now walked very rapidly, despite his short legs. I hurried to keep up, my heart pounding because I knew that we might be at the end of the chase.

Burl Ives was not on the porch and we did not tarry to ask where he was. Blackie plunged through the swinging screen door, paused to get his bearings and then turned left down a shaky wooden staircase. I continued to hurry after him.

The basement was moist from the humid atmosphere and the corridor through which Blackie led me had low ceilings reminiscent, I thought, of a film-version Andersonville. Actually the names on the tightly packed doors indicated that it was a faculty office area—probably "temporary" offices constructed in 1947.

We paused in front of a larger door on which was painted in gold and silver Gothic letters the words "Art Department."

"In there we will find the end of our chase?" I asked Blackie, whose myopic eyes were blinking rapidly.

"I honestly don't know," he said breathlessly. "Shall we find out?"

"By all means."

"It's your feast day," he argued with singular lack of logic. "You go first."

I pushed the door open.

The large room we entered was a studio for artistic work of all kinds—sculpture, paintings, mobiles, even photographs competed for every empty space. A small college could not, I supposed, afford more than one studio.

A young woman in her late teens, short and dainty in an artist's smock, was working on a plaster figure of Santa Claus, easily twice her size. My namesake was built like a heavyweight boxer instead of a jolly old Father Christmas. She was the only person in the room.

"Hi," she said cheerfully. "Everyone has gone home."

"A wonderful Claus," Blackie said, admiring her work. "Just right for the day."

"I think he is a very strong man," the girl said, pausing to consider her creation. "Don't you, Father?"

"Climbing down all those chimneys is good for muscle tone," Blackie agreed. "Uh, this is my colleague, Mr. Broderick—Nicholas Broderick, in fact."

"Happy feast day," the pixie giggled. "I think Santa Claus is cute, don't you, Mr. Broderick?"

"I'm prejudiced."

"We're looking for Angela," he said smoothly. "I'm kind of her cousin."

"Oh, Angie is never here after lunch. She works in the afternoon. That's her stuff over there. Isn't it neat?" She gestured toward a stack of canvases.

My heart stood still as I looked at the first canvas. It was a gold and silver sunburst, like nothing that Catherine had ever done, yet maybe with her mark on it. Behind that painting there were almost a dozen such explosions of color, most of them light and ethereal—the paintings of an Ariel spirit. A few were more somber, a sun rising over industrial smoke stacks perhaps.

"She does a lot of that old-fashioned abstract stuff." The girl wiped wet plaster off her hands. "I'm Cindy, by the way. But lately she's been catching up with the modern emphasis, realism and that sort of thing."

The second stack of paintings depicted quiet scenes on the campus, and the inside of a church, which I assumed was the college chapel.

"Very nice," I said, my voice choking.

"Familiar style?" Blackie raised a questioning eyebrow.

"It's changed a lot," I said slowly, "but it reminds me of earlier work."

"Angie is a real neat kid," Cindy commented as we went through the canvases. "She's a lot more talented than the rest of us, but she spends as much time helping us as she does on her own work."

"Kid?" I said, wondering if I was deceiving myself again.

"WELL, not really old, anyway. Twenty-five or twenty-six. Hey, you're not supposed to look at that one." Cindy turned a vivid red. "Angie shouldn't have left it here."

It was a nude of Cindy, depicted with astonishing skill and respect as a chaste and fragile imp.

"It's not at all obscene, Cindy," I said truthfully. "It's a wonderful painting. You should be proud to be in it."

"Well," she said, pleased and flattered, "it IS kind of embarrassing." She giggled. "Angie says I should give it to my husband as a wedding present. All I need now is to find a husband."

I slid the portrait back into the stack, not wanting to kind of embarrass her anymore.

"I'm sure he'll be proud too, doubly proud."

In both technique and vision the nude was a total transformation of Catherine's work from the past. Maybe it was indeed the work of another woman. But a woman who, like Catherine, was obsessed with the human form.

"We'd better be getting along, Nick," Blackie said. "You say Angie works in the afternoon. Do you know where we could find her right now? We'd like to surprise her at work with our St. Nicholas Day present."

"You can't miss it." Cindy began to pour more plaster into the bucket from which she was working. "On the left by the golf course turn. The Howard Johnson's."

"That's what she said." Blackie nodded. "In the restaurant?"

"Right. She's hostess there from one till nine. Then she does her homework and comes here at seven-thirty for Mass. I don't know how she manages."

"Always was very devout," Blackie agreed.

A few minutes later I drove the T-Bird into the parking lot of the Howard Johnson's. We both sat in it silently.

"Someday you'll have to explain how you figured it out," I said softly.

"Maybe neither of us will want to know," he replied with equal softness.

"I'm afraid to go in."

"So am I," Blackie agreed.

"God knows what we'll find."

"The painter of those sunbursts. And the comically erotic elf girl."

"Right you are. Isn't this the place where the man said, 'Damn the torpedoes'?"

"Admiral Farragut on August 5, 1864. He meant mines, of course, not torpedoes in our sense."

"Full speed ahead." I pushed out of the car and, with my heart pounding and stomach twisting in and out of knots, walked as confidently as I could toward the door of the restaurant.

I was terrified of what I might see inside. A woman broken and battered by physical torture? A pale shadow of the Catherine I had loved for so long? I resolved that it would not matter. I still loved her and I always would.

Inside the door, the hostess, in beige slacks and white blouse, was chatting with the cashier, her back turned to us. It looked like a dizzingly familiar rear view.

"Two," said Blackie, his voice choking on the word.

The hostess turned around slowly. "This way please," she said.

Long blond hair, horn-rimmed glasses and blue eyes.

Not Catherine.

<u>140</u>
ANGELA

She fell several times in the mud as she pedaled back to the *centro* in the rain. The Indians in the little *barrio* at the edge of the forest were not ready to follow the simple public health instructions she had given them. So there was another outbreak of dysentery. They might take the antibiotics she had dispensed. And then again they might not. Some of the kids would, of course. Her weird magic with kids still worked, even in the Indian *barrios* at the foot of the Sierra. The adults were nervous about her presence, fearful doubtless that the revolutionaries would come down out of the mountains again and the Federals would come up from the *campo* and they would be caught in the crossfire as they had been before.

After an especially muddy fall, she dismounted from her bike and slushed through the mud on foot, hunching down under her poncho. She would be glad when the late winter rains stopped and spring came, even if it heralded the awful summer heat. The beginning of her fourth year at the *centro*, four years in which nothing much had been accomplished.

Charles deFoucault had labored among the Tauregs for fifteen years and made not a single convert. But he was into religious goals, and the *centro* was in the vanguard of a revolution, one which seemed to be going nowhere.

Then Father Ed appeared with his jeep. They fastened her bike on the back of the jeep and she jumped inside, removing the hood of her poncho with considerable relief.

"Thank goodness you showed up," she said. "It would have been a long walk."

"And we can have the talk which has been delayed for so many weeks."

She felt a sting of fear. She still desperately wanted his approval. And the poor man seemed so tired. He had been ill much of the winter. His hair was almost completely gray now, and his face was lined with worry and sickness. The revolution was not going well. And the *centro* was plagued by dissent, most of it stirred up by Lorna's incredible bitchiness, which he ought not to tolerate.

"I suppose so," she said, wishing the talk could be delayed.

"You're not happy with us, are you, Cathy?"

"We're doing social work, Ed, and a little community organizing—and we're not very good at it. We talk about revolution and about the sweep of history. But the people won't listen to those things and we didn't really mean them ourselves until the guerrillas showed up. Now we're providing some support they can't really use to gunmen who aren't popular with the people and whose only achievement is keeping the junta in power."

"That's a heavy indictment, Cathy," he said sadly. "Revolutions take time. Look at Cuba."

"I don't know about other countries, Father Ed. But here it seems that we are supporting a revolution that no one wants."

"We are the vanguard of the people," he insisted sternly, "leading the people before they know they need to be led."

"Maybe if we were not foreigners that would be all right. But we're North Americans imposing our view of social justice on this country when the ordinary peons don't want that view. And we talk revolution until someone says we're Marxists, and then we say that we're merely missionaries, not politicians. We try to have it both ways—reformers and revolutionaries, natives and foreigners. And we're not accomplishing anything. The natives don't trust us because we're allied with the gunmen and the gunmen don't trust us because we're foreigners."

"Only a Marxist revolution will bring justice to this country." His massive hands were tight on the wheel of the jeep. "You know that, Cath." He drove over to the side of the road and stopped the car.

"As it has in Cambodia or Poland or China," she said, realizing that she was using arguments she had heard from Nick and Blackie.

"As in Cuba," he said stubbornly. "I've been there, Cathy. I know that it does work. For a while you have to take away the old bourgeois liberties. But a poor country can't afford them. And for a while you have to force the people into a revolution, but they or at least their children will be grateful. And certainly you're not supporting the junta? Your vision hasn't eroded that much, has it? A government of torturers?"

"The revolutionaries torture too. You saw the bodies of those Indians they thought were working for the government. And what about those women and children who died on the bus they blew up? And the three hundred silver miners?"

"I've told you, Cathy," he said wearily, "told you time and time again: There are no revolutions without losses. If the Movement is to win, it must first disrupt the economy of the country and force the people to rise up against the government."

"Why are we stopping?" she asked, noticing finally that the car was no longer moving.

"I can't argue and drive at the same time."

The rain continued to pound on the canvas roof of the jeep, a tattoo of protest against their folly.

"And so we helped them blow up bridges and destroy railroad tracks. Then the peons couldn't market their crops last summer and have been even hungrier than usual all winter."

He slammed the steering wheel with such violence that it frightened her. "Goddamnit, do you think I like to see them hungry? It's all part of the essential revolutionary contradictions. We must deepen the contradictions to achieve the revolution."

"I used to believe that. But now that I see what the contradictions are doing to the peons and the Indians . . . and I know that we are taking money out of the country which could be used to improve their living conditions. Does turning money over to the Mafia deepen revolutionary contradictions, Ed? Oh, don't look surprised. I know I'm a naive flake, but I'm a Chicagoan and I can smell 'Outfit' on those couriers from fifty yards away."

"And you are preparing to desert the revolutionary cause, to betray the Movement," he shouted, furious at her.

"I have to follow my conscience, Ed," she said in a tiny voice. "Don't I?"

"Conscience is a luxury for rich North Americans. The poor and the oppressed can't afford to have consciences."

"I don't agree," she said hotly. "These people have ethical standards as much as we do. They don't lie. They are good to their families. They love their children—"

"False consciences," he interrupted her. "And now you want to leave us and go home? You've lost your revolutionary zeal and you want to quit?"

"I need time to think, Ed," she pleaded.

"There is no time." He pounded the wheel again. "Not when the poor are suffering. And you are going to take back the money you gave us? Money that is rightfully ours now."

How could he know that? Did someone show him the letter I smuggled out? Or did Lorna guess?

"I didn't say that."

"Oh, but you're thinking it, Cathy. You're thinking it. You're planning a crime against the people. Which is as bad as committing a crime against the people."

Down the road she saw lights of several cars.

"That's not true, Father," she said, feeling the tears well up in her eyes. She wanted to make his pain and suffering go away. "I won't desert you."

"Yes, you will," he sobbed, caught now in deep emotion. "You are guilty of treason against the people."

Police cars. Military police, white stripes on the cars, white arm bands on the soldiers. And one man, under an umbrella, in a tightly fitting white uniform.

Don Felipé.

They approached the car with pistols drawn, automatic weapons at the ready. A fat sergeant held the umbrella over the *comandante*.

"So we have found ourselves a little revolutionary." He smiled and lovingly fondled the riding crop under his arm. "So nice to meet you again, Doña Caterina."

At first it seemed unreal, impossible. The soldiers in the rain, the guns, the sardonic smile of Don Felipé, the sobs of Ed. She was being arrested . . . no, it had to be a nightmare.

They got out of the car. Ed embraced her. "This is for the best, Cathy," he whispered, "believe me. You will have to suffer, but that will pay for your sins. No one will ever know—you can count on it—that you lost the faith. And in your suffering you will regain your faith. The world will always remember you as a brave revolutionary who suffered and died for Christ the liberator."

She sagged against him, hardly believing any of it. It was a game, a joke.

Ed kissed her. "I love you, Cathy. I will miss you. This is for the best. I know it's for the best. It will purify you and it will purify the Movement. At last we will have our heroine, our martyr."

Even then, knowing that he had betrayed her, she could not hate him.

The *comandante* handed Ed a thick packet. Money? she thought. Father Ed sold me to him for money?

She went unresistingly to the police car, too numb from shock to fight back.

In the police station, Don Felipé was the first to rape her. She realized soon that he could not have sex without tormenting his partner. Only when he hit her bare buttocks with his riding whip was he able to force himself into her.

As the whip cut into her flesh, she repeated over and over to herself the incredible words: Father Ed sold me, Father Ed sold me.

Then the other police took turns raping and sodomizing her. Fifteen, twenty times. She lost count.

And that was only the first night.

141
ANGELA

About four o'clock in the morning they cut her down from the ceiling and dragged her back to her dank, vile-smelling, whitewashed cell, where she moaned softly and yearned for death.

An hour or so later Luisa, the matron, brought her torn prison dress and ointment for the cigarette burns. She feared Luisa more than López, because the women who raped her were more vicious than the men. No one, however, was more cruel than Don Felipé.

"Cover yourself, Communist cunt," Luisa sneered. "And take care of your burns. Don Felipé is merciful today."

She cringed. The only thing more terrible than his cruelty was his mercy.

Today they would use the electricity again.

Then she slept fitfully for an hour or two. When the sun had risen and sent a thin shaft of light through the slit in the wall, beginning to turn the cell into a furnace again, Luisa wakened her with a kick and threw her the clothes she had worn when she was arrested, slacks, blouse, shoes, underwear, even her purse.

"Dress, Yankee pig," she ordered.

Her clothes hung loosely. She had lost perhaps twenty-five pounds. She must look terrible. But then, it did not matter anymore how she looked. No one would see her again.

The *comandante* delighted in teasing his prisoners. He would bring some to the gates of the barracks, hinting at freedom, and then laugh as they were sent back to the cells or to the execution yard.

There was little will or personhood left in her. She had been broken, just as he said she would. Yet she resolved she would not permit him the pleasure of seeing her anticipate release. She tried to pray again. How long had it been since she had spoken to God? How long had she been here? Was there a God in Esmeralda?

She could find nothing to pray for except death.

Then the *comandante* himself came, smelling of shaving cream and cologne, his immaculate uniform neatly pressed.

"Ah, my dear, you do not like our prison uniforms. You insist on wearing your *norteamericano* clothes. But they do not fit you well? Have you been on a diet?" His hands began to explore once again. "Well, never mind, at Punto Malo we will have many lovely dresses from which you may choose. Much more chic than these ugly things."

Punto Malo, the *comandante*'s seaside villa, was far down the coast, at the foot of the mountains that contained the recently reopened San Tome silver mines. Other prisoners had been taken there and never returned. Perhaps they were freed. Perhaps they were killed and their bodies pushed over the edge of the high cliffs. No one knew.

"Come now, my dear." His little effeminate giggle no longer rasped on her nerves. "Give me a kiss until we meet tomorrow."

She kissed him. She was totally dependent on him, as all prisoners are on their torturers. For the torturer has the power to grant the only thing his victim wants—a temporary suspension of pain. Her resolutions not to accept degradation had lasted only a few days.

Once she thought she would be as brave as Joan of Arc at the stake.

López and García escorted her to the auto yard into which she'd been brought the first night in the rain. Her eyes blinked helplessly in the glare of the sunlight. How long since she had seen the sun and the blue sky? The *comandante* personally tied her in the backseat of an old Ford painted khaki, one hand strapped to either side of the car.

"We want you to have a very comfortable ride over the hills and down to the *campo*." He giggled again. "It would not be proper for my weekend guest to have an unpleasant journey."

Eight or ten hours on bumpy roads with her arms, already sore from a night on the hook, tied above her. Yet another ingenious torment.

The two sergeants guffawed.

When they had come down out of the hills and emerged on the broad *campo*, they raped her, as she knew they would. It had happened so often that she was almost indifferent to it. Yet there was still enough of her left to recoil when they began.

It amused them especially to take her in the back of the car with her arms extended in the form of a cross. "Just like Jesus," López joked.

They left her naked from the waist down, so she would be cool, they said, on the hot ride.

Through eyes narrow with pain, hunger and exhaustion she barely noticed the wheat fields and the grazing cattle of the plains. She slept a little and then was awakened by the toothachelike pain in her arm muscles.

Dimly, as if seeing something from a great distance, she realized that the strap on her right hand was loose. It could be scraped against the window edge. Don Felipé had not tied it well. Was it another trick?

In the middle of the afternoon, they stopped the car for their lunch, noisily consuming cold meat and fruit and guzzling beer. They teased her with offers of food and water and made her plead.

She had learned how to plead.

They gave her a half cup of water and a few slices of orange, making her beg for each bite.

She had learned how to beg.

Then they took off their side arms and raped her again, more brutally this time.

She concentrated on the strap around her wrist, an imprisoned animal gnawing at its trap. As the car bumped down a gravel road and then turned on a two-lane highway, she slowly worked her aching arm backward and forward. Each movement sent a current of pain down the arm and into her shoulder, almost as bad as the electricity that had so often raced through her breasts. She bit her lip to silence the cry of pain.

The countryside was slowly changing as they approached the southern end of the Higuerota Mountains, which ended in the sea at Punto Malo. They had left behind the wheat fields and the grassy cattle country. Now the land was more rocky, with scrub plants, underbrush, an occasional grove of citrus trees and a few discouraged cornfields.

The sea, as best she could remember the map, was ten miles away and along it ran the railroad to the silver mines.

A quarter of an hour later they stopped in a small *barrio*—a gas station, a store, a cantina and a few huts. The owner of the station eagerly filled the gas tank when he saw López's pistol aimed at his stomach.

There was laughter and song and women's voices from the cantina. López wanted a drink. García disagreed, then relented.

"Don't go away, little one," López snickered. "We will be back. If you had any modesty you would put your pants back on. Be good. When we return, we may give you some more water and some more affection."

The two fat sergeants waddled toward the cantina. They were both already half-drunk. García had neglected to bring his pistol.

It was no longer necessary to pretend. She pulled, yanked, tugged and twisted at the strap, grinding it against the metal which held it to the frame of the car. Her wrist was bleeding now and the pain in her arm was unbearable. She fainted once as she suppressed a scream of agony. When she regained consciousness, the sun was sinking toward the sea and the noise from the cantina was louder. It seemed that half of the strap was still intact.

She gave up. Another diabolic torture. Don Felipé had left the strap loose because he knew she would torment herself trying to shred it. Why permit herself to be a victim again?

Then all the rage and the anger that were still inside her exploded. "Goddamn him," she shouted, and pulled on the strap with all her might.

It broke.

Feral cunning replaced anger. With shaking fingers she untied her other hand, pulled on her clothes, seized her purse and jerked a water container over her shoulder.

Garcia's forty-five lay in the front seat. "A cannon," Lorna had called the weapon. She jammed it into her purse, pushed open the door of the car and, heedless of the pains shooting through her muscles and nerves, hobbled across the road, around behind the cantina and into the brush.

At first she weaved and stumbled. And once she fell on her face, scraping her nose and bruising her thigh. Then her perceptions changed. The world seemed to lapse into delayed-action photography. Another being took control in the center of her brain. Her flight across the brush country toward the railroad was now that of a crafty escaped cat. Her steps were unerring, her decisions shrewd, her anticipation of problems flawless.

She paused to regain her breath and take a sip or two of water from the container. Stupidly she had grabbed the one which was already half-empty. Nothing could be done about that. She checked her purse. The money she had when she was arrested was still there—100 escudas, not enough for a ticket to the capital. Her passport, a half-empty bottle of aspirin, a notebook and ballpoint pen.

And the gun with her last Pope John rosary tangled around it. Was it loaded? She slid the magazine open. Six neat shells. A game of Don Felipé's? Would he give her a loaded cannon? He would, perhaps, if he did not know about Lorna's insistence on weapons training. She flipped the safety catch off and then back on. She was now in control of her own fate. And with control came new confidence.

As twilight turned to dusk, she resumed her careful progress across the rocky land toward the seacoast. Finally it grew so dark that she could no longer see where she was going. Afraid of breaking a leg or losing her direction, she stopped. There had been moonlight the night before when she was dragged across the courtyard to the torture room—a full moon, she thought. It would rise over the mountains and illumine the brush country, lighting her path and giving her direction—away from the mountains.

She fought against an instinct to continue rushing into the blackness. She must wait. Calculation now was essential. She could not permit herself to panic again.

She found a circle of medium-sized rocks, eased her way into a cleft between two of them and sat down, breathing heavily. I must keep control. I must keep control.

First of all, another small drink of water, then the pistol on the rock, safety catch off, then rest, build up my strength, wait till the moon.

I must not fall asleep. They are searching for me. If I sleep, they may find me before I can use the gun on myself.

She remembered that there was a bottle of aspirin in her purse. What might it do to someone who has been tortured for weeks? She shrugged and swallowed three of them with a gulp of water. The worst it could do was kill her.

It was a mistake to ease some of the pain. The night sounds of the semidesert were peaceful and reassuring, the rustle of leaves in the light wind, a distant bird protesting some disturbance, a pro forma yapping of a dog or a coyote. The noises of freedom. I am free now. I may not be tomorrow but I am free now. She fought sleep desperately. But her weary body would not cooperate. Her head kept nodding and then her cheek sought the cool comfort of the slab of rock in front of her.

She awoke with a start—voices, and the countryside glowing under a full moon sitting majestically on the top of the mountains, an Inca goddess on her throne.

God, what a painting it would make.

She saw them coming from a distance—two men with flashlights even though they didn't need them, shouting and cursing. López and García. Had they been lucky or had she left a trail? It really didn't matter, did it?

Was Don Felipé somewhere watching her and enjoying the chase?

She banished that thought. He didn't know that she could use the gun. How did they do it in the films? Put the barrel in your mouth and pull the trigger? It couldn't hurt for long, could it?

Her hand on the gun, nursing it like it was the face of a sick infant, she huddled behind the rock and waited.

"Those rocks, she might be hiding there!" López sounded very worried. Perhaps it was part of the scenario. How had they found her so quickly? They were too stupid to follow a trail. Had a helicopter been watching her?

As they came near, she slid the gun across the rock until it was even with her mouth, and slowly moved the barrel so that the muzzle pointed at her teeth. How much did the orthodontia cost when I was in seventh grade?

Pull the trigger now.

No, you have to steady it with both hands and put it in your mouth. Brace your hands on the rock.

This is suicide. It's a mortal sin. God would understand. He loves me.

Does He really? Then what are you doing here?

The sergeants were only forty yards away, stumbling and bumbling toward her. She braced the gun the way the revolutionaries had taught her and clamped her teeth on the barrel.

Then she had another idea.

She turned the gun around and pointed it at the approaching men.

She was sweating profusely. Perhaps she should wipe her forehead dry. Beads of sweat were creeping into her eyes, making it hard to see. No, she would keep the gun pointed at López.

She blinked the sweat out of her eyes and wondered whether she had the courage to pull the trigger. She remembered what the rifle bullet had done to the chest of the teenage soldier and shuddered.

"She is there!" shouted García. "She has the gun!"

She aimed the gun at his head. "Don't come any closer or I'll shoot."

López laughed. "Come now, pretty one, you would not shoot your old friends, would you?" His hand reached slowly for his own pistol.

"Don't touch it or I will kill you," she warned, this time with a more confident voice.

Garcia's laugh was less contemptuous than Lopez's. "You do not know how to shoot the gun, cunt; you will blow off your own head."

"Come closer and find out," she snapped.

They hesitated, García the more uncertain of the two.

384 / ANDREW M. GREELEY

"She will only have one shot and she will miss," López reassured him. "Then we will teach her the lesson she needs."

"What if she doesn't miss?"

"I would rather face her shooting than the *comandante*'s."

She waited till they were only ten yards away. "One more step toward me and I will kill you," she said, now icy calm.

López laughed sardonically. "A woman cannot fire such a big gun." He reached quickly for his own weapon.

For an instant she thought of turning the automatic on herself. Indeed, she decided to do that. It was safer. End life. She hunted for the right words of prayer and pulled the trigger. But the gun was still pointing at López's forehead.

Her shot was off target. It tore into his chest, which exploded in a gush of blood. His gun slipped out of his fingers and fell noisily on the ground just as he himself collapsed like a tower of children's blocks.

In the slowest of slow motion, she saw García leap for the gun. She fired again, blowing away his shoulder. Then, as he screamed in pain, she calmly and deliberately pulled the trigger a third time, sending a bullet crashing into his skull.

Now the only sound under the moonlight was the gurgling of López's final, blood-choked breaths. Finally it stopped.

She tried to keep her nerves steady. I must not break down now. I must stay in control. I must not be sick. The stench of exploding ammunition assaulted her nostrils and reached for her stomach.

No, I will not be sick, she insisted. I have work to do.

And I must get the ammunition clip from the other gun and fill my water container.

I must do it now. I do not have much time.

She hesitated, afraid to see what her marksmanship had accomplished.

But the lust for life of the animal—a she-cat with bloody fangs—was strong. She forced herself to walk the few yards to the dead bodies. Trying not to look at them, she lifted the gun off the ground, slid out the clip of ammunition and put it in the pocket of her slacks. García had been carrying the water container. She had to roll him over to lift it off his remaining shoulder.

When she saw the hideous mess which had been his face, she retched and for a moment lost control. Then, grimly ignoring the blood on the container, she pulled it away.

On unsteady legs she walked back to her little fortress, realized that her hands were too unsteady to fill her own water can from the one she had removed from the dead man's body, and then understood that she would be wise to take both of them. She rubbed as much of the bloodstain off on the ground as she could, reloaded the ammunition clip in her own automatic and, without looking back at the corpses she had made, began walking away from the mountains toward the sea.

The sun was high in the sky and the Sierra hidden in mists the next morning when she staggered across the railroad tracks and collapsed on the beach of the Golfo Plácido in the shade of a huge rock some giant must have thrown there long ago.

She had stolen some bitter oranges from a citrus grove at sunrise and had appeased the worst of her hunger pains.

Now she must plan, a shrewd, deadly beast on the run. First she must swim in the quiet gulf. The seawater would hurt her wounds perhaps, but she would be clean and refreshed. Then she must hide till night and follow the railroad track to the nearest *barrio*. If there was a station, she would wait till dawn and buy a ticket, not to Santa Marta but to Tonoro and then change for Río Secco. She would find Angela in the crypt in the basement of the old church and then ride the bus with her to Santa Marta.

She would have to beg the money for the second ride. Well, she'd learned how to beg. And what if Angela wasn't waiting for her in the church? Only Margaret could have betrayed that secret.

Or someone might have found it accidentally.

If worse came to worst she still had her automatic.

They might send helicopters to search for her. But unless someone found the bodies of the two sergeants or unless they were spotted from the air, a search would have the whole *campo* to explore.

And it might be fifty miles to the next station.

She would have to take her chances.

So she stripped off her clothes and plunged into the gulf. The water was warm and soothing, stinging her wounds only slightly. She floated for a few minutes, absorbing strength and healing from this primal source of life.

In the mists in one direction was a dim outline of the low mountains reaching from San Tome to Punto Malo. In the other the north end of the *golfo* was bounded by Azuera, a tiny smudge on the horizon. She was about halfway up the *golfo*, she estimated, not too far from Tonoro.

Then she returned to her rock and leaned against it in the sunlight to dry. She was alive and free, as she'd thought she would never be again.

A quiet sea breeze caressed her, the vigorous twang of salt played with her nostrils. The waters of the ocean glistened. Her senses were all still working. Her woman's body was bruised and wounded and dreadfully thin, but still more or less intact. She was not dead yet. Perhaps the remnants of her body could be salvaged. It's still in one piece even if it is a hurt and tattered plaything for psychopaths. And her mind? Would the images and memories of degradation and agony ever fade? Probably not. Worry about that later.

She reached a hand up to heaven, partly in defiance and partly in plea. "Get me out of this and I promise you I'll put my life back in order. I promise, I promise!"

She put on her underwear and folded her shirt and slacks in a neat pile close to the rock, as she'd done in the tub room when she was a postulant. Perhaps tonight she could find a river or a stream in which to wash them.

Before she fell asleep, she opened the notebook they had left in her purse and, with the pen that was attached to it, made a quick sketch of the scene, ocean, beach, rock and railroad track. If she survived, she would paint it someday.

A train rumbled by on the tracks. Hunched down against the rocks, she saw that it was a local. Tomorrow with any luck she would be on the train, headed for home.

Wherever home was.

She finished the sketch.

It was the first time in years that she had drawn even a sketch. She then ate another stolen orange, took two more aspirin and slept till late afternoon.

When she awoke, she was seized by terror. Where was she? What had happened? She reached for the gun and remembered.

She was stiff and sore and felt weak and ill. She stifled those sensations. She could not afford them. She waited till twilight before she peeled off her bra and pants and dove into the ocean again. She remembered her first experience skinny-dipping at Grand Beach. It had seemed so delightfully wicked then.

While she was in the water, she heard the churning hum of a helicopter. It was coming from the south, from Punto Malo perhaps? She debated whether to race for her rock and decided against it. She waited till what she thought was the last minute, took a deep breath and ducked under the gently lapping waters of the incoming tide.

She counted to sixty, and then when she thought her lungs would surely explode, she permitted her mouth to break the surface and gulp air.

The second time she was able to count only to thirty.

But when she peaked above the surface, she saw that the copter was far down the beach.

If they come back in the moonlight, they may see me on the tracks. I'll have to take my chances of walking in the dark. Why didn't you take the flashlights?

Then she remembered the dead bodies and vomited her last orange into the ocean.

At sunset she put on her blouse, slacks and socks. Thank God she had worn sensible socks instead of pantyhose when she was up in the hills the day they arrested her. But she had to force her feet into her shoes. Damn. They've swollen from all the walking. I've got to find some cold water somewhere. Maybe a stream.

They would hurt as she walked. It could not be helped. Probably her feet would hurt less than when they suspended her by her arms and beat the soles of her feet the day after she was arrested. She had hobbled for days and then forgot about her feet because there was so much more and so much worse pain.

So she limped wretchedly down the tracks, assuming that no helicopter would be out late in the day.

She barely heard the freight train roaring up from the south. A horn screeched behind her; she glanced over her shoulder wondering where the car was and then saw the light of the train like a one-eyed monster almost upon her. At first she was paralyzed, unable to move, hypnotized by the gigantic eye, which grew bigger with every second.

Then animal instinct revived and she hurled herself off the track and tumbled down the embankment. The engine thundered by, its wind wake punching at her face. She lay at the foot of the embankment, gasping for breath. What if the engineer reported seeing her?

But it was dusk and he would hardly have had time to see what she looked like.

She climbed wearily back to the tracks and hobbled northward to . . .

Well, to whatever was there.

But she soon gave it up. It was too dark to see even the cross ties of the tracks. Clouds had rushed in from the ocean to obscure the stars. They would hide the moon too. But rain would give her cool water for her feet.

She found a depression by the side of the tracks in which rainwater might gather and waited. In the distance lightning flashed across the sea and thunder rumbled. The storm seemed to hesitate lazily, and then, gathering momentum like a bull, it charged at the shore and the mountains beyond.

Now lightning crackled over her head and thunder boomed all around. She saw the rain dashing across the sea, sizzling in the lightning flashes. Then the rain and the wind hit with a fury that pressed her down against the side of the embankment. There was no place to seek shelter, so she hunched her head between her shoulders and tried to absorb the storm's anger as she had absorbed the torment of her prison.

At least the cool rainwater relieved some of the swelling in her feet.

It lasted perhaps an hour. Then, soaking wet and discouraged, she began to trudge down the tracks by the light of the furtive moon.

She passed two *barrios*, neither of them large enough for a station, before light broke sky above the mountains.

There was no point going on now. She should find a spot on the beach and wait till it was dark again.

But she had to slip along in the half-light on the wet beach for almost a mile before she found a sheltering rock. There would be no bathing in the sea today. The storm had whipped up the ocean and the surf was big and dangerous. Nor would she risk hunting for a stray orange grove for food. A highway had appeared like an unannounced stranger to accompany the tracks. Trucks rumbled along on it frequently, big blue ones from the silver mines and smaller, khaki military vehicles. The helicopter appeared three more times during the day, flying low over the beach and forcing her to dig in next to her rock. The final time the survey seemed perfunctory, as though the crew did not really expect to find their prey.

She tried to remember the map of Costaguana. Where did the highway merge with the railroad? She could picture the two converging but she had no image of the names of the towns, if there were any on the map hanging in Ed's office.

Ed. Will he learn that I have escaped?

When the tide raced in, she had to retreat quickly to the far side of her rock because the waters swirled around it and filled the hole she had dug for herself. Until the tide started to ebb, she would be dangerously exposed to traffic on both the railroad and the highway.

Despair returned. She was tired, sick, weak, hungry. Her feet hurt. Her body ached from weeks of rape and torture. She was eight thousand miles from the United States, in a hostile country, equipped with only a gun—of which she was increasingly afraid—two water cans she had partly refilled during the storm, and a purse with a notebook and 100 escudas. And a rosary.

She untangled the rosary from the gun—it seemed attracted to the weapon like a magnet—and tried to pray. No words came but she clung to the beads.

Why not quit? Who was she to think she could escape a whole army?

There was no good answer to the questions. But there was no easy or painless way to quit. The temptation to self-destruction had receded, though it was still an option that was better than going back to the torture cell. What would Don Felipé do, she wondered, to a woman who had killed two of his lackeys?

Clinging to the rosary, she napped fitfully and dreamed not of Don Felipé but of Nick and Grand Beach. She was surprised when she woke up. She had not thought of Nick since the day she was arrested. What would he make of her present predicament? Probably would have figured it served her right.

When the moon rose she doggedly began her trek, this time on the highway, ducking into the ditch whenever she saw the lights of vehicles.

She heard a rumble from the south and then saw a cordon of lights sweeping either side of the road. A motorized patrol—a car, two trucks, and a couple of motorcycles—was coming up the highway at slow speed, with spotlights probing the darkness. She had time to scurry off the road and hide behind some scrub on the other side of the ditch. Might it be Don Felipé, directing the search himself?

She would kill him, if he found her. That would be her final service to humankind, eliminating Don Felipé. They could do nothing more to hurt her than they would do for killing López and García. Grimly her lips tightened. She hoped the convoy would stop. Kill Don Felipé and then herself.

But it went on, its lights exploring the darkness lazily, as though the military police were only going through the motions.

Then she stumbled into the outskirts of a larger village, a town almost, the pungent stench of latrines reminding her of the buckets into which her head had been repeatedly shoved at Esmeralda, when the hugely amused Don Felipé threatened to drown her in excrement.

"Each inch, my beloved, can drown you as effectively as eight hundred feet of water. You do not like the taste and the smell of our little pool? What a pity! You must try it again. My, your pretty face is so dirty, we must return it to the pool to wash it clean."

The gagging reflex came back to her throat. She heard Felipé's giggle, tasted the foul liquid, felt it rush up her nostrils, and wanted to die again.

I'll never get over it, she thought, fighting to silence the gasping, retching sounds ripping at her body. I'll always be a freak.

But she did control her body and exorcise the tastes and the smells and the terrors of the torture room.

I will not quit, she vowed. Never. They will not take my soul away from me.

As she picked her way carefully through the town, some dogs barked indifferently at her, but the night was too hot for them to worry about an intruder. She left the road and picked her way behind a row of houses and toward the center of the town.

Then, without warning, someone jumped from the dark, seized her, clamped a stiff hand over her mouth and enveloped her. She flailed against her attacker. It backed off and then embraced her again, its grip lackadaisical and uncertain.

She stopped hitting and laughed at her own terror, shutting off the laugh an instant before it became hysterical. She was fighting a ghost, but a harmless ghost, a clothesline full of clothes. Then she had an idea. She groped along the line until she found a cheap dress, one that might fit her. It looked blue or gray in the moonlight, buttons in front and belted. She removed her blouse and slacks, folded them neatly on the ground, stepped into the dress and buttoned it. The girl was more buxom than she was in her present condition. No matter, she would blend now with countryside, especially with a scarf tied over her head to protect her from the sunlight.

Sorry, *señorita*, but my clothes cost more than yours. It's a fair trade. I hope you don't see me tomorrow morning.

She walked back to the road and, without trying to hide, limped for the center of the town. A couple of men, in front of a cantina, made some perfunctory lewd remarks, which she ignored. Her Spanish was good, but she did not want them to wonder about a strange accent.

In the plaza there was a railroad station, a *municipato* and an old church. It was hard to read the grimy schedule on the station wall in the dark, but as best as she could tell, there was a train for Tonoro at 9:15. The church door was open and she slipped into it, finding a chair near the back on which to sit and rest her feet. She debated taking off her shoes and decided not to. A girl in this town might walk barefoot during the summer but not on a train ride.

She saw the outline of a Christmas crib in the flickering lights of the votive candles. The wise men were kneeling by the manger. So it was early or middle January. She had been in prison for two months.

It had seemed like two lifetimes.

What a story to tell my grandchildren: how I escaped from the fascists.

Dummy. You won't even have children. What man would want you now?

In the morning she purchased her ticket to Tonoro and used her remaining escudas to buy a cup of foul coffee and a stale roll.

She walked boldly by two civil guards, hoping that they would not notice a thin peasant woman with a bruised face, a cheap dress and a scarf tied low over her forehead.

The train was crowded but she found a seat by a window. She had dumped the water cans in a trash heap near the church. All she was carrying now was her purse, bulky with its automatic. If anyone wanted to search it, she would have to pull out the weapon, switch off the safety and shoot before they could get it out of her hands.

She doubted that she could move that quickly.

As the train pulled out of the station, wheezing and lurching, the same military convoy that had passed her the night before rumbled into the plaza. Don Felipé stepped out of the car, his white uniform dirty and unpressed. She saw him talking to the civil guards as the plaza slipped away behind her.

It was a three-hour ride to Tonoro with many stops. At each one of them she expected military police to board the train and swagger down the aisle. She opened her purse and squeezed the safety off.

But they never came.

At Tonoro she begged for the fifty escudas which would buy her ticket to Río Secco. She chose well-to-do people who seemed to be tourists from Santa Marta, perhaps at the end of a Christmas vacation.

But at first she had little luck as she walked the broad plaza with the great seventeenth-century cathedral radiant in bright sunshine on one side. How quickly her middle-class pride had returned. Free only a couple of days and she already found it hard to beg. After several failures she sat on a bench in front of the cathedral, sweating profusely in the summer heat. Her ingenious plan had fallen apart, for a crummy eight dollars.

She watched an old woman approach a bespectacled young man—a university student clearly. He contemptuously tossed her a few bills.

She then realized that she was not humble enough, not desolate enough in her pleas. She thought of López and the orange slices and approached a smartly dressed young woman about her own age with two children and pleaded for a little money to return to her sick mother—"Only fifty escudas, *señora*," she whined piteously.

The woman reached in her purse and pulled out two fifty-escuda notes. "Buy yourself something to eat, *señorita*," she said kindly. "You look very hungry. I will pray that your mother lives. And you will pray for me, no?"

Tears of gratitude poured down her cheeks. "All my life I will pray for you and the children," she whispered.

The young woman smiled. It was a Costaguana exaggeration, though a graceful one. "I appreciate your prayers. We all need them."

But I mean it. I really do.

She had to wait three hours for the local to Río Secco. It was just as well. She would rather be in the anonymity of a city than risk recognition in daylight in a town where many might recognize her and where she even might encounter some of her colleagues from the *centro*.

Was the *centro* still there? She decided she did not want to find out.

She ate lunch in the shade of a sidewalk café across the plaza from the cathedral. She was careful about her lunch—soup, fish, an orange. Nothing too heavy on a dubious stomach. She took out her notebook and tried to sketch from memory the face of her benefactor and the two children. She worked very carefully and after considerable effort was satisfied with the woman's gentle smile and the children's wide eyes. She thought about trying to depict the rest of the woman. But she was unable to draw the first line of a female body, even a clothed one. No more nudes for this artist. Instead, she reconstructed the shapes of the crib scene illumined by candlelight in the church the night before. The rough traces were inadequate and she slammed the notebook shut. What a crazy time to draw pictures!

She walked back to the railroad station and bought her ticket. There was enough money left to replenish her aspirin supply. So she left the station and returned to the plaza looking for a *farmacia*. Her feet were still hurting her and she was afraid of what would happen when she removed her shoes. At least there would be cold spring water at Río Secco. After she bought the aspirin, she hobbled back to the station.

A squad of military police was waiting at the station when she returned. She clutched the purse under her arm, and opened it to be ready for them.

But the white-helmeted soldiers paid no attention to her as she slipped by them on the platform. When the main-line train from the south to Santa Marta stopped, they swarmed onto it, leaving a handful of people to board the three-car local for Río Secco.

So I was right. They think I will go directly to Santa Marta—to the American embassy perhaps.

She had planned to take a cab from the bus depot to the embassy, but that might be part of Don Felipé's amusement—arrest her in sight of safety.

She would have to think of something else.

Of course, they may not be looking for me at all.

It was almost dark when the train, exhausted by its climb up the hills, puffed to a stop at the tiny station in Río Secco. Her heart sank as she climbed off the train and saw Lorna sitting in the car of the *centro* across the dusty street.

How could they possibly have known?

Was Lorna part of it?

But the woman did not seem to notice her. Maybe that was part of the trick too. Maybe they were waiting for her to reveal to them the hideout for Angela.

Or maybe a skinny woman in a cheap dress doesn't look much like the spoiled middle-class whore I used to be.

Limping on her sore feet, she walked by the car and across the small plaza to the church. She turned to look back. Father Ed . . .

The priest came out of the bus depot and climbed in the car. Lorna drove it down the street toward the church. She pressed herself against the side wall, huddling in the semidarkness and hoping they would not notice her.

Lorna did not turn on the car lights, resolutely demonstrating that she was not an energy pig.

She leaned against the wall to calm her pounding heart long after the car had passed her. Then she slipped into the church, lifted a votive from the rack at the entrance and walked up to the main altar. The key to the gate leading to the crypt was where she had left it. She opened the gate, swinging it outward gently so that there would be no sound, though there was no one else in the church, and picked her way down the dusty stairs into the murky dampness of the underground cemetery.

What if someone had taken Angela away.

She turned the corner, almost enjoying the dry, worn-out smell of old death, counted five alcoves, and then forced the cover off a stone casket, half expecting to find nothing.

Angela was exactly where she had left her—money, traveler's checks, passport, everything.

Good-bye, Cathy; hello, Angie.

Catherine waited till the moon appeared, crept out of the church and slipped down the alley to the spring-fed creek. She bathed in the creek, soaked her feet and became Angela.

Her Angela clothes fit badly. She would have to hope that she did not appear peculiar enough to attract attention. By the moonlight she carefully applied her makeup, while her feet continued to soak in the stream. Then she dried her feet, put on pantyhose and her old shoes. The heels would have to wait till the airport.

She wrapped the old clothes in a bundle to drop at the rear of someone's hut on the way back to the church. The few traces of her Catherine identity she tore into pieces and threw into the stream. Her old purse would go in a trash can.

She saved the notebook with its sketch of the beach where she had bathed the first day of freedom.

And the automatic?

Dangerous to carry it if she were searched. Dangerous not to have it if she were captured. She shrugged and put it in her Angela purse and went back to the church.

And then, not confident that anyone would be listening, she prayed, muttering the rosary automatically for the young mother who had given her the sixteen dollars, the difference perhaps between life and death.

She ached to sit on a chair for the rosary, but felt that the woman deserved prayers on her knees, even if the rough stone floor of the church rubbed harshly against them.

In the middle of the fifth decade of the rosary, the murmured words slowed down and stopped, like a car running out of gas. She had asked for nothing, wanted nothing from whatever might lurk in the church—save for blessing for a generous woman. But that which was in the church intruded just the same, assuring her that she was loved, deeply, powerfully, passionately loved.

I don't want that, she protested, knowing full well that what she wanted was irrelevant.

Well, where have You been? she demanded, realizing that too was a ridiculous question.

Then there was no more time or space, only a vast and reassuring peace.

Although the worst was over and she was now Angela, complete with her long blond hair, blue eyes and thick glasses, and despite the peace that had transiently but overwhelmingly possessed her in the old church, she teetered on the edge of panic on the bumpy ride down to Santa Marta. For the first time escape seemed a real possibility and not a dream. Her animal craft and cunning deserted her. She was a frightened and broken woman running for her life.

Using all the willpower that she had left, she stilled her nerves at the Central Station in Santa Marta. She ignored the various military personnel who were swarming through it. There were always police and soldiers in the Central Station. Trying to appear calm, she walked across to the airport limo and bought a ticket. "International," she told the driver.

"*Si, señorita.*" He nodded respectfully.

If the schedules had not been changed, there was a Pan American flight to Miami in midafternoon. Don Felipé might not know about Angela. In the interrogations he had never mentioned that subject. Perhaps this was safer than the American embassy. One had to choose.

She put on her high-heeled shoes in the limo. I've got to last in them, no matter how much they hurt, till I'm on the plane. She stored the old shoes in her carry-on bag. They were loyal friends, and besides, she might need them in Miami.

Miami . . . was she really going there? It seemed impossible.

As she left the limo at the departure entrance of the sumptuous modern airport, built by American aid money, of course, she wished that she had left the automatic in the stream at Río Secco. Soldiers were checking everyone who entered the terminal.

I will tell him that I carry the gun for my own protection, she told herself. No reason to kill him. I am, after all, an American citizen.

The soldiers were paratroopers, reputed to be enemies of the more extreme members of the junta.

Casually she flipped her passport open for the handsome young lieutenant in a blue beret who barred her entrance to the door.

"Good afternoon, Teniente," she said in English, austerely polite.

"Good afternoon, *señorita.*" He smiled appreciatively.

Good God, I still can't be beautiful, can I? Maybe he likes haggard and haunted women.

"I hope you had a pleasant visit." He returned her passport.

"A wonderful country," she said. "Even when it is troubled."

The young officer frowned. "I hope that when you return, it will be less troubled. Have a pleasant trip to America, Señorita Carson."

"*Gracias*, Teniente," she murmured, wondering how much charm was left in her smile.

The ticket agent assured her that there was "*mucho*" room on the Pan Am flight. She purchased her ticket, paid for it with traveler's checks, cleared immigration, ignoring the officious leer of the inspector as he stamped her passport, dropped her automatic in a waste container in the women's room and passed serenely through the metal detection system.

Her carry-on bag was opened, but they did not search the lining for the 450 hundred-dollar bills that were neatly arranged inside.

She did not permit herself a sigh of relief when the flight was called, nor even when she boarded the plane. She wanted to hug the cabin attendants but restrained herself. Only when the 747 was airborne did the sigh of relief come, and then copious tears.

"Just a nervous reaction, hon," she told the anxious young attendant. "No, nothing to drink . . . well, a Coke maybe."

A long time before I have to worry about calories again.

The young woman brought her the Coke and a copy of yesterday's *New York Times*.

Her picture was on the front page.

"Relatives Protest Death of Catholic Missionary," the headline said.

Mary Kate and Joe Murphy had been to Santa Marta searching for her body. The government told them that they had no information about her. Father Edward Carny, the director of the Centro San Ysidoro, said that she was a modern martyr. Mary Kate told reporters that they would much rather have a living cousin than a martyred one. The Rev. John B. Ryan, another cousin, observed that the attitude of the American ambassador suggested he thought Ms. Collins deserved to die in a prison camp.

Angela folded the paper thoughtfully. Catherine was a failure at everything she had ever done—daughter, lover, religious, wife, painter, revolutionary. She had even failed at martyrdom.

But Catherine was dead now, wasn't she? And Angela was alive.

Angela knew what she would do.

142
BLACKIE

It was only when we were seated at the table and I saw the look of despair on Nick's face that I realized he didn't recognize her. Wig, glasses and blue contact lenses, a simple disguise which could fool a lover completely.

Not, however, a cousin.

The air around me was tense with a drama about to explode. Nick was suffering from frustration and loss, which would in a few moments be converted into the terror of new opportunity. Cathy's back, still turned toward us as she tapped menus on the cashier's counter, was stiff with fear and also perhaps anticipation.

What was she thinking? She probably wanted to run and also to embrace both of us. Did you ever really think, Coz, that you could escape from us?

I watched her take a deep breath and then turn toward us. Her face showed neither anger nor fear. Rather, she seemed amused.

"Take good care of these two," she said to the waitress as she placed menus on our table. "They're old friends."

Nick looked like he had crash-landed on an erupting volcano.

"It's Catherine?" he asked in disbelief. "It doesn't look . . . "

And then she returned, glasses off, and stood anxiously above us. "I might have known you two would find me," she said, a postulant caught by mother general and her top assistant.

"Blame him," said Nick, pale and frightened again.

"Please don't make me go back," she begged.

Cathy looked more like a novice than she ever had in the novitiate—trim and neat, solemn, reflective. She wore no makeup and did seem to be, as Cindy had said, a woman in her middle twenties. Her face was thinner than I remembered it, her chin a little less determined. If there was any sparkle left in her eyes, it was hidden by the blue contact lenses she was wearing. Only a hint of preoccupation around her eyes suggested what might have happened to her in Costaguana.

"We're not going to make you do anything, Catherine," Nick said slowly. "Right now we're just incredibly happy you're still alive."

"I'm Angela now, not Catherine," she said firmly. "What do you want of me?"

"Only to talk," he replied. "And that only if you want to."

She hesitated, playing with the plastic menus in her hand. "What do you want, Blackie?"

"A cheeseburger with mushrooms and everything else, except the onions, ketchup and mustard. And two milk shakes, one chocolate and one strawberry."

That earned me a faint smile. "You know what I meant, silly."

"Oh, THAT. Well, maybe I could sit in on your talk, if you are going to talk to us, that is."

"Of course I'll talk to you." Did I see a lower lip tremble? "Not while I'm working, though."

"Do you have a supper break?" Nick asked with the respect he would normally use for someone-important's grandmother.

"Yes." Her faced hardened. "But I'm having supper with a friend; he teaches at the college . . . oh, Blackie, don't look so worried. He's not a priest and never has been."

"We're staying at the Stars and Bars." Nick recovered smoothly. "Could I pick you up here after work and bring you over for a drink?"

"I'll walk over," she countered. "Pretty snooty place."

"Why not?" I asked. "Your estate is paying for it."

In truth, that remark obtained me a vintage Cathy grin.

"Take it up with the executor. Ten-thirty, Nick? I'll be there. I promise."

"She doesn't look bad at all," Nick said. "A little thin, maybe, but . . ."

"Alive," I said.

When the waitress brought our order, Cathy, glasses back in place, swept by our table.

"Happy feast day, Nicholas."

"Thanks." He turned purple in embarrassment.

"I don't have your perspective," I remarked. "But one could say she looks better than ever."

Nick's eyes had followed her as she walked back to the cashier's table.

"One sure could."

<u>143</u>
NICHOLAS

Promptly at ten-thirty Catherine walked into the Dixie Lounge of the Stars and Bars, glanced around the room searching for us in the darkness, somehow discovered us in the light of the red votive-type candles that flickered on the tables, and approached our booth in the farthest corner as awkwardly as a peasant might approach the throne of the pope.

She was wearing a beige sweater that matched her slacks and had abandoned the blue contact lenses and blond wig. Now she was unmistakably Catherine. I had a memory flash of her walking down the beach in summertime, adoring little kids trailing behind her.

"We make these dark-wood, red-light bars for y'all who come down here from the north," she said, in perfect imitation of the waitresses in both the restaurant and the bar. "Might I join y'all?"

Without waiting for an answer, she joined Blackie on his side of the booth.

A pianist was playing bland, "easy listening" music, occasionally murmuring soothing lyrics about love into the microphone. Song lyrics lie, I thought. There were only a few people in the bar, not much revelry in honor of my patron.

"What would you like to drink?" I asked formally.

"Soda water with lime," she said primly.

"Smoke?"

"No, thanks," she replied, with a half-smile. "I've returned to the disciplines of the novitiate."

And then none of us knew what to say. The chase was over, the prey cornered, the quest ended. And I forgot what it was I wanted to talk about.

Despite her flip words, Catherine looked frail and vulnerable. She reminded me of a twenty-year-old who had been arrested by the Feds for trying to smuggle in her boyfriend's hashish—he'd shoved it into her purse as their plane landed. She was the kind of pathetic victim you want to put your arm around.

And I wanted passionately to put my arm around Catherine's thin shoulders.

"What cooks, Coz?" said Blackie.

"How much time do you have?" I asked, wondering if there was a boyfriend to go home to.

"As long as you want. You can drive me home when we're finished. It's just around the corner. I walk to work and to school usually. It's good exercise. And, Coz"—she brightened briefly—"would you believe that my car is an orange bug?"

"I would indeed believe it. As to the questions, my first one is whether we're talking to Cathy or, God protect us from the nickname, Angie?"

Catherine grabbed both of our hands as if we were going to pull her out of an undertow.

"Nick . . . Blackie . . . I thought I'd never see you both again. You're the only ones I truly miss." She bent her head. "I told myself that it was part of the sacrifice. Now I'm so damn glad to hold on to you that I think I'm going to cry."

She did, but for only a couple of seconds. Then she regained her composure, wiped her face with a tissue, and lifted her eyes to face us. Pretty she still was. More beautiful than ever, as Blackie had suggested, yes, indeed. But the glitter was gone from her eyes. The vitality drained away.

"Still into making sacrifices?" Blackie asked casually.

"I guess." She nodded. "But this time it is for me. Where should I start?" Mischievousness flickered in her eyes and then died.

"Were you really in Esmeralda?"

"Yes," she said grimly. "That part of the legend of St. Catherine is mostly true."

"And you were released?" he continued. It was not where I would have started, but I was so busy admiring this familiar stranger that I still couldn't think where I would have started.

"I don't know." She folded her hands. "I know that sounds strange. I'm inclined to think now that I was released. Then I thought I escaped. Maybe it was a combination of the two. I'll probably never be certain."

"Do you want to tell us about it?" he asked gently.

"I'm terribly afraid to tell you and want in the worst way to tell you. Does that make sense?"

"We're prepared to cope with paradox," Blackie said.

She raised a speculative eyebrow. "You may have to, even contradictions."

And with flickering red-votive light alternately illumining and obscuring her face, she told us about her escape.

She told her story in a simple, straightforward voice, almost as if she were a reporter describing the experiences of another woman. When she was finished, she lapsed into silence, her thin, impassive face looking like the statue of a real saint in the dim red light of the votive candle.

The light went out. Nick relit it, in one competent movement of a Stars and Bars match.

Cathy looked from Nick to me and then back, puzzled by our silence. "Don't you believe me?" she asked hesitantly, a penitent facing not one but two hostile confessors.

"That's not why we're quiet," Nick replied, his knuckles white on the counter of the booth.

The entertainer was still singing about eternal love, a soft, melancholy, bittersweet emotion if his music was to be believed.

"If anyone asked me whether my cousin is the kind of woman who can escape alone and unaided from a hostile country, I would say yes, of course, why not?"

"I will never be the same," she said uncertainly, wanting our reassurance that she would.

"It will always be part of your life," I said. "The issue is whether you emerge a better or a worse woman because of it."

She nodded solemnly. "My shrink says that. She also says I must learn to talk about it in such a way as to free others from the burden of guilt. I try."

"It would make me a Communist for the rest of my life," Nick said bitterly.

"Why? They do it. I've seen the bodies of peons they thought were government spies. And the English in Northern Ireland, and the French in Algeria. And we've done it too, especially in Vietnam. When sick men and women have total power over others there will always be torture. The only safeguard is good habeas corpus procedures." She smiled slightly. "See, Nick, I've studied about it and even know legal terms."

"Ours are the best in the world," he said promptly.

"Damn right. Surprised, Blackie? I've become a patriot."

"Nothing you do will ever surprise me again, Coz."

The quicksilver mists had dogged her down those railroad tracks,

402 / ANDREW M. GREELEY

swirled around her in the plaza while she begged for eight dollars and finally, just so there would be no doubt, flashed into view in the church at Río Secco. And then haunted her home to therapy and to reading books on civil liberties. Such mists are expended only on someone very special.

But they take away no one's freedom.

"I don't understand . . . " she said, afraid that somehow her story had offended us.

"We're silent, Coz, because of admiration for heroism."

She waved her hand contemptuously. "A frightened animal running for its life. Anyway, I'm sure Felipé intended me to escape. I think I surprised him by going to the airport, not the embassy. But maybe he would have let me get in the embassy too."

"Why would he want you to escape?" Nick asked.

"Perhaps so he could deny I was ever in prison."

The waitress came again. I ordered my second Jameson's, a second vodka and tonic for Nick and a second soda water for Cath.

She wasn't telling us everything, of that I was certain. She had another reason for suspecting that the escape might have been rigged.

"He was so crazy that he changed his mind about life or death while taking a prisoner to the execution yard. Maybe he wanted me to escape and then wanted me back. I don't know. Even today I'm afraid he will catch up to me, that he will come into the art studio with his white uniform and his riding whip. . . . "

"He's dead, Catherine," Nick said. "I have a picture of his body. Do you want to see it?"

She nodded thoughtfully. Nick removed the picture from his ever-present briefcase.

She stared at the photograph. "It's him, all right. The para brigade had reason to hate him." She shuddered. "I'll be afraid of him as long as I live. He's still in my dreams, almost every night."

"Yet you did outsmart him, whatever his plans were," I insisted.

She paid no attention to my modest praise. "Nora Cronin—you know the bishop's gorgeous sister-in-law—boarded the plane in Caracas. I suppose she was visiting one of her foundation places. She walked by me and didn't recognize me. I knew that Angela would succeed. So I checked into a hotel in Miami. . . . "

"The Biscayne Inn," I observed.

"That's right. I found a woman gynecologist the next day at Mercy

Hospital and told her to put my body back together. She wanted to hospitalize me and I said no way. It took about a month to straighten out the basic mess. I've been going back there on vacations to finish the plastic surgery. Then I came up here, settled down with a shrink and an art teacher and gave Angela a chance to live."

"And have done reasonably well," I said.

"I don't know. I have a job. I see my therapist four days a week. I'm finally learning how to paint. I sleep pretty well some nights, a couple of hours anyway. My body is finally functioning more or less properly. It took a year for some of the systems to start working again. I put on most of the weight I lost, though I simply can't make the last seven or eight pounds. The people at school seem to like me. The shrink says I'm ready to try a normal sex life again, and I tell her I wouldn't know what one is. I go to Mass almost every morning. I teach art to black kids at a Catholic school one morning a week. Oh, sure, I still have a cause. I suppose I will always have one. But this time it's something I can do— it isn't saving the world. I'm living my own life finally, and I'm happy with it." Her lips quivered. "And I don't want to have to give it up."

"And none of this is counted as meritorious, is it?" I demanded.

She dismissed it with another brusque hand wave. "Pure survival instinct. I was a nasty little rich bitch with terrible guilt feelings because of the way I was raised. And I tried to satisfy those guilt feelings by becoming a nun, and then a radical, and then marrying Roy, and then turning to revolution. I was using all those things and people for my own purposes. I'm mostly over being angry at my parents. Poor people, they couldn't help themselves. . . . What looked liked generosity and dedication was pure selfishness. Angela doesn't need to assuage guilt feelings. I know it's all dreadfully middle class, but I guess I've learned you can't identify with the poor unless you first identify with yourself."

"It sounds like you've figured a lot out," Nick said, somewhat stupidly. But he was so hopelessly in love with this brave and resourceful woman at the moment that one could hardly expect him to be clever. They would have one of their fights shortly.

"Big deal," she said, still angry at poor Cathy. "Anyway, I didn't even realize about the martyr thing for six months. I didn't read the papers. The paratroop revolution was three weeks old before I knew about it. My *teniente* is someone important now. . . . And I heard some of the kids from school talking about the miracles at the Hill, and then Rosie's stupid statue. I don't know who worked the miracles. But it wasn't me. And can you imagine what they will all say if they ever find out I'm not dead? I've messed enough things up in my useless life. I don't want to do it again."

"You stack the deck, Coz. The accomplishments are dismissed as instinctive responses and the neuroses as your own fault."

She grinned ruefully and consumed half her glass of soda water, as if she wished it were something stronger. "That's what my shrink says. That and I should experiment with a normal sex life, as if any man could want a woman who has been raped a couple of hundred times."

"He would if he loved the woman," Nick said. "It wouldn't matter."

"The hell it wouldn't," she replied bitterly. "Men care about those things."

"You haven't told us how you were arrested," I said, suspecting that she was hiding something important.

She examined her soda-water glass glumly. "I don't want to talk about it."

"Still, maybe you should."

"Goddamn it, Blackie, do you have to know everything?"

"No, but I think I have to know that part of the story."

She took a very deep breath, grabbed for Nick's hand again and told us how it happened. Small wonder she wanted to keep it a secret.

<u>145</u>
NICHOLAS

"I'll kill the bastard," I exploded, feeling my face twist in rage. "The lying, murdering hypocrite."

Catherine patted my hand. "Don't be angry, darling. He's more the victim than I am. He's insane now, don't you see? He always had a little character flaw. The church made it worse by the way it treated him. They took away his school, then his parish, then his community organization, then the school down here. Each time his pain became a little worse and he became a little more insane. But his intentions were always good . . . he merely lost the ability to see them in perspective."

"You make him seem so goddamn innocent."

"No, he's not innocent, just sad. And crazy. And now you see why

I think Don Felipé might have wanted me to escape. If I had gone to the embassy and told the press what had happened to me, it would not have harmed the *comandante* at all. Men and women who were maimed more than I was attracted no attention from the world. But if it was revealed that a revolutionary priest had turned me over to the *comandante*, it would have been a disaster for the Movement. Funny thing, I never even thought of denouncing Ed."

The moment she'd sat down across from me in the booth at the Dixie, sexual electricity had begun to bounce back and forth between us. No matter how many evil events had happened since then, the memory of those nights on Copacabana was still pulsing in our bodies. I wanted her more than I had ever wanted anything in my life.

And, sadly, I could not have her. She was Angela now, not Catherine. And she had a boyfriend with whom she shortly was to have a normal sex life.

"His personal charisma became demonic," Blackie observed. "He couldn't understand why the charm that worked on others didn't work on his superiors. Then he couldn't understand why it didn't change the world. Then he finally couldn't understand why those whom he once influenced began to desert him. You're right, Coz, he's a victim too, but that doesn't make him any less dangerous."

"You have to come back and stop him," I insisted.

"You can talk to your friends from the FBI." Cathy was undaunted, but her seeming calm was deceptive. "I'll give you details about the currency operation—I suppose you know he was smuggling money for the Mafia?"

"We know, all right."

"Can't the courts keep him from using my money?"

"Maybe they can," I admitted grudgingly. "If they want to. Right now, however, he stands to inherit seven million dollars of your money. He can use it to betray others the same way he betrayed you."

"You won't let him do that," she said firmly.

"It's your responsibility, not mine," I shouted.

"They'll martyr me again," she cried. "Do you know what women like Lorna will say about me—for the rest of my life? Haven't I suffered enough because of Ed Carny?"

"That's self-pity, Catherine. Do you want to give him money so he can hand other young women over to torturers because he needs a martyr?"

"You stop him, goddamnit. I've done enough."

"Actually, Cousin, you'd win," Blackie interrupted before we could turn our fight into a donnybrook. "Ed has gone too far this time. A few of his radical friends will support him. But he's made a worse mistake than Dan Berrigan made when he attacked Israel and was labeled an anti-Semite. He dealt with the enemy. You offer to take a lie detector test and he refuses . . . it's the end for him."

"I don't care," she wailed, ignoring the two other patrons at the other side of the bar. "I won't go back."

"You have an obligation," I said. "And please don't shout. There're other people here."

"I don't care if there's an army," she hissed. "I didn't earn the money. It's been a burden all my life. I'm finished with the obligations that that money imposed on me. I want to be left alone to lead my life in peace."

"There is no peace," Blackie said laconically.

"Your family, your friends, all the good things you could do with the money, the Ryans, the kids I know you want to have—don't you owe all of them something? Leave Ed out of it. What about all of us who love you?"

"You stupid asshole, haven't you been listening to me? I told you I don't want it. I'm finished with that life. What did my friends and family do to protect me from an indifferent father and a crazy mother? Or the nuns? Or Roy? Or Ed? Or Don Felipé? I'm sick of my family and friends. Where were they when I needed them?"

"You wouldn't let us help you when we wanted to," I said, meaning, of course, you wouldn't let me help you when I wanted to.

"You were no damn good to me," she sobbed. "I don't owe you a thing. I want to live my own quiet life. Fuck the seven million dollars."

"Those of us who love you are unimportant?" Blackie asked, cocking an eye. "Come now, Cousin, you must not permit this reenactment of past battles with Nicholas to lead you into positions you do not espouse."

"Of course, they're important," she said finally, the fight draining from her face and her shoulders slumping. "Not a day passes when I don't weep for the loss of all of you. I can never go back, not because I don't love you, but because I do."

"Tell me," said Blackie, whose bland expression had remained unchanged during our confrontation, "do the black kids you work with at the Catholic school react the same way the children at Grand Beach did? Do they see in Angela what the Chicago Irish kids saw in Catherine?"

"What do you mean?" She was wary, hostile.

"Come on, Coz, you know what I mean. Do they expect Angela,

as a perfect stranger, to wipe their noses, heal their hurts, tie their shoes, dry their tears and play their games? Is Angela, on appearance, everyone's favorite surrogate mother?"

"Damn it," she said, blushing faintly. "Yes, of course she is. I guess it wasn't the curly hair after all, huh?"

"Interesting, isn't it?" Blackie said, sighing heavily. "Cousin"—he changed the position of his empty tumbler—"I propose to preach. That is, after all, what priests are for."

Catherine tilted her chin at an expectant angle. A slightly intrigued smile crept across her face. Her eyes danced alertly. "Then preach away," she said.

"I am accounted an excellent preacher, not that that is a great accomplishment in the present state of the art," Blackie began, more nervous than I had ever seen him. "I don't worry about my Sunday homilies, because I feel they are well within my professional competence. Still, I worry about this sermon, because it is the most important one I will ever preach, and I'm not sure my skills are adequate to the task."

"Go on," she said.

"Indeed. I propose three points. First, on the nature of martyrdom, need I tell you that a martyr is a witness not so much to the power of faith, which may be impossible to demonstrate, as to the presence of God's love in the world which makes all things possible. Death is one kind of witness, which Christians have historically considered of enormous value as a sign of what is possible because of God's love. But so too is life. And living takes longer than dying and offers more challenge, and hence witness, to most of us, who will not be called on to shed our blood. I do not discount the importance of your suffering in Esmeralda, as you try to. Your suffering was the result of service to poor people who needed your help. And you did serve them, no matter how mixed your motives might have been and no matter how far short of your goal of total social renewal your service might have fallen."

"But—"

"Congregation does not reply till father is finished. . . . Your most powerful witness to the presence of God's love is your escape, and your reconstruction of your life, neutralizing not merely the horrors of Esmeralda but in great part the previous horrors of your life. You show us that it is possible to do what we must spend most of our lives doing, neutralizing horror and beginning again. I will entertain none of your neurotic nonsense about how flawed these accomplishments are. Work those out with the good Doctor Friedman. All our efforts are flawed. You are powerful witness, Cousin, for all the flaws and the incompleteness that may still limit that witness."

"But—" she tried again.

"Silence in the congregation, please. . . . Moreover—to make my second point—you have always wanted to be a remarkable woman. I suggest that now you realize that you have sought for remarkability outside yourself when it was in fact always lurking within you, unformed, nascent but ready to blossom. You attract people, you influence them, they admire you and follow you. That is no great merit, as such—you were born with those abilities. Nonetheless, now, because of your sufferings in both Esmeralda and Mobile, you are about to flower as a woman, a painter, a leader, a witness, a wife and mother, a citizen, a fighter for justice. And indeed you can readily become the woman of towering importance that in your deepest self you always suspected, hoped and feared you might be."

Big tears were forming in her eyes. Her face was contorted in agony as conflicting emotions struggled for victory. "I can't . . . "

As much as I realized Blackie was using the best arguments, I wished he would leave my poor tormented Cathy alone.

"Let me finish. I cite but one example. A woman who can suffer so much of the horrors men have inflicted for millennia on the helpless bodies of women and still celebrate the splendor of the womanly body, as you did in your painting of your friend Cindy, is enormously important for all of us. It won't be easy. Ed's allies will go after you, and so will others. Yet many more will listen and admire and perhaps understand a little of what is possible if one knows that God loves us. It doesn't really matter whether you walk across a small stage here or a big stage back home; there will always be promise and pain and possibility for you. You have tried too often to escape personal responsibility by fleeing to the safety of moral obligation. As the priest in charge, I won't permit that again. You don't have to come home—not as you thought you had to become a nun or had to marry Roy or had to fight for revolution. But come home or not, you are inevitably a witness. You were born one, Coz, and you always will be one, like it or not."

Large tears were spilling down her face. And both hands were in mine.

"It's so beautiful, Blackie, but I can't . . . "

"I think you can. But I repeat: It's your choice, Cousin Catherine."

"Catherine is dead." Abruptly she removed her hands from mine and stiffened. "Angela is alive."

"That is the one thing that has been said in this conversation that is simply and categorically untrue. Angela has never existed and doesn't exist. She is dead because she never lived. Catherine, on the contrary, is very much alive, because astonishing as it would have seemed to us even twelve hours ago, she never died. The only issue is what's next for Catherine."

She bowed her head. "I'm so tired."

"Catherine, we need you to protect others," I said obtusely.

"Protect?" She snarled at me like a caged animal. "Who protected me? Where were you when I was being tortured? Men have always used me—my father, Roy, Ed, Felipé. You're the same as they are!"

"I beg, dear Cousin, to disagree," Blackie interjected in a tone that allowed no dissent. "Nick doesn't belong in that category and you know damn well he doesn't. In fact, if you were honest you would admit that he's been less the user than the used."

Her shoulders sagged and the tension went out of her back. Her face collapsed.

"Oh, Coz," she said, "I'm such a dolt." She turned to me abjectly. "I'm so sorry, Nick. I'm so sorry that I shouted and I'm sorry for the terrible, untrue things I said. Please, please forgive me."

She touched my hand.

"Hell, yes." I grinned at her. For someone who had never apologized to me before, she was certainly good at it.

"I'm so tired," she pleaded. "Can we continue tomorrow? At lunch, after my workshop? I promise I won't run out on you again."

"Sure," Blackie said cheerfully. "We'll catch you if you do."

"I know," she said softly, her hand still on mine. "Would you take me home, Nick?"

Blackie regarded his empty tumbler grimly. "Can I close with a quote?"

"Sure, Coz." She kissed him on his forehead.

"From a fat old Italian gentleman who admired you when you were seventeen: 'Teaching, Caterina, requires a lot more work than dying.' "

She wept all the way to our T-Bird.

PART
SEVEN

146
BLACKIE

I was delighted to escape from both of them. The sexual tension was embarrassing, like that between a husband and wife of many years in the elevator of a strange hotel the first night they are away from home. One enjoys their fondness for each other, applauds their rediscovery of mutual appeal, and feels only slightly less awkward than if one had stumbled into their bedroom.

At the end of the conversation, despite their shyness and hesitation, Nick and Cathy were reduced to two terribly lonely human beings who wanted each other. As a nonstarter in such enterprises, I was clearly out of place. Hence I got out of the place and returned to my celibate bed in the Stars and Bars Motel.

I had preached my damnably pedantic sermon. Now someone had to incarnate the words, put flesh on them. Ball in your court, Nicholas Thaumaturgos.

I was much too sad to go to sleep. There were desperate and healthy longings in both their bodies, Nick to heal and Cathy to be healed. Yet the odds were that the only events in her apartment would be some vehement couplings which would leave them both dissatisfied and unhappy, Nick still not sure that he could be a man for her and Cathy not sure that she could ever be a woman for anyone.

They surely loved each other, however inept and inadequate their love had always been. And tonight they loved each other more than ever. Coupling was an attempt to open up the connections of love. Surely the quicksilver mists would seep in through the windows of her apartment. It was precisely the kind of situation, fluid, uncertain, problematic, in which grace is most likely to be effective. The sheer unfamiliarity of circumstances lowers the barriers of human resistance. Their emotional condition would make it difficult for them to set their hearts against God's goodness.

On the other hand, the two of them had long practice in the art of throwing up barriers.

So I prayed, for want of something better to contribute.

Perhaps I had made another one of my idiot mistakes. If only Mary Kate and her husband were in Chicago and not in Hong Kong and I

could have had her advice. We had to move quickly if we were to prevent
Ed Carny from getting his paws on her money. But what did the money
matter? Perhaps we should have given Cathy more time. But who could
say that more time would not have been a disservice to her? And how
much longer could Nick go on loving a ghost?

So I had made a gut decision. Once I knew that it was probable
that Angela Carson was Cathy and that Angela/Cathy was at St. Peter's,
I felt we had to have a confrontation. Foolishly I did not think through
the implications. I did not suspect that we would argue and that then
their hormones would take them off to bed.

Dummy.

Or genius maybe.

But because I wasn't sure, I worried and prayed some more.

When was I sure that Cathy was alive? I suppose that, despite my
efforts to convince Nick that the dead must bury their dead, I never gave
up hope. Yet I only believed that Angela was Cathy when I saw her in
the Howard Johnson's. We Irish are prone to expect the worst.

I began to believe it likely that Cathy was still among us when I
called St. Peter's, and asked them if I could speak with Angela Carson
in the art department. Unlike the other Catholic liberal arts college I
had called, they did not say immediately either that they had no art
department or, after some confusion, that there was no Angela Carson
in that department.

It had occurred to me that if Angela were Cathy and that if Angela/
Cathy were trying to start a new life, she would turn to what was her
greatest creative joy. Moreover, I also wagered with myself that she would
seek out a Catholic college because it was an environment in which she
would feel at home until she mobilized her resources to move into the
larger world of, let us say, a state university.

I was prepared to go after the state universities if my census of
Catholic institutions failed.

And given the brisk and direct style that was part of Cathy's character
and of which there were hints in Angela Carson's behavior as we had
traced it, I further wagered that she would not travel far from Miami to
find a place to begin her life again.

Rather unintelligently I began with Miami and worked north. I
should have realized that Cathy or Angela/Cathy would have sought a
school distant from a large metropolitan area, especially one where the
inevitable Rosie O'Gorman might appear.

It was a stab in the dark, but then stabs in the dark were all that was left to us.

I sat next to the phone, quite literally shaking like a leaf when the switchboard operator at St. Peter's said, without any need to check, that Ms. Carson was not in that afternoon.

Still, a man of less faith—when push comes to shove—than Nick, I was not ready to believe even when we saw the paintings and it seemed that the sunbursts and lovely elf girl were her work. I hoped they were, however; for the sunbursts hinted at a new Cathy. And the naked elf child was to some extent a self-portrait.

I prayed the sun was bursting now for both of them in their apartment. And that she was strong enough to be elf girl for him.

Yet the probabilities were that Cathy would become frightened and bitchy and Nick would become timid and diffident, deferring as always to what a woman said instead of what she meant.

My arguments about martyrdom would never in themselves convert St. Cathy, virgin and martyr, to Ms. Cathy, mother and witness. They were not strong enough to make her endure yet more pain. Not unless she was convinced that Nick could love her with the mixture of tenderness and firmness that she needed and wanted could she change. That he could be kind and sweet and gentle and reassuring was as certain as the rising of the sun, but that he could be strong enough to settle for none of the counterfeit Cathys that would appear every day was much less certain.

A lot riding on one romp in the hay? Indeed, yes. But this was the turning point in their story—not just any act of sexual intercourse, but one in which love either began again or ended permanently. Sex engulfed in the mists.

And could I imagine myself playing the role Nick was playing and enjoying it enormously?

Is the pope Catholic?

So I prayed that those devious and ingenious mists would seep into the nooks and crannies, the weak links and the interstices of their souls and create BANG! a surprise.

Realistically I could not imagine a scenario for surprise.

How would I respond when Cathy, still suffering terribly, began to blame me for her pain?

I had not the slightest idea.

And poor Nick had not even considered that possibility.

Mindful that this was the feast of the wonder worker, the patron of unexpected surprises, and also mindful of where we were, I made my own prayer the prayer of Admiral David Glasgow Farragut on the bridge of the U.S.S. *Hartford*: "Nicholas, full steam ahead!"

147
NICHOLAS

"I'm sorry I was so bitchy," she said softly, touching my arm briefly. "I'm plain scared, I guess."

The woman next to me in the car, an intriguing mixture of diffidence and self-possession, was not like the Catherine I remembered—more quiet and yet more confident. God knows her vulnerability and determination were an appealing combination. It was hard to picture her gunning down her tormentors, leaping into a ditch in the middle of the night, begging for eight dollars and bluffing a paratroop officer, probably my friend Capitán Pedro Ramírez. A whole new Catherine to know and enjoy if she would give me a chance.

The gypsy Ariel of the past had apparently disappeared. Yet there had been a fit of the old flounce when she sat next to Blackie, Catherine of yesteryear settling down for a night of conversation. If the loss of Ariel was the price to pay for a living Catherine, I would cheerfully pay it.

"I have a long record of not saying the right thing at the right time," I admitted.

"I know what you were saying, Nicholas," she sighed. "I could see it in the warmth of your eyes and strain in your fingers. I chose to fight your words, because I didn't want to deal with what you meant."

Two apologies in one night. Now what should I say?

I decided not to say anything. We rode the rest of the short ride to her apartment in silence. She lived in a concrete two-story, a college dormitory-like building, softened by balconies and rapidly growing trees, and several old but comfortable-looking cars, including her orange bug, parked in front of it. Some of the windows already glowed with Christmas decorations, and the doors were painted different colors to provide a pathetic touch of respectable lower-middle-class individuality.

Catherine leaned her head wearily against the seat rest of the T-

Bird. Considering me dubiously, she drew her beige sweater more tightly around her shoulders. "Are you sure you want to come in?"

"I didn't know I was invited."

She hesitated and then smiled shyly. "You're invited."

We held each other's hands as we walked up the outside stairs at one end of the concrete block, like two teenagers coming home from a date.

And like a teenage girl, she released my hand and stood with her back protected by the door when we came to her apartment.

"Maybe you shouldn't come in."

I kissed her with a quick teenage kiss.

"Am I still invited?"

She nodded and opened the door.

The apartment was convent-neat, two rooms and a kitchen, furnished in inexpensive Motel Modern. The only touch of Catherine's personality was two dazzling sunbursts, one lavender and the other misty green, on the walls of the living room and a Christmas crib, carved from wood, in which only Mary and Joseph were present in this time before Christmas.

Catherine lit a vigil light in front of the crib.

"Lovely figures," I said.

"Thank you." She smiled at me, like a child who has been praised for a drawing she has brought home from kindergarten. "I made them. I've been experimenting with wood carving. The porch of the art building seems to demand that one whittle."

"Blackie says that Burl Ives sits there in a rocking chair and spits for two hours every day."

"Blackie is incorrigible." She laughed fondly, making me jealous, as she always did when she seemed to love Blackie more than me. "It's not Frenchman's Bend and I'm not a Faulkner heroine, but I guess I should be complimented. . . . Do you think Blackie knows what we're doing?"

"What are we doing?"

"I'm making a pot of blackberry herbal tea. Will you drink some?"

"Sure." I wondered if blackberries were an aphrodisiac and decided that they probably weren't and I didn't need one anyway. I loved her so much that I felt at the edge of giddiness.

On her way to the tiny kitchen, she discarded her sweater and then, convent training asserting itself as a second thought, picked it up from the chair on which she'd tossed it and hung it in a closet.

Monica's advice rang in my brain: "When a man thinks he is being ridiculously, absurdly, impossibly slow, he has arrived at the remote fringes of what a woman wants and needs."

She sat at one end of the couch, whose springs weakly protested the presence of two people, and I sat at the other while we quietly sipped our blackberry tea.

Maybe, I thought, it is an aphrodisiac after all.

I took off my glasses and put them in the pocket of my jacket.

"Can you find me with those off?" She too was on the edge of giddiness.

"They're only reading glasses. I think I can find you."

"They make you look very distinguished, a wise, learned counsel. And also, as I said once before, marvelously cute. . . . " She paused, took a deep breath and continued. "That was the only sensible thing I said at Copacabana. If you don't mind another apology, I am sorry especially for what I said and did there."

"You don't have to apologize . . . " I began.

"I want to clear that out of the way," she said, bowing her head and in her contrition radiating irresistible appeal. "I won't do it again."

We both backed off, looking for something to talk about. I heard another instruction from Monica. "Every inch of a woman's body is potentially erotic. Take your time and touch her everywhere, but be as light and delicate as if she were chiffon frosting."

"Lovely sunbursts," I said, trying to focus for the moment on something besides the delectable chiffon frosting at the other end of the couch.

"So many compliments for the frightened little woman. Thank you. They're Angela at her best. Her worst are sick and ugly, but I throw them out."

I took the cracked teacup out of her hand. "Is it Angela or Catherine I am about to kiss?"

Her brown eyes clouded over with fear. "Catherine. . . . "

"They're both quite appealing." My lips brushed hers, lingered, absorbed a taste of response and then departed. Still two adolescents necking on a couch.

We were both shy, awkward, embarrassed. And eager.

"I don't want to use you, Nick." She bowed her head and pressed her hands together. "I care for you too much to experiment with you just to find out whether I'm still a woman."

"I don't feel that I'm being used. I don't think this is an experiment. And I'm sure you're still a woman."

My second kiss was a little longer and the taste of her response a little sweeter. We had graduated to our very early twenties.

"You always were a hell of a good kisser," she laughed.

It would be a long and careful night, but I had nowhere else to go and nothing else to do.

Catherine was like a bride on her wedding night, passive and unresisting, but also uncertain and terrified, doubting not so much her lover as herself and trying to trust totally both his love and his skill.

And I was a confused jumble of desire and concern, frantic lust and worried tenderness. Everything I did might affect both of us for the rest of our lives.

I opened one button on her blouse and then another.

Catherine gulped. "Oh, did you think you were invited here for that?"

We both laughed, nervously and artificially, and clung to one another for strength.

She was wearing a rosary around her neck, the crucifix hanging between lace-covered breasts. The rosary from her escape, of course.

"I'll take it off if it distracts you from the creature's merchandise."

"It enhances rather than distracts."

"Nick, I love you so much." She leaned toward me to brush my lips and then pulled away as though she had been too bold.

"Don't be afraid of me, Catherine," I said, opening the other buttons and sliding the blouse off her shoulders and down her arms.

"It's not you; it's me and my damn memories." She stumbled over the words.

I kissed her throat, her shoulders, her back, tasting the soft saltiness of her skin.

"Your therapist"—I hesitated between the bra and the slacks and opted for the slacks—"has told you that you're ready for sex again and that the memories are not an insurmountable barrier."

"How did you know that?" she said, helping me slide the slacks down her legs.

"And Angela seems to like sheer lace more than Catherine did, in very small amounts, that is." My hand crept under some of that lace to touch a round cone of breast, smooth and white as Irish linen.

"Angela," she agreed, with a very deep breath, "is a bit of a tart. No, that's not true. She would like to think of herself as a bit of a tart. Oh . . ."

"Did I hurt you?" I pulled my hand away.

"The creature is jumpy, Nick," she said with stars in her eyes as she recaptured my hand. "You only scared me. Good scare."

I drew her head against my chest and unfastened her bra, kissing her back and pathetically thin shoulder blades. I chose a small area on one of the shoulder blades and caressed it with my index finger, carefully and slowly, as if I were healing all of her through that one spot. She sighed peacefully.

Then I moved her lightly away, disposed of the flimsy bra and captured each breast, caressing it gently and pushing it against her ribs. God, I said to myself, I hope I am not going too fast.

"Nick, you're the only man in the world who would do this for me."

"The pleasure's mine," I said as I began to kiss and nibble at my twin captives, feeling confident that the Person watching me from her rosary did not mind sharing her and indeed had always intended to share her with me.

I'm doing all right, I told Him, but don't desert me now.

There was a thin white scar down the side of her right breast. Someone had caused her excruciating pain there. I touched the mark with my index finger and tried the same healing magic I had exercised on her shoulder blade. For long, delightful and painful minutes, I caressed the scar. She closed her eyes and threw back her head, I hoped in pleasure and not in painful memory.

Then she opened her eyes and absorbed me. "Oh, Nick," she said weakly.

"Catherine," I replied, my finger pausing. Our eyes locked. And time stood still. Minutes, hours, years, eternity passed us by.

"You really ought to take all the creature's clothes off," she sighed, breaking the spell. "See how she compares . . . "

"I know that already, Catherine."

"Verdict?" she said when I had finished stripping her. She cocked an eye at me, in which all the old Catherine imps danced again.

Not a nubile teenager anymore—I tried my best judicial face—but a woman blessed with the durable beauty of the Ryan clan: firm, conical breasts; slender waist; flat belly; lovely ass; elegant thighs and legs. "Ah," I said, "the creature would do more than keep the bed warm at night. And best of all she's Catherine and she's alive."

I can't wait much longer. Damnit, you have to wait.

"Tell me more about this creature," she insisted.

"She looks like one of her own sunbursts," I said simply, taking the creature into my arms again and holding her tightly.

"A little underweight sunburst, don't you think?" she said critically, like a director appraising a chorus girl.

"Maybe a little thinner, but I confess that I was so taken by other aspects of the creature that I hardly noticed." I brushed my hand over one of her breasts again.

"Thank you," she said in the same pleased and modest voice that she had used when I praised her paintings.

"Do you mind if I say you remind me of a bride on her wedding night—anxious, eager and trusting?"

She touched my cheek with her fingers, "Nick, you're wonderful—though I wonder what you know about brides." She giggled. "This bride will try not to be too much of a drag."

There were white marks on her body, the scars of torture. But they were, somehow, not ugly—the result of an accident long ago—and they did not spoil the attractiveness I had praised. Nor had they caused shame to Catherine, for she had obviously been sunbathing in a bikini.

"You still wear sex-object swimsuits," I said as I undressed, and instantly regretted touching the ideology of the past.

But no harsh memories were stirred. "They are not into nude sunbathing in Mobile yet."

"Maybe I should take you to some place where they are."

"An interesting proposition, noble sir. Let's break up into small groups and discuss it."

And following as best I could the precepts of my instruction, I began my infinitely delicate final preparation of her body, treating her as if she were a tissue-paper doll. I was conscious of how much pain her lovely body had suffered and then conscious only of how much I loved her.

Catherine's fists were clenched and her lips pressed together tightly. But her body seemed to be mine for whatever I wanted and grateful for whatever I did, the bride giving herself totally to her husband.

My head was throbbing and my loins aching, but she was not ready despite her best efforts. Love must postpone lust yet a little while.

Catherine wrenched herself free from my caressing hands and probing lips, twisted off the couch and dashed into her bedroom, slamming the door shut.

I hesitated. Perhaps it was too soon. Perhaps I was not the one to bring her womanliness back to her. Perhaps it was all a terrible mistake.

Desire more than anything else made me open the door. Catherine lay on her bed, huddled under the spread in a tight little ball like an embryo in the womb.

I sat next to her on the edge of the bed. The taut little knot beneath the spread was barely visible in the light filtering through the doorway from the living room. Her bedroom, like everything else in Angela's life, was prim and spare, almost monastic.

"Can I help?" I said foolishly.

"Get out." A voice of a hurt child, muffled by the pillow into which her head was sunk. "Leave me alone. You're as bad as the rest of them."

One last shot before I left.

"I love you, Catherine. I won't hurt you the way the others did."

"Goddamn bastard. If you hadn't failed me, they wouldn't have hurt me."

It wasn't fair, and yet it was fair, in ways I only dimly understood. Monica said I should never have let her become a nun. That was the first of many failures.

"Can't I make up for those failures?"

"Fuck off!" she snarled.

I left the bedroom and softly closed the door. How had I blown it? I must have done something wrong. Perhaps I should have waited another day.

I put on my shorts. Perhaps tomorrow would be easier.

Tomorrow would not come.

I hesitated, still burning with passion for her. No, it was not going to end this way. Goddamnit, Catherine, no more flakiness.

I went back into the bedroom and pulled the spread away from her clutching fingers.

She was indeed thin, a twisted ball of skinny yarn, with elbows and knees and shoulder blades pathetically protruding.

"Get out, please." From anger to pathos. It won't work, Catherine my beloved.

I began to pry apart the strands of the ball of yarn, separating the tightly pressed bones from one another. She resisted doggedly.

I held the stiff, harsh body in my arms, feeling the wild heartbeat pounding under sadly fleshless ribs in rhythm with my own.

"I'm not going to hurt you, Catherine. And I will not force myself on you. But I am not letting you go, either."

Every bone resisted me; every muscle was tense with fear and hatred. I hung on, determined that my fire would melt her ice.

Minutes passed—I don't know how many. Gradually she became passive again. The bride was ready to satisfy her husband's lust.

"All right," she said in grim resignation. "Finish what you started." Copacabana again.

I don't know where my words came from. "Not on those terms, Catherine."

"Well, what terms?" The familiar impatient Catherine rage, which would never again, I vowed, fool me.

"That I am your lover and you want me." The words came from the same wise voice whispering inside my skull.

"Oh, THAT." She laughed softly. Her disinterested and indifferent body became warm and moist and affectionate. "My God, why didn't you say that in the first place?" She moved my hand back to her breast and held it there.

I felt her nipples grow hard. My lips claimed one, then the other. "I'll always love you, Catherine. Always."

"I don't know why," she murmured.

Belly, thighs, loins—my hands and mouth everywhere as she exhaled very softly, like a spent balloon settling into a child's embrace. "Give me long enough and I'll explain."

I turned on the lamp next to her bed. Perhaps I should have had more respect for her modesty. But I was leaving my hesitations behind. Damnit, I wanted to see her clearly.

"Voyeur," she sighed happily.

Our renewed love was hardly spectacular. The most my passionate thrustings could call forth was a soft sigh of pleasure as she shivered briefly beneath me. It was enough.

"Thank you for waiting," she murmured complacently as she cuddled sleepily in my arms.

"I wasn't going to leave," I lied.

"I mean always," she said as she fell asleep.

In the middle of the night, I felt someone kiss my chest.

"Are you awake, darling?"

"I am now, Catherine. Something wrong?"

"Maybe it was an accident."

"I don't think so."

Her aggression against my chest was tentative and maidenly.

"I want proof."

"Lustful wench. Can't a man have a good night's sleep?"

"Please." There was so much pathos in the word that I couldn't continue my joking.

"Lights off?"

"No."

I turned on the bed light and pulled back the sheet. Her body was covered with sweat.

"One thing that hasn't changed." She smiled, wiping her face with the end of the sheet.

"Five pounds more wouldn't hurt," I said, pretending to consider her objectively.

"Even ten." She laughed. "I drink two milk shakes every day. And eat two helpings of chocolate ice cream. And I still don't gain an ounce. Remember when I used to count calories? . . . Oh, do that again . . . Your mistress must be quite clever. Or do you call her your mistress?"

I stopped my preliminary activities. "Mistress?"

"You know more about a woman than I was ever able to teach you. Don't stop, please."

Mischief sparkled in her eyes, not transiently as it had before but now like it had come to stay. "The woman is all right," I admitted. "Earthy peasant type."

"I hate her." She laughed again. "Absolutely hate her." Then, as though a drug had been injected into her veins, she stiffened. "Nick, we shouldn't be doing this."

"Shut up," I said.

"All right, Ape-Man," she said softly.

The second time together was much better, not wild passion, heaven knows, but confident and settled affection, binding two sweaty bodies even more closely together.

It would require many such interludes of binding, I thought, before I could begin to teach her some of the refinements I had learned, but now such education seemed a possibility.

And I fell asleep, inordinately proud of my masculinity.

149
ANGELA

Cathy was more pleased with herself than she had any right to be.

As she floated between sleep and wakefulness again, she knew where she was and who it was who was holding her, whose strong hands were cupped around her ass. And she hesitated now between fear and self-satisfaction.

He thinks I'm his virgin bride, she thought. And maybe I am. Roy didn't count. I thought I was called to be a bride of Christ. Now only a bride of Nick.

Then she considered that Nick might be Christ for her—might always have been, the only hint she had of God's love. It was a delightful thought and a terrifying one. She banished it hastily and firmly, but it still lurked on the edges of her consciousness.

Wait till I tell Marian Friedman, she thought. Twice in one night, and not all that bad the second time either. Sort of routine marital fucking, but this time he had some fun too. Rape victims can be good lays, not great lays, but good lays. You may have a future, kid, as a sex object.

The first good night's sleep in years. So it does beat tranquilizers, after all. . . .

But only with men who are pathetically in love with you and should avoid you like you were an occasion of sin.

Occasion of sin . . . how long since she had thought of those words? Father Ed had warned her in high school that Nick might be an occasion of sin.

Ed. She shuddered. Demonic, Blackie had said. Well, maybe. Yet I went along with it for years.

And what I'm afraid of now is not that I will wake up tomorrow and find López and García working me over again. Or Don Felipé kissing me with a knife at my throat.

I'm afraid I will wake up and find Nick here still. I can't cope with him. I love him too much to give him up and I love him too much to burden him with me. I wasn't right for him ten years ago and that was before they wrecked me.

I should never have let him in my bed. Poor dear man. Look at those lines around his eyes, so clear in the morning sunlight. Worrying about me made some of those lines, didn't they, darling? Two quick fucks hardly make up. But at least the second time you got something as well as giving.

As long as you are stuck with me, you'll be the giver and I the getter. I must absolve you from me.

But I was nice, wasn't I? You're waking up, beautiful Ape-Man. You'll have to leave now, you know. Before I throw you out. I would love to sit on the edge of the bed, stark naked, and lasciviously devour a dish of chocolate ice cream. Drive you out of your mind, my adroit young lover. Oh, God, would that be fun!

And who is this mistress, anyway?

150
NICHOLAS

I was awakened by the sun streaming through the windows and the motion of a beautiful woman stretching deliciously beside me.

"Persistent so-and-so slept with me last night," she laughed, quite satisfied with herself.

My masculinity, still pleased, reacted instantly.

"Hey," she shouted, "I'm not going to run. . . . " And then, realizing that she had indeed run only a few hours earlier: "Well, not anymore. Take it easy."

"I don't want to take it easy."

"Who is this mistress person?" She pretended to push me off until she had a satisfactory answer. Now her resistance was all pretense.

"Her name is Monica—or was."

"Did she die?" The sparkle in her eyes was extinguished by compassion.

" 'Course not. She gave me my walking papers."

"Oh." The sparkle flickered momentarily. "Because you were in love with a dead woman?"

"We'll talk about her some other time." I swatted her playfully, forgetting how sex and pain had been contorted in her life. "My God, I'm sorry, Catherine. I didn't mean—"

"Didn't hurt," she interrupted me briskly, rubbing the offended part of her anatomy. "A man should swat his woman's rear end occasionally. That's one of the things it's for." An impish snicker. "Remember when you spanked me for pouring sand in your lemonade? Oh, Nick," she said, giggling uncontrollably. "Remember? Wasn't I an obnoxious little brat?"

"Did I hurt you then?" I asked.

"I loved every second of it. You couldn't hurt a woman even if you wanted to." She frowned, her mania snuffed out. "And you've had enough reason to want to, God knows."

"You were spectacularly obnoxious then—and haven't changed a bit, especially the spectacular part."

I began to kiss appropriate parts of her anatomy.

Our third union in the new dispensation was not high passion; neither of us was capable of that. But it was high comedy, playing and probing, tickling and teasing, romping and rolling, laughing and tantalizing. And she became my gypsy Ariel again, light, delicate, comic, frolicking with a man's body for the first time and quickly learning how such frolic is best done. For my Catherine and me at that moment, humor and amusement were much better than furious passion. The raw hungers of Copacabana would perhaps return with time, but in a context in which they would not become, to use Blackie's word, demonic. The fireworks could wait.

"Nine-thirty," she said reluctantly when the comedy abated. "Do you mind if I make my ten-thirty workshop? I'll meet you and Blackie for lunch at one."

"Ah, Blackie." I sighed in mock resignation and struggled out of her bed.

"Go on." She grinned impishly. "You can hardly wait to see him and hint at what a great lover you are."

I pulled on my shorts—the rest of my clothes were still in her living room—and, hands on hips, stared down at her. "And I'm not?"

"I didn't say that." Her eyes were soft with gratitude.

"Let's be clear about it, woman," I said, still enormously pleased with myself. "You're mine now and I'll stand for no more foolishness."

"A possession?" she said, hinting at a willingness to rekindle the old ideological fires.

I was still listening to the mysterious voices in the back of my head. "Nope, a love. My love is imprinted on you for the rest of your life. The only claims I have are from that."

"And if I persist in acting flaky?" She was considering me intently, a rumpled, floral-patterned, pink sheet held protectively at her breasts, covering the crucifix of her rosary too.

"I'll insist you stop."

"And if I don't?"

"I think I demonstrated last night—the first time—how I'll react. I won't force you and I won't let you go."

She blushed, a new bride taking orders from her strong young husband. "I think I'll be able to remember that . . . and if I run again?"

I leaned over, peeled off the sheet and kissed her soundly. "I'll come after you."

My lips sought her breasts, and my tongue touched a nipple, making it firm again; my teeth, now confident and at home, grazed her flesh.

"Hey, Ape-Man, your teeth are sharp. Cut it out." She giggled pleasurably. "And I suppose you'll drag me back by the hair of my head, like I'm some prize seal?"

My free hand, the one not holding her breast prisoner, made gentle promises to her thighs. Then I released her and stood above her, folding my arms in what I hoped looked like the pose of a conqueror.

"Only figuratively. Anyway, Catherine or Angela or whoever you are this morning, the running days are over for both of us." I said it with all the male power my voice could manage and still tried to keep it tender. I thought I'd succeeded.

"I'm Catherine, of course, Ape-Man, sir." She pulled the sheet back over her body. "And while I think it might be fun to be dragged around figuratively, I won't run from you anymore, darling."

"Don't try," I said, astonished at my firmness.

"And I have to go back to Chicago with you?" she asked humbly—ready, I think, to obey if I told her to.

"I don't know, Catherine. That's all negotiable. We can talk about it at lunch. I'll give you all the room you need. The only thing that is unnegotiable is you and me. Is that clear?"

Her brown eyes filled with large tears. She looked away from me, joyous and embarrassed. "Yes, Ape-Man, master, sir."

There was a moment of silent relief. We were both happy to have crossed the most dangerous reefs.

One more kiss.

"God, Nick, you'll drive me out of my mind . . . don't . . . oh, God . . . Now please get out of my boudoir and let me dress for art class. It's going to be hard enough to concentrate as it is."

I turned to look at her as I left the bedroom. She was a leprechaun nymph, a slightly more mature and more bridal version of Cindy, delighting in both her conquest and mine. "Out," she said happily.

"I'm going," I said with equal happiness.

I put on the rest of my clothes in the living room and had my hand on the door when Catherine appeared behind me, now wrapped in her sheet.

"Thank you, Nick. I love you." She hugged me as she did in the days of her passionate adolescence. "And you're so damn gorgeous." She touched my chest and arms, losing control of her floral covering. "I simply have to paint you."

"You'll make me vain," I said unsteadily.

"Fat chance." She continued to cling to me as though her future depended on me, standing on tiptoe, hands locked at the back of my neck, naked torso pressed against my shirt. "I don't know how I can stand to wait till tonight."

Study a woman's reactions as you would a witness, Monica had instructed me. This woman had a powerful need for close physical contact. Hugs wouldn't always do the trick, but they would be essential.

So much the better for me. Naked in my arms in light of day, Catherine had the firm, long-legged elegance of a disciplined woman athlete. She must have spent much time and energy on the respectful maintenance of her battered body.

Fragile and yet very strong. I drew her even closer.

"Maybe we can have an early supper and dump Blackie."

"Fair enough. Now go away and let me dress for school."

Neither of us wanted to end the embrace. I pressed my lips against hers, pushing deeply, demandingly.

"Come up for air," she said, the sheet now abandoned on the floor. "But don't stop."

We clung to each other as if there was no one else in the world and our only task was to sustain our embrace forever. All the years spun off, like a heat shield from a returning space capsule. We were young lovers again, bright with hope for the life that was just beginning.

"Go 'way, so I can make my workshop," she said with little conviction.

"I would, but a naked woman is hanging on to me."

"Ape-Man." She pushed me affectionately out of the door.

Outside, the warm winter sun of the southland was shining and the horizons of my life seemed limitless.

But I was still afraid.

151
BLACKIE

I was sitting at the side of the motel swimming pool, reading Marcel Proust and trying to pretend that it was not cold. December is December, even in southern Alabama and even with a heated pool.

Nick had not appeared at breakfast and was certainly not in his room. Presumably the events of the night had not been unsatisfactory. However, I found the confrontations between Proust's Narrator and poor Albertine less than compelling.

Finally he appeared in swimming trunks and terry cloth robe as though it were August, the picture of self-satisfied male complacency.

"How's the water?" he asked with elaborate casualness.

"Warmer than the air. Do we have plans for the day?"

"Catherine has a ten-thirty class. She will meet us for lunch here at one o'clock."

"Ah."

"I'm going to swim some laps."

"Fine."

So he swam his laps like a man who had triumphed at all of life's important games.

After some forty minutes of churning heroically against the water of the pool, he rejoined me, breathing heavily and content with himself.

After waiting in vain for my question, he gave in. "I think the worst may be over."

"She will return and take on Ed?"

Nick frowned at the thought of the ineffable Father Carny, maker of martyrs. "I don't know. We'll have to work that out. We can start talking about it at lunch. I think we'll have to give her all the room she needs. If necessary, I can stall the estate matter for months."

"Indeed."

"The important thing is that she is Catherine again, not Angela. And she has promised that she will not run away."

"That is progress," I conceded. "You must have finally drawn the line last night."

He looked at me nervously, his confidence shaken for the first time that morning. "I think I did, Blackie. I sure gave it my best try."

But when we entered the dining room of the Stars and Bars a few minutes before one, Nick attired in blue sport coat with color-coordinated shirt and tie, his confidence had returned. He had finally won the battle. The woman was his.

All right, Nick, if you can make it stick.

He chatted merrily about the various legal ploys that could stall the plans of Ed and his friends to take possession of her money. There were, it seemed, two strategies—delaying the probate and delaying the finding of her legal death. With some reservations, my scholarly legal companion appeared to favor the latter, although, as he admitted, the critical question was which approach was most beneficial to Catherine and most supportive of her and most likely to provide her "all the room she needs to find herself."

"It seemed to me that she had found more of herself last night than ever before," I said mildly.

The distinguished lawyer was shocked. "Good God, Blackie, have you forgotten what she's been through?"

"It seems to have facilitated her maturation," I said pedantically. "Most people don't grow up, no matter how high the cost. Maybe it was a *felix culpa.*"

"That's cruel," he said automatically.

"A tortured and adult Cathy is better than an untortured and juvenile Cathy," I said, persisting in my defense of the crooked lines of God.

The minute hand of the clock swept inexorably toward one-thirty and my heart descended with it.

"I'll make a call," Nick said, pushing his chair away from the table with studied confidence.

A few minutes later he returned, his confidence shattered like that of a pitcher whose clean-up hitter has just struck out with the bases loaded.

"She didn't show up for class," he said grimly.

"Maybe she fell asleep," I said tentatively.

"No answer at the apartment, either."

Sometime between his departure and one o'clock Angela Carson had reappeared and disappeared.

"What shall we do?" I asked, knowing damn well what I would do.

"Let's check the apartment."

So we checked the apartment.

The door was locked and the curtains were drawn. No sign of the orange bug.

On the back of the building, next to some neatly stacked garbage cans, we found a door with the word "Manager" stenciled in neat letters.

The manager person, it turned out, was a flighty southern belle of some sixty-five summers.

Miz Carson left this morning. Oh, 'bout eleven o'clock. Paid up her lease, which had six months to run. Packed her luggage in that cute car of hers and said she would phone with a forwarding address.

Then St. Peter's College. No trace of her in the art building. Our friend Cindy said she had not been to the workshop that morning. Everyone was surprised. Angie never missed class, not even when she was sick.

Finally, late in the afternoon, after we had discovered which of the Doctors Friedman was the one Cathy was seeing, we were in that person's office, uncomfortable in her contempt.

She was a thin, intense woman with black hair, black eyes and a New York accent. And she was not going to tell us anything.

Nick explained that I was her cousin and that he was her lawyer, that we intended her no harm, that we would not violate her privacy or interfere with her new life, that we had had a pleasant talk with her the night before and had no reason to think we had frightened her, and that we were both astonished and worried by her sudden disappearance.

"I cannot discuss my confidential relationships with my clients," said Marian Friedman for the tenth time.

"Surely she has been in touch with you? Can't you at least tell us that?"

"She called to end the therapy" — I spoke for the first time—"didn't she?"

"There was such a message with my answering service." She nodded her head in reluctant agreement.

"And she promised she would mail you a check and stay in touch by phone and of course you will not be able to tell us when she does that. . . . "

"I cannot—"

"—discuss your confidential relationships with your clients." I finished the sentence before she did.

"No more than you can—"

"—violate the seal of confession."

Nicholas was not able to leave things to me. "And if I tell you that her life may be in grave danger?"

"I won't believe you," she replied tartly.

The game was up. Angela, in any event, was too smart to tell anyone where her next stop would be, if she knew, and she probably didn't.

"You surely wouldn't deny," I said in my most professional voice, "that the prognosis for her is quite hopeful?"

Her eyes flickered at me. "No, I certainly wouldn't deny that at all."

"Especially since, despite what she has suffered and despite her great and very real fears, she clearly possesses enormous ego strength?"

I had graduated from insect to mildly interesting toad in Doctor Marian's eyes.

"Indeed, she does."

"Come on, Counselor," I said. "The good doctor has told us all she can."

On the way out, I casually mentioned that I assumed she had heard of my sister, Dr. M.K. Murphy. I watched her eyes widen and her mouth open before I closed the door.

"What was that about?" Nick asked in the chill twilight outside.

"Doctor Friedman told us that her patient was making remarkable progress until we came along and messed it up, that she still needs therapy and that she's strong enough to find it wherever she goes."

"That's good news, I guess," he said sadly. "I don't know what I did wrong."

"Nothing," I said in a rare burst of compassion for the poor geek. "Absolutely nothing. Cathy panicked. She slipped out of the quicksilver mists, damn her. Come on, let's go after her."

He was shocked at the suggestion. "But how? She's run again, even though she said she wouldn't."

"How? Will you stop being a lovesick clod long enough to remember that you are an officer of the court and that this woman has possibly perpetrated a monumental fraud? Give the state police her license number; tell them to check with Chicago for your credentials and have them bring her in. What could be easier?"

"I don't have her license number," he said, giving a fair imitation of the prince of Denmark in a stew.

"Alabama BEK 144."

"How do you know?"

"I memorized it last night. Figured it wouldn't hurt to have it."

Damnit, Watson, even an aroused lover should have thought of that.

"We can't do it, Blackie. We can't do it."

I knew it. As sure as the tide rose in Mobile Bay, as sure as the Union had won the War between the States, I knew it.

"You have to give her the room she needs?" I said, conceding that I was beaten. They had both slipped out of the mists.

"I have always respected Catherine's freedom," he said with deep sadness. "And I always will."

"But you told her you wouldn't let her run away again," I said, guessing what he had probably said in the golden glow of post-orgasmic elation.

"I also told her that I would always respect her freedom," he insisted. "Come on, Blackie, maybe we can catch the late plane to O'Hare."

Back to the ice and snow of isolated hearts and frozen brains.

152 BLACKIE

On December 22 of the bicentennial year of our resilient republic, I sat in the court of Judge Janice Fielding, in nondescript lay garb, for the empty ritual of a hearing on the motion, argued by Counselor McNally, to declare that Catherine Collins, virgin and martyr, had indeed been chopped to pieces by Comandante Felipé Gould in the courtyard of Esmeralda Prison almost two years before.

The hearing would be brief. Although the two witnesses to her execution were present, it was not likely that they would be asked to testify. Since the executor of Ms. Collins's estate would not demand the right of cross-examination, their sworn statements would be enough.

Moreover, the executor would not strongly object to the motion. He knew already that Judge Fielding, a handsome black-haired woman in her early forties, who had just announced a brief recess, would rule in favor of the plaintiff. He also knew that if he appealed, his appeal would be quickly turned down. The matter had been settled.

"The fix is in," Nick whispered in my ear as I came into the courtroom.

"They got to Judge Fielding?" I said in disbelief. "How?"

"I don't know. Not threats and not cash. Political pressure of some sort. Promise of a seat on the federal bench maybe. Same with the appellate court. The Outfit wants that money."

"Did they threaten you?"

"Not in so many words. McNally talked about support if I should run for State's attorney or seek the U.S. attorney's office. Remarked about what a fine senator I'd make. Assured me it wouldn't do any good to fight, because the matter was settled. Some vague hints about unnamed angry people who might be deeply offended. Typical."

"And you were not going to fight anyway."

Ed Carny came in with a bevy of angry-looking, middle-aged women, who had to be radical nuns. He smiled and waved at us.

My fingers itched for his windpipe.

"It's her money, Blackie," Nick said wearily. "And she has the right to spend that money to buy herself more time."

Bullshit, I thought.

"I still can't believe Judge Fielding is going along."

"The point is, Blackie" — Nick gathered up his papers and prepared to walk to the front of the courtroom—"that neither Judge Fielding nor anyone else thinks there will be injustice. Catherine Collins is dead."

Dead and buried.

The courtroom filled up rapidly as the curious came to learn more of the gory details of the Acts of St. Catherine. There were, as well, at least a dozen reporters. And some bearded hippie types (in designer jeans) with drawing pads were already sketching the featured players of the drama for the evening news, as cameras were barred from the courtroom (they were poised like high-tech vultures at the door).

Judge Fielding, managing to look quite chic in her judicial gown, returned from the brief recess.

Her bailiff called the court to order and the dismal process began.

I paid little attention. The will would still have to be probated, but it was all over. It was the anticlimactic climax, the unhappy ending to an unhappy drama.

Cathy was alive but I doubted that we would ever see her again. It was, I told myself, perhaps just as well. For Cathy Collins there would never be peace or happiness. Perhaps for Angela Carson there would be. The world would have its virgin and martyr. And the woman who was hailed would have her own life.

On the whole, and all things considered, not an ungraceful outcome.

Ed Carny had won, goddamn him.

And he was beaming enthusiastically next to McNally in the front of the court, surrounded by his adoring fans.

Worse still, in his own twisted mind, I'm sure, he thought justice was triumphing. Justice for Cathy and justice for the poor and the suffering of the world.

I could bring it all to a halt. But that was not my intention. I would still settle with Ed Carny, somehow, some way, someday.

I felt someone touch my arm, an extremely attractive woman, deftly made up, wearing an elegant blue suit with white trim, and smelling of very expensive perfume.

She kissed my forehead.

"I figured that Ape-Man up there"—she gestured in the general direction of Nicholas B. Curran—"would come after me again and haul me back by my hair and it would be more dignified if I did it this way. Besides"— she laughed—"it saves you a lot of unnecessary work."

She kissed me a second time, touching my lips and permitting a mist of tears in her large brown eyes. "So far, Coz, resurrection has been fun."

She grinned and winked. Then, rear end swinging a little more than usual, as it had when she'd brought Nick his lemonade laced with sand, she flounced up to Judge Fielding's bench.

BANG!

"I think I can make a contribution, your Honor," she said brightly, an arm materializing around Nick's waist.

Janice Fielding was quite upset.

"And who are you, young woman?"

"The decedent, your honor," she said in that tone of the pious novice at which she was so practiced.

I slipped out of my seat and quickly left the courtroom. There would be a wedding the day after Christmas—for Cathy would want him in her marriage bed as quickly as possible. I must look over the ritual and prepare my homily.

And I did not wish the tears that were pouring down my cheeks to appear on television.

But as I left, I heard Edward T. Carny bellow, "She's been brainwashed!"

Oh, he would put up a good fight. And his claque of thin-lipped, feminist nuns would rally to him. But, unless I did not know my Cathy, she would have a carefully prepared statement for the press conference afterward. Presumably, with Nick at her side, she would offer to take a lie detector test. Might even say that her ordeal had left her unfit for any man and at the same time propose to Nick while the TV cameras whirled away.

So, despite the loyalty of his supporters, Ed Carny would begin to slip and his decline would soon be rapid.

Against the combined wonder-workers Nicholas and Catherine, the forces of evil traditionally have been no match.

Ed Carny was finished.

In a few days I would permit myself to feel sorry for him.

After I had enjoyed winning.

The quicksilver mists had done their devious and insidious work. Cathy had seen more vigor and determination in Nick than was actually there. She thought he would come after her. Perhaps she thought so because she wanted to think so.

And perhaps in seeing her man as one who would be strong to and for her, she had gone some of the way toward creating that man.

I could see the picture. Somewhere in the Sunbelt, Arizona or New Mexico would have been my guess, the orange bug was in a service station in the middle of the desert, its motor being inspected by a very polite and very slow mechanic. Cathy, in shorts and a T-shirt, would be striding back and forth impatiently, hardly aware of the quicksilver mists racing across the desert and swirling above her. She missed Nick. She loved him. Did he love her? Of course. She didn't deserve his love, but she had it. His love was a given, a presence, a reality that would always be there. He would come after her this time, as he said he would. But how soon would he catch up? How many more lonely nights without him? Then, as the mists enveloped her, the tantalizing thought: Why waste time? After all, so much has been wasted already. Why make him go through the motions when . . . ?

438 / ANDREW M. GREELEY

When it would be so easy to end the stupid chase right now.

You could be in a marriage bed with him by the Saturday after Christmas. Only a week away. Why drag it out?

And again: Why waste any more time?

And then the bug was ready. To the astonishment of the polite mechanic, the pretty woman turned it around and drove in the direction from which she'd come.

As the orange car perked down the ruler-straight road, the driver was oblivious to the mists dancing around her.

But the mechanic must have frowned in bemusement. Gosh darn, if it didn't look like there were wisps of cloud trailing behind the VW.

Nicholas and Catherine, Nick and Cathy, would live happily ever after. That is to say, they would have only three or four serious fights each week. Cathy would continue to test him to see if he would take a stand and he would continue to flunk that test most of the time. At least one day a week they would not speak to each other—my homily was beginning to take shape. And on five days their life would be ordinary and routine.

But on the remaining day . . . ah, perhaps on that day they would know the love which is reputed to reflect the Love that launched the universe in a vast BANG.

Maybe even a day and a half some weeks.

Not much, perhaps. Only a little bit—a little bit of light in the gloom, a little bit of life in the entropy, a little bit of love in the indifference.

Maybe that is enough. Maybe, even, it is everything.

That gave me an idea for a Christmas homily, part of which I could also use at the wedding mass.

And as I walked down Dearborn Street in the brightness of a cold crisp December morning, past the grinning Calder flamenco, I heard St. Bernard's Christmas hymn, which said that the little bit of light, the tiny tad of sweetness which is enough, is also everything.

Mane nobiscum Domine
Et nos illustra lumine
Pulsa mentis caligne
Mundum reple dulcedine
Jesu flos matris virginis
Amor nostrae dulcedinis
Tibi laus, honor nominis
Regnum beatitudinis.